THE BIG SKY

DEBORAH E. HAMMOND

Copyright

DEDICATION

To my Grandfather Harry, the horse whisperer; my uncles Ezra and Gordon, the cattlemen and to Bill; the love of my life.

CHAPTER ONE

BUENA VISTA, NEW MEXICO – MAY, 1885

The train wound through some of the most beautiful country that Catherine had ever seen. She had never expected the sky to look so large. I guess this is what it is like in the west, Catherine thought. I can't wait to see Father and see the ranch. Life as she knew it would never be the same again. She was on a train alone coming to a new life in the west and she was excited as she had ever been. The last horseshoe bend in the railroad line meant that she could see the caboose of the train from her railroad car. Not far now.

When she arrived at the train station for Buena Vista, she could not believe her eyes. It was a real western town just like in the picture books, except this real western town would be the closest town to her new home. She descended the steps leaning on the strong hand provided by the train conductor. He had looked out for her during the long journey and found that he was very glad indeed that he would soon be turning the young lady over to her Father. It may have been exciting for her coming all this way, but he was a nervous wreck, concerned for her safety and well being on such a long journey. He advised her that her luggage would be brought up shortly.

A true life cowboy was standing next to the train studying Catherine as she emerged from the train. Yep, he thought; that must be her. She looks just like her Father described her; young, midnight black hair, blue eyes and a figure that a man would not soon forget particularly in this part of the world where women like this are not seen except in picture books. Her Father had omitted the last part, but then he would have as he was her Father. Jake thought bad about thinking it at that moment, but it was his first thought and would not be his last about this particular visitor. That hat she is wearing could get her killed in this sun. I need to get her back on that train and home where she belongs.

Jake Nelson stepped forward to greet the young lady descending from the train. "Ma'am, are you Catherine McCullum?" Jake asked. Those disturbing blue eyes trained on Jake for the first time.

"Yes sir; I am Catherine McCullum. And you sir?" Catherine asked. Her voice was as soft and feminine as the rest of her. Good Lord, Jake thought, I need to get her back on that train.

"I am Jake Nelson ma'am. I am here to meet your train," Jake replied.

"Did Father send you to meet me?" she asked smiling.

"No ma'am; that is why I am here. Your Father couldn't meet you Miss McCullum. Your Father is a neighbor to me and a real good friend. Miss McCullum I hate to be the one to be the bearer of bad news, but your Father is dead," Jake said grimly. He watched her face try to register the news that he had just broken to her. Whether it was the news or the combination of the news and the sun and its heat, Jake was unsure, but Catherine fainted dead away and fortunately he was close enough to catch her fall. Damn, Jake thought, what do I do with her now? He shouted for the station master who had seen the young lady faint and came running. "Chet, pick up her gear and bring it into the station. We need to get her awake again so that I can get her back on that train and back east where she belongs. Good Lord Chet; people die from sun stroke out here. Just look at that hat she is wearing. No wonder she fainted. Help me get her inside," Jake said.

Jake gently lay her down on the train station bench and Chet got her a glass of cold water. Jake removed his bandana and placed it in the cold water and placed the cold, wet bandana on her forehead. He took off the fashionable but useless hat and stroked her forehead with the bandana dipped in the cold water. Now what do I do with her he thought.

"Maybe you should take some of those duds off of her Jake. She looks like she has ten pounds of clothes on her," Chet Stoner offered.

"Well it was either the heat or the fact that I had to tell her that her Father died. Either way, she went out Chet. This is no place for a lady like her. I loved her Father, but he had no business bringing her out here Chet. I need to get her back on that train and back home as soon as possible," Jake repeated to Chet Stoner this time and not to himself.

Jake noticed Catherine's eyes start to flutter and he moved the cold bandana to the back of her neck to try and bring her back to life. Those amazing blue eyes opened then and looked at Jake so very intently. His first thought was that a man could lose himself in those blue eyes. He put that thought away as it was imperative that he convince Catherine to get back on that train. She looked at him so very strangely and then tried to sit up.

"Miss McCullum, you fainted outside. We brought you in here because we thought it might be the heat. Don't try to get up too fast as you might pass out again. We have some cold water here for you. Don't try to talk too much either until you get yourself straightened out. Can we get you anything else?" Jake said worriedly.

"No thank you Mr. Nelson was it? I am so sorry to be a nuisance but I thought you said that my Father had died?" she asked with an incredulous stare.

"That's right ma'am; I am so sorry to have to be the one to tell you, but like I said, he was a neighbor to my spread and a real good friend. He told me that you would be on this train and that is why I am here to meet it. I need to get you back on this train before it moves on ma'am. Do you feel well enough to sit up now?" Jake asked again worriedly.

"Oh yes Mr. Nelson; thank you so much. This must be your bandana. The cold water certainly did the trick." She saw her hat lying on the bench and looked at it strangely. Everything was strange now that she knew her Father had died before she could even say goodbye.

"I took off your hat ma'am so you could lie down on the bench. You know people die from sunstroke out here ma'am. You need a real hat not something like this flimsy thing. But that doesn't matter now. I know you will be going back home real soon so hats don't matter much I suppose." Jake asked himself why he couldn't stop talking, but of course the reason was he had had to tell her the bad news and knew she was trying to process it and get her head wrapped around the fact that she was all alone in New Mexico. Damn, he thought again, I wish she wouldn't look at me with those blue eyes again.

"Thank you so much Mr. Nelson for coming to meet me and for being the one who had to tell me this terrible news. I will not be returning to the east however Mr. Nelson. This is my new home. I would like to see it now if you would be so kind to drive me there. I need to get my luggage from the train also. As for the hat, well I will take care of that once I am home and settled. Would you be so kind to drive me home Mr. Nelson?" Catherine asked sweetly.

"Well I'll be . . . ," Chet interjected.

"Oh Miss McCullum, this is Chet Stoner the station master. He will gather up all of your things and then I can take you out to the house. Once you see everything, I can bring you back to the station so that you can take the next train home," Jake replied.

"Oh no Mr. Nelson; you don't understand; this was my Father's dream. I am home. I just need to see my Father or where he is buried and then I need to get on with getting settled. I am so glad that we are neighbors Mr. Nelson. It is good to know that I will have one acquaintance in this new land." Catherine swung her legs off of the bench then and steadied herself for a moment before trying to stand again.

Jake looked at Chet who just shook his head and went outside to gather up Catherine's luggage. Maybe she has had too much sun already, Chet thought. Well if anyone can make her see reason, Jake will be the man for the job.

"I will borrow a wagon and take you out to your Father's spread," Jake replied. "If you should change your mind about leaving again, I can bring you back when you are ready."

"As I told you Mr. Nelson; this is my Father's dream and I am here at last. Thank you very much Mr. Nelson for meeting me and telling me this horrible news. It must have been very hard for you. You are a good friend indeed," Catherine replied smiling weakly again.

Jake took her arm as she tried to stand. She looked up at him then and smiled. The smile carried with it the deepest dimples that he had ever seen. I wish she would stop smiling at me, Jake thought. I need to get her to see reason and return home, but that will be hard if she keeps looking at me with those blue eyes and those dimples. Good Lord Jake; get a hold of yourself and go get a wagon, he thought glumly.

"Ma'am you might want to rest here while I go borrow a wagon. Chet will be back with your luggage in just a minute. You wait here alright?" Jake said.

"Alright Mr. Nelson; I will wait right here," Catherine replied softly.

When Jake went outside, he saw Chet huffing and puffing with the endless suite of luggage. "She must have brought everything she owned Jake. I never saw so much luggage for one person in my life. Hopefully there is one good hat in there somewhere," Chet stated glumly.

Jake walked down to the livery station and borrowed a surrey wagon to get Catherine and her luggage out to the ranch. He hoped to make her see reason before the day was out.

When he returned to the train station, Chet was standing outside with the pile of luggage. He helped Jake load the luggage and waited while Jake went inside to retrieve Miss McCullum.

"I think we have everything on board Jake. Good thing you borrowed the large surrey otherwise you would have left Miss McCullum behind," Chet muttered.

"Thank you very much Mr. Stoner for all of your help. I am so sorry to be a nuisance. I will find my feet I promise and then no more fainting. That simply won't do when one is going to live in the west," Catherine said smiling again with those deep dimples.

"Oh, it was nothing ma'am. Jake will take real good care of you from here. Nice to meet you ma'am; bye now," Chet said smiling. Good Lord Jake thought; all she has to do is smile and everyone around here turns to mush, me included.

Jake helped Catherine up into the surrey and took the reins. They set off for the spread with a wagon full of luggage. Thank you very much Cameron for giving me the task of meeting your daughter's train. I know you are smiling about this somewhere in heaven, but it really isn't funny, Jake thought to himself.

Once outside of the town, Catherine noticed that the air started to cool. She had never seen such beautiful country and understood why her Father had instantly fallen in love. When she thought of her Father, she couldn't grasp that he was gone and that she would never see him again. How will I live without seeing my Father again, she thought? I have to keep myself intact until we get to the new house. It won't do to faint and then have an emotional breakdown on the same day in front of a man that you have never met before even if he was a great friend of Father's.

Catherine gave herself a moment to stare at the profile of this now silent cowboy who was a great friend of her Father. He certainly looked the part with his cowboy hat, bandana, chaps and boots. I guess this is how everyone dresses out here, Catherine thought. His profile was perfectly straight and he had high cheekbones, dark eyes and reddish brown hair and a beautiful mouth if she was being honest to herself. He was tall like her Father, about six foot three. Oh yes, he is the quintessential cowboy and now that he has stopped talking, I am not quite sure what to say to him, Catherine thought worriedly.

"Have you lived here long Mr. Nelson?" Catherine asked.

"I wish you would call me Jake. Everyone around here calls me Jake. Mr. Nelson was my Father don't you know," Jake replied. Well of course he was Jake; who else would he be? Why can't you think clearly around this little piece of fluff? She may have been Cameron's daughter, but she is certainly not meant to be in New Mexico. "I have lived here all my life. My spread and your Father's spread are neighbors. We share the same water supply which is truly something in this part of the world. That is how we became such good friends. Would you like to see where your Father was buried Miss McCullum?" Jake asked.

"If I am to call you Jake then you must call me Catherine," she replied with a smile. "And yes, I would like very much to see where Father is buried. How did he die Jake?"

"He was carried off with a fever Catherine. He had done too much too soon after having pneumonia. As you know, his chest was not the best and I think he always tried to do more than he was able. But I expect you know that Catherine," Jake replied tenderly.

"The doctor told him to come west for his chest. I think it helped a great deal, but you are right, his chest was always a problem. Has he been gone long Jake?" Catherine asked. She was looking at him with those distracting blue eyes again so he decided to keep his gaze on the horizon rather than looking at her when he talked. He found he could concentrate better when he did so.

"He has been gone for two weeks now Catherine. I guess the letter missed you as you were probably traveling before it arrived," Jake replied. "I buried him at his favorite spot

Catherine where our two spreads meet. There is a little oasis there of trees and well, he loved that more than any place on the property. He couldn't wait to show you. I am very sorry Catherine; I know this has been a terrible shock for you," Jake said looking intently at her now. He could see the tears and the fact that she was trying to keep herself in check. I shouldn't have told her about it being his favorite place. Damn if she starts crying I am done for, Jake thought.

"Thank you so much for taking such good care of him. He was very lucky to have you as a friend. I am sure that he loved the oasis because it reminded him of home. It is so green and beautiful at home that he probably thought it was the closest thing. Not that it isn't beautiful here of course; just a different kind of beautiful. The sky is so large here and so blue. One doesn't expect that when one reads the stories about the west," Catherine said wistfully.

"Are you sure that you wouldn't want to go straight home first and then maybe I can show you where he is buried tomorrow? If you decide to take the train tomorrow I could show you on your way back into town," Jake asked.

"Oh no Jake; like I told you before; this was my Father's dream. I need to make a go of it now for his sake. That is why I have everything that I own in the luggage behind us. Mr. Stoner was right on that front," Catherine replied smiling bravely.

They drove on in silence then each lost in their own thoughts. Catherine's first thought was to stay in control and not let her grief overcome her in front of a stranger regardless of the fact that he was Father's best friend. Jake's thought was that Catherine was as stubborn as her Father. He just hoped that she didn't get hurt just trying to survive in this country before he could convince her to go home.

A half hour later they arrived at the green oasis that Jake had described. Catherine thought it was the most beautiful place that she had ever seen. "Why this must be what the Garden of Eden looked like Jake. No wonder Father fell in love with this beautiful place," Catherine exclaimed. He looked at her then and saw the wonder in her eyes. Oh no, Jake thought; this is not a good sign. She is looking at this place just like her Father did. I will never get her back on that train if she looks like this at her Father's favorite spot. He drove on to her Father's gravesite. Once there, he took her hand and helped her out of the surrey. She is such a little thing he thought. She will not survive in this country. He walked with her up to her Father's gravesite and stood with her as she closed her eyes and prayed for her Father. He could see the tears coming down her face, but she tried very hard not to say anything to give herself away. She is trying to not break down in front of me, he thought. He took her hand then and she looked up at him with her eyes drowning in tears. "It is alright Catherine; you can cry. There is no shame in crying for a good man," Jake said tenderly.

He watched her take her hankie from her tiny purse and wipe her eyes. She was trying so hard to stay in control. He wondered how long it would take for her to break down completely. She is stronger than I thought. That's not a good sign either, Jake thought. How am I going to get her back on that train?

Catherine stood at the gravesite for a few moments and then turned to Jake with a weak smile. "Thank you very much for bringing me here Jake. You are right of course; this was the perfect final resting place for my Father. With the exception of being with my Mother, nothing could be better for Father than to be here. I will be able to look after his gravesite now. I will come here every day in the future," she said smiling again weakly.

She turned then and walked back to the surrey. Jake helped her back in and they took off for her Father's spread. Once she sees how hopeless this all is, she will want to go home, Jake thought. Damn I hope she wants to go back home otherwise, what am I going to do with her? I can't leave her all alone in that big house. She probably doesn't even know how to fire a gun. She probably has never even held a gun, he thought glumly. This is all just a big mess. People need to stay where they belong and not go traipsing all over the country. Particularly soft little women like Catherine. Damn he thought; there I go again.

When they arrived at the ranch, Catherine smiled again widely. "This is such a beautiful house Jake. Did Father have it built or was it here when he bought the property?" she asked.

"Oh no; your Father had this built especially for you. He said he had seen a picture of a place like this in Australia and thought it would look just dandy here. Everyone thought he was crazy, but here it is and it sure is beautiful. Let me help you down Catherine," Jake said.

Jake came to her side of the surrey again and helped her down. She walked up the front porch steps as if she was well and truly home. This is going to make things even more difficult now that she is in love with the house, Jake thought. No matter where I turn, obstacles. Thank you again Cameron for putting her in my charge.

"Thank you again Jake for bringing me home. Is there anyone that can help us with the luggage?" Catherine asked.

"Oh yes; Ramon will help you with whatever you need. Ramon, your new mistress is here and needs help with the luggage," Jake stated.

Ramon smiled at Catherine and proceeded to unload the surrey and the endless luggage suite that Catherine had brought to her new home. When he had finished, he asked which room the mistress should be taken to. "Take her to Mr. Cameron's room Ramon until Catherine can get things organized. I will say goodbye now and take the surrey back to the livery stable. I will ride over tomorrow and see how you are doing. Goodbye now Catherine," Jake said smiling.

Catherine looked up at him again with those deep blue eyes and the dimples that went on for days "Thank you again

Jake for all of your help and for being such a good friend to Father. I won't forget it," she said smiling shyly.

And I won't forget you Catherine. I doubt that any man worth his salt could forget you, Jake thought.

CHAPTER TWO

The next day Jake rode over from his ranch to see how Catherine was doing. On his way to the English Rose, Jake saw a rider heading to the oasis. Since very few people rode in this area, he thought he would know whoever it was. He kept looking at the riding figure and realized after a few minutes that the figure was a woman. She was dressed in a black felt Spanish style hat, white blouse, gaucho pants and a bolero vest. The rider was riding side saddle also which was certainly a foreign sight in this territory. Is that Catherine, he thought? She is heading for the oasis so that would make sense. He thought he would go to Cameron's gravesite and wait just to make sure that it was indeed Catherine. Who else would be out here but her, he thought? He didn't have long to wait. The woman was heading in the direction of Cameron's gravesite for sure.

When the horse arrived at the oasis, Jake smiled at the rider. It was Catherine. She looked so different from yesterday that he would have had to look twice to make sure it was her. She had her hair pulled back in a pony tail which made a lot more sense for this part of the world. The hat was definitely one to protect both her fair skin and against the sunstroke that he had warned her about yesterday. He thought she must be a very good rider if she was riding side saddle. He never could figure out how women did that. Cameron hadn't mentioned that his daughter could ride. Maybe she took that up after he left Delaware.

"Hello Catherine; I wouldn't have known that it was you if I hadn't seen you up close. I see you took my suggestion about the hat," Jake said smiling.

"I did indeed Jake. I had packed for more practicality, but I just didn't dress for it yesterday. I wanted to dress especially for my Father yesterday, but I take your suggestions seriously because you have lived here all of your life. I don't want to faint again Jake and I need to learn how to live here so that I can make a go of things. Were you heading over to the English Rose then?" Catherine asked smiling.

"I was Catherine; I was just heading over to make sure that you were alright and didn't need anything. I am glad to see that you took my suggestion seriously. I wouldn't want to see anything happen to you on your first day in this country. The hat is very practical and the outfit certainly is right for our part of the world," Jake replied smiling.

"I thought I would come here every day because I am nearer to Father when I come here," Catherine replied quietly. "I am so glad that I ran into you to save you the trip all the way to my home," Catherine replied smiling.

That smile again, Jake thought. That smile and those blue eyes are absolutely hypnotic. I must remember not to look into those eyes if I am going to keep thinking straight.

"Oh I was headed that way anyway Catherine. I wanted to introduce you to the hands on the place and let you know a few things that your Father had wanted you to know," Jake said smiling.

"Thank you again Jake. Did you want to head that way now? I will just put these flowers on Father's grave and then we can head on," Catherine replied.

Jake watched her place the flowers on her Father's grave and thought again how concerned he was for her safety. She was out riding on her own in a country that she didn't know on a side saddle of all things. What if she encountered a rattler? She could be thrown or worse. He would have to take another try at talking her out of staying here for her own good. And for his own good as well, he thought.

The two rode on then headed for the English Rose. He had asked her Father once the source of the name. He had explained that an ancestor had built a ship for his lady love and he called it the English Rose. He said further that his daughter Catherine was the image of her ancestor who had also been named Catherine and who had been the image of

13

the English Rose for her future husband. That must be a beautiful family, Jake thought to himself. I have got to stop thinking about this lady and get her back east where she belongs. He had to admit that she was a very good rider, but as for shooting and protecting herself, that was something he doubted strongly. He would have to question her about those skills and maybe if he couldn't convince her to go home, he could at least teach her to protect herself.

When they arrived at the English Rose, the crew was sitting in front of the bunk house. He wasn't sure why, but he planned on putting a stop to that right away. "Men I don't know if you have had the chance to meet Miss McCullum yet. She is Mr. McCullum's daughter who has come all the way from Delaware to the territory here to follow her Father's dream. I expect to see each and every one of you earning your keep and making sure that this place runs real smooth. If I find out that you are not earning your keep and not doing what you are supposed to be doing, you will have me to deal with me on top of Miss McCullum. Do I make myself clear? Good, get to work then and don't make me tell you again," Jake said angrily.

Catherine watched this exchange and thought that Jake certainly had the ability to motivate in addition to being very sweet when he wanted to be. He certainly was the most handsome man that she had met in her life, although he seemed to treat her like an imposition on his all male, western world. Maybe he was just being concerned for her welfare and didn't have time to show the finesse she was accustomed to in the men from back home. "Won't you come in for a cup of tea Jake?" Catherine asked shyly.

"Maybe not tea Catherine, but I will take a cup of coffee if one is offered," Jake replied.

"Oh I am sorry; I forgot that strong coffee is the drink of choice. I am sure that Ramon will have some on the stove. Won't you come in?" Catherine asked.

Jake followed her up the porch stairs and into the house and her Father's library. He decided he would have another run at asking her to reconsider returning home.

"So how are you getting settled here at the ranch? Quite a change from back east I guess. I noticed that you rode your horse side saddle today Catherine. Do you know how to ride astride? It might be safer for you in case your horse was spooked by a rattler or some other animal. Do you know how to shoot Catherine? Knowing how to shoot is a vital skill out here in case you would be put upon by some wild animal or someone up to no good. You should really ride with someone else when you are out to make sure that someone could go for help in case something were to happen to you," Jake stated firmly.

"Are you trying to persuade me to go back home Jake? I appreciate your concern for me and I will learn to do all of the things that you just mentioned. I know you are only concerned for my safety and well being. I am sure that Father put you in charge of me and I appreciate you are only doing as Father asked. But let me be very clear again; I am not going back home Jake. This is my home now and I intend on making this work. If I need to learn to ride astride, I am prepared to do so. If I need to learn how to shoot, I am prepared to learn how to do that as well. I have already changed my hat and my attire Jake and I have been here less than one day. I don't intend on fainting every day so you don't have to worry about that either. Now, is there anything else that you need to tell me to learn how to do on my first day here?" Catherine asked smiling that dimpled smile again.

"No Catherine I expect not; but like you said, you need to know how to do these things and how to supervise your men so that they don't run over top of you. There is a whole list of things that you need to learn how to do Catherine and I just don't want you to have any problems you see. You are correct in that your Father asked me to watch out for you. I am trying to do that, but there are so many things that could go wrong before I even have the time to show you how to protect yourself or run the ranch like it should be run," Jake said firmly.

"I appreciate your concern Jake and I think you are so very kind to watch over me as you are doing. No wonder you and Father were such good friends. I think he had a wonderful friend in you Jake. Out of curiosity Jake; how many ranchers are there in this valley?" Catherine asked.

"Why on earth would you want to know that Catherine?" Jake replied surprised by the subject change.

"I thought it would be nice to invite neighbors for a get together here at the house in celebration of Father's life and so that I might get to meet some of my closest neighbors," Catherine responded.

"Well I would have to think about it Catherine. I am your closest neighbor and I am about two miles away. How big a circle would you want to draw to invite folks?" Jake replied.

"You are my closest neighbor and you are two miles away?" Catherine responded wide eyed.

"You see what I mean about someone riding with you? By the time you were found to be missing, you could be dead from sunstroke or hurt by falling off of your horse. You must be careful Catherine at least until you learn the lay of the land out here. Can I count on you to have the good sense to be careful?" Jake asked worriedly.

"You can indeed Jake; I promise. What would be the best way to invite my neighbors over to the house for a get together?" Catherine persisted.

"I would have one of the boys ride out with invitations, but I will need to sit down with you and get you names of the families on the surrounding spreads. You might want to get settled a bit before you plan on any fancy parties Catherine," Jake replied.

"Alright Jake; perhaps tomorrow you can sit down with me and we can make a list of the surrounding families within whatever size circle you view as appropriate. Could I also have a shooting lesson tomorrow Jake?" Catherine asked smiling.

"Well I guess so provided you don't ride out on your own. I will come here in the morning and then we can ride out somewhere private for your shooting lesson. How would that be Catherine? And don't forget to have them saddle a horse astride for you alright?" Jake continued.

"That sounds wonderful Jake; thank you so much for helping me. I am sorry to be such a nuisance, but I promise I will learn quickly so you can get back to your ranch work. Would you like a piece of cake to go with your coffee?" Catherine asked smiling that beautiful smile again.

"Yes Catherine; thank you that would be very nice," Jake said smiling in spite of himself. Damn, not only did I not convince her to leave; now I am going to be her teacher. I wish she would stop smiling at me and offering me cake, Jake thought glumly.

CHAPTER THREE

Jake was as good as his word the next day. He rode over first thing in the morning so that Catherine would not get into her head to ride out alone. She might be a good rider, but anything could happen in this country and he couldn't face the thought of something happening to her when Cameron had placed him in charge of her welfare.

When he arrived at the English Rose, Catherine was waiting for him on the deep front porch. Her Father had been so right about the design of that house. The deep porch gave shade and shelter to its occupants and helped to keep the inside of the house cool as well. He knew how fair Catherine was and probably thought he needed to keep her in shade until the trees grew around the house. Her Father had thought of everything including making me her protector, Jake thought glumly.

"Good morning Jake; are you ready for our first lesson?" Catherine asked smiling.

"More importantly Catherine, are you ready for your first lesson? Have you ever fired a gun before Catherine?" Jake asked.

"I have never even touched a gun before Jake; but don't worry; I am a very fast learner," Catherine replied. Her horse had been saddled for her just as he advised with the Western mount. He knew it would be a change for her, but like she said, she was a fast learner. He thought it much safer than the side saddle riding she had done yesterday. They headed out and he thought to take her to the oasis for her lesson. He knew from experience that she would be pitiful when she first started, so he didn't want to embarrass her in front of the crew. Besides she said she wanted to go to see her Father every day and Jake knew that Cameron would have loved that idea. His baby girl was with him even though he wasn't there to see it. Catherine had gathered wildflowers again for her Father's grave he noticed when he helped her up into the saddle.

As they rode along to the oasis, Jake noticed that Catherine was excited by everything that she saw and asked questions about every little thing. She is just like her Father in that respect too, Jake thought; they learn about everything by being excited by life. "It must be quite a change to be away from the ocean like this Catherine. Do you miss the water?" Jake asked.

"I will always love the water Jake. It is where I was born and reared and the water means peace to me always. The thing about this landscape is that it reminds me of home in so many ways. It is so much more beautiful and green than I thought it would be and there is a sea of grass rather than a sea of water. The cattle must love this beautiful green grass," Catherine replied.

Jake looked over the fields and thought that to himself, it was just grass; something to feed the cattle. It had always been here and he had never given it any thought. I guess it took someone looking at a thing with new eyes to realize its beauty. He thought that no one with eyes could keep from seeing Catherine's beauty. Why on earth would she want to be here when she could be home surrounded by her pick of men Jake wondered?

"So what drew you and your Father to want to come to New Mexico?" Jake asked. "I know what your Father told me, but what draws you here?"

"Father always had a dream to see the west. I think after Mother died it was the thing that kept him going. We are a big family so I have brothers who will take care of the family property in Delaware. He just had that same spirit of adventure. My great-great-great Grandfather came from Scotland to build ships in the United States. He settled in Lewes, Delaware where he met my great-great-great Grandmother Catherine. I am named for her. She was originally from England and decided to remain in Lewes,

Delaware after her first husband died. They must have been great adventurers to come all that way to the other side of the Atlantic to find their happiness. I think a lot of that spirit infused my Father and I must have inherited it as well," Catherine said smiling.

"But why would you want to stay here Catherine when you could be anywhere in the world? Why you could visit and then go back home where the rest of your family is found," Jake replied.

"Yes but this is where Father is now and after all; he built this house for me didn't he? I couldn't very well just visit and then walk away. That would be denying his dream Jake," Catherine responded.

"I understand that, but this ranch and New Mexico; it was your Father's dream Catherine. He would not have wanted you to put your life aside to pursue his dream," Jake countered.

"I suppose it became our dream Jake. I am the only girl you see and my Father and I had a very special relationship. I am not going to stay here if I am not happy Jake. You mustn't worry about me. If things don't work out and I am not happy, I can always sell the ranch and go back home I suppose. I just want to enjoy being here and explore what life is like in New Mexico. I know it seems strange to you because you have lived here all of your life, but just coming here on the train was an adventure in itself. I want to see if I can make this new life work just like my great-great-great Grandmother made her new life work in Delaware. It is a family trait I guess," Catherine replied smiling. "What about you Jake; do you have brothers and sisters?"

"No Catherine; it's just me. My Mother died when I was born and I think my Father just never got over her and couldn't imagine starting over again. You have to remember too that there aren't a lot of women out here Catherine. There are some in town and some that you spend an afternoon with, but not your whole life," Jake replied.

"You mentioned those ladies that you spend an afternoon with; would they be ladies in saloons?" Catherine asked wide eyed.

"How did you know about that Catherine?" Jake replied frowning.

"Father and I used to read all of the novels about the west and they mentioned ladies in saloons quite frequently. I supposed they were the ladies that you spent an afternoon with but I was just wondering," Catherine said smiling mischievously.

"Well I don't think that is a proper thing for you to be thinking about much less asking about," Jake replied embarrassed. "Not everyone spends afternoons in saloons with ladies," Jake replied. His cough told Catherine that she had hit upon a sore subject and should just move on.

"So did you give any more thought about the circle of friends that we should invite to the house for Father's celebration of life get together?" Catherine asked.

"Well like I told you; we should just draw a circle on a map and then I can tell you the name of the spread owners in that area and you can invite them over I guess. Were you thinking about a real party?" Jake asked.

"From my great-great-great Grandfather's side of the family there are wakes that are held after someone dies. People get together to tell stories about the person who has passed and then that person lives on in the minds of everyone present. My great-great-great-Grandfather was partial to whiskey, so there were refreshments and everyone had a good time remembering the person who had passed versus remembering only the sadness of that person's passing. It has come down through the family although we became Episcopalians when he married my great-great-great-Grandmother," Catherine replied.

"It sounds like you have a really wonderful family history Catherine. I can't imagine you wanting to leave that all behind," Jake replied.

"Are you trying to convince me to get back on that train again Jake?" Catherine stated smiling. "I promise if it doesn't work out, I will go back home. Can't I just enjoy myself here first before deciding whether I will stay here forever or not?" Catherine asked.

"I guess so Catherine assuming you mind what I tell you about all of the things that can hurt you out here," Jake replied.

"Did you give Father the same lecture?" Catherine asked sweetly.

"Well no; of course not because he was a man wasn't he," Jake replied.

"So you are just telling me all of these things because you think that as a woman I can't take care of myself?" Catherine asked smiling just as sweetly.

"Well you have to admit Catherine; that hat you had on when you got here could have gotten you killed from heat stroke. And what about you riding side saddle; your horse could have gotten spooked and there you would be lying on the ground with no one around to help you. It is just different Catherine; it just is and you need to understand that," Jake replied heatedly.

"Alright Jake; I understand what you are telling me, but you have to admit that I have done everything that you have recommended now haven't I? I have even come out on a beautiful day to learn how to shoot and I have never even touched a gun before. But you told me it was important for me to learn to defend myself so that is what I am planning to do. Don't I get some credit for following directions from someone who lives here?" Catherine asked sweetly.

"Well yes; I guess so Catherine. I just don't want to see you get hurt that's all. Your Father asked me to look out for you and that is what I am trying to do. I have never been responsible for someone else before and I am just trying to make sure that I do it right. Now here we are; let me get set up and then we will get on with the lesson," Jake replied. He was muttering to himself so Catherine assumed she must have upset him again somehow. All she was doing was asking questions. Why he was so touchy she just couldn't understand.

Jake set up a row of cans against a rolling area of terrain. Catherine assumed that he would want her to shoot at the cans when it came time for her lesson. Since she had never touched a gun in her life, she was hopeful that she could just shoot straight never mind trying to actually hit something. She decided to let that comment alone since she didn't want to upset Jake again. He came back to stand next to her and to teach her the proper stance. "Now Catherine; do you see how I am standing? I want you to turn and face towards the targets. With your right hand I want you to take this gun. I have loaded it so be careful with it. You need to point a loaded gun towards your target only and never towards a person or yourself. Do you understand that Catherine?" Jake asked earnestly.

"I do understand Jake; thank you," Catherine replied.

"Alright then; face towards the target, take the gun in your right hand, and bring it level. Now before you squeeze the trigger, I am going to stand behind you. It is not because I don't trust you mind, it is because the gun will have a bit of a kick. You are not used to that and I don't want it to knock you down. Alright take the gun in your hand, aim and gently squeeze the trigger," Jake stated.

Catherine planted her feet hoping that the recoil of the gun would not knock her over. She didn't know what to expect, but did as she was bid. The gun went off and Jake caught her as the recoil brought her backwards. "Did I do it right Jake?" Catherine asked smiling.

"You did Catherine; you just need to practice so that you can actually hit something alright; let's try again," Jake replied.

Catherine continued with her practice until the gun was empty. He told her then to always count the number of shots that she had fired and how many were left in the gun. In the event of an attack by a wild animal, that would be important to know and remember. "There is so much to remember Jake. I don't know if I will ever get it right," Catherine replied.

"After you get the hang of it, I will teach you how to use a rifle. It is not as important that your aim is good as you will at least wing whatever you are shooting at. Do you feel more comfortable now that you have done it a few times?" Jake asked watching her intently.

"At least I know what to expect now so that is something. Thank you for teaching me Jake. Can we do this often so that I can get better with practice?" Catherine asked smiling.

"Sure Catherine; we can practice whenever you want. Someday you might actually hit the target," he said smiling.

"Well I didn't expect to be an expert on the first day. Were you an expert the first day that you learned to shoot?" Catherine asked teasingly.

"No of course not; but then I was ten years old at the time wasn't I," Jake replied with a wink.

"We just have different life experiences Jake that's all. There really wasn't a great need for me to learn how to shoot at home. Only men went hunting and then just for sport not to actually protect themselves or their family. I can understand why it could be life threatening not to know how to shoot here. Thank you very much Jake for teaching me and for being so patient with your instruction. I have asked Ramon to make lunch for us as a reward for your kindness. He made some of that cake that you like also. Would you like to stay for luncheon Jake?" Catherine asked smiling.

"Well thank you Catherine. That is real nice; you know you don't have to feed me every time you see me," Jake responded smiling.

"I know Jake; I just wanted to thank you for taking your time again in teaching me something important. I know you are a busy man and I just wanted to thank you. If I take out a map Jake, will you circle the area for the invitations while we are having lunch?" Catherine replied.

"Well sure Catherine if you want me to. Let's get these targets gathered up so we can use them again. I am sure we won't need new ones for quite some time," Jake said laughing.

"I will ignore that taunt. You wait and see; I will learn how to do it I promise," Catherine said smiling again.

Jake and Catherine returned to the English Rose where Ramon had luncheon prepared along with the special cake that Jake liked. When they had finished luncheon, Catherine took Jake along to her Father's library. She found a map and a pencil so that they could draw a circle and make a list of neighbors to invite to the wake for her Father. Jake noticed a small painting then on her Father's desk that he had never noticed before. "Is this a painting of you Catherine?" Jake asked.

"No; that is my great-great-great Grandmother Catherine. She is the one that I was telling you about who came from England and married my great-great-great Grandfather Cameron. I was named for her and as you can see, there is quite a resemblance. Father always kept it on his desk because he said it was like a reflection of me when I would be grown. Her uncle sent it along to Lewes, Delaware before she came to America so that her first husband would know what she looked like before she got there. I guess it convinced him because he sent for her after he received it," Catherine replied smiling.

"One look at that beautiful face would convince anyone Catherine," Jake replied softly.

Catherine looked at him then and smiled her beautiful smile. Why does she have to smile at me like that, Jake thought. Who knows what I will agree to next.

*****

Jake and Catherine met on a daily basis for her shooting lessons as Catherine called them. Within two weeks, she was able to actually hit one of the targets with a pistol. She smiled such a radiant smile after that accomplishment that Jake felt bad for teasing her. He next gave her a rifle to try. He warned her that he would need to stand right behind her and catch the recoil himself for fear that she would fall backwards. He shot the rifle himself first to show her how it was done. Although the rifle recoiled when Jake shot, his strength kept it from pulling him backwards. He knew that Catherine would not be so fortunate. When she was in place and had the proper stance, Jake moved behind her and placed his hands at her waist. "I am just trying to make sure that you don't fall backwards when the rifle recoils alright Catherine. Don't be afraid; I have you alright. Now fire when you are ready." Catherine very carefully and slowly pulled the trigger waiting for the inevitable recoil. Jake caught her as he told her he would. She looked up at him then so amazed that she had shot a rifle and amazed at the strength of the recoil. "I don't think I will be very successful if we need two people to fire one gun," Catherine said smiling. Whether it was the closeness of Catherine or her success in firing the rifle, even Jake had to smile down at her this time. His hands at her waist felt too good and too natural to him. He was finding it more and more difficult to keep his distance, particularly when she smiled at him in that way.

When they finished the day's lesson, Catherine asked Jake if he had had a chance to make a list for her of all of the neighbors who should be invited to a get together at her house. "I do have a list Catherine. I made a circle of all those who I thought would have known your Father and would want to visit. Now keep in mind that folks in this part of the world will take any reason to get together because we do it so seldom. Usually we have parties only after the cattle go to market each year or for weddings and things like that. I don't remember one for a wake like you described it, but your

Father was very well liked so I am sure that people will come from far and wide to do something special for him. He was a very special man," Jake replied.

"You never told me how you two first met," Catherine stated.

"It was at the oasis as he called it. He rode over to tell me that he had just bought your spread and that he was building a house for his beautiful daughter to come visit. He told me all about you and that you had always wanted to see the west just as he had wanted to visit. He told me that you two used to read every novel about the west that you could get your hands on. We started to meet halfway then and he would ask questions about cattle and hiring hands and all of the things that he would need to know to get a place up and running."

"When the house was built, he would ask me over for dinner and we would visit. I never had a neighbor like your Father. I don't think I had anyone who I was as close to since my own Father died. He was a real special man Catherine. You were lucky to have him in your life," Jake stated.

Catherine had tears in her eyes when he finished telling her that story. "Thank you so much Jake. That is so lovely to hear. I miss him so much every single day. I can't believe that I will never hear his voice again. I am so glad that he had you as a friend and that you were here when he passed," Catherine said crying.

Jake could tell that the loss was still very raw to her. She tried to keep the grief of her Father's passing bottled up, but it came out at unexpected times like this. He hadn't meant to make her cry and didn't know what to do to make her stop. He took her hand then as he had the first day that he took her to the oasis. "Like I told you; there is no shame in crying for the death of a good man. I hope someone cries like that for me when my time comes. Like you said; you need to focus on keeping his spirit alive Catherine by hearing stories that folks will tell you about him. We can invite the folks at Buena Vista to your party also. Maybe old Chet Stoner might have some stories about your Father. I bet you haven't seen him since the first day you arrived. We ought to go into town so you can invite folks face to face and then let the boys handle the outer spreads. What do you say? We will go into town tomorrow instead of your shooting lesson. Why if you keep on; you might end up better than me so I need to slow you down some don't I?" Jake said teasing.

"You are just saying that to be nice, but thank you all the same Jake. I just miss Father so much. I want to keep his dream alive here. Thank you for helping me so that I learn what I need to learn to stay here," Catherine said smiling.

"Have you made up your mind to stay then Catherine?" Jake asked worriedly.

"I don't know for sure do I Jake. I still like it very much and would like to hope that I could stay here. I don't know for sure but I would like to try," Catherine replied smiling bravely.

"Well you don't have to make up your mind just yet; give it time before you know for sure alright? There is a whole lot of world out there to see and maybe you haven't seen all that you want to take in yet," Jake replied worriedly.

"I don't have to see it all by myself do I? Maybe I would like to see the rest of the world with someone else. It is more fun after all to see a new place with someone else so that you can talk about it; don't you think?" Catherine said sweetly.

Jake had never thought about that, just as he had never thought about most of the things that Catherine told him. He had certainly never thought about exploring the world or even a part of it beyond Buena Vista. Maybe she is on to something, Jake thought. It sure would be fun to go exploring with Catherine. Shoot she made going to the oasis something to look forward to. What if she decided to stay? For the first time since her arrival, he found himself thinking about that outcome and it was not an unhappy thought. Whether he liked it or not, Catherine was starting to become an important part of his life. He didn't fear it like he once had; in fact, he was starting to look forward to their daily meetings whether it meant teaching her to shoot or lecturing her about this, that, or the other thing. He noticed that she never got angry, but instead always thanked him for whatever insight that he had shared with her that day. He had never met anyone like Catherine before and he guessed that he would never again.

CHAPTER FOUR

The next day Catherine and Jake set off for Buena Vista to invite the people there to Catherine's party. Jake knew the people who had been close to her Father and he would take Catherine to them, introduce her to them and then she could invite them to her gathering in her Father's honor. He decided to take the surrey wagon this morning because he thought it only fair to transport her in style. He wasn't sure if she would wear one of those useless hats again from back east, so he thought he had better keep her covered as well. He thought then about how many times during the day Catherine crossed his mind and also considered the things that he would tell her when he next saw her. He realized that he wasn't frightened by that admission any longer and had even learned to like it.

When he arrived at the English Rose, he found that he was correct in the attire that Catherine had chosen. She might wear gaucho pants and a Spanish style hat when she was riding or around the ranch, but since they were going calling she wore one of her "back east" outfits as he called them. The hat had a larger brim than the first one that he saw her in, but the dress was at least ten pounds of material as Chet Stoner had correctly assessed. She had one of those new bustles on her dress which amazed him because he couldn't understand how a lady could sit in a dress like that. The dress had long sleeves, was rose in color and emphasized her assets to an uncomfortable degree as far as Jake was concerned. He noticed that she pulled out one of those useless umbrella things which she explained was a parasol when she went out in the sun. She was definitely dressing for going calling and he was sure that no one in Buena Vista would have ever seen an outfit like that before.

"So is that one of those dresses you brought with you in that load of suitcases you carried on the train?" Jake said smiling with one eyebrow raised as he leaned against the surrey.

"It is indeed Jake. I know what you are going to say, but I simply could not go calling in my riding clothes. You can understand that can't you Jake? Thank you so much for bringing the wagon with the cover. That will help since my hat is not as large as my usual riding hat. You aren't going to get upset again are you since I am not wearing my riding hat?" Catherine asked smiling.

"No Catherine because I see you have one of those new cover things to put over your head so maybe you will be alright provided we don't stay in the sun for long," Jake said teasingly.

"It is called a parasol Jake and it is designed to keep sun off of you so you don't get freckles," Catherine replied smiling.

"Is that a fact Catherine? Well most folks that I know get a tan and not freckles. Leave it to you to worry about freckles," Jake said shaking his head.

"It is my great-great-great Grandmother's legacy I guess. I have her skin as well as her coloring and looks. They say she looked like a marble statute when the town first saw her, so I expect she had to worry about freckles also," Catherine said thoughtfully. "So do you have list of people that we will invite from town?" Catherine asked.

"I don't have a list but I know who to introduce you to and who to invite because I know the places that your Father went and the people that thought highly of him," Jake replied. "Just how many people do you plan on inviting?" Jake asked.

"As many as you think appropriate Jake. It is a large house and we can always spill outside if there are more people than room. Why do you never take me to your house Jake?" Catherine asked innocently.

Jake was surprised by the quick change in subject which he found Catherine did to a disturbing degree. He was thoughtful for a moment before answering. "Well for one thing it wouldn't be proper would it? There are only men at my house and well, what would people think if I brought you there?" Jake started coughing again so she thought she had hit on another inappropriate topic.

"What people would be around to ask questions Jake? Your men would be out in the fields. Do you have anyone who looks after you Jake; what I mean is there someone like Ramon who cooks for you?" Catherine continued.

"Yes Catherine; not to worry I have a man who cooks for me at my house. You don't have to worry if I am getting enough cake and coffee. Honestly, what did you think went on in my life before you appeared?" Jake said shaking his head again.

"I didn't ask you to make you angry Jake; I was just making conversation. I am sorry if I am a nuisance. I try not to be really I do. I just like having someone to talk to, that's all," Catherine replied quietly.

"Are you homesick Catherine; is that what these questions are about? I suppose you had lots of people at home to talk to so it must be hard to be all on your own. I myself am used to it. I have Hector who is my cook and of course the men on the crew when we are out doing chores on the ranch. I enjoyed the company of your Father of course because he was a highly intelligent person to talk to. You are very intelligent to talk to when you aren't talking about parasols and useless hats," Jake said laughing.

"Sometimes I don't understand you at all Jake Nelson. You can be so very sweet and then you treat me like I am a nuisance in your way. I just don't know what to make of it," Catherine said impatiently.

"I guess because I am not used to being around a lady such as you Catherine. You ask me some of the most confounding questions. Were you always like this or has the west just brought this out in you?" Jake said laughing again.

"I am just curious; that's all. If you have known someone for close to a month and you have never been asked to their house you are just curious that's all," Catherine replied impatiently.

"Well just so you know; my house is a very masculine affair and not frilly and fancy like your house. There are no fancy women there if you were wondering so you don't have that to worry about either. I have a cook who prepares food for me so I don't starve even if he doesn't make cake like Ramon. I am perfectly content in my very masculine house. I enjoy being with you Catherine we are just two different people that's all. I don't go calling to other people's houses; just yours. I don't carry people into town or teach them to shoot; just you. Now have I answered all of your questions for the day or is there something else that you would like to ask me?" Jake turned his full attention to her then and to those magical blue eyes. She looked very shocked at first, but then smiled one of her deep dimple, magical smiles. He realized too late that he had made a mistake in turning to her just then. He found it hard to look away when he was captured by those hypnotic eyes and that magical smile.

"No thank you very much Jake; I don't have any more questions. I hope I have not been too inquisitive. I was just curious; that's all. I am glad that you have someone to look after you just like I have Ramon. It is not good for someone to spend all of their time alone even if they enjoy being alone," Catherine said quietly.

"Well here we are in town already and you can get ready to go calling. That is certainly the dress for it," Jake said shaking his head again.

Jake took Catherine to each of the businesses in town that he knew her Father had frequented. Like Catherine he had been a very social person, so he had made friends with each of the vendors and they liked him in turn. They were happy to come to the wake for Catherine's Father just as they were pleased to meet her. Jake watched as she charmed each and every one of them and smiled as she did so. They watched Jake watching her as well and some of them thought that they might be seeing a match in the process. Jake had never been one for socializing, although he was as good a man and as good a friend as anyone could have. He came to town when he needed something and the rest of the time he kept to himself. It had always been that way until now. Many of the folks in town wondered if Catherine had anything to do with that also. She sure was pretty enough and that dress she was wearing was unlike anything that any of them had ever seen. The ladies of the town especially took to that dress and asked her many questions about it and her hat and parasol. Jake thought to himself that he should bring her into town more often. That way she wouldn't ask so many confounding questions of him.

When they made their way down to Chet Stoner at the train station, he saw them coming and came out to meet them. "So I see you are still here Miss McCullum. Are you enjoying life here in New Mexico? I thought you were going to wear a real hat to keep from getting sunstroke. Haven't you told her about that Jake?" Mr. Stoner inquired.

"I have Chet and she has been real good about it, but she is calling on folks today so she thought she needed to dress up for all the people she would meet around here. I am not sure why she thought that, but I guess that is what they do back in Delaware. Is that about right Catherine?" Jake said smiling.

"Well yes Mr. Stoner. I wouldn't go calling unless I dressed for it. I wanted to invite you to a party at the English Rose. I am holding a party to honor my Father and hope that you will come and perhaps your wife if she would like," Catherine answered sweetly.

"Well that is real nice Miss McCullum. I will be real happy to come to a party at your house. We don't have many parties around here unless someone is getting married or the cattle are being brought to the rail head here. That is real nice. You aren't getting married are you Miss McCullum?" Chet asked smiling.

"Oh no Mr. Stoner; this is a party to honor my Father. I have asked people to bring their stories about him and in that way, we will all remember him with happy stories and not with sad stories. Do you understand?" Catherine replied.

"Well that is nice, isn't it Jake? Have you ever heard of a party like that Jake?" Chet asked.

"No Chet; I think they do parties like this in Catherine's family. This way she gets to meet folks around here also. Well, we will be moving along Chet. I have to get Catherine out of the sun even if she does have one of those parasol things to keep the sun off," Jake said with a wink.

"Thank you again Mr. Stoner and I so look forward to your coming. Here are the particulars as to date and time for you and your wife. I hope to see you both. Thank you again," Catherine said with that magical smile and magical eyes. Who wouldn't be taken in by both of those things, Jake thought.

"Well, I guess that is everyone that would have known your Father Catherine. Should we head back to the English Rose or did you want to visit with your Father on the way home?" Jake asked.

"I would like to visit with him if that is alright and then Ramon should have some lunch ready for us when we get back to the English Rose. I asked him to make that cake you like Jake just in case you were staying for lunch," she said smiling.

"Well that is real nice Catherine. You know I like that cake don't you and Hector of course doesn't make that cake as I have told you," Jake responded teasingly.

Jake helped Catherine back up into the surrey and they proceeded onto the oasis for Catherine to visit her Father. She was very quiet on the trip back and after a while Jake thought to start the conversation again. He thought he may have been a bit hard on her on the ride in. "So Catherine; is there anything else that you want to ask me while you have me captive in the surrey?" Jake asked teasingly.

"Oh no Jake; I don't want to pry as you made it very clear I was asking too many questions on the way to town. It's just . . . well . . . that is how people get to know one another isn't it by asking questions?" Catherine asked

"I guess so Catherine. I am not a big one for conversation probably because I spend so much time on my own. You are right though; that is how people get to know one another. Ask away Catherine; I promise not to be so grumpy this time," Jake said smiling.

"So what do you do for fun Jake? I know you have the chores with the crew on the ranch, but what do you do for fun when all of your chores are done?" Catherine asked.

"Well I like to read and of course I go up to my cabin in the mountains when I have the time," Jake replied.

"Oh that is lovely; reading is one of my favorite things as well. Are the mountains far from here Jake?" Catherine asked.

"Not so very far away, but most of the time I am doing chores on the ranch as you mentioned. I sometimes go hunting in the winter and there is a beautiful lake there so there is good fishing as well," Jake replied.

"Well that sounds just lovely. Are there any fish at the oasis Jake?" Catherine asked.

"No that area has not been stocked. It is some wonderfully cool water though especially on a hot day," Jake replied. "Do you know how to swim Catherine?"

"I do know how Jake. One does learn of course when one lives at the ocean. I have never been swimming in a lake though," she replied.

"Well maybe one day when we are out on our shooting lesson, we can have a swim Catherine; what do you think?" Jake said smiling.

"Are there any animals that we need to be concerned about? I know you said there are animals here that could injure or kill a person so I was just wondering," Catherine replied.

"I am glad that you remembered that. I don't think there would be anything in the water that would harm you. We would keep our eye out for snakes and such, but they could be anywhere. That is why I told you about not riding alone remember?" Jake replied intently.

"I do remember Jake; that is what made me think of it. You would only tell me for my own safety and not just to scare me," Catherine said very intently.

"That's good Catherine. That will keep you alive out here. You know I wouldn't let anything happen to you alright? Your Father made me promise to be responsible for you Catherine so while you are here, I am responsible got it?" Jake responded.

"Is that why you want me to go back home to Delaware so badly?" Catherine asked quietly.

"Now I didn't say that did I Catherine? Now don't start putting words in my mouth alright. I am just saying that I am responsible for you and I take that commitment very seriously," Jake said shaking his head again.

"I didn't mean to make you angry again I just wondered if you were regretting making that promise to my Father, that's all," Catherine stated looking intently at Jake again.

"I wouldn't regret any promise I made to your Father Catherine. I don't make a promise if I don't intend to keep it. You just keep that in mind alright?" Jake replied. He smiled at her then and made the mistake of getting captured again by those intensely blue eyes and that wondrous smile. There I go again, Jake thought; turning to mush.

*****

The next day Catherine began her party planning in earnest. She sat down with Ramon and asked for any ideas that he might have for a buffet for the party. He was surprised to ever be asked such a question, but suggested that he barbeque half a beef and make some Spanish inspired dishes so that they had a combination buffet. "That sounds like a wonderful idea Ramon. Could we have some of that special cake that you make that Mr. Nelson likes so much? I think that is really fine cake Ramon. You do such a wonderful job when you make it. Mr. Nelson always comments on how much he enjoys it," Catherine stated smiling. Ramon thought that Miss Catherine set a great store by what Mr. Nelson thought and maybe she was sweet on Mr. Nelson, but he kept that opinion to himself. He was smiling to himself when he returned to the kitchen; maybe someday I will be making a really special cake for Miss Catherine; a wedding cake. She is a real sweet lady; just like her Father. I sure do hope she will stay.

Jake made his usual ride over in the afternoon and Catherine told him about her conversation with Ramon. "Do you think that there are any other items that I should add to the menu Jake? I want to make sure that I don't forget any local delicacy that the neighbors might enjoy," Catherine asked.

"So long as you have plenty of beer Catherine I think people will be happy. Ramon will do a good job as always. Did you ask him to make some of that special cake that he does so well?" Jake said smiling.

"Oh yes Jake; that was one of the first things that I asked him to make. I know you enjoy it whenever you visit. Would you like a piece now along with a cup of coffee?" Catherine asked smiling.

"That would be real nice Catherine. Maybe we can have it out on your porch. That surely was a good idea your Father had. It keeps you in the shade and keeps the house nice and cool," Jake replied.

"Father truly thought of everything. It was meant to be his dream house, but I guess it just wasn't meant to be," she said with tears in her eyes. "I will be right back with your coffee and cake," Catherine said smiling.

She is such a soft woman Jake thought. I still think she is not meant to be in this country, but I think I will miss her if she decides to leave, he thought glumly.

*****

From that day forward, Catherine checked her list each day in preparation for the planned party. She wanted to make sure that nothing was left to chance. She asked Ramon if he would like to have some additional help in the kitchen or outside on the day of the party. He told her that the ranch crew would help him with the barbeque and he could take care of the inside chores. Jake rode over as was his usual routine and suggested that Catherine take a break from her party planning and come out with him for a shooting lesson and a swim. "If you don't keep up your practice Catherine, you may forget what you have learned thus far. Keep in mind, I want to be able to gather some more targets once you have hit all of my original ones," Jake said teasing.

"Alright Jake; I will get changed and find my bathing costume," Catherine replied.

Good Lord Jake thought; I hope it doesn't have ten pounds of material like some of her other clothing.

Catherine went upstairs to change into her riding outfit and found her bathing costume, towels, a blanket and some snacks for the oasis. She wasn't sure what type of bathing costume was customary in New Mexico, but she had an idea that her Delaware version was probably not going to be appropriate as Jake liked to remind her constantly. She breezed through the kitchen on her way out and cut some of

Jake's favorite special cake and wrapped it for their after swimming snack. She wasn't sure how to carry coffee with her, but filled up the canteens so that at least they had water with their cake.

After some minutes, Catherine came out on the porch to meet Jake who was enjoying the shade of the porch. "I was wondering if you were going to bring a trunk Catherine. I know you like to pack pretty heavy as well as dress pretty heavy, so I wasn't certain how long I would be sitting here," Jake said teasing.

"I think I am doing very well in learning to pack lighter. Besides, we are going to the oasis not across country. Honestly I guess I will never live down my luggage suite from my first day here," Catherine said smiling.

"Don't worry Catherine; we only tease people that we like," Jake said laughing.

"What do you do with everyone else?" Catherine asked curious.

"We just ignore them Catherine," Jake replied smiling.

They set off for the oasis, both smiling and enjoying each other's company. Catherine had learned that she didn't need to fill each moment of time between them with conversation. Jake had learned that Catherine was not overly curious; she just was trying to think of things to talk about with her usually taciturn friend. Jake and her Father had learned the peace of a comfortable silence and perhaps Catherine was learning the same. He had to admit that her questions were never boring, but then neither was Catherine. She had the same zest for life as her Father and the same desire to constantly learn and improve everything that she observed.

When they arrived at the oasis, Jake thought they would try a shooting lesson first and then use the swim as a reward for Catherine's continued good sense in wanting to learn something useful. He set up the targets as usual and then stood behind her in case she needed him to catch her from the gun recoil. He handed Catherine the loaded gun and she aimed and carefully shot at the assembled targets. To Jake's surprise, Catherine hit each of the targets on her first try. She smiled up at him and he was as happy as she that she was making progress. He would still stress to her that he didn't want her out riding alone, but she was making progress. The skills that he had taught her could be just as valuable in her own front yard as in the open country. He was pleased that she saw the wisdom of that education.

"I think that you have earned a swim for that progress Catherine. Let me check out the area here for you to make sure there isn't anything that will scare you in the vicinity and then I will show you a place that you can change before slipping into the water," Jake stated smiling.

"I am sure that my Delaware bathing costume won't be the thing here, but I packed it anyway," Catherine said smiling.

"So you were planning on wearing a bathing costume were you?" Jake said with a wink and a smile.

"Well, yes Jake; what do you wear when you swim?" Catherine asked wide eyed.

Jake set off checking the area for any animals that might scare Catherine. She was still waiting for an answer to her question, but thought that she would find out soon enough. He reminded her of her brothers back home when they got mischief into them and decided to skinny dip in the ocean. She did miss them at that moment, but she knew that they all had lives of their own and families of their own. As the youngest and still at home with her Father, she had been so excited to set off on this adventure. She was still excited, but sometimes the smallest things made her think of her Father and of her family back in Delaware. The water was probably the trigger this time and the closeness of her Father's grave was always the trigger at this beautiful oasis.

Jake came back then with the still present smile on his face and told her that all was clear. There wasn't anything that he had found that would scare her, but she was still to keep a close eye and scream if there was anything that she didn't recognize. He showed her a discreet area where she could change. "I will be changing over there," Jake pointed across the water "just so you know Catherine," Jake said smiling again.

"Alright Jake; thank you for checking for me. I don't like scary things when I swim just so you know," Catherine replied warily.

"Alright Catherine; nothing scary when you swim; got it," Jake said laughing. He is in an awfully good mood today, Catherine thought. I wonder what is going on other than us taking a swim. Maybe it is because I stopped asking questions. Yes, that must be it. I must remember to be quieter in future. But if I am quiet and he is always quiet; when will we ever speak? Maybe that is the reason that he is in a good mood; neither of us are talking. The man is a puzzle for sure, Catherine thought.

"I cut some of the special cake for you Jake. I thought you might like some after our swim," Catherine called across the water. She didn't hear a response so she thought that Jake had not heard her. "I said Jake; I cut some of your favorite cake to bring with me today. Did you hear me?" Catherine called out. At that moment she heard a splash and realized that Jake must already be in swimming. She finished changing and looked for an easy way to enter the water without jumping in. Her brothers had always done that and she preferred to tip toe into water and not make a big splash of it. If you made a splash you got your hair wet and well; men just didn't understand.

As she came around the tree, she spied Jake with his hair wet and his shirt off swimming in the oasis water. She thought he looked so peaceful then enjoying the oasis and she thought he was the most handsome man that she had ever seen, particularly with his shirt off as he swam. She still wondered what he was wearing to swim in, but thought it best to let that thought go for the moment. She was covered from head to toe in her bathing costume and thought that would probably generate a laugh or two from Jake. I am glad that at least occasionally I can make him laugh even if I am the butt of the joke. She started to gradually tiptoe into the water and had to admit that it was wonderfully cool on such a hot day. Jake spied her at that moment and thought he had never seen one woman wear more clothes than Catherine McCullum. Even when she swims she has on more clothing than most people do when they go to town.

"Catherine; do you think you have on enough clothes there to go swimming? If you start to sink under all of that weight, just call out and I will come rescue you. Honestly, I have never seen anyone wear more clothing than you do. Chet said he thought you had at least ten pounds of clothes on the first day that we saw you get off the train," Jake said laughing.

"I am glad that I can make you laugh occasionally even if I am the butt of the joke," Catherine called from across the water.

"How do you even feel the water if you have all of those clothes on Catherine; at least take off the hat if nothing else," Jake called out.

"I guess I could take off the bathing hat. Alright, you convinced me Jake; happy now?" Catherine called out. She got out of the water and placed her swimming bonnet with the other clothes in her discreet changing area.

When she returned to the water, Jake was right next to her. She didn't realize that he had moved from his side of the water. "Now at least you can get your hair wet Catherine," Jake said smiling. "Now watch; there is a serious drop off a foot or so from where you are standing. I don't want you to have a fright. Just ease down because there is like a step that leads down to the water. When you get to that edge, sit down and I will help you," Jake said smiling.

"Alright Jake; am I near the edge now?" Catherine said watching intently.

"Yep, you sure are; now sit down and I will help you. Are you any good at treading water Catherine?" Jake asked.

"I guess so Jake; it just depends on how long I have to tread the water," Catherine replied warily.

"Well you see where I am and where the water is on me?" Jake asked. "My feet are touching the bottom, so you are not going to be anywhere near touching the bottom unless you tread water the whole time you are in the water. Sit down now and let me come get you," Jake stated.

Catherine sat down on the sloped step and Jake stood looking up at her. He was smiling she presumed because of her endless layers of clothing. He put out his arms then and told her to let go. "I have you Catherine; just slide off the slope there." Catherine did as she was bid and Jake's strong arms caught her. She put her arms around his neck then and they were face to face and eye to eye. "Do you want to hold me this way, or do you want to ride piggyback?" Jake asked

"This is fine Jake, but you won't be able to swim very well will you?" Catherine asked shyly.

"The whole object is to feel the cool water Catherine. I am enjoying that very much. Why don't you put your legs around my waist and then I can take you out to the deep part," Jake said smiling.

"You mean this isn't the deep part Jake?" Catherine said panicking.

"Don't worry Catherine; I have you. Just let yourself enjoy the cool water. If I get tired, I can bring you back to the shallow portion. Enjoy yourself Catherine. Do you remember asking me what I liked to do for fun? Well this is one of the things. You were right; I just don't do fun things very often I guess because there is always something to do on a ranch. There are endless chores and always something that needs tending. Sometimes I guess we all need to take a step back and have a little fun," Jake said smiling

Catherine smiled then and thought this is why he is in a good mood. He is doing something fun for a change. I should have suggested this a long time ago, but I guess I thought he would never want to do something fun with me. I wonder what has changed?

"Are you enjoying the cool water Catherine?" Jake asked watching her intently.

"I am Jake. You are right it is so heavenly. This truly must be what it felt like in the Garden of Eden; perfect beauty and perfectly cool water," Catherine said smiling.

"If this was the Garden of Eden, you would be wearing a lot less clothes now wouldn't you?" Jake said laughing.

"And there would be a snake Jake. I don't like snakes one little bit," Catherine said frowning.

"Or other scary animals," Jake replied with a wink. "Should you give me a list of those scary animals so that I know what to look for in the grass when we swim?" Jake said laughing again.

"You are in a very good mood today. Did something happen to put you in such a good mood?" Catherine asked smiling.

"Well I am at the oasis and I am swimming and you hit all of your targets for the first time . . . and I am holding you and I am about to kiss you for the first time," Jake said moving closer to Catherine. She looked at him so intently then after he made that statement. He moved closer to her and kissed her gently at first and then more intensely as her grip around his neck tightened. She felt as if she was floating; kissing Jake and being kissed by him, the coolness of the water, the beauty of the oasis and the big blue sky overhead. When he pulled away from the first kiss, her eyes were misty and the incredible blueness had become even darker. She wasn't frightened and she wasn't pulling away. He decided to kiss her again to see if she reacted the same way. He moved closer to her this time and she met him halfway. He kissed her more passionately this time and her grip around his neck continued to tighten. He thought if he kissed her again, she might just cut off his breathing accidently. He had never felt anything that felt more right than this moment in this place, kissing Catherine and being kissed by her. When he released her this time, he told her to bend backwards and put her hair in the water. She did as she was bid and the feeling of freedom was wonderful as she floated in the water. She closed her eyes and felt the beauty of the moment and the beauty of the day. She didn't know what had prompted the change, but she thought she wanted this day to go on forever.

"So did I hear you say something about cake earlier?" Jake said smiling. I will take you over to the slope again and meet you in a few moments for cake," Jake said smiling.

"Why do you need to meet me Jake?" Catherine asked.

"Because I need to put something on if I am going to sit and have cake with you," he said with a mischievous grin. Her eyes widened and she started blushing. Her reaction just make Jake laugh all the harder.

"You are just like my brothers back home," Catherine replied. "They were always going skinny dipping."

"I am not your brother Catherine," Jake said quietly.

"I know that Jake. I'm just saying, girls are supposed to cover up from head to toe and boys get to go skinny dipping whenever they like. I'm just making a comment that's all," Catherine answered.

"Well after we have our cake, you can always go skinny dipping if you want to; I won't tell," Jake said laughing again.

"A kind offer but I feel that I must decline," Catherine answered primly.

"Suit yourself Catherine; you don't know what you are missing," Jake said laughing again. "Now, here you are at your slope again. I will put you back on the slope and go over and change. I will meet you over on your side of the oasis for the always special cake which you said you had cut especially for me. Is that correct Catherine or was I hearing things also?" Jake said grinning.

"That is correct Jake. Are we going to go swimming again after we have cake? I ask only because I need to know if I should change out of my swimming outfit back into my riding clothes," Catherine asked casually.

"We can if you want; this is your day. We are having a day of fun for a change and we can go back swimming again as many times as you like. Hopefully there will be enough cake for each snack after we swim," Jake said with a wink.

Jake and Catherine had their snack resting on the blanket that she had packed. She had stayed in her swimming costume just in case she could convince him to take her swimming again. He sat looking at her covered from neck to toe and shook his head laughing again. He sat with his trousers on and his shirt still off.

"So I suppose you stayed in your swimming costume to see if you could encourage me to go swimming again; is that about right?" Jake said smiling.

"Well you did say we could go swimming again if I wanted to and . . . well, I enjoyed it very much," Catherine replied.

"I enjoyed our kiss also," Jake said smiling and watching Catherine intently.

"I did too Jake," Catherine said blushing again.

"I noticed that Catherine. I was afraid you might accidentally cut off my breathing if I kissed you again seeing how your arms were around my neck so tightly," he replied grinning.

"I was just surprised I guess. I was always afraid that I was being a nuisance Jake. I guess I wasn't always a nuisance," she said smiling shyly.

"No, not always a nuisance Catherine; you are a real pleasure to be around when you are not asking a million questions every minute," Jake said grinning again.

"Well my word Jake; how on earth do people get to know one another if they don't ask questions of each other."

Catherine replied. "I certainly answer any questions that you ask of me; don't I?"

"You do indeed Catherine; I guess I am just not used to people wanting to know about me and what I do and what I enjoy. It takes some getting used to, but I think I am getting the hang of it Catherine," he said smiling.

"It is nice to think that someone else is thinking about you; don't you think?" she said smiling again.

"Well now that we are dried off again, do you want to take another turn swimming?" Jake asked. "You can always decide if you want to do that skinny dipping that we talked about," he replied laughing.

"Again, though I appreciate your thoughts on the subject, I must politely decline," she said with mischief.

"Alright then; suit yourself. I will meet you at the slope again in five minutes," Jake replied.

The two rejoined again in the water of the oasis and Jake took Catherine out to the deep portion again. He explained to her that the oasis was spring fed so that even during periods of drought, there was water here and in the surrounding area. It made this area even more magical to Catherine and she could readily understand why it was so very cool even on the hottest of days. Jake watched her intently again as he tread water in the deepest section of the oasis. He told her to put her head back in the water again and to feel its coolness. As he pulled her up and she placed her arms around his neck again, he kissed her again and she tried this time to not strangle him when she placed her arms around his neck. The kiss became quite intense as he slowly rubbed her back and sides. He decided that he better not extend the kiss further, but had a grin on his face as he once more took her to the slope. "I think that is enough swimming for one day Catherine. Ramon will probably be watching for you and for me for that matter. I will meet you on your side in a few minutes," Jake said smiling.

Catherine returned to her discreet changing area and thought it had become the most beautiful day of her stay so far in New Mexico. She hoped that Jake would stay for dinner as she didn't want the day to end. She didn't know what had prompted this change in heart on the part of Jake, but she knew that she had been hoping that he would see her as something more than a nuisance and not just the responsibility that her Father had imposed on him. She had a fanciful thought then that her Father was looking out for both of them and that coming to this beautiful oasis over the past several weeks may have been their opportunity to forge a new relationship. She thought if she was going to stay in New Mexico, she wanted to stay with Jake and she wanted him to want her to stay more than anything. She smiled at that thought and at the fact that she would relive this day in her mind over and over again.

When they returned to their horses, Catherine asked Jake if he would like to stay for dinner if he didn't have any other plans. "That would be real nice Catherine. Maybe Ramon made some more of that special cake while we were out," Jake said with a wink.

As soon as they returned home, Catherine went inside to bathe and change. "I will be just a few minutes Jake. I thought maybe we could have dinner out on the porch if you like since it will be nice and cool there," Catherine said smiling.

"I am going to go down to the foreman's bunk house and take a quick bath. I will be back in a few minutes Catherine," Jake replied.

Catherine raced upstairs and bathed and then tried to find something in her closet that didn't have ten pounds of material. She finally hit upon a light summer frock that had a sweetheart neckline and was made of lavender cotton. It did not have the bustle that had become so fashionable, but instead had a gathered waist and short sleeves. She would have to carry her shawl with her because she got cold so quickly, but she thought at least Jake would not tease her about the excess of material. She pulled up her hair with a lavender ribbon and placed a choker at her neck and matching earrings. She hoped that she looked like she wore this sort of thing every night for dinner and not that she had changed especially for him. When she came downstairs, she checked in with Ramon and told him that she would like to have dinner with Mr. Jake out on the porch as she thought it would be lovely and cool. Ramon smiled after she left the kitchen and thought that the wedding cake he had been planning might be getting closer to reality. He wanted very badly for his new mistress to stay in New Mexico because she and her Father had been the kindest people that he had ever worked for.

Jake came walking up the path to the house shortly thereafter and smiled as he saw Catherine waiting on the porch. She had changed into a dress that did not have ten pounds of material for once and was in fact so light that he saw she already had her shawl at the ready. He had sensed the change in their relationship all day and here was more proof; Catherine was looking just like a woman who was being courted. Since he felt like he was courting her for the first time, he was glad that feeling was being reciprocated. He couldn't wait to kiss her good night after dinner and thought that might be even better to anticipate than Ramon's cake.

CHAPTER FIVE

After much planning and even more anticipation, the day of Catherine's party arrived at last. The food had been prepared by Ramon and the barbeque was being overseen by the rest of the crew. Tables had been set up outside so that there was plenty of room for the company who would attend. Torches were set up at various locations so that the party could go into the night should the party attendees wish to remain. The stage was perfectly set.

Catherine had debated for over a week what she should wear. As Chet and Jake had repeatedly teased her, she had quite the extensive wardrobe. She knew now that she was dressing not only for herself, but for Jake's tastes as well. She understood that he was not an advocate of the new bustle style and preferred her in more simple dress. He had commented on the lavender dress that she had worn the night of their dinner and she was pleased that she had finally worn something that did not provoke teasing. She wanted to hit that same balance and yet wear something that would be memorable in light of the importance of the night to her and to the community. She finally hit upon a rose pink gown with a gathered waist and satin skirt. The neckline this time was more daring because it was a gown designed for the evening. The neckline was in a deep v and was off the shoulder. The sleeves were short and she would have another shawl ready should the party go late into the evening. She was amazed at how cool the evenings were here in New Mexico even if the days were intensely warm. Her hair was placed in curls with a ringlet descending on the left side of her neck. She had wound rose colored ribbons through the curls and had placed a rose pink choker around her neck and earrings to match. She thought that she had hit upon the correct balance of simplicity and beauty and hoped that Jake would be pleased

After one look at Catherine and the gown that she had selected, Jake was anything but pleased. He was pleased that she was as beautiful as always, but not pleased that she would be so revealed to the community for the first time. "Catherine, you were more covered when you were at the oasis swimming. You need to go upstairs and change your gown right now; that is all there is to it Catherine. I will have to follow you around with a gun if you wear that dress," Jake stated heatedly.

"Jake it took me all afternoon to get ready. I can't just go upstairs and change now especially when I see my guests starting to arrive. Look Jake; there are wagons starting to arrive in the front yard. I simply won't have time Jake. I so wanted you to be pleased for a change. I didn't wear ten pounds of clothing like you always tease me about," Catherine said anxiously.

"For once you didn't wear ten pounds of clothing and now is the time that you need to be more . . . covered," Jake said pointing in the vicinity of her décolletage.

"Jake this is a gown directly from Philadelphia, Pennsylvania. It is the height of fashion and does not have a bustle. I promise you everyone will think it lovely and nothing untoward will happen. I won't go off somewhere on my own and you will be right here won't you?" she answered soothingly.

"Catherine there are men coming here who have never seen a woman like you least of all a woman like you in a gown like that one. It took me a long time to get used to seeing someone like you, but I have been around you every day. These men are on ranches without women and then they will see you. Do you understand my meaning Catherine?" Jake said worriedly.

"I think I do Jake but certainly these men are gentlemen or they wouldn't be coming to my house to honor Father," Catherine replied.

"Alright; I see I cannot change your mind. Please just put your shawl around you or something," Jake said anxiously.

"The first guests are here Jake. Would you be so kind to stand with me because I won't know them will I? If you stand with me and introduce me to them then you are close by in case something untoward would happen. The crew is outside with the barbeque in case you would need back up against some unknown assailant of women in evening gowns. Do you feel better now Jake?" Catherine said smiling.

"Just don't smile like that Catherine. I am used to that smile now but trust me these men will not be used to that smile and what it does to a man," Jake said anxiously.

"I think I will be fine so long as you stay beside me," Catherine said again seriously but with the mischief in her eyes. She took one of his hands in her hands then.

"Don't worry about that Catherine; I am not going anywhere," Jake said earnestly.

With that, the first guests arrived on the porch. Catherine went to greet them in the hallway and Jake stood at her side so that he could introduce her to them as they came through the door. As Catherine predicted, every woman who arrived commented on her beautiful gown and presumed that it had come from the east. They had never seen a gown like it and thought she was beautiful in it. Jake tried to valiantly smile each time he heard a compliment on the gown. He watched the line as they came to the door to check for any who would give him cause for concern. When they spied Jake towering over Catherine and the majority of her guests, the majority gave him a wide berth. They knew Jake to be a good friend and a good fellow, but with a temper when riled and a reputation for protecting those he cared about. The word had gotten round Buena Vista that Jake just might care about the lady who was their hostess and they could truthfully say that they couldn't blame him. She was the prettiest woman in the county for sure and had a smile that would melt a January snow.

All had gone well with the receiving line until the end of the line. When Jake spied two individuals coming towards

Catherine, she saw him tense and his eyes narrow to a squint. She had just noticed that action when two men approached her. They were the very last people waiting to meet her and Catherine noticed that the rest of the guests gave them a wide berth as well. Jake introduced them as Angus Delaney and Duncan Carmichael. Both shook Catherine's hand, but she noticed that they both had the same cold eyes and their smiles never reached their eyes. It was as if the appearance was a mask for the true nature beneath.

"Angus, Duncan; what brings you here tonight?" Jake asked rudely.

"We heard about our charming hostess and wanted to meet her of course. Besides, anyone who owns the spring will be of interest to us. Ma'am, nice to meet you," the elder of the two stated and both then moved away.

Catherine turned and gazed up at Jake. He gave a weak smile and then taking her elbow, led her outside. The guests had made themselves comfortable at the arranged tables. Jake decided to give a speech and welcome the guests and ask them to say a few words about Cameron McCullum. He placed Catherine in an adjacent seat and stood next to her as he delivered his words.

"Thank you all for coming today. Our hostess Catherine McCullum is the daughter of Cameron McCullum who most of you knew and admired. In her family there is a tradition of honoring the individual who has passed with stories about their loved one. Miss McCullum was not here when her Father passed away, so she arranged this party to meet her neighbors and to hear their stories about her Father. I would like to welcome everyone here since I know you all and ask you to share your stories about Cameron McCullum. Thank you again for coming and I will start with my memories of Mr. McCullum."

"The first time I met him, he was coming to the oasis to let me know he was buying the property that would become the English Rose. Of course there were others who had interest in the property," here Jake glanced knowingly at Angus Delaney and Duncan Carmichael "but Mr. McCullum was the successful buyer and never looked back. He saw the design for the house here from a picture of a ranch in Australia. Everyone wondered about this house design when he talked about it, but once they saw it built, it made a whole lot of sense for our territory. The porch is nice and deep and provides shade and keeps the inside of the house cool. Mr. McCullum was a real visionary and a man that I was honored to call friend. I for one will miss him, but am glad to welcome his daughter Catherine here to Buena Vista. For those of you who have met her you know that she has a lot of spirit and energy like her Father. I ask you all to raise your glasses to Cameron McCullum and to his daughter Catherine." Jake smiled down at Catherine then who had tears in her eyes.

"I would welcome anyone here today who would like to tell other stories about Mr. McCullum as I know it would mean a lot to Miss McCullum," Jake continued.

Judge Wilkerson was the next person to stand. "Cameron McCullum came to me when he decided to buy the ranch that would become the English Rose. He asked me to tie up that property purchase real tight because he didn't want there to be any problems for his daughter Catherine who you have met today. He knew he had health problems, but he never let it stand in his way. We had a number of great conversations in my office concluding the transaction for the purchase and the work on the building of the house and outbuildings. I like Jake here will miss those conversations and miss someone who has so many visions for the future of our territory. To Cameron McCullum," Judge Wilkerson tipped his glass in Catherine's direction.

Chet Stoner was next to stand. "Miss McCullum, I was at the train station when your Father first arrived. Although he didn't have as much luggage as you when he arrived," he gazed at Catherine above his glasses with that remark, "he had a dream and saw that dream become real. I know that he watches out for you every day and is real happy to see that you have come to stay here in New Mexico. To Cameron McCullum," Chet tipped his glass in Catherine's direction as well.

On and on the stories and well wishes continued. Catherine would in turns laugh and cry at some of the stories that were told about her Father. Jake several times placed his hand over hers when he saw that she was starting to lose her composure. He knew the purpose of the wake was to bring the loved one back to life in the minds of those who knew him and he knew that they were doing Cameron credit by this day's work. Finally Jake stood again and asked that everyone take advantage of the great cooking by Ramon and the boys. A buffet line began and the party began in earnest.

"Thank you so much Jake. This means the world to me and I know would mean the world to Father also if he was here to enjoy it. I think maybe he is here in spirit and I am so glad at the number of people who have come out to honor Father," Catherine said with shining eyes.

"I told you that folks in this part of the world like a party because we don't get together that often. Now, you stay put for a few minutes and I will get you a plate from the buffet alright? Chet, will you and your wife stay here with Catherine while I get us both a plate?" Jake asked.

"Sure will Jake; you take your time. I am going to ask Miss McCullum here if she has gotten any lighter weight dresses since she got here or if she is still wearing ten pound dresses," Chet winked at Jake and then smiled at Catherine when he said it. "You know I don't mean anything by teasing you right?" Chet asked.

"I do know that Mr. Stoner. Jake explained to me that you only tease people that you like; the rest you just ignore. I feel honored to be one that you tease," Catherine said smiling her magical smile.

"There are some here today that you won't see me tease, but it's a party so we won't get into that. This is sure a nice idea and a nice way to honor your Father. I haven't seen this many people together since the last time we brought the cattle to the rail head. That is a party that is worth going to Miss McCullum. I sure hope that you will be here to see that this year. Are you still planning on staying on here at the English Rose?" Chet asked.

"I do plan on staying Mr. Stoner. I love it here. Everyone has been so kind and I love the house that Father built for me. It is so very special and like Jake said, the design makes for shade during the day and keeps the inside so very nice and cool," Catherine replied. "I am so glad to meet so many of my neighbors also. I hope to see them more frequently."

"Well there are some that I don't need to see frequently, but since this is a party, we won't get into that will we? Well, I see old Jake heading this way so I guess we will get on up and get in the buffet line. Thank you again for inviting us and it sure is a nice party," Chet replied.

Jake returned to Catherine's side then and smiled as he sat down with two plates. "I got you a little bit of everything Catherine. I don't know which ones are your favorites, but everything looks mighty good. I see there is special cake up there also. Did you have anything to do with ordering that for the party?" Jake asked grinning.

"I always make sure that Ramon makes some of the special cake Jake. I know it is your particular favorite and who knows; others might like it as well. But it is really for you because I know you like it," she replied with shining eyes. Jake squeezed her hand again and they started in enjoying the buffet treats.

"Ramon is such a wonderful cook. I hope no one tries to steal him away once they taste his specialties," Catherine said frowning.

"I don't think you have anything to worry about Catherine. Ramon tells me that you and your Father have been the kindest people he has ever worked for. He thought the world of your Father and thinks the world of you too," Jake responded. "I think a lot of people think that way Catherine," Jake said grinning.

Unbeknownst to Jake and Catherine, their every move and gesture was being watched by Angus Delaney and Duncan Carmichael. "Just look at them Father; Jake has definitely staked his claim with Catherine McCullum. I had heard talk in town, but I had no idea until tonight that she was such a beauty. I don't know if I can make headway with her, but I need to try. We need that spring Father just as we needed it when McCullum snatched it away from us. I will do everything that I need to do to get that property back," Delaney replied frowning.

"Patience son; there are legal remedies that we can pursue. There is always a lawyer who wants to make some money and can tie things up for quite some time. Despite what Judge Wilkerson says, there is always a way to break a sale or find a reason that a sale wasn't properly recorded. We will take that up but in the mean time, you see what you can find out about Miss McCullum and you start pressing your attentions on her tomorrow. You can ride over and thank her for the party and take it from there. You will know what to say son; if you have one gift it is the gift of gab. You will know what a woman wants to hear. Once we have her tied up, we will have the property regardless of what Jake Nelson has to say about it," Duncan Carmichael replied.

As was predicted, the party wore on with the attendees enjoying the food, the beer, the company and the beauty of the English Rose. By the time all of the attendees had left, the party had wound into the night. Jake stood protectively by Catherine's side as he had promised and would always rely on Chet Stoner or the Judge to be with her in case he needed to make a trip to the buffet line for more beer or cake. He watched those that he had worried about earlier in the day and kept a particularly close eye on Angus Delaney and

Duncan Carmichael. Like many in attendance, he knew their story and he knew their methods. He just needed to make sure that Catherine was warned as he did not want anyone or anything to upset her, particularly snakes like those two. Catherine had said that she wasn't partial to snakes and he needed to make her understand that there were two legged snakes as well as the kind found in the grass.

Jake remained until all of the guests had departed. He took Catherine's hand and he led her up the porch stairs. She was on the third step of the stairs so she could look him in the eye for once. "Jake, can Ramon make up a room for you so that you don't have to go back to your place this evening? I hate for you to ride alone in the darkness," Catherine said worriedly.

"I'll be fine Catherine. I have ridden that path so many times that my horse knows it as well as me. Besides, it wouldn't be proper and I won't have anyone say anything improper about you ever," he said earnestly.

"What about a bed in the foreman's bunkhouse? No one could say anything about that?" Catherine continued.

"No, I will be fine. But thank you for worrying about me. I do want to tell you one thing not to scare you but because I want you to be aware. Angus Delaney and Duncan Carmichael were not invited to your party. They would not have known your Father and they certainly would not have had kind words to say about him because he bought the spread here from the man who was trying to keep it away from those two. They have had a burr under their saddle about that sale ever since. If either one of them come around here Catherine, I want you to promise to send one of the boys after me. I will tell Ramon the same thing. Will you promise me that you will do that for me?" Jake said worriedly.

"Of course Jake; are these men dangerous? I noticed that you were not entirely welcoming to them when they came through the receiving line this evening," Catherine replied.

"No one in this county would welcome them Catherine. They are the type of men who take and never give back to the community or to anyone but themselves. The man who sold the spread to your Father was trying to keep it out of their hands because of the oasis. Water in these parts means life. We can all make a good living from the grass, but we cannot over graze or increase the herd to the extent that we can't feed or water them. If those two had their way, the range would be over grazed and the water would be dry. They only believe in quick money and then I guess they will move on. The folks who were here tonight Catherine want to spend their lives in this valley. They work every day to keep their herds healthy and the land healthy. Your Father understood that and did everything that he could to keep the English Rose in balance like the rest of us do. There is more to the story and I will tell you that as well, but that is the part of the story that concerns the English Rose and you. That is why I needed you to know," Jake responded.

"I understand Jake. There is always someone trying to ruin paradise Jake. It has been like that since biblical times. This is as close to paradise as Father or I would have ever seen, so we would want to do everything possible to preserve it. They are I guess the snakes of the Genesis story. Am I right?" Catherine asked.

"You are right on target Catherine as always. Now, I will ride over tomorrow to visit and I can tell you the rest of the story about Angus Delaney and Duncan Carmichael. For now, you need your rest. Good night Catherine and I will see you tomorrow," Jake replied smiling. He leaned in then and Catherine placed her arms around his neck. He kissed her lightly at first and then very intensely. He smiled when he pulled away and said that when she was on the third step, they could just about see eye to eye. He took her face in his hands and smiled. "Oh by the way; I really do like your dress Catherine. You are beautiful in that dress. I guess I am not used to sharing you that's all," Jake said smiling. She waited on the step until she had seen him climb on his horse and ride away.

In the hallway Ramon had listened and heard Mr. Jake ride away. He had had a talk with Mr. Jake about Delaney and Carmichael and Ramon was ready. He would not let anyone hurt Miss Catherine and he had learned firsthand of what Delaney and Carmichael were capable. He had promised Mr. Jake that someone would ride to get him if those two snakes showed up on the English Rose. He would let the crew know tomorrow also so that they could be on the lookout as well. Delaney and Carmichael had now seen Miss Catherine and unless he missed his guess, they would be back.

*****

The next day Catherine slept in so that she could recover from the party and the lateness of the hour. She thought about the two men that Jake had warned her about. She didn't yet know the rest of the story, but she had to assume that they were both dangerous men who in their own way had terrorized the people of the valley. Jake had told her that he would tell her more when he visited today so she wanted to be ready. She dressed for riding and went down for breakfast. Ramon heard her in the dining room and came out to offer her breakfast.

"Miss Catherine, Mr. Jake told me to be on the lookout for Delaney and Carmichael. He thought that they might be coming here today. I want you to know that I know to send someone after Mr. Jake if they come to the English Rose. The rest of the crew will also know to do that Miss Catherine. They are bad men and Mr. Jake is right to worry about you," Ramon stated.

"Jake told me that they are snakes in the grass Ramon. Can you share any stories about what they have done to make so many people afraid of them?" Catherine asked.

"They are the type of men who can never have enough Miss Catherine. I worked for them at their spread. They treated me and all the people who work for them like they are slaves and not men. I know how to do my job Miss Catherine. I am a good cook and I take care of the people that I work for. Not so in their house. Whatever was done was not enough, not right and always could have been done better. When I came to work for your Father, he had nothing but praise for my work and it has been the same since you have been here. I have never worked for kinder people than the two of you and it makes me want to work even harder every day."

"These two have tried to buy ranches from people who were having a hard time making ends meet. They tried to cheat those people when they were down. They try to overgraze the land. The land will always provide if you take care of it, just like people will always work hard if they know they are appreciated. There are many other stories Miss Catherine and some stories that are not nice for a lady to hear. Mr. Jake will tell you some of them but not all of them. He does not want you to be alone with them Miss Catherine because you are alone here on the ranch during the day. I will always be close by and the other members of the crew will be close by as well, but they are out on the range during the day much of the time," Ramon said earnestly.

"Thank you so much Ramon. I appreciate you sharing this with me so that I can be on my guard. I know that you and Jake only have my best interest at heart," Catherine replied smiling.

After her breakfast, Catherine sat in her Father's library to write some letters home. She wanted to share with her brothers the party that had been held to honor their Father and the wonderful stories that had been shared. She had not yet told them about Jake, but she thought that soon she might need to share with them that a very special person was in her life. As she was writing, she heard a horse enter the front yard. She smiled as she hoped that it was Jake and perhaps he would want to go swimming again at the oasis. She went out on the porch to welcome Jake, but found instead that Angus Delaney was tying up his horse on the hitching post outside of the house. He looked up when he saw Catherine and smiled that same cold smile that she had first noticed last night. She hoped that Ramon was close by and also hoped that Jake would soon be on his way.

"Good day Miss McCullum; I wanted to ride over to thank you for the wonderful party last night. I have been remiss in not riding over to meet you before now. I have heard such wonderful things about you from the people in town. I could not have been prepared for such a beautiful woman although I guess the naming of this spread as the English Rose should have been my first clue. Your Father certainly thought of you when he named the ranch. May I come in Miss McCullum?" Delaney asked.

"Oh I am sure that you will find the porch is one of the places that I entertain the most. May I get you a cup of tea or coffee?" Catherine replied.

"A cup of coffee would be most welcome Miss McCullum." Delaney had sat down on the porch so Catherine thought at least she didn't have to worry about him being in the house. She went inside to fetch the cup of coffee and to alert Ramon. He had already heard the arrival of the horse bearing Delaney and had slipped out the back to alert one of the crew members. He told Catherine to not worry as he would stay in the hallway close by if she needed him and that Mr. Jake would soon be arriving at the ranch.

Catherine went outside with the offered cup of coffee. She did not offer any of Ramon's special cake. She thought after hearing Ramon's story from this morning that Delaney had forfeited the right to any of Ramon's delicacies. "So what brings such a lovely and refined lady to the wilds of New Mexico?" Delaney said smiling.

"New Mexico was a dream of both my Father and of me. We have read about it for so many years. Unfortunately my Father's stay here was a short one, but I have fallen in love with the English Rose and with the territory," Catherine replied.

"Well it certainly is not the place for a lady such as you. Why you should go on to San Francisco or another city of refinement. I cannot imagine you wanting to bury yourself here. Why there must not be a person of your intelligence for fifty miles around here Miss McCullum," Delaney stated.

Catherine thought to herself that there was a fine man not two miles away but decided to keep that thought to herself. "We all have our own dreams Mr. Delaney. I have found both the people and the territory to be very warm and inviting," Catherine replied. Present company excluded of course, she thought to herself.

"Perhaps you would enjoy a trip into town or to a neighboring town. We have a very fine surrey wagon and we would be happy for you to visit our ranch. It is a true place of culture in this wilderness. We have the finest home in the valley if you will excuse my boast. I would love for you to see it sometime," Delaney continued.

"Well that is very kind I am sure. How far away is your ranch Mr. Delaney?" Not far enough for me, Catherine thought to herself.

"We are but a short way away in New Mexico terms. Our ranch is about ten miles away, but of course it seems like another country. We only employ the finest hands and staff. Our cook is from San Francisco and can provide for the most rarified palates. I am sure that you find the local cuisine to be very taxing having grown up in the east," Delaney replied.

"Not at all Mr. Delaney; I have enjoyed each of the Spanish dishes that I have sampled while here in New Mexico. I find that it is always better to respect the local culture and tastes wherever one travels don't you think?" Catherine replied smiling.

Delaney did not respond to that comment and Catherine saw he was not happy with the direction of the conversation. If he thought that Catherine would melt in his arms, he was in for a surprise. Delaney was not the first man in the world who tried to charm her. If he had known her better he would quickly understand that she was a woman who was more interested in honesty in a friend or a relationship than gab, but of course he did not know her and if Catherine had anything to say about it, he never would.

"May I refresh your coffee Mr. Delaney?" Catherine stated smiling.

"No Miss McCullum; I must be going. I would not want to overstay my welcome. I enjoyed our chat. I thank you again for the party last night and will look forward to expanding our friendship. Good day Miss McCullum," Delaney said upon leaving.

"Goodbye Mr. Delaney," Catherine said smiling. Goodbye and good riddance. She was never so happy to see the back of someone and could not wait for Jake to come for his daily visit. She was hoping that he could shed more light on the Delaney-Carmichael connection and on the rest of the story that he had promised her last night.

Delaney and Jake were bound to encounter one another that day or in the days to follow. As Delaney was leaving the ranch, Jake was riding over from his property through the oasis. "Are you heading over to see the charming Miss McCullum Jake? However did you keep her a secret for so long? I will be enjoying getting to know her Jake. May the best man win of course Jake; but I am always the best man," Delaney stated arrogantly.

"Well Angus; there is always a groom and a best man at every wedding isn't there? I don't really see you being either in this case," Jake replied riding onto the English Rose.

When he arrived at the house, he saw Catherine nervously pacing on the porch. He was immediately worried when he got off his horse and took the steps two at a time until he reached the porch. "Catherine I saw Delaney as I was riding over. Did he upset you in anyway?" Jake asked worriedly.

"He is detestable Jake. He thinks that he is better than everyone else and that every woman he meets is supposed to swoon. Please tell me the rest of the story about this man and Carmichael. Ramon shared his story with me this morning. I just want to know how to be better prepared," Catherine said wringing her hands.

"Sit down Catherine; I don't want to see you upset. We can handle Delaney and Carmichael; we just need to all be on our guard; that's all. Now let me go in and get a cup of coffee and some of the special cake and we will have a good talk," Jake said soothingly.

"I will get it for you Jake. You sit down; it will help me to do something with my hands after sitting with that snake. I will be right back," Catherine said smiling.

Well Jake; it has come to this sooner than you thought. You are going to have to let your feelings be known so that you can keep Catherine safe. You are not about to let her fall into the hands of Delaney and Carmichael. I don't think that would happen, but Catherine isn't going to sit here by herself for the rest of her life either assuming that she is planning on staying here which I think she will do. Every time we turn around there are Delaney and Carmichael trying to grab something else in this territory. Well I for one do not plan on sitting still and letting that happen. I think there are others who will agree with me and maybe we can stop this thing once and for all. Catherine came through the screen door then with a cup of coffee for Jake and a piece of Ramon's special cake which was always ready for a visit by Jake. Catherine smiled when she placed the cake and coffee in front of Jake. He took one of her hands as she did so and smiled up at her.

"So do you want the whole unvarnished story of Delaney and Carmichael or the short story Catherine?" Jake said earnestly.

"I think I need to know as much as possible about those two Jake. You were right in thinking that Delaney would come to the English Rose this morning. Ramon thought the same and shared with me his story of working for those two and how they treated their people. He is just the most arrogant, self important person that I have met since I came to New Mexico. To hear him tell it, his house is the best in the valley and his people are the best in the valley and his food is the best in the valley and I am just going to swoon to see everything that he owns. You may not know this about me Jake, but there are other men in the world who have tried to charm me before, but I am not a woman to be easily taken in especially by someone who is all style and no substance," Catherine said heatedly.

"I have never seen you all riled up Catherine. It sure brings the blush to your cheek. I should have told you about Delaney and Carmichael a long time ago," Jake said smiling.

"Don't try to change the subject Jake. What is the story with these two men?" Catherine continued.

"Well the story is not a happy one as I am sure you can understand. It goes all the way back to my Father and Carmichael. They were both in competition for my Mother and of course my Father won that one. Then of course I told you about the sale of the spread that would become the English Rose right out from under Carmichael's nose. That didn't make them any happier. I am not sure what Ramon has told you, but I am sure that he only told you the parts that were fit for a lady to hear. These two like to strike when people are down and then try to buy their ranches for a song when they are having financial problems. I told you last night about the over grazing worry that the responsible ranchers in the valley try to prevent. They treat their hands like slaves and they treat every woman in the valley like she is dying for love of them. They haven't run across one like you before though who is both smart and beautiful and who doesn't take kindly to someone trying to charm her. That will be a new experience for them and I am not sure how they will respond. They are both so dangerous that I don't want to know how they will respond. I am sure that Delaney saw that we had an understanding you might say last night, so that just made him more dangerous and not less when he came calling today," Jake replied.

"Do you mean to say that he would come calling today because he saw that you and I were . . . well friends?" Catherine asked.

"I am afraid so Catherine. By the way, are we just well . . . friends?" Jake replied watching her intently.

"I don't know Jake; we certainly aren't enemies and you certainly don't treat me like I am just another possession that you want to add to your collection. You have been honest with me and you have always tried to help me and teach me things so I take from that you care about me . . . when I am not being a nuisance that is," Catherine said smiling weakly.

"You were never a nuisance Catherine. I told you; I felt responsible for you and your safety because your Father gave me that responsibility; didn't he? I have never been responsible for someone else before and it made me nervous at first. I started to find that I liked being responsible for someone and I liked it when that person was worried about me too. We are definitely not just friends Catherine and I am not your brother either as I made it clear at the oasis," Jake said emphatically.

"I never said you were my brother Jake; I only said that you liked to get into mischief at times just like they did," Catherine said smiling.

"I will not let Delaney or Carmichael ever make you feel uncomfortable in any way. I know what they are like and Ramon knows what they are like. It is better for you to be prepared than to be taken unaware by people like that," Jake replied smiling.

"What about the kind of stories that a lady should not hear about Jake?" Catherine asked quietly.

"Well you would ask me that Catherine; let's just say that Delaney is actually Carmichael's son but they have different names because Carmichael was not married to Delaney's Mother at the time," Jake replied.

"Oh; I see . . . so they are truly two of a kind and not in the good way," Catherine replied.

"I am afraid so Catherine. I have heard other tales about them, but I don't want to spread stories that I can't prove. Let's just leave it at the fact that they are not men that you want to have anything to do with and the respectable people in this valley will tell you the same," Jake replied.

"Would you like to stay for lunch Jake? I know you are busy and I am sorry for taking you away from your ranch chores, but since you came all this way; would you like to stay for lunch? I am sure that Ramon will have some excellent dishes left from last night's party," Catherine said smiling.

"I will be happy to stay to lunch Catherine. I could tell that you were nervous when I saw you pacing on the porch. I don't ever want you to feel that way in your own home Catherine," Jake said.

"I didn't let him any farther than the porch Jake. I thought if I entertained him out here I didn't have to worry about him being in the house and me not being able to get rid of him," Catherine said grinning.

"That was a real good plan Catherine. Don't worry; we will deal with them together. Now, let's see what Ramon has made for lunch," Jake said smiling.

*****

While Jake and Catherine ate their lunch, Delaney returned to his Father's ranch the Triple B. When he tied his horse to the hitching post, Carmichael could see that he was not happy.

"So how did it go with the girl this morning Angus?" Carmichael asked before Angus could sit down.

"Not well Duncan; not well. She is not like any that we have dealt with before. You know she is beautiful, but she is also smart. I felt like I was fencing with her the whole time that I was on that porch. She didn't even have the decency to let me in the house. I sat on the front porch with her drinking coffee. I can't abide women like that Duncan; you know that I can't. We will have to find some way of making sure that Miss McCullum decides to return to Delaware. We don't need her kind here Duncan not one little bit. If people like her keeping coming to this valley, we aren't going to be able to control it and I am not having that either. It is bad enough dealing with the Jake Nelsons of the world without having smart women in cahoots with him," Delaney said heatedly.

"Relax Angus; relax. We will find out something worthwhile on our Miss McCullum and if we don't; you can always take her down a peg or two. I am sure if you had your chance at her, Nelson wouldn't be interested anymore. He is probably a man who would only want a virtuous woman Angus. When you are done with Miss McCullum, she won't want to live in New Mexico and Nelson won't want her. Maybe we will be rid of the both of them, fingers crossed," Carmichael responded.

*****

Before Jake left the English Rose, he asked Catherine if he could speak to the crew man to man. She agreed readily, but didn't know what he would need to discuss with them. Jake went into the bunk house and closed the door behind him. "Men, you know that I asked you all to make sure you did for Miss McCullum whatever you would have done for her Father and of course whatever you would do on any spread. You have done that I am thankful for all of your work. I have a new request concerning her; I am going to ask that you all keep a close lookout for Miss McCullum when it comes to Delaney and Carmichael. You all know what those two are capable of and I need to know that you are all looking out for her. Keep a close eye out and if you see either of those two heading to the English Rose, head back to the house as soon as you can. I appreciate your working together and working as well as you have been doing for Miss McCullum. Thank you again," Jake said.

Catherine watched Jake come out of the bunk house and move towards his horse. He came up on the porch again to say goodbye. "I enjoyed lunch today Catherine. I don't want you to worry about anything. Like I told you, we all look out for each other here in this valley. We are all going to look out for you too. Walk with me a little Catherine," Jake asked.

They left the porch and headed down the lane towards the oasis. "Catherine, I asked you before how you saw the two of us and you said that we were friends; is that how you see me Catherine as your friend?" Jake asked watching her intently.

"Well, I don't think of you just as my friend. Sometimes you are my guardian angel and sometimes you are a teacher and sometimes like when we were at the oasis, you are much more than a friend. But I don't know how you feel do I?" Catherine asked smiling her most magical smile.

"Well Catherine; I don't go around kissing my friends do I?" Jake answered smiling.

"No, I expect not Jake," Catherine replied shyly.

"I want you to know how special you are to me Catherine. I would not have anything happen to you for anything in the world. I want you to rely on me and to call on me just as you did today. You are never a nuisance; in fact you are a joy to me every time we are together. I want you to know that also," Jake said tenderly.

"Thank you Jake. That means a great deal to me. Thank you for saying that." Catherine looked up at him with those magical eyes and that magical smile that he had so come to love. He lifted her up then very slowly off of her feet and she placed her arms around his neck.

"We need those steps back on the porch you know; it makes this a whole lot easier," Jake said laughing.

"Or the oasis so we can be eye to eye," Catherine said grinning. Jake leaned down then and kissed Catherine very passionately. It was like sealing a new understanding of their relationship. Jake hadn't actually told her that he loved her, but she felt that love all the same. He would never let anything happen to her and he wanted her to stay here. She felt that now each time that they were together and it strengthened her resolve to do just that. Let the Delaneys and the Carmichaels of the world come at them, she was going to stay in New Mexico and stand her ground. Because standing on the ground next to her was the man that she knew she loved.

CHAPTER SIX

Two weeks later, Catherine was again sitting in her Father's library in the morning working on ranch business. She loved working in his library because it made her even closer to him. She could sit at his desk and use his chair and his pens and make that day to day connection with him. She knew that he had built this house with her tastes in mind and she knew that he looked out for her every day just as Jake did here in New Mexico. She frequently thought that she had two angels looking out for her; one on earth in the person of Jake and one in heaven. If she counted Ramon, she might actually have three guardian angels. She thought again about Delaney and Carmichael and how even back to the biblical days, there had always been snakes trying to ruin paradise. She hoped that the good people of Buena Vista would join together to keep that from happening. As she sat at her Father's desk, she again heard an approaching horse in the front yard. After the last encounter, she warily approached the front window to look out at who may have arrived. She hoped that it was Jake, but was newly wary. She heard Ramon coming into the hallway at the same time as they were now both wary of approaching horsemen.

"I don't know the man Miss Catherine. I will stand on the porch with you when you greet him," Ramon said earnestly.

Catherine went out on the porch to greet the lone rider. She noticed that a few members of the crew were moving towards the porch also. The entire ranch was on alert and she assumed the crew's wariness resulted from Jake's discussion with them as well. "May I help you sir?" Catherine asked from the porch.

"Are you Catherine McCullum?" the rider inquired.

"I am indeed; how may I help you?" Catherine again asked warily.

"You have been served Catherine McCullum. I have papers here that I am to deliver to you personally. Good day ma'am." The rider handed the papers to Catherine and mounted his horse and rode away.

"Should I have someone go get Mr. Jake?" Ramon asked.

"Let me look at these papers first Ramon, but I would guess that we will need Mr. Jake in short order. These look like legal papers and I assume they are from Delaney and Carmichael," Catherine replied. She went back to her Father's library and sat down with the papers. Ramon had stayed nearby in case she needed him and needed Jake. "Yes Ramon; please send someone over to ask Jake to join me. I think we are going to need to go in and see Judge Wilkerson," Catherine replied. She went upstairs then to get dressed as she didn't want to go into town in her riding clothes despite teasing by Jake and Mr. Stoner. If she went calling, she would always go looking like a lady. That is how she was raised and that was how it would always be.

After she finished dressing, she resumed reviewing the papers in her Father's library. She took them to mean that Delaney and Carmichael were somehow challenging her Father's purchase of the English Rose and questioning the recording of the property documents. She knew that Judge Wilkerson had taken care of that very paperwork for her Father before he was appointed Judge and she also knew that he would not take kindly to this newest effort on Delaney and Carmichael's part to push around their weight and try to take something that did not belong to them. When Jake arrived, she would ask him to drive her into town and they would get this thing straightened out. She went out and asked one of the crew to have the surrey wagon prepared and ready as she needed to go into town. The wagon was prepared and when Jake came into the yard, he saw that Catherine was ready for travelling. He just didn't know where and why at the moment. He swung down from his horse and headed up the porch steps two at a time again. He found her in her Father's library when he entered the house.

"Oh Jake; I am so glad that you are here. Would you be so kind to drive me into town to see Judge Wilkerson? I have been served with papers from Delaney and Carmichael this morning. They are challenging the purchase and recording of the English Rose as if to imply that Judge Wilkerson made some mistake when he took care of Father's paperwork. I will not stand for it and we will fight it in any way that we need to do. I will not let Father's dream be taken away Jake," Catherine replied heatedly. Like the prior encounter, Jake saw the color in her face. She was dressed for calling and ready to do battle. If it hadn't been Delaney and Carmichael again he would have commented on that pretty blush to her cheek, but it was them and he needed to get her in town and get this thing settled. He was not having it and he knew that Judge Wilkerson would not stand for it either.

"Come on Catherine; I see you are already dressed for calling. Let's go see Judge Wilkerson and get this fool thing taken care of. They are just going to keep coming at you until we start fighting back. I will not have it Catherine and I know that Judge Wilkerson will make short work of it. Are you ready to go Catherine?" Jake asked.

"I am Jake. Let me tell Ramon that I am heading into town so he can have lunch ready for us when we return." In a moment she was ready to leave and the two set off for Judge Wilkerson's office.

"You know Catherine; this is just another of their games. This is what they do; they keep pushing until someone pushes back and says enough. I know that Judge Wilkerson will be ready to do just that. They will try the law and then I am not sure what they will try next Catherine. Are you ready for that sweetheart; are you ready for whatever dirty trick they try next?" Jake asked watching Catherine intently.

"I will fight them at every step Jake. They will not take my Father's dream away. They will not take my dream away Jake. Who knows how many other people in this valley have been hurt by those two? At some point it has to end. Judge

Wilkerson will advise us how we start bringing their reign of terror to an end," Catherine replied heatedly. "You just called me sweetheart for the first time," Catherine said smiling.

"That was a quick change in subject," Jake said smiling. "I wondered if you had noticed and it seemed that you did," Jake said taking her hand. "We will get this settled sweetheart; Judge Wilkerson will know what to do," Jake said smiling.

When they arrived in town, Jake tied up the wagon in front of the Judge's office and handed Catherine down from the wagon. They walked into the Judge's office and asked if they could see him. They were immediately shown into his office.

"Well this certainly is a pleasure; what can I do for you two young people," Judge Wilkerson said smiling. He noticed that Catherine was dressed for calling and he hoped that they had the news that he had been waiting on; they wanted to get married and wanted him to marry them.

"Judge, Catherine was served papers this morning from Delaney and Carmichael trying to bring into question the sale of the English Rose to Cameron. We knew that you handled that sale for him and that you would know what to do to fight this," Jake said heatedly.

"There is always some lawyer trying to make a quick dollar by trying one of these stunts. I will have this settled in short order you can be sure. We will file for a summary judgment and have this taken care of quicker than you can get to town from the English Rose. Don't worry Miss McCullum; I am not going to let anyone take that ranch from you and destroy your Father's dream. I will file the paperwork immediately and we will get this thing addressed. Now is there anything else that I can do for the two of you? Miss McCullum certainly looks like she is ready for calling today Jake," Judge Wilkerson said winking at Jake.

"She always looks like she is dressed for calling when she comes to town Judge. She doesn't come to town unless she is dressed for calling do you Catherine?" Jake said smiling.

"It is just how I was raised Judge. You certainly don't go visiting unless you are dressed for calling," Catherine said smiling.

"Well of course; that is how a real lady is raised Jake. Catherine I wonder if I might speak to Jake for a few minutes?" Judge Wilkerson asked.

"Of course Judge; thank you very much for your help. I will just step down to the General Store for a few minutes Jake. Thank you again Judge and we will see you again very soon I hope," Catherine said smiling.

After she had left the office Judge Wilkerson asked Jake to sit down so that they could talk man to man. "Jake I am not surprised by those two snakes or anything that they do or try to do. What I need to talk to you about man to man is Catherine. I know you have been watching out for her and I know also that you have warned the crew at the English Rose to watch out for her. A report has surfaced that has both the Sheriff and I worried sick. We have sources inside their hacienda Jake and some of the reports that come out would make your hair stand on end. We have reason to believe that Delaney may have plans to abduct Catherine. It seems that they have in their pea brains the idea that if she were abducted by Delaney that you would no longer have any interest in her. She would either be forced to marry Delaney to save her reputation or would be forced to return back to Delaware. I know it sounds crazy Jake, but I can't put anything past either one of them," Judge Wilkerson said heatedly.

"You don't know this Jake but Delaney has a bad reputation for beating up women. He usually only goes for fancy women and they are too afraid to file a complaint with the Sheriff or with the courts. Ruby keeps a cabin in the back of her place and the girls who have been beaten up go there to recover. I have met with more than one of them Jake, so I know what I am talking about. I know that a lot of people have heard rumors in the past and just put it down to gossip. Let me tell you Jake it is not gossip; I have seen it with my own eyes. His Father had the same problem and that is why your Mother had the good sense to marry your Father and not Carmichael. Jake if these two were to abduct Catherine, there is no telling what could happen to her. She may never recover from it and you will probably get yourself killed trying to save her. I know that you two have an understanding Jake and I think they figure that she is staying here because of you. My question is this Jake; are you ready to make a commitment to this girl? If you are, this is the time to do it so that you can protect her from the fate that may await her," Judge Wilkerson said.

"You have certainly given me a lot to think about Judge. I had heard the rumors before also and even though I know they are snakes, I guess I never thought they would go that far. I never knew the reason that Mother chose Father other than just good sense, but I can certainly understand now," Jake replied earnestly.

"I wanted to give it time Judge; I wanted Catherine to decide to stay here because she loved it and not just because of me. I know she loves me and I certainly love her; I just wanted to give her time to grieve her Father and to settle in here. I wanted her to see the entire year of weather and everything else that life can bring here in the valley before she decided. I don't think we have that time from what you are telling me Judge. They will try to use her as a pawn and if they hurt her, you are correct; I will probably get myself killed trying to get her back. I just don't want her to do anything that she doesn't want to do Judge," Jake said worriedly.

"I know Jake but you know as well as I that you can't make a woman do something that she doesn't want to do.

Have you ever tried telling Catherine to do something and she said no?" Judge Wilkerson asked smiling.

"Well I did ask her to change her gown on the night of the party and she would have none of it," Jake said smiling.

"No son; I mean something really worthwhile?" Judge Wilkerson asked.

"Well I told her that she needed to wear a real hat in this sun and she did it the very next day. I told her to only ride astride instead of side saddle and she did that the next day too. I told her not to ride out alone and she hasn't done that since the first day she was here. I told her to learn how to shoot and I gave her lessons and she can hit all of her targets now and she had never even touched a gun before coming here. I don't know about shooting someone or something, but she knows how to handle a gun now," Jake replied grinning.

"It sounds like she listens to good advice when she hears it. Jake you don't want something to happen to that girl that she may never recover from. If you feel for her like I believe you do, you need to do something about it sooner rather than later," Judge Wilkerson advised.

"You are right Judge. Can you meet us at the English Rose in the morning? If you can, I will ask Catherine on the way back today to marry me. If you marry us at the English Rose, we can make it to my cabin in the mountains before word even gets out to Delaney and Carmichael. By the time that they find out, I will have spirited her away and they will have to come up with something else to come at us. I know they will try, but at least we can fight them together and I can protect her myself. I will prepare the crew at the English Rose and my own crew so that is a good number of men to fight off whatever is coming our way," Jake replied.

"Good man Jake; I thought you were coming to ask me to marry you today, so I knew that I needed to share this information with you. I wish you had more time Jake, but I think you have both run out of time. If they know that she is there on her own, she is very vulnerable. I know you won't stay at her house without the two of you being married as you don't want to sully her reputation. Those bastards will have no such reservations Jake and you know it," Judge Wilkerson responded.

"Alright Judge; I will go pick up Catherine and try to convince her to marry me on the way back to the English Rose," Jake said smiling.

"I don't think it will be that hard son. The whole valley has seen how you look at her and how she looks at you. Her Father knew what he was doing when he placed her in your hands. I think he was giving her to the best man that he knew and he was right Jake. It was meant to be," Judge Wilkerson stated.

"You have just given me an idea Judge. I think I know just how to ask her. Thank you again and we will see you in the morning at the English Rose," Jake replied.

Jake went down to the General Store to find Catherine. When he entered the store, she was standing talking to Mrs. Downes who was showing her some of the latest material that had been received for fall of the year. Catherine turned then when she saw Jake in the doorway. Her smile told him all that he needed to know. She smiled at him as if he was her entire world. She absolutely lit up when she smiled at him. He knew that she was his entire world and to think that someone was planning on hurting her was more than he could bear. "Are you ready Catherine?" Jake said smiling.

"I am Jake; thank you Mrs. Downes; I will be in later to look at your pattern selection for fall. If you can help me make up some of the dresses that we discussed that would be just fine," Catherine stated smiling. Jake held the door for her and held her hand as soon as they left the store. Catherine looked up at him again, surprised by the fact that he was holding her hand. She smiled that smile again and he knew that his course was an easy one; he would ask her to marry him on the way back to the English Rose.

"Is everything alright Jake; did the Judge have worries about the summary judgment?" Catherine asked worriedly.

"Oh no Catherine; he will start on that right away. We talked about some other things going on in the valley. We will talk about it some more later on Catherine," Jake said smiling. Jake helped her back into the surrey wagon and they headed out for the English Rose. He thought about the first time that he had driven her out to the ranch and how much he was trying to convince her then to get back on the train. He knew that she would never leave now unless it was to visit her brothers. He wished he could send her back there now to be safe, but he knew that it was time that the entire valley took a stand. Catherine was just the most recent victim and he wasn't going to let her be hurt for any reason on earth. It ended here and now. He drove them to the oasis on the way back to the English Rose. He knew how he wanted to ask her to marry him and where.

"Are we stopping off to see Father's grave Jake?" Catherine asked. "I think he would want to know what is going on and that we will not let anything happen to the English Rose," Catherine said earnestly.

I will not let anything happen to either English Rose, Jake thought. He had hoped that he would have more time to court her. He certainly had enjoyed courting Catherine, but he also knew that he would enjoy being married to her even more. The life ahead of him spread out before his eyes as if he were reading a story book; Catherine and him married; Catherine as a Mother; the cattle being brought to the rail head each fall; the parties that they would hold for the community. All of it was dependent on the answer that she would give him and the way in which Delaney and Carmichael were dealt with in the days, weeks and months to follow. They could not live their life in fear and neither could the rest of the valley. But for now, he needed to keep Catherine safe and he knew how and where to do so. He drove over to Cameron's grave just as he had done on the first day that he brought her to the

English Rose. He had something to ask her and he needed to have her Father's blessing as well. When they arrived at the gravesite, he helped Catherine down and they went to stand at her Father's resting final place just as they had done so many times before this day."Catherine, I have something to ask you today and I want your Father to be witness to that question. I know that he placed you in my hands because he was doing so for a reason. He wanted you to be taken care of and he wanted me to take care of you. As I told you before; at first it was a responsibility that I was not comfortable holding. I had never been responsible for anyone but myself and of course my ranch. As I came to understand what it would be like to be responsible for you, I found that there was someone who wanted to be responsible for me as well and that felt very good indeed. I am asking you Catherine in the presence of your Father for your hand in marriage. Will you do me the honor of becoming my bride Catherine?" Jake asked earnestly.

Catherine looked up at Jake with her beautiful eyes and her magical smile. "Yes Jake; I will be honored to be your wife. You are the best man that Father could have ever chosen for me. Once I realized that I wasn't a nuisance to you, I knew there was no one that I would rather be with than you Jake. You taught me what I needed to know and you have been my guardian angel and so much more ever since the first day that I arrived in Buena Vista. The answer is yes Jake; I will marry you," Catherine said smiling with shining eyes. Jake lifted her up off her feet very gradually and brought her to his level to kiss her very intensely. She put her arms around his neck making sure she didn't cut off his breath in the process. Her Father who had brought them together may not have seen them together on earth, but he certainly watched from heaven along with her other guardian angels; Jake's parents and her Mother.

"I know this is sudden sweetheart and I apologize for that, but Judge Wilkerson will be coming in the morning to marry us at the English Rose. I will explain all to you tomorrow, but trust me it needs to happen in this way Catherine. Do you trust me sweetheart?" Jake asked worriedly.

"Of course Jake; you have never done anything but take care of me from the very first. I would always trust your judgment," Catherine replied.

"Let's get you home because I am sure that Ramon will want to make a very special cake indeed for tomorrow. We don't have much time and it won't be the wedding that I would have wished for you, but it will have all of the same love behind it Catherine. I will devote my life to making you happy and making you the most loved woman in the valley; that is my solemn vow before your Father and before God," Jake replied smiling. Jake helped her back into the surrey wagon and held her hand for the remainder of the trip. He knew that a lot of activity was going to spring to life when they returned to the English Rose. He would get Catherine settled and then return home and pack for their trip tomorrow. Once the wedding was concluded, he would take her to his mountain cabin. No one knew its location except him and he knew that he would keep her safe until they could get a longer term plan in place.

On arriving at the English Rose, Jake took Catherine inside the house and made her promise to stay inside for the rest of the day. "I have so much to do Jake that it will not be a burden. Are we going to spend our honeymoon here Jake or do I need to pack for a trip?" Catherine asked.

"We will be taking a trip Catherine. Pack with warm clothes for night and lighter clothes for the day. Don't pack any of your ten pound dresses as we will be very simple in our surroundings. Make sure that you wear your riding clothes to leave here tomorrow. I will explain everything that you need to know tomorrow. Thank you Catherine for making me the happiest man in New Mexico and probably the whole world," Jake said smiling. She went to stand on the third step of the staircase so that he wouldn't have to lift her up. Jake kissed her again passionately and told her that he loved her with all of his heart. He would be back to make her his bride in the morning.

Catherine stood at the screen door and watched him mount his horse and ride away. She waved and blew him a kiss. He waved and smiled as he rode away. Just one more day Catherine and all of your dreams will come true, she thought. She went directly to the kitchen to tell Ramon what had happened so that he could prepare a cake and breakfast for the Judge, Jake and the crew in the morning. Ramon smiled from ear to ear as he heard the news. He thought to himself that Mr. Jake would keep her safe. He didn't yet know the plan, but he knew that Mr. Jake would keep her safe.

CHAPTER SEVEN

The day of the wedding arrived clear and beautiful. Catherine knew that so much of the day was still a mystery, but she also knew that she was going to marry the man that she loved and the man that her Father had especially chosen for her. Jake did not know that she had brought her Mother's wedding gown with her in her multiple suitcase luggage set. She had no idea if she would ever wear it, but she did know that as the only girl, it fell to her to maintain the dress. She had packed it when she left Delaware and now would wear it to marry the man that she loved. He would be surprised that she had her own wedding gown waiting for him, but then he would be happy as well that she was having a real wedding if not the wedding of her dreams.

Ramon had worked through the day to make her the wedding cake that he had planned. He hoped that Mr. Jake and Miss Catherine would have another real wedding in the future with the whole town there to share their happiness just as they had been there to honor her Father. Today was important because Mr. Jake had to protect Miss Catherine from what was being planned by the two snakes of the valley and he needed to do it now before something worse happened. He had heard the stories from the hacienda and he knew that nothing worthwhile ever came from the Triple B.

Catherine had risen early and prepared for the morning's events. She had taken out the dress the prior night and made sure that it was ready to be worn. She had also packed her nightgown, robe and slippers as her warm items and packed different shirts to wear with her riding clothes as well as jackets. They were the simplest items in her wardrobe and since Jake had told her no ten pound dresses, she knew that she needed to dress simply and for practicality. She still didn't know the complete story yet, but feared that Delaney and Carmichael had something to do with the expedited wedding. She knew that whatever was coming their way, she just wanted to be with Jake and the location made little difference to her. She hoped that they would live at the English Rose going forward. She knew that Jake was aware how important the Rose was to her particularly when it had been built for her by her Father. She was just excited that her love for Jake was reciprocated and that the two would marry today. Everything else including the legal maneuvering would be sorted out in short order.

She went downstairs to check in with Ramon about the cake and the wedding breakfast. He had everything in hand and told her she needed to stay above stairs in case Mr. Jake came early. He mustn't see her until it was time for the wedding. They had chosen her Father's library as the location of the wedding as it held so many special memories for Catherine. Her Father's personal items were there as well as the miniature of the first Catherine in their family; the one who was the mirror image of the present day Catherine. Everything was set and ready. Catherine had only to dress and to present herself at the appropriate time to marry Jake.

Judge Wilkerson arrived with his wife shortly thereafter. Ramon showed them into the library and explained that this was the room where Miss Catherine wanted the ceremony to take place. The Judge could see the many influences of her Father in this room and understood why it had special meaning for Catherine. Jake had had many great conversations in this room with her Father, so it was special to him as well. Mrs. Wilkerson went upstairs to see if she could be helpful to the bride. As she knocked on the door, Catherine was dressing and Mrs. Wilkerson explained that she was there to help.

"Your help will be very much appreciated Mrs. Wilkerson. I seem to be all thumbs today and am having trouble finishing off my corset," Catherine replied smiling. She had already completed her hair and all of the clothing items were laying on the bed for her to change into.

"Your gown is simply lovely my dear. Is this a family gown?" Mrs. Wilkerson asked.

"Yes this is my Mother's gown. I am the only girl you see so it came to me for safe keeping. I know that Jake and Mr. Stoner teased me about my endless luggage suite when I first arrived, but this was one of the items that I brought from home along with all of my other possessions it seems," Catherine said smiling. Mrs. Wilkerson helped her with the corset and thought that she had never seen such a tiny waist. Catherine must have taken after her Mother in that respect as well as the dress looked like it had been designed for a doll. The dress was ivory satin with two pieces; a bodice that had an oval shaped neckline with a bow at the bust line. The corset meant that the bodice was pulled into a deep hourglass curve. The skirt was A-lined with ruffles at the hem. A full length veil fell from a floral headpiece. It was traditional yet classic; the type of wedding gown that could be worn in the 1860's or the 1880's without thought to decade. Catherine's tiny feet were encased in ivory satin shoes. She had a cameo around her neck that had also belonged to her Mother. Ramon had picked flowers from the garden for her this morning and they lay on her dressing table gathered in a large rose ribbon. She would indeed be the English Rose today. Mrs. Wilkerson hoped like Ramon that this ceremony could be performed again for the whole town when the dreadful matter before them was resolved. She was not sure how much Catherine knew of that matter and did not want to scare her any further. She assumed that Jake would explain everything to her once he had spirited her away. It was all positively medieval and she hoped that her husband could do everything in his power to stop the evil that was permeating their valley.

"Jake Nelson is without a doubt one of the best men that I have ever met Miss McCullum. He will be a wonderful husband as he has been a wonderful friend and neighbor to everyone in the valley. You have nothing to fear Miss

McCullum about that man and his love for you. Everyone in the valley sees it and we all know that you will both be very happy," Mrs. Wilkerson stated. She decided she had better stop talking now because she was going to cry even if the bride didn't. Who had ever heard of trying to kidnap a girl so that she would turn over a ranch to someone who didn't need any more ground and was a monster to boot? Well it will all be sorted and that is an end to it.

There was a knock on the door then and Ramon let Miss Catherine know that Mr. Jake was here and they were all ready for her when she was ready. "Thank you Ramon; I will be down in just a few minutes," Catherine replied. She looked so radiant that Mrs. Wilkerson felt certain that she didn't know the true reason for the expedited wedding. Jake could tell her once he had her safely hidden away.

"Well Mrs. Wilkerson; I think I am ready. Do I look alright?" she asked shyly.

"You are so beautiful Miss McCullum. Jake will certainly have the most beautiful bride in the valley. Are you ready then? If so, I will go on downstairs. Ramon says you are to be married in the library. I will see you there my dear. Don't forget your hanky." With that Mrs. Wilkerson left Catherine's room and she was left to contemplate for a few minutes before going downstairs. She said a quick prayer of thanks, looked at the picture of her Mother and Father and turned to go downstairs.

She walked down the stairs alone and turned at the bottom to go into the library. When she reached the door, everyone stood and turned to see the bride. Jake was standing next to the Judge and when he turned, he smiled from ear to ear. She thought he was the most handsome man that she had ever seen and he knew that she was the most beautiful bride. She looked just like a doll come to life. He remembered her saying that people in Lewes, Delaware had thought her ancestor a marble statute come to life; Catherine was a tiny, precious doll to him and he would vow to keep her safe. She looked throughout the room and saw Ramon smiling ear to ear and the members of the crew. Not all were inside because many had volunteered to keep look out for Delaney and his crew. No one wanted a skirmish today of all days. She walked over to stand next to Jake and he took her hand and kissed it.

Judge Wilkerson smiled also. He was not happy about how the wedding had been expedited, but he was happy that his warning to Jake had brought it about. He wanted nothing to happen to the beautiful woman in front of him and the good man he was about to make her husband. He knew that Jake would spirit her away. He knew also that the native peoples of the mountains who Jake and his family had protected for decades would be the best protection for them both until Jake could safely bring her home. The Judge had asked Jake before the wedding to give him a week to bring in the US Marshal to investigate the many claims against Delaney and Carmichael. He would get word to Jake when it was safe to bring her home. Until then, as the Judge reminded him, he would be on his honeymoon with the most beautiful woman in the valley. Jake smiled then and said that he had thought of that and it was a happy duty indeed.

When the Judge had concluded the vows and Jake had given Catherine his Mother's ring, the Judge stated that Jake could now kiss his bride. They all wondered how that would be accomplished since Jake was so tall and Catherine so tiny. The Judge figured that they had a solution for it and so they did. Jake lifted Catherine and she put her arms around his neck. The Judge thought that they must have practiced that before because they did a good job of it.

The group moved then to the dining room for a quick breakfast and Ramon's wedding cake. Ramon was packing special treats for the bride and groom to take to the place of hiding that Jake had prepared for his bride. As happy as Ramon was to see this wedding, he would be happier when the bride and groom were spirited away. He knew that the

English Rose crew would be following them to Jake's ranch and that the Trinity crew would then follow them to the base of the mountain. After that only Jake knew the destination and he was not talking. In this way both crews had deniability when Delaney and Carmichael's crew came to look for Catherine. Jake had requested that the crews move the herds into the home paddocks until this matter was over as he did not want any of the men in the far flung pastures until the issues could be resolved. He had told his men the same. Both crews would now look out one for the other as the two ranches were now joined by the marriage of Catherine and Jake. The oasis that had brought them together was now the center of one much larger ranch. All of that would be worked out at a later time as well. Jake now needed to get Catherine to his place of hiding as quickly as possible.

Once she had completed her breakfast, Jake asked Catherine if she needed help getting changed out of her wedding dress. She blushed deeply at that comment and Mrs. Wilkerson volunteered to help her change. Jake was going to change in the library into his riding clothes. Everything except Ramon's treats was already on the pack horse that would accompany them into the mountain. Ramon quickly wrapped food for his mistress and her new husband. The crew was ready to mount and accompany Catherine and Jake to the border of his ranch.

With Mrs. Wilkerson's help, Catherine quickly changed into her riding clothes. She looked around her room one final time and went downstairs to meet Jake and her next adventure. He was already out next to her horse and took her hand when she reached the bottom of the porch steps. Judge Wilkerson stood with Jake. The plan had been finalized and they would meet again hopefully in a week's time. If the Judge needed longer, he would get word to Jake through the chain of security that would now keep them safe.

Catherine thanked Judge Wilkerson and Jake helped her to mount her horse. In the space of an hour, they had been married, had their wedding breakfast and now were setting off. Catherine knew that something was not right, but she also knew that her new husband had the support of the valley as always and that both her crew and Jake's crew had been mobilized to get them to safety. She knew that Delaney and Carmichael were at the bottom of it all and that Jake would tell her everything when they got to the place they were going. She just looked over at Jake and smiled whenever she could gain his attention. His jaw was set and she knew that he was focused on the destination ahead of them.

When they reached the border of Jake's ranch, the English Rose crew turned and returned back to her ranch. Jake's Trinity crew took over then and escorted them until they reached the base of the mountains. When she saw the mountains ahead of them, she knew that their destination must be Jake's mountain cabin. He had mentioned it before and she knew that he only went there to hunt, fish and swim. She didn't think he was taking her there to do any of those things, but she also knew that he would explain when they arrived as he had promised.

One hour into the mountain trail, Jake let out a whistle that sounded like a bird call to Catherine. The whistle was met with another whistle and then another until Catherine realized that they were surrounded by a group of native peoples. She had never seen real life native people in their own surroundings before. She wondered if Jake had ever brought her Father here or anyone for that matter. She felt as if she was in the middle of one of the novels read by her and her Father when still at home in Delaware. It was a feeling both strange and comforting as she knew from their faces that Jake was a friend to these people. They smiled at her and talked to Jake in a language that she had never heard before. Jake seemed to both understand and speak the language. He pointed to Catherine and touched his heart. He must be explaining that I am now his wife, she thought. They waved to Jake and closed ranks behind them. The trail continued on and they continued climbing higher and higher into the mountains. She understood now why Jake had told her to pack warm clothes for the night and cool clothes for the day. She thought that it must grow cold here at night and was glad that she had her warm robe, nightgown and slippers with her.

For another hour they climbed higher into the mountains. Jake kept turning to make sure that she was alright. She knew that no one had ever made this trip with Jake and the higher they climbed, she had a fleeting thought that not only the native people would protect them, but that they were moving closer and closer to God and he and her family angels would protect them as well. She saw a clearing ahead of them then and a rustic cabin that was nestled in the woods. She thought it looked like something from the Brothers Grimm Fairy Tales. She would ask Jake who in his family had built the cabin and all of its history. There was time for many questions, but she would try not to burden him with questions on this day of all days. She had decided that whatever had been the reason for their expedited wedding, she did not want that reason to mar her wedding day. She would ask that Jake explain everything to her tomorrow. As for today, she only wanted to tell Jake how much she loved him and have him tell her the same.

When they arrived at the clearing, Jake tied up the horses and helped Catherine down from her mount. "I know that you are probably tired from all of that riding, but you did so very well in keeping up Catherine. I know I pushed hard, but I just wanted to get us here and to make sure we were here by sunset. Even for a person who knows the way, you don't want to be on the trail after dark. I know you will have a million questions for me and I promise that I would tell you all. Let's get the horses unpacked and then we can have a good long talk," Jake stated.

Catherine walked a bit to stretch her legs after the long ride. She felt that she had entered yet another oasis. This oasis was more tree lined and had a sparkling lake, the tree canopy and the rustic cabin. It was another perfect Eden as far as she could see and she was here with the man that she loved most in the world. The rest of the world and whatever had prompted their flight was behind them. It was time to focus on her husband and their honeymoon.

When they reached the porch, Jake smiled down at her and lifted her off her feet. "It may not be our permanent home Catherine, but it is our first threshold. I love you my darling girl and I am so happy to bring you here. I have never brought anyone here before Catherine; you are the first. It was built by my Grandfather who was also the first to ranch at the Trinity. I know you have a million questions my love but first, let me get a fire going and check out the cabin for you. Did you bring warm clothes like I suggested?" Jake asked.

"I packed exactly as you told me Jake. I have warm things for the nighttime and I have cooler things for the day. And there are no ten pound dresses anywhere to be found although Ramon has certainly packed us ten pounds of food. He just kept wrapping things before we left so I am not sure everything that we will have to eat. He is such a wonderful man Jake; they have all been so wonderful to me darling," Catherine said with tearful eyes.

"And that is the first time that you have called me darling. I find that I like that a lot Mrs. Nelson. You may have to call me that all the time from now on," Jake said grinning. He put Catherine down on her feet then and kissed her as he slowly released her to the ground. "Alright first thing first; let's unpack the horses and I will gather wood for the fire. It will get cold tonight in these mountains so we should have a fire going quickly," Jake stated smiling.

Catherine released the items from the horses and brought all of the items that she had packed into the cabin. She thought it must be exactly like Jake's house. He had told her it was a very masculine affair. The cabin had animal skins on the walls and in front of the fire that she assumed Jake or his family must have hunted. There was one large front room with chairs and a table and a massive fire place. Beyond this room was a second massive room with an equally massive bed. She assumed that Jake's family must have all been tall like him and like her own Father and brothers. There was a smaller curtained area beside the bed chamber which appeared to be a private changing area. She wondered if Jake's Mother had requested that innovation or if Jake had prepared it. She thought then of her great-great-great Grandmother's description of the magical cottage that she had lived in with her husband. She would have to remember to tell Jake about that as he would love the comparison. She decided that this was a magical cabin just as the original Catherine and Cameron had had a magical cottage.

She went to the door then to look out on the lake and the clearing in front of her. She wondered if they could swim in this lake or if the water would be too cold for swimming. Knowing Jake as she did, she thought the cold would not bother him although it would certainly bother her. Jake was coming up the path than with an armful of wood for the fire. He had said that it was important that a fire be started as the nights would be cold here. She had noticed a heavy quilt on the massive bed and was relieved to see that there would be blankets. When she thought of that massive bed she also briefly thought of her wedding night. She decided to file that thought away for the present time also. She knew how much Jake loved her and that he would be patient with her and whatever was to occur between them tonight.

She watched as Jake started a fire in the massive fireplace. There was still so much that she didn't know about the expedited wedding, Jake's relationship with the native people and the beauty of this cabin. She would sit down at the table and wait for Jake to tell her the many stories that she needed to know. This would be their first conversation as man and wife as the expedited wedding and breakfast did not count. She could feel the urgency all morning of the need to leave the English Rose as quickly as possible. Ramon had conveyed the urgency as well as Jake, the Judge and the crew. She didn't know the reason that she had been spirited away, but she knew that somehow Delaney and Carmichael were behind it.

Once the fire had taken hold, Jake took her hand, sat down and pulled her onto his lap. "Well Mrs. Nelson; would you like a snack after travelling all of that way? I am sorry that we had to keep such a pace but we needed to get here before dark as I told you before," Jake said smiling.

"I know Jake; so you said. Jake I am only going to ask you one question today about why we are here; does it have anything to do with Delaney and Carmichael?" Catherine asked quietly.

"It does my love. Do you want me to tell you the whole story now or just the short version?" Jake asked.

"There always seems to be a short version and a long version when it comes to those two. If you don't mind Jake, I would like to wait until tomorrow to hear the long version of the latest tale. I don't want them to ruin my wedding day Jake," Catherine replied.

"I know it wasn't much of a wedding day Catherine and I will make that up to you as soon as this whole sorry mess is over. You looked so beautiful my love. Was that your Mother's wedding gown?" Jake asked smiling.

"It was my Mother's wedding gown. I know that you and Mr. Stoner teased me about my endless luggage set when I arrived, but it was one of the things I brought with me. As the only girl in the family it was my dress to keep and maintain so I brought it with me. Wasn't it lucky that I had a dress just waiting for you to ask me to marry you?" she said grinning.

"Well if not that dress Catherine, you could have worn one of the other many other dresses in your closet," Jake said laughing.

"I know darling; but it wouldn't have been the same now would it? Jake, did your Father build this cabin or did your Grandfather?" Catherine asked.

"I would have to say both of them built it. My Grandfather built the large room that we are sitting in and that was the entire cabin during his time. Then my Father built the bed chamber. I built the small dressing room to the side and may need to build something else to please my wife as my Father and Grandfather built parts to please their wives," Jake replied.

"Tell me about the native peoples that we met when we came up the mountain Jake. It was like a story book to see them in real life," Catherine stated.

"When my Grandfather first came into the valley he had five head of cattle with him. The winter that year was one of the harshest in memory. He cut out one of the head of cattle to make sure that the native people would not starve. That established the relationship between them and my family. Each year my Grandfather and then my Father would cut out a steer to make sure that the tribe made it safely through the winter, The mountain is sacred to them Catherine. The Trinity ranch is the portal to the mountain that they regard as sacred. It is my responsibility to protect that portal and to protect the mountain just as my Father had done and my Grandfather had done before him. We always had a wonderful relationship with the native people. We have learned their language and we all look out for one another. As Ramon said, you protect the land and the land will protect you. Likewise you protect the people and the people will protect you. You are safe here my love and you will always be safe on this sacred mountain. No one knows how to get here except for me and the tribe of course. You will find small gifts on our porch each day that we are here because they know that we have just been married," Jake said smiling.

"That is such a lovely story Jake. Is that why you never entertain at the Trinity?" Catherine asked.

"Well I was being honest when I said that the Trinity is a very masculine affair and nothing like what you would be used to at the English Rose. But it is also true that I do not entertain there as I do not want people to become overly curious about the mountain and the people who live here. The way I figure it, they have lost so much land to folks like Delaney and Carmichael. What little bit that they still oversee belongs to them and to no one else," Jake replied.

"Are there fish in the lake Jake? I remember you saying that you came here to hunt, fish and swim," Catherine asked.

"There are fish and we can have fresh fish every night if you like. I know you had fish in Delaware and this will be like those fish though not the same kind of course," Jake replied.

"Jake what happens if Delaney or Carmichael comes to either the English Rose or the Trinity while we are here? Won't they start looking for us?" Catherine asked worriedly.

"Both crews can honestly say that we are not at either ranch. They can wonder where we are, but both crews honestly do not know. They only know that we are not at either ranch. You are not to worry about that today either Mrs. Nelson. You are to worry only about your husband on your wedding day and I am only to worry about my bride. It will get dark soon so I will go out and bring in some water from the lake for us to bathe. How does that sound my love?" Jake asked smiling.

"It sounds like it will be very cold Jake," Catherine replied worriedly.

"Ah but that is why we have the fire place so that I can heat some for you. You see, I think of everything or at least I tried to. There will be something that I will have forgotten in my haste to pack for our trip but as long as I have my beautiful wife in my arms, nothing else matters to me," Jake said smiling and kissing Catherine very tenderly.

Catherine went back to the bed chamber then and the small dressing area beside it. She thought that she should lay out her clothes in case she was unable to see after darkness set in. She still could not shake the thought that she was in a lovely, secluded cabin like the ones in the Brothers Grimm stories. In all it had been a very eventful and educational day. She still had so much to learn about the valley and its people, but she knew that Jake would teach her everything that she needed to know just as he had done since the first day that she arrived in Buena Vista.

When Jake returned with the water and it had been heated, she would start getting ready for bed while there was still light. She wasn't sure what would happen tonight, but she knew that she was married to the best man that she knew and he also happened to be her guardian angel, teacher and friend. She thanked her Father then for selecting him for her and her Father in heaven for sending him to her. She was so full of love on that day that despite the obstacles ahead of them, she found it difficult to do anything but smile. She would have much to write about to her brothers when she was able to return to the English Rose and to her diary. There would be much to write about indeed; just like the novels that she and her Father had read about the old west.

Jake brought her a basin of heated water a few minutes after. She told him that she would go ahead and change for the night before they lost the light. When she said the words, *lost the light*, he thought of one of the things that he had forgotten to pack; he had brought no candles for the cabin and he was sure that he had none in the cabin from previous visits as he had always woken up by the sun and gone to sleep when it was dark. "It is alright my love; as long as we are together we don't need candles," Catherine replied smiling.

"I wanted very much to see your face when I made love to you for the first time. Don't worry Catherine; everything will be fine. I will take care of you and you will take care of me just like we talked about," Jake said smiling.

Catherine went back to the dressing room and changed out of her riding clothes. The warm water felt so wonderful after the long day of riding. She took out her lavender soap that she had especially packed for their trip and began to get ready for the night ahead.

While Catherine got ready in the dressing room, Jake went out on the porch to wash and clear his head. He was amazed at how calm Catherine was given the hurry to leave the valley and retreat to the mountains. He knew that there would be many conversations over the next few days to discuss the way forward, but one thing he did know for sure; he had married the love of his life. He had loved her from the first time that he set eyes on her; he just didn't know it at the time. He had tried very hard to push her away thinking that he didn't want the responsibility of a wife and one from the east to boot. What he had truly feared was falling in love with such a magical creature only to have her decide to return to Delaware and her family. That fear was now behind him. They might go back for a visit to Delaware and her family would hopefully come out here to see the English Rose; but for now the love of his life was changing for him and he would make love to her tonight; tenderly and with much care.

When Jake had finished washing, he closed and bolted the front door. It would be dark soon and the cold would soon begin as well. He knew how easily Catherine became cold and he would keep her warm that was for sure. He stoked up the fire and sat unwrapping some of the treats that Ramon had sent along with them. One of these containers would definitely house either special cake or wedding cake and he was looking for one or the other. It was funny how he never ate cake until he started visiting the English Rose. Many things had changed since he started visiting the English Rose. Catherine came out of the bed chamber then dressed for the winter frost. He smiled when he saw her and thought; well

Jake, she did exactly what you told her to do. She has on a nightgown, robe and slippers that most people would wear in December.

"Catherine, are you dressed for the winter frost there darling? I know I told you to dress warmly for the nights but I meant warm for August not warm for December," Jake said laughing.

"Well I did exactly as you said Jake and you know that I get cold so this is what I brought. It feels very comfortable right now so I expect it to feel very good indeed when it starts to get cold tonight," Catherine replied.

"You know that I will be here to keep you warm Catherine. You won't be sleeping alone anymore my love," Jake said smiling.

"I know that Jake," Catherine said blushing "but you always tell me to follow your directions so that is what I did. From now on, you can see what I will be packing and can tell me if it is too warm or too cool for wherever we are going," Catherine said smiling. "Don't forget Jake; I didn't know where I was going so it was hard to pack properly," Catherine continued.

"Especially without bringing that entire set of luggage with you. I am very proud of your packing for this trip by the way. Otherwise we would have needed two pack horses or maybe more," Jake said grinning. He was just starting to relax after the worry of getting them to the cabin. He also planned on enjoying his wedding night regardless of how expedited the wedding had become.

"Catherine I need to ask you a question before we get ready for bed. Do you know what takes place between a man and a woman when they are married?" Jake asked tenderly.

"Well no Jake; I know that we have kissed and that I have liked that very much and that you have held me and I have liked that very much and you have held my hand . . . but no Jake; I don't know. I know that you will teach me everything that I need to know because that is what you always do right?" Catherine said smiling shyly.

"That is right my love. I will teach you and it will be my great joy to teach you. Please know that I love you and that I would never do anything to hurt you. I only want to make you happy always. You understand that right?" Jake asked tenderly.

"Of course Jake; you held me when we went swimming at the oasis and you kissed me for the first time and it was wonderful Jake. I felt like I was floating," Catherine replied wistfully.

"That is how I want you to feel tonight as well Catherine. Remember when I told you to just feel; that is what I want you to remember tonight as well; just feel Catherine; just feel my love for you and that wonderful feeling of floating," Jake said smiling. He took her hand then and led her into the bed chamber. It was already so dark that he could barely see his hand in front of his face. He turned back the covers, sat down on the edge of the bed and stood Catherine in front of him. He slowly untied her robe and taking it off, placed it across the bed. He reached up then and felt for the buttons to her nightgown. He unbuttoned each one of them feeling the buttons rather than seeing them. When he had unbuttoned her nightgown, he slipped it over her head and held her tiny waist in his two hands. Catherine placed her hands on his shoulders then and he pulled her down onto his chest. He felt rather than saw her silken hair fall beside his face. He drank in her lavender scent and kissed her deeply. She placed her arms around his neck as she had done so many times since he first kissed her. His hands circling her waist began to rhythmically stroke her back and bottom. Jake groaned then deep in his throat and Catherine sighed which he captured with his deep kiss. Jake mated his tongue with Catherine's and she softly moaned telling him that she liked that action. He rolled her to her back and stood up to remove his trousers. When he returned to the bed, he took her face in his hands and continued to kiss her deeply. His hands began to stroke her neck and travelled further to her silky breasts. He heard her quick intake of breath at that juncture. Jake stopped then and told her it was alright; "Just feel Catherine; feel my love for you," Jake said.

His hands returned to her breasts as he caressed and cherished her, his mouth returning to her full and parted lips. Catherine became restless under his touch and his hands slowly moved to her abdomen and to her outer and inner thighs. Her skin was as soft and silky as he had always thought it would be. He thought his own hands too rough and calloused for such silken skin. She thought his hands the warmest thing that she had ever felt and she never wanted him to stop touching her.

Jake returned again to her mouth and mated his tongue with hers in preparation for the lovemaking that was to follow. He gently touched the inner recesses of her intimacy then and she again gasped with that touch. Jake quietly reassured her that all would be well and that he wanted her to feel his love for her. She relaxed against him again slowly and restlessly moved against him, craving his touch. Her response to him prompted him again to caress her gently and prepare her for the lovemaking that was to follow. "Catherine love; put your arms around my neck. I am going to come inside you love. Please don't be afraid; I love you Catherine," Jake said huskily. Catherine placed her arms around Jake's neck and he slowly entered her preparing himself for the pain that he knew would follow. She cried out this time in pain and he felt the warm tears against his chest. Jake stroked her face and kissed her deeply waiting for the pain to subside. He kept saying words of love and assurance to her that he would soon make it better and that she would soon feel his love for her again.

After what seemed like a life time to Jake, she slowly relaxed against him again and placed her arms again around his neck. It was the signal that he needed to move whilst inside her. She held onto him and held him so tightly that he feared neither would be able to breathe. She cried out his name and he felt the tears again against his face. He met his climax then and cried out his love for her.

When he could at last again breathe he kissed Catherine and stroked her face. He couldn't see her face, but wanted to make sure that she was alright and that the tears he felt were indeed tears of joy and not of pain. When at last he could move, he rolled to his back. He gently pulled her to him to come to rest on his broad chest. She snuggled against him and again he felt the warm tears as he pulled up the quilt and kissed the top of her head. "Catherine," he said into the darkness; "my love; are you alright? Have I hurt you too badly Catherine?" Jake said worriedly.

"No Jake; it did hurt at first, but what followed was so magical that it just made me emotional. I couldn't stop crying Jake. I love you so much," she said tenderly.

"I will take care of you my darling girl. I will hold you all night and keep you warm. I love you Catherine and I always will," Jake said tenderly.

"I love you Jake. Thank you so much for being my wonderful husband and taking such good care of me. I love you so much Jake," Catherine said quietly.

Jake held Catherine as he had never held another. He thanked God and Cameron McCullum for the gift of his beautiful Catherine. Exhausted, they both fell deeply asleep; contented in each other's arms and with the knowledge that they were safe in the arms of the sacred mountain.

CHAPTER EIGHT

The next morning Jake woke with the sun as was his custom. He smiled when he realized that Catherine was still in his arms, asleep across his chest as she had fallen asleep the night before. Though he was accustomed to getting up first thing, this was one morning that he would stay in bed. He felt safe in the assumption that they had both earned their lie in after the stress and travel of the day before. He knew that there were many things that he would need to tell her today as he was sure that she would no longer wish to be kept in the dark. For now his sleeping beauty was perfectly relaxed and perfectly at peace and he wanted that to continue for as long as possible. When he thought of the love that he felt for this woman and that someone would want to needlessly hurt her and use her as a pawn to gain even more ground and even more money, he grew so angry that he could have killed with his bare hands. The thought of anyone hurting someone as soft and gentle as Catherine made him see red. He was content in the knowledge that he could protect her here and with the Judge's help and the US Marshal, hopefully he could protect her again in the valley. The Judge had been right of course, if they had come for Catherine, he would have readily killed to get her back.

As he lay listening to the sound of her breathing, he felt her stir and begin to stretch. Each movement of her body was gentle torture for him because after last night, his first thought had been to make love to her again at first light when he could see her beautiful face. He would try to resist that urge at least for now as he knew that she would need to process the events of yesterday and of last night. The first thing that he expected was that she would be very shy. He had anticipated this fact when he draped her robe and nightgown across the bed after they had been removed the previous night. It had killed him to not see her face and her beautiful body as he made love to her for the first time, but that would come and if candles were the only thing that he had forgotten in his haste to depart, he could readily forgive that flaw.

He felt her movement again and she raised her head so that she could see his eyes. He was smiling down at her and she grinned then looking like a mischievous imp. He pulled her up until she was eye to eye with him and kissed her deeply. When she pulled away, he saw the same magical deep blue of her eyes, misty now with the love that they had just shared. "Good morning Mrs. Nelson; did you sleep well my love? You were in the exact same spot where you fell asleep last night, so I think you must have been very comfortable," Jake said teasing.

"I was so very warm Jake. You said that you would keep me warm and you did. It was like sleeping with a hot water bottle only the hot water bottle never became cold," she said smiling.

"Well that is high praise indeed Catherine. I have never been compared to a hot water bottle before, but I am glad to have been of service. Is that the only thing that you remember about last night?" he said grinning.

"Oh no Jake; it was magical; you were magical; I don't know how to describe it except to say what I thought when I first saw your cabin and the clearing; this is truly the Garden of Eden and there are no snakes here or at least if there are, they are the ones that travel in the grass only," Catherine replied smiling.

"You are so right Catherine and if this is the Garden of Eden, you will not be wearing any clothes while we are here will you?" Jake said grinning mischievously.

"I didn't say that Jake Nelson and you know it," Catherine replied primly.

"Did you bring your head to toe bathing outfit again? If anyone from the tribe sees that outfit they will never recover," Jake said laughing. He was trying very hard to make her laugh and to overcome her shyness at waking up with her husband for the first time and without her nightgown in the bargain. He didn't think she had quite thought of that yet or if she had, she was not yet sure how to address it without calling attention to the fact. He waited to see what she would do next.

"Jake I have a question for you," Catherine said.

"Of course you do my love. You always have questions for me," Jake replied grinning.

"You know I don't ask questions to be a nuisance Jake; that is how I learn things. I was wondering . . . Jake . . . do married couples make love every night?" Catherine asked shyly.

"Well I have never been married before Catherine so I can't really answer that question. I suppose that each married couple finds their own way on that particular issue. Did you want to make love each night my love?" Jake asked smiling.

"I was just wondering and wanted to make sure that I knew what to expect or at least knew what one was supposed to do. I told you Jake that I have no knowledge in this area and I just want to be a good wife to you," Catherine replied.

"I know that my love; I don't think there is a right thing or a wrong thing only what is right for Jake and Catherine; it will be what is right for us and no one else. It is truly no one else's business; don't you think?" he replied. "Now Mrs. Nelson; I am going to get up and make us some coffee or tea in your case and see what Ramon has packed for us for breakfast," Jake said grinning.

"Do you want me to cover my eyes?" Catherine asked wide eyed.

"No indeed Mrs. Nelson; we are married now. Don't expect me to go to the other side of the oasis to change when we are swimming anymore either!" he said kissing her and rolling her to her back so that he could exit the bed. She remained in the bed until he had gone into the front room and then quickly grabbed her robe. He may not be covering his eyes, but she was definitely going to cover herself. This was all too new for her and she had to become accustomed to many things at once. She slipped to the changing area and began to sort out her riding clothes. They were as casual as she had packed and she wanted something casual to wear during the day. She wondered if she should wear her corset since she wore it every day at home. "Mrs. Nelson would you like some heated wash water in there?" Jake called out.

"That would be lovely Jake; thank you very much," Catherine replied.

When Jake opened the front door, he found two items on the front porch left by his friends from the tribe. He had expected gifts during the week since they knew that he and Catherine had just been married. It was not a surprise to him to see two items left during the night or earlier this morning. The first was a skirt for Catherine in the soft leather worn by Native American women. The second was a baby container to carry a baby from one location to the other. He thought the second gift might make Catherine blush, but it brought to mind his mental images of Catherine as a Mother. He knew that she would be a wonderful Mother and it was but one of many happy future experiences that life held for them.

He brought the items into the front room of the cabin and placed them on Catherine's chair. He met the day then and captured the water needed for bathing and warm drinks from the nearby lake; the day had dawned clear and cool as was customary for their mountain retreat. Later today it would become warmer and Jake would do his best to coax Catherine in the lake for swimming. He smiled then when he thought of her Delaware bathing costume and hoped that he could convince her to wear less in this sacred clearing than she did when swimming in the oasis.

When he returned to the cabin with the water, Catherine was standing at the door with her heavy robe wrapped around her. She drank in the beauty of her husband; his muscles and his body so different from her own. "Aren't you cold Jake; you don't have on a shirt?" Catherine said worriedly.

"I am fine Catherine. This is a summer day my love; what are you going to do this winter?" Jake asked smiling.

"I guess I will just have to rely on my husband to keep me warm," she replied smiling.

"That I can easily do since I have been compared favorably to a hot water bottle," Jake said laughing. "Did you see the gifts from our friends from the tribe? There is something there for you especially and something that we will need in the future," Jake said smiling. He watched her intently as she went to the chair to see the gifts.

"Jake this is absolutely beautiful; just look at the exquisite beadwork. It must have taken ages to make," Catherine replied smiling. "May I do a thank you note to your friends?" Catherine asked.

"We will find our way to thank them; don't worry. We will not see them this week as they will want us to have our privacy. Did you see the other gift as well? That one will have to wait for use later on. It is used to carry a baby Catherine," Jake said smiling.

"Oh I see Jake; you are right; that one will have to wait for a while longer," she said smiling and blushing.

"You will make a wonderful Mother Catherine. You will care for our babies the way you look after me and everyone else that you love," Jake said tenderly. Catherine smiled then and picked up the baby carrier lovingly. Jake went to her side and kissed the top of her head. "Are you going to wear your robe all day Mrs. Nelson or do you plan on getting dressed? Once it gets warmer, we can go swimming in the lake. If you like, you can always go skinny dipping. Now is your chance Catherine as there will be no one around but me," he said laughing.

"I am not quite sure that I am ready for that Jake Nelson and you already know that. Besides you know how cold I get; I couldn't possibly think of getting into cold water without by bathing costume," Catherine replied primly.

"You did not bring that bathing costume to this mountain did you? You know you had on more clothes when you went swimming than you wore to your Father's wake? That was the reason that I wanted you to change your dress; that and the fact that I wasn't used to sharing you of course," Jake said grinning.

"But everyone loved my dress Jake just as I told you they would." Her face clouded for a moment then when she thought about her Father's wake and the appearance of Delaney and Carmichael. "Jake you don't think that Delaney got some crazy ideas into his head that night do you; I mean when he saw my dress?" Catherine replied worriedly.

"Delaney and Carmichael get all kinds of ideas into their pea brains Catherine and no one knows why other than their own greed and lust for power. You haven't asked me yet about the long story involving them. Do you want to hear that love or do you want to wait until later?" Jake asked worriedly.

"I think I would like to wait until later Jake. I am having such a glorious time with you that I don't really want to think about those two until we have to Jake," Catherine said quietly.

"I think that is a very smart answer indeed. I for one do not intend on letting those two snakes ruin my honeymoon any more than I would let them ruin my wedding day yesterday. Why should we give them a moment's thought when we are safe on our mountain with the best security that any two people could possibly have? There is plenty of time to talk about those two and that time is not now. I have your water warmed Catherine so you can get ready and later we can plan on swimming once it gets warmer," Jake said smiling.

As Catherine returned to her dressing area, Jake thought about all that he would need to tell her. It would be shattering to her to think that two people could be as vile and evil as Delaney and Carmichael, but at least he had spirited her away before their plan could be put into place. Had she been taken to the Triple B Hacienda there was no telling how many people would have been hurt trying to get her back home. He had done what he promised her Father he would do; he had kept her safe and in the bargain, had found the love of his life.

*****

While Jake and Catherine were safely secreted away in the mountain cabin, Delaney and Carmichael made good on their plan. As predicted by Judge Wilkerson, Delaney appeared at the English Rose with two of his men in tow. He tied up his horse and called to the house. Ramon was quick to arrive at the screen door and two of the crew came running from the bunkhouse. They had expected his appearance and they were ready for whatever he had planned. "I have come to see Miss McCullum. I need to urgently talk to her as there are matters involving the English Rose which need to be resolved," Delaney yelled to Ramon.

Ramon to his credit remained calm. He had the support of his fellow crew members who he saw gathering from the home paddocks. "Miss Catherine is not here Mr. Delaney," Ramon responded.

"What do you mean she isn't here? Where is she; out riding somewhere with Jake Nelson no doubt. When is she expected to return?" Delaney replied angrily.

"She did not say Mr. Delaney. Is there a message for Miss Catherine when she returns?" Ramon responded.

"If there was a message I most certainly would not be leaving it with a cook. I will return in short order and I expect to see Miss McCullum on my return. I will not accept no for an answer," Delaney replied. With that, Delaney and his two crew members left the English Rose in the direction of the Trinity. Ramon asked one of the crew members to saddle his horse. As requested, he would be advising Judge Wilkerson that the expected visit had occurred. Unless he missed his guess, Delaney was now headed to the Trinity ranch for the same reason. When he found Miss Catherine missing from both ranches, the next visit would be less pleasant. Ramon hoped that help was on the way as he expected tensions to increase in short order.

As Ramon predicted, the Trinity was the next destination of Delaney and his men. Delaney received the same answer from the crew at the Trinity ranch. He was by this time furious. He decided that he would return to both ranches in the morning and Catherine had better be presented or things were going to become ugly fast.

The foreman of the Trinity also went in search of Judge Wilkerson as soon as Delaney and his men had left the ranch. He had also been instructed to advise the Judge when Delaney appeared and both Ramon and he had carried out their mission. The Judge had gotten word to the US Marshal the day before after returning to town from the wedding. As he had feared, Delaney was ready to carry through with his plan and that plan had happily been foiled by Jake's quick thinking and by the seeming disappearance of both Jake and Catherine. Only the native peoples knew the true location of the bride and groom and they certainly weren't talking and most definitely did not leave the sanctuary of their sacred mountain to share their intelligence. Jake would keep Catherine in the mountain cabin for at least a week before they returned to the English Rose. If they saw the sign from the Judge that more time was needed, they would remain in the cabin for the arrival of the US Marshal. Jake knew that there was plenty of game and fish in the vicinity of the cabin and he knew he could keep them fed for as long as they would need to remain.

While the crew from the English Rose and Trinity reported to Judge Wilkerson, Delaney and his two men returned to the Triple B. Carmichael was on the porch anticipating their return. "Where is the girl Angus? Didn't you go in search of her to bring her back here to see some sense?" Carmichael called out.

"We went to both ranches and she is at neither. Nelson is missing from the Trinity as well so something is afoot; if they went off together than I say good riddance to both of them. I can't see Nelson leaving the Trinity for long however, even if he sent Catherine McCullum back home to Delaware where she belongs. I am going to both ranches again tomorrow and I will have answers. If I do not receive answers, I will have heads. This is not over; not by a long shot," Delaney responded heatedly.

*****

While the turmoil circled both ranches; the bride and groom remained blissfully unaware of the undercurrents that were occurring in the valley in their absence. As the day progressed and the temperature became warmer, Jake carried through with his suggestion that Catherine join him for swimming in the lake. She had indeed packed her bathing costume but after being teased by Jake on multiple occasions, borrowed a shirt from Jake to swim in instead. He admitted to her that he was unsure which costume would cover her more as his shirt was nearly a dress for her. She rolled up the sleeves and the hem of the shirt came well below her knees. He had to smile when he saw her as it occurred to him then just how tiny she was when he saw his clothes on her small frame. Since she was smiling that magical smile, he decided to refrain from teasing her further. He was just glad that she seemed so relaxed and so happy and would do nothing to end that joy.

"Catherine honey I will show you the best place to enter the lake. Like the oasis, there are several places that drop off sharply, so I don't want you to be frightened. I know you like to tip toe into the water rather than jumping in, so I will show you the best places to do so. I have gone swimming in this lake since I was a child so there are few places that I don't know about around the lake edge," Jake said smiling.

"Are you going to go skinny dipping again Jake?" Catherine said smiling mischievously.

"Well I can't wear my shirt can I since it has become a dress on you my love," Jake replied laughing. "I might just have to wear my jeans for the first swim because I expect it to be a little on the cool side. The longer that we are in, the warmer it will seem; you will see," Jake said grinning.

"Alright Jake; I will take your word for it as a gentleman. It is beautiful here and the water is so very clear. I believe you can see directly to the bottom Jake," Catherine replied.

"You can indeed my love; all the better when one is skinny dipping don't you think?" Jake replied grinning.

"You and your skinny dipping; I am wearing less clothing now in your shirt I might remind you, than I did when we went swimming at the oasis," Catherine replied primly. "Do I get a piggyback ride or will you hold me like you did at the oasis?" Catherine smiled shyly.

"I think I should be entitled to hold you as I did at the oasis since I am your husband now after all; besides, I have lots of questions for you for a change," Jake replied smiling. "Now come to this point here and start to move forward. I will tell you when to stop. I will go out in front of you and you will see where the drop off is by the height of the water on me," Jake called to Catherine.

Catherine walked slowly into the water at the edge of the lake. She called out at the temperature of the water, but Jake kept insisting that she would get accustomed to it the longer that she was in the water. At about five yards in, he turned to her and told her to stop and to sit down as she had done at the oasis and he would come to get her to take her to the center of the lake. She did as she was bid again and Jake put out his arms to catch her. "Put your legs around my waist Catherine;

that's it. Now I have you my love. Isn't this wonderful? Once you get used to the water, put your head back and feel the water again Catherine just as you did at the oasis," Jake said smiling. "Who knows, I might just need to kiss you again; just so you know," he said grinning.

"I will try very hard to not cut off your breathing Jake when I put my arms around your neck," Catherine said laughing.

"That is most appreciated my love; the first time that we went swimming and I kissed you; I was afraid by the third kiss that you might accidentally do just that," Jake replied laughing.

"I know Jake; it was just a new experience for me, that's all. It just felt heavenly; under the big, blue sky and in the cool water and with your arms around me and kissing me for the first time. It was all very beautiful and new," Catherine said smiling.

"When you talk like that to me Catherine, you know I might just have to kiss you again," Jake said smiling. He moved closer to her then and kissed her very tenderly and then more intensely as she responded to him in her customary manner. Her arms circled his neck but she was careful to not restrict his breathing this time. He held her and stroked her back as he expanded his kiss. "So Mrs. Nelson; I have questions for you for a change. Tell me about your ancestor Catherine; the one in the miniature. How is it that you know so much about her when she was your great-great-great-Grandmother?" Jake asked.

"Well she kept a diary and of course she and my great-great-great Grandfather were very well known in the community. She was the niece of a baronet from England. Apparently her uncle had a very serious gambling problem and was in debt to a gentleman who lived in Lewes, Delaware who was very wealthy. When the uncle couldn't pay the debt, he sent the miniature that you have seen of my ancestor. The man agreed to accept Catherine in exchange for the debt being satisfied. She was sent all the way from England to marry a man that she had never even met. The night that she came to Lewes it was blowing a gale. She was brought to the church, married to him and he went out to save his fleet in the gale and was killed that very night. Then she inherited all of his holdings and my great-great-great-Grandfather came to Lewes to serve as a ship designer and builder. They fell in love and got married and they built ships and raised children. They even survived the War of 1812 right there in Lewes. It was all in her diary. You will need to read it when we go home to the English Rose. It is in Father's library. Jake . . . we will be able to go home to the English Rose again someday; won't we?" Catherine asked worriedly.

"Of course my love; there is a current dust up with Delaney and Carmichael again and we needed to get away from that for a time, but of course we will go home to the English Rose. You know our two ranches are now combined since we married. It will be a wonderful life Catherine. We can combine our cattle and take them to the rail head each fall and we will hold parties for the community just like we did for your Father's wake. In fact once the dust settles, I would like us to get married again so that the whole community can be there. I want you to have a proper wedding Catherine just like you would have dreamt of all your life," Jake replied.

"The important thing is the marriage Jake not the wedding; but I see your point. Everyone was so kind when they came for Father's wake. I would love to share our happiness with everyone. This dust up that you spoke of; is that the reason that Judge Wilkerson wanted to talk to you the other day?" Catherine asked worriedly.

"Yes it was my love; but I don't want you to worry; Judge Wilkerson has it all in hand. He has called in the US Marshal to take care of the newest scheme by Delaney and Carmichael. We will have the help that we need to turn this valley back into the paradise that it once was before those two monsters started their games," Jake replied.

"Tell me about your family's story Jake," Catherine asked.

"Well my Grandfather came to the valley like I told you with five head of cattle. The Trinity lies directly adjacent to this mountain. My Grandfather would find gifts that had been left for him from the people of the tribe, so he started to leave gifts as well. Like I told you; that first winter was the harshest in anyone's memory. He didn't have much but he cut out one of the steers for the people of the tribe to keep them alive during the winter. They never forgot that and our family has been close to them ever since. My Father continued the same custom and I have continued it. When I was a boy, I would come to the mountain with the young men and they taught me how to shoot with a bow and arrow and how to do trick riding. There isn't a thing that they can't do on horseback and I learned all of that growing up. It was a wonderful childhood for a boy especially; hunting and fishing and swimming whenever I wasn't doing chores," Jake said smiling.

"And were there beautiful native girls in the tribe as well?" Catherine said casually.

"There were beautiful native girls but they were more like sisters as I was that close to the people of the tribe. It didn't seem right somehow. As close as I was growing up; it was still two different worlds. Where would we fit in as one of us would be leaving behind all that we knew of our own people? That is what frightened me so much when you first arrived. I kept trying to put you back on that train because I thought; I am going to fall in love with her and then she is going to go back to Delaware and I can't leave the Trinity and she won't be able to stay. It was a problem for a long time Catherine. I kept trying to push you away but every time I would look into those beautiful blue eyes of yours and see that magical smile; well, it just wasn't going to work to send you back was it?" Jake said stroking her cheek.

"I didn't want to go back Jake. Of course I love my brothers and their families but they have their own lives don't they? This was Father's dream and it became my dream and from the moment I got off that train it was just so very different and so beautiful. I just wanted to learn more and more and I wanted to be with you every day and yet I was afraid that I was a nuisance, so it was just very confusing for both of us; until of course the day at the oasis. Then it was no longer confusing because I knew that you wanted to be with me and I knew that I wanted to be with you so it was just a matter of time," Catherine said smiling.

"I wanted to give us more time my love; I wanted to keep courting you and for you to see a full year of weather here and to see the cattle round up when we bring the cattle to the rail head in the fall and to see the parties and all parts of life here in the valley. We just ran out of time Catherine and I knew that I needed to keep you safe from whatever crazy schemes that Delaney and Carmichael had come up with next. I am so sorry that we didn't have more time to just court and be together. But I also knew how happy I was going to be being married to you so it was not a hardship for me. I hope that it wasn't for you either," Jake said stroking her cheek again.

"How could it ever be a hardship to be with the man that you love Jake? I was so happy when you asked me to marry you. I knew that something had happened because everything was happening so fast and then we had to leave with such haste and I could tell from Ramon and the Judge that we somehow couldn't get away fast enough. I knew that something was wrong, but I just didn't know what. You still don't have to tell me Jake until it is time that we go back because I don't want them to intrude upon our time here. This is sacred Jake because this is you and me and the foundation of our marriage. We know that we love one another; all the rest will come in time. I will tell you my stories and you will tell me your stories. I know from everyone who knows you that they all think you the best man and the best friend and the best neighbor that everyone has in the valley. My Father chose you to look after me when I arrived because he knew that I wouldn't go home, especially after seeing the English Rose and the house that he had built for me. In a very real sense, he chose you for me because I guess he knew what I held as important in a man that I would marry and that is your very real goodness and how you help anyone who would ever ask for that help. That is why I first fell in love with you and then, well, it just grew from that point on didn't it?" Catherine replied tenderly.

"I think that sums it up pretty well Catherine. I also think that you are starting to get way too cold Catherine because you are starting to shake and your lips are turning blue. Let's go get you warmed up and maybe get me warmed up too; what do you say?" Jake asked grinning.

"I think I had better Jake because as wonderful as the water feels it is also starting to get very cold as well," Catherine said shaking.

"Just hold onto me Catherine and I will get us both warm very quickly." Jake carried her from the lake then to the waiting blanket and then onward to the cabin. Once inside, he told her to take off her wet clothes and towel herself off. He also told her to put on her nightgown and her robe and he was going to make sure that she was very warm again in short order. Her eyes became very wide at that statement and then she smiled the impish grin again and went to the changing area to do as Jake had suggested. When she had gone into the bed chamber; Jake took off his jeans, toweled himself off and wrapped himself in one of the blankets. He thought to be discreet again in anticipation of his shy young bride's reaction. He smiled when he thought about Catherine and the love that he felt for her growing with each moment spent with her. He knew that his course had been the correct one even if he had not had the time to court her slowly as he had hoped to have. He thought again of her Father and his faith in placing his greatest treasure in Jake's hands. He would not disappoint Cameron or Catherine as he found now his greatest delight in taking care of that treasure each and every day. He closed and bolted the front door again and then returned to the bed chamber and his new bride.

Catherine came out of the changing area with her winter nightgown, robe and slippers on. "Catherine love; come here. Are your feet freezing?" Jake asked smiling.

"They feel like ice cubes Jake," Catherine replied.

"Sit here love and I will rub the warmth back into them," Jake stated. Catherine sat on the edge of the bed and Jake took each foot and rubbed the warmth back into her tiny feet. "You have the tiniest feet that I have ever seen on a grown woman. My friends from the tribe commented on your size when they saw you," Jake said smiling.

"What did they call me Jake?" Catherine asked.

"It would be loosely translated as *little bit,*" Jake replied smiling.

"Is that a good thing Jake?" Catherine asked.

"It is a very good thing Catherine. It seems that they like everyone else find it hard to imagine how one so tall ends up with one so tiny. I myself feel it just confirms the saying that opposites attract," Jake said smiling.

"I don't think we are opposite in the things that really matter Jake. We both believe in family and in doing the right thing and standing up for what really matters in the world; don't you think Jake?" Catherine replied.

"I think you are entirely right Mrs. Nelson. Now that your feet are starting to return to normal temperature, why don't you take off that winter robe Catherine and come over here," Jake said smiling. As she took off her robe, he went to the other side of the bed, took off the wrapped blanket and got beneath the covers. Catherine turned to him then and he pulled back the covers on her side of the bed for her to enter.

As he expected, she snuggled close to him as soon as she was settled in the bed. He pulled her up on his chest as he had done the night before and placed one arm around her waist and his hand on her cheek. She leaned into his hand as a kitten would lean into a stroke. He smiled then and thought about the gentle nature of his beautiful bride. She was right; they were alike in all the ways that matter the most. She would make a loving home for him and he would keep her safe from all variety of outside influences that would try to harm her and his family. "Catherine I am going to need to get you a summer nightgown. We may have to send all the way back to Delaware for it, but I will need to buy you something that doesn't look like you are packing for an Arctic expedition," Jake said smiling.

"Well you told me to pack for cold nights Jake, so I did exactly as you said," Catherine replied smiling.

"So you did love; so you did," Jake replied. She looked up at him with anticipation of what was to follow. He leaned in then and kissed her first in a very gentle manner and then with more intensity as she responded to his kiss. He loved the way she responded to his kisses. He knew that she was feeling the same feelings for him as he did for her each time they kissed. It made him smile to think how alike they were in that aspect of their relationship as well. He slowly unbuttoned the row of buttons on her nightgown that reached from her neck to her waist and beyond. When he had finished, he then slowly pushed the gown down her shoulders to her waist. The vision before him was very like the statute description that Catherine had told him about the first Catherine who had come to Lewes, Delaware. She was a perfect hourglass and her skin milky white in its color but not cold like marble but very warm and silky. He placed his hands in her dark hair and drew her closer to him for another intense kiss. She placed her arms around his neck and drew him closer to her as they mated with their tongues, their hands on shoulders and backs as they drew each other closer.

Jake moved her than to her back so that he could cherish her with his lips and hands. He traced kisses from her neck to her breasts and back again to her full lips. The nightgown was discarded then and placed across the bed. Jake continued his exquisite torture, caressing her body and following those caresses with kisses that reached her breasts. Catherine responded to his caresses with soft moans, her hands caressing Jake's shoulders and his muscled arms. As Jake slowly and gently suckled her breasts, Catherine arched her back and called his name. His hands slowly caressed and cradled her abdomen and continued lower until he was caressing her silky thighs. When at last he felt that he could no lower delay, his hands slowly found and entered her most intimate recesses. Catherine moaned again and responded to his touch. Jake again returned to her mouth, kissing and mating his tongue with hers to mimic the lovemaking that was to follow. Jake entered her this time without fear of the pain that had been inflicted the night before. Catherine wrapped her arms around his neck and pulled him closer to her. Her tears began again at the emotional outpouring of her love for Jake and his for her. He called out her name when his climax came and she did the same moments later. His head fell to her neck and he felt again the wet tears on her cheeks.

When at last he had regained both his breath and his composure, he kissed her cheeks and she opened her magical blue eyes to smile at him. "I love you Catherine; you are my whole life," Jake said tenderly.

"I love you so much Jake; I never knew that love could be like this. Thank you my love for making me so happy," Catherine said through tear stained eyes. Jake kissed her eyes then and rolled to his back bringing her to rest again on his broad chest. He knew that they would sleep now and he would hold her content in their love and at peace in that warmth and love.

CHAPTER NINE

Jake woke the next morning amazed at the fact that they had slept the late afternoon and night away. He knew that he had missed supper because he was starving. He looked down again to see the peaceful Catherine sleeping in his arms. He couldn't help but be amazed that she could sleep in one place as peacefully as she did. As he had been advised the previous morning, he was as warm as a hot water bottle and Catherine was content staying warm in one place with Jake. He slowly moved her to her back so that he could get up and start to gather water to make coffee and breakfast. He knew he was starving and thought Catherine might be also when she awoke. He wrapped the blanket around him from the afternoon before and placed her robe across Catherine as he expected her to get cold as soon as he left the bed. In short order, Catherine awoke and was confused for a moment as to Jake's whereabouts. She heard him then in the front room building a fire. A moment later she heard the front door open and she thought he must be gathering water again for their morning breakfast and for washing. She thought that she could happily stay in this cabin for as long as they would be here. She had never felt such complete and utter contentment and happiness than the time that she had spent with Jake. She hoped that he felt the same.

Jake returned to the cabin with the water that he had gathered and more wood for the fire. He saw her in her winter robe and smiled that she was awake. He set down the water and the wood and then carried in the gift for this morning from his friends. There was a pair of moccasins on the front porch that were so tiny that they could only be meant for Catherine. He thought it funny that anyone else would think the moccasins belonged to a child if they had not seen Catherine's tiny feet. He would ask her to try on the skirt and moccasins this morning after breakfast. For now he was on a mission to find the country ham that Ramon had wrapped for them as he was starving. This honeymooning could certainly work up a powerful appetite in a man, he thought to himself smiling.

"Mrs. Nelson, are you awake and ready for your warm wash water?" Jake called back to Catherine.

"I am Mr. Nelson. Did you sleep well my darling? I slept so amazingly well again, but I am now starved as I think we missed dinner last night," Catherine called out from the bed chamber.

"I believe you are correct Mrs. Nelson. It is but a small price to pay for my honeymoon bliss. I am searching for some of Ramon's country ham to make biscuits for us. I know it is here somewhere in all of these parcels that he wrapped for us. I believe he packed food like you pack clothes," Jake said laughing.

"I will ignore that comment as you have already commented on my excellent packing skills for this particular trip. I did not bring my suite of luggage nor any of my ten pound dresses as you and Mr. Stoner refer to them. How on earth did that description start anyway?" Catherine asked.

"The first day that you were in Buena Vista you fainted and Chet thought that maybe your dress had something to do with that faint. He said that he had never seen anyone wear more layers of clothing than you and maybe that was the reason for your faint. He of course has never seen your bathing costume or he would know that you wear more layers of clothing than anyone he has ever seen. There is another gift for you Catherine. I will place it in your chair," Jake stated.

Catherine came out to the front room so that she could see what had been left for them today. She saw a pair of moccasins waiting on her chair. "Oh look Jake; they will match my skirt from yesterday. I will have to model them for you after we have breakfast. They are so very soft; they feel just like slippers," Catherine said smiling. "You really must let me know how I can thank your friends for the lovely gifts

Jake. They are such lovely people for welcoming me as they have done," Catherine replied smiling.

"That is how they are love; you are instantly one of their tribe because I have chosen you as my wife. You are family in their eyes and in their hearts. Now sit down and eat some breakfast Mrs. Nelson before you blow away. I will have to make sure that we don't miss any meals going forward; however good the reason," Jake said grinning and kissing Catherine.

*****

On this the second day of Jake and Catherine's disappearance, Delaney made yet another visit to the English Rose. He brought with him two crew members again as he had done the day before. When he hitched his horse to the hitching post, he came this time up on the porch, banged on the door insolently and called Catherine's name. Ramon was quick to come to the door and the crew members in the bunkhouse were quick to run to the main house. Whatever Delaney was selling, they were not buying. "I told you that I would be back for Catherine McCullum today. Where is she? I will not take no for an answer." Delaney brushed rudely by Ramon when the door was opened and started calling Catherine's name in the house. There was of course no answer, but he went from room to room looking for Catherine as if Ramon had lied to him the day before when he stated that she was not available.

"Mr. Delaney, I told you yesterday that Miss Catherine was not here. She is still not here and she has not left word of when she may return. Mr. Delaney kindly leave this house as Miss Catherine is not here as you can see," Ramon said fiercely.

"You will not talk to me like that Ramon; not you or anyone. I don't know what sort of game is being played here, but I can tell you that I will have none of it. When the English Rose is mine, you will be the first one out of the door and the rest of you," he said gesturing to the crew beyond the house "will be the next ones to go. Just think on that while you defend Catherine McCullum and Jake Nelson. You will be out of a job as soon as I am master of this house," Delaney yelled menacingly at the assembled men.

Delaney mounted his horse again and again the threesome took off for the Trinity. Ramon asked that his horse be saddled again and again he took off for Judge Wilkerson's office. He was to give a report on any threats made by Delaney and today's visit would certainly qualify in that area. Delaney would never get into his head that Mr. Jake and Miss Catherine would never give into the likes of Delaney and Delaney and his Father would come to understand that when the power of the US Marshal came their way.

The same scene was played out again at Jake's Trinity ranch. Likewise Jake's foreman set off for Judge Wilkerson's office so that he too could report on the visit by Delaney and his ranting and ravings. If this is how he was after two days, they did not want to see him after a week.

Delaney and his two henchmen returned again empty handed to the Triple B. When Carmichael saw that Catherine had once again eluded Delaney, he turned and went back inside the hacienda. Delaney realized that to his Father, he had again failed and his mind searched for answers to the mystery of the disappearance. As he entered the house, he thought he had come upon the answer. "I believe we have a spy here in the hacienda Father. I believe that Nelson and Catherine found out my plans for her and made off in anticipation of that. I will be questioning the staff until I can make one of them break and tell me the truth. I am not accepting this behavior lying down. These people are making a fool of me and I will not have it." Delaney stormed out of the house then nearly taking the door off the hinges in his haste to begin questioning the staff. Carmichael knew that his son had an uncontrollable temper once he had been set off and knew too that he would be kept occupied for at least a day with the questioning that was to occur. His only concern was that Angus not kill anyone in his determination to obtain answers. Were that to occur, even Carmichael may be powerless to help him.

*****

As the Triple B drama continued to swirl, Jake and Catherine continued on the second full day of their honeymoon content in the secluded surroundings of the mountain cabin. Catherine modeled her new skirt and moccasins for Jake who thought they were very fine indeed and that she looked just right for the mountain cabin. She told him that they were the softest thing that she had ever worn. "They couldn't have made anything to fit you better than if they had measured you; I think they look real nice Catherine and they are perfect for the cabin," Jake pronounced. "After yesterday, I thought it might be nice for us to just fish today rather than getting in the water. I don't want you to get that cold again and I am not even sure that your Delaware bathing costume could save you from that temperature. Have you ever been fishing before darling?" Jake asked.

"I have been surf fishing with my brothers before but I only watched. I never actually did the fishing. Do I have to touch anything scary Jake?" Catherine asked anxiously.

"No darling; I will put the worm on the hook; all you will have to do is hold the fishing line and then if you get a bite; I will show you how to bring it in alright?" Jake said smiling.

"Alright Jake; I will bring the blanket from yesterday and we can have a picnic lunch at the lake also. How would that be?" Catherine asked smiling.

Jake smiled at the thought that the simplest of things were automatically more enjoyable if they did them together. This was definitely the case today as he could not imagine Catherine fishing until the thought came to him as he went after wash and coffee water this morning. Catherine gathered food for them from the multiple packages that Ramon had organized and she placed them in the baby carrier due to the lack of a picnic basket among the items in the cabin. She thought then to make a list of things that they could bring the next time they visited that would make the cabin cozy for them. Candles were definitely on that list and now a luncheon hamper as well. She gathered up the blanket that they had used the day before and she and Jake set off hand in hand for the lake and a good spot for fishing.

Catherine watched with amazement as Jake assembled everything that they would need for their fishing expedition. He had fishing poles that he kept at the cabin and dug for the needed worms. He knew that she would be uncomfortable with the worms and baiting the hook, so took care of that as well. Once all was prepared, he handed Catherine the fishing pole and made himself comfortable on the blanket. He thought then that he was the most relaxed that he had been in years. Even with the multiple threats by Delaney and Carmichael hanging over them and over their ranches, sitting with Catherine in this secluded place brought a whole level of peace that not even their scheming could penetrate. After an hour or so, Catherine looked at him with wide eyed surprise as there was a bite on her line. Jake came to sit behind her and held the pole so that she could see what was needed to bring in the fish. Her first catch was a small fish so he brought it in, showed it to her and then released it back into the lake. He would have her try for a larger fish that they could then have for their dinner. They were not long in waiting as a larger fish was caught on Catherine's line and together they brought it in for the waiting bucket. "You don't have to worry love; I will clean it so that we can have it for our dinner. You have caught your first fish Mrs. Nelson; how does that feel?" Jake said smiling.

"It feels just like the day that I shot all of my targets for the first time Jake. I am truly learning things that are useful for life here in the valley," Catherine said grinning. "My brothers will not believe it when I write to them about all that has happened since my arrival," Catherine stated.

"Let's see if we can catch one more and then we should have plenty for dinner darling," Jake replied. In the interval, Jake sat behind Catherine and she leaned into him while she held the fishing pole. Never had something so simple seemed so magical to Catherine.

"I thought when I first saw the cabin that it reminded me of the enchanted cabins in the Grimm's Fairy Tales Jake. This is truly a magical place because you are here and it is so peaceful here. I understand now why you love it so," Catherine stated.

"We will have to think of the addition that we want to make to the cabin just like Grandfather and Father made their mark here," Jake replied stroking her arms.

"Maybe we could add a room for the children to sleep in," Catherine replied.

"Well you know; I just slept outside when I was growing up," Jake answered.

"But what if we have daughters Jake? You wouldn't expect them to sleep outside would you? If they get as cold as I do; they would freeze," Catherine answered smiling.

"A room for the children might be a nice idea at that Catherine. That way Mom and Dad could still have the privacy of our bed chamber," Jake said grinning.

"I like that idea Jake. There will be plenty of room for children at the English Rose you know," she said smiling.

"Yes there will Mrs. Nelson; boys to teach to ranch and girls to teach to be beautiful ladies like their Mother," Jake replied.

"Do you think that we could ever go home again to Delaware so that you could meet my brothers?" Catherine asked.

"Of course love; I want to meet them and they can teach me how to surf fish. That sounds like something that would be worthwhile to learn. I want to see the ocean and I want to see where you grew up. You must have been the cutest little girl because look at how beautiful you are now," Jake said nuzzling Catherine's head. "You know Catherine; we may just have to take another nap again after all of this fishing and the luncheon basket," Jake said laughing.

"Just so you don't miss your supper again Jake. I don't want you to blow away either," Catherine said grinning.

"Well, if we don't catch another fish in an hour or so, we will cook up this one for supper and then have a nice nap," Jake replied. "Yep I think a nice nap might just be in order Mrs. Nelson," Jake said grinning.

"That's funny Jake; I don't remember you talking about taking naps so frequently before we were married?" Catherine replied mischievously.

"I am going to tickle you for that Mrs. Nelson? Are you ticklish by any chance?" He started to tickle her and realized that beneath her shirt and the leather skirt she was wearing her corset. "You are not sitting here fishing in a corset Catherine? Tell me you are not wearing a corset to sit on the ground and fish," Jake said in amazement.

"Of course I am Jake; I always wear a corset unless I am swimming or sleeping of course," Catherine replied.

"Well that needs to stop this minute. Why on earth do you have a corset on when your waist is no bigger than my two hands?" Jake asked.

"Because silly a lady always wears a corset. It is how I was raised Jake from the time I was twelve years old. It is just how things are done," Catherine replied.

"Are you trying to tell me that you rode your horse all the way from the English Rose in a corset?" Jake asked amazed.

"Of course Jake; I had it on under my wedding gown so of course I wore it here under my riding clothes. I am just used to it darling so you mustn't worry," Catherine stated in a matter of fact manner.

"As Chet Stoner would say; I'll be . . . Catherine, you do some of the darnest things I have ever seen. This is one for the books; sitting on the ground on a blanket fishing with a corset on," Jake continued to shake his head in amazement. "That makes as much sense as wearing your ten pound dress on the train into Buena Vista," Jake said grinning.

"But Jake, I thought that Father was meeting the train didn't I? As it was the future love of my life was meeting my train so it was meant to be that I was dressed for calling. There is always a method to my madness Jake; don't worry; you will come to understand that in time," Catherine replied.

"If I live to be one hundred years old I will not understand someone sitting on a blanket fishing with a corset on so you can get that out of your head right now," Jake replied laughing.

"Jake I think you are scaring away the fish darling. Aren't you supposed to be quiet when you fish? I seem to remember my brothers telling me that when I was a little girl and still allowed to go out with them," Catherine replied laughing.

"Oh you will definitely pay for that comment. You wait until I have you without your corset on for our planned nap. I will see if you are ticklish alright and you will pay for that remark. You telling me to be quiet; that is rich indeed coming from the lady of a million questions," Jake said laughing and holding Catherine around the waist.

"I told you Jake; that is how people get to know one another remember? Besides darling Jake, how am I going to learn things if I don't ask questions?" Catherine replied. "Honestly Jake everyone knows that," Catherine said laughing.

"Shush, you will scare the fish and then I will never get my nap," Jake replied.

"Why don't you have one of the snacks that I made for you? I put them in the baby carrier since we don't have a luncheon hamper here yet. I will place that on my list for our next visit," Catherine replied.

"So what else is on your list for our next visit to the cabin? None of your ten pound dresses I hope to match your ever present corset," Jake said laughing.

"No my love; only a picnic hamper and candles so far; but there may be other things that we add as the week goes along. I want to make the cabin nice and cozy for our future visits," Catherine replied.

"I like the idea of candles. I want to be able to see your beautiful face when I make love to my wife," Jake said kissing Catherine's neck.

"You know, you just might be interfering with my concentration while I try to fish, as well as scaring away the fish. I really must complain about this breach of fishing protocol," Catherine said teasing.

"I don't think there is a fishing protocol Mrs. Nelson just so you know. There is also not a dress code in case you needed to be informed for our next fishing expedition. I see you packed some of Ramon's special cake in your improvised luncheon hamper. You know; your magical smiles and Ramon's special cake are among the reasons that I fell in love with you," Jake said smiling.

"I will have to tell Ramon that when we get home. He is so wonderful to me and has been treated so very badly by Delaney and Carmichael. I am so glad that he is with us Jake. I wouldn't want him to ever be treated badly again," Catherine stated wistfully.

"You are not to worry about that love. Ramon loves working for you; he has told me so before just as much as he loved working for your Father before you. He is very contented at the English Rose and we will do everything in our power to make sure that he stays that way," Jake replied. "Now Mrs. Nelson; I think we have had enough fishing for one morning. You have one of these treats in this luncheon hamper and then we will get to working on that nap that I have been planning," Jake said kissing Catherine's neck and cheek.

"Well since you are the teacher of all things related to nature; I will bow to your advice my love. I did catch my first fish so that is something of which to be proud," Catherine replied smiling. They gathered up fishing equipment, luncheon basket and the day's catch and headed into the cabin for their planned nap.

After everything had been put away from the fishing expedition and Catherine had eaten her lunch from the hamper, Jake took Catherine's hand and then headed to the bed chamber. Jake stood Catherine in front of him as on the first night and started to unbutton her shirt. After he had done so, she moved to unbutton his shirt as well. "Is this alright Jake?" Catherine asked shyly.

"Of course my love; didn't I tell you; it will be Jake and Catherine's way. There are no rules only what is right for us." She sat down on his lap then and he watched her intently as she unbuttoned his shirt and kissed the exposed skin on his neck and upper chest. He pulled her shirt from the leather skirt and exposed the corset lying beneath. Again he shook his head trying to understand wearing a corset under a shirt to sit on the ground and fish. This was but one of the paradoxes of his beautiful wife. He slowly looked for and found the ribbons to the corset and began unlacing them. When the corset had been removed, he reached in and unlaced her skirt as well. She was sitting on his lap then in her chemise, looking at him in the same misty eyed manner as the first time that they had kissed. Jake pulled her to him and pulled her down again on his chest, undoing her hair as he did so. Her silky hair fell against his cheek as he kissed Catherine deeply. Her arms came around his neck as was her custom. Jake stood up then and removed his trousers. For the first time, he was nude before Catherine. "Don't be afraid Catherine; we are as God has made us," Jake said tenderly. "You are the other half that I have been seeking my whole life," Jake continued.

"I wouldn't be afraid Jake; not of you ever. I think you are the most beautiful thing that I have ever seen. You look like a statute in one of my picture books with your muscles and your strength. And you have the most beautiful mouth that I have ever seen on a man," Catherine said smiling.

"I have never heard of a man being beautiful Catherine; that is indeed a first," Jake said smiling and lying down on the bed.

"Well it is the truth Jake. The first time that I saw you one of my first thoughts was; there is a true cowboy in the flesh. When you drove me to the English Rose and I peeked at you while you were driving I thought; he has one of the most beautiful mouths that I have ever seen." She traced his mouth then with her finger and Jake kissed it for her trouble.

"Now Catherine; you still have on your chemise and it has the smallest buttons that I have ever seen. You will have to unbutton it for me darling because I can't even get my fingers around those small buttons. They look like they were made for doll clothes," Jake said smiling.

"I will undo them for you Jake," she unbuttoned her chemise and then looked at Jake next in anticipation of what she should do next. He spread her chemise and traced a line of kisses from her mouth, to her neck, to her breasts and finally to her abdomen. "You are the most beautiful woman that I have ever seen Catherine. You are the one who looks like a statute, but your skin is so silky and so warm even if you do get cold easily," he said smiling

"Only for you Jake," Catherine said shyly.

"Only for you Catherine," Jake responded. He kissed her deeply at that moment. The chemise was quickly abandoned and there was no more talking from that moment onward, but only caressing and making love. With each day together, their relationship had continued to build. As their intimacy grew, their love continued to grow as well. The simplest things like the fishing at the lake when done together were instantly the best of times for them both. If Jake had any more doubts that their wedding had been too hasty, they were quickly dispelled as they spent more and more time together. As Catherine had said, he would tell her his stories and she would tell him hers and they would forge their relationship from the foundation of this magical time together without worries or the strain of the outside world. Let the insanity surround them; high on their sacred mountain the only thing that intruded into their world was their love for one another and it was very good indeed.

*****

On the next day, Ramon headed into town to again confer with Judge Wilkerson. This time it was not about a visit by Delaney or Carmichael. Neither ranch had had a visitation from those two for a day, but the news coming out of the Triple B hacienda was far more troubling than a visitation. It seemed that Delaney had gotten into his head the thought that he was being spied upon by his staff. And with that idea had come cross examination of each of the staff members on the hacienda. Employees were being interrogated to try to determine if and how information was leaking from the hacienda to the surrounding ranches and most particularly to the English Rose and the Trinity. Ramon knew the source of the leaked information and he advised the judge that the crew of the Triple B were in danger. He knew that Delaney was just unhinged enough to not only threaten the crew, but to possibly carry through on those threats.

"Ramon, I don't want you to worry anymore about what is going on at the Triple B. I have had word from the US Marshal that he is due here in three days. Catherine and Jake will be able to return to the English Rose and we will also have a Circuit Court Judge here to take on this nonsense legal challenge from those two. The Judge is due here in a week so the US Marshal will be present when that case is heard as well. Knowing Delaney and Carmichael as we do, if that case is not decided in their favor, there is no telling what they might try to do. I for one will not sit here and wait for someone to be hurt or placed in further danger by those two and their threats. Keep strong for just a little while longer Ramon. Trust me that help is on the way and I believe resolution of this insanity once and for all," Judge Wilkerson replied.

"Thank you very much Judge. May I share this information with the foremen for the English Rose and the Trinity ranch also?" Ramon asked.

"You may indeed Ramon. I am sure that they will be very happy to know that they will not need to shoulder this burden much longer," Judge Wilkerson replied.

*****

The next day at the mountain cabin, Jake went out for water for bathing and coffee and found another gift for the newlyweds. A handmade blanket had been left on the porch just as the skirt, basket and moccasins had been provided previously. Jake smiled when he saw the gift and thought how appropriate it would be for Catherine who was always cold. He thought of something then that he would like to show Catherine today and it would involve a short trip on the mountain to another special location. He knew that Catherine would enjoy it and he would love showing it to her. It was yet another place that had not been seen by the outside world which made it all the more special in Jake's eyes.

As he entered the cabin with the water for washing and coffee, he heard Catherine in the bed chamber moving about. "Mrs. Nelson, did you sleep well my love?" Jake asked from the front room. "There is another gift for you which I think it most appropriate indeed," Jake called smiling.

Catherine came to the front room then and looked on her chair. When she saw the blanket she was enchanted. "Jake this is just beautiful. I have never seen such beautiful work as your friends create. I really must find a way to thank them Jake," Catherine replied.

"As I told you my love; that will be taken care of, have no fear," he kissed the top of her head again. "I am taking you to a special location today. We will be riding for about an hour from here so make sure that you take your jacket for this morning. You probably won't need it by mid day, but it will feel good when we first start out," Jake said smiling.

"Is this another surprise Jake?" Catherine asked wide eyed.

"It is indeed my love. I have never taken any one to this spot. I think you will enjoy it Catherine," Jake replied. "Here is your warm water my love. You get dressed and I will rustle some of Ramon's wonderful treats for our breakfast," Jake responded. He thought then that Catherine was as wide eyed as a child when it came to the beauty of the valley. Her Father had been the same way. They were both excited by life and couldn't wait for the next adventure. He had never been around people like that in his experience before and decided it was a wonderful way to live. It was just one more amazing thing about his new wife and their new life together.

Catherine hurriedly washed and dressed in her leather skirt, a white shirt and moccasins. She would have her corset on but didn't plan on letting Jake know that fact. She thought it was so funny that he would be surprised that a lady would wear a corset everyday of her life. What else would I wear, she thought? It would be as if he was surprised that I washed twice a day or ate three times a day. Men just don't understand these things I suppose. Men put on a shirt and a pair of pants and are ready to go, she thought smiling. She grabbed her warm jacket just in case she needed it as Jake had advised. She could always put it across the saddle in the event that it became warmer later in the day. Dressed for the day, she went out to her chair to eat some more of Ramon's wonderful biscuits and country ham. She thought if they were able to return by the end of the week, he would have outfitted them for their entire stay. She looked forward to returning to the English Rose even if she did not look forward to whatever behavior by Delaney had necessitated the need for their hasty wedding and escape to the mountain.

Jake was shaving out on the porch when she came out to eat her breakfast. She was still amazed that he could stand on the porch without a shirt as he washed and shaved, but she guessed that he was just used to it and that weather didn't bother him as it did her. She hoped that she would become more accustomed to the weather the longer she was here. As Jake had told her, he wanted her to see a full year of weather before making up her mind to stay. She decided that weather was the least of her concerns after the magic of the past few days. She had encountered hurricanes and gales in her home in Delaware and they were of little concern to her so she would become accustomed to the cold as well even if she had to dress in layers and of course sleep with her always warm husband.

"What are you smiling about Mrs. Nelson? You look like the cat that swallowed the canary in there?" Jake said grinning.

"I was just remembering how warm you keep me at night and how lovely it is to be so warm. Then I wondered how you can possibly shave and wash on the porch without a shirt, but I put it down to the fact that you are accustomed to the weather and as you said before, this is just a summer day in the mountains," Catherine replied smiling.

"I am glad to be of service in keeping you warm at night. I can honestly say that I happily sign up for that service. As to the temperature; you are right, it is just a matter of getting used to it and knowing that the day will be warmer soon. I see you are properly attired in your jacket my love. Are you about ready to get going?" Jake asked.

"I am ready when you are my love. Do you want to give me the once over to make sure I have dressed properly for wherever we are going?" Catherine asked.

"I will happily give you the once over Mrs. Nelson. I think you are very properly dressed although you will probably want to put on your riding boots rather than your moccasins," Jake replied smiling. Catherine went into the changing area and took off her moccasins and placed on her riding boots and her felt riding hat just in case it was needed. When she had returned to the front porch, Jake had brought one of the horses up to the porch which he had saddled. "We will just take the one horse love as I know exactly where I am going. Besides, riding double will be a pleasure," Jake said grinning. He brought the horse over to the porch steps and took her hand to pull her in front of him on the horse. His arms were around her waist and off they climbed to Jake's special location for the day. There was a slight mist that Jake knew would burn off by mid day. It gave the mountain an even more magical look. Jake thought then about the Grimm Fairy Tale description that Catherine had given to the cabin and the clearing. She would definitely think of that when she saw their destination for the day.

They climbed even higher on the sacred mountain. Along the way they saw all sorts of wildlife. Catherine noted that Jake had his side arm as always and his rifle. He was always prepared for whatever may occur which she assumed was the reason that he had stayed alive all of these years. His training with the tribe was probably also important in that preparation.

After an hour or so riding along the mountain ridge, Catherine heard a loud sound. She was trying to identify the sound and the closest that she could come in her mind was the sound of the ocean. She knew that could not possibly be right, but it certainly sounded like rushing water. In a few moments, they came into another clearing and the sight before her explained her confusion. The sound that she had heard was a waterfall. It was water which fed the lake in front of their cabin. The water rushed at a near deafening level. The waterfall and the terraced stone layers over which the water ran gave the site a magical quality. It definitely looked like a place that could only be found in a storybook. She assumed that it would be a sacred place as well and she could definitely understand why. Catherine turned then to Jake who was smiling from ear to ear. "This is another of my special places Catherine. I wanted you to see this. It is the most sacred of all the places on the mountain and one that has to be seen to be believed," Jake stated.

Jake took the horse over to one of the stone steps and pulled alongside so that Catherine could step down from the horse to the ground. He tied up the horse and joined her at the base of the waterfall. She looked at him then with that same wide eyed smile from earlier this morning. He was so correct that this was something that he wanted to share with her and something that she needed to see. She walked from stone step to stone step taking in the beauty of the space. He pulled his canteen from the horse and filled it with the rushing water and returned it to Catherine. "Take a drink of this sweetheart. This is the purest water that you would ever want to drink and probably the coldest. I don't think that even I would be comfortable skinny dipping in this water," Jake said smiling.

Catherine drank deeply from the water from the canteen. It was definitely bracing and tasted like the purest water that she had ever tasted. "Jake, this is one of the most beautiful places that I have ever seen. I can understand why this is a sacred place. Is this a location that your friends would use as a sanctuary because it certainly feels like one doesn't it?" Catherine said with eyes shining.

"It does indeed Catherine. If ever there was a person in the world that doubted the story of creation; they should be brought to this spot. It is a very spiritual place Catherine and I wanted very much to show it to you," Jake said placing his arm around her shoulder.

"I understand why this mountain is sacred to all who come here Jake. Thank you so much for bringing me here. When we approached I thought that I was hearing the ocean again because that was the closest thing that I could compare it to. The sound and the mystery and the magic remind me so much of the ocean. If you bring me here Jake, it will be like bringing me to the ocean whenever I get homesick. Thank you so much Jake for this wonderful surprise."

"It was a place that I wanted to bring you to sweetheart. Like you said, it is special to share a place such as this with someone that you know will appreciate it. I have always loved the places on the mountain and now I know that you love them as well. We will bring our children here also Catherine and teach them about the importance of caring for this sacred mountain; I pray that it will always be this pristine and beautiful," Jake said smiling.

*****

Their special time together and the time spent building their relationship slipped by much too quickly for both Jake and Catherine. He knew that they would soon need to return to the valley and to the pressures that remained there. He hoped that the Judge would soon get word to him that it was safe to return. He had not yet told Catherine everything that she would need to know about the threats to her, but he knew in time she would come to understand that they would face whatever needed to be faced together. They along with others in the valley would face the people who had tried hard to ruin the paradise that was Buena Vista and he would try hard to reverse that trend.

On the fourth day of their mountain stay, Catherine asked Jake if he would show her some of the trick riding that he had learned growing up. Jake was not one to boast, but since he had told Catherine about his childhood experiences, he agreed to show her. She sat on the porch of the cabin so that Jake had plenty of room to demonstrate his trick riding. He described each of the different riding maneuvers that he was doing so that she would understand what he was doing and the original purpose of that action. He also explained that the native peoples did not use the same saddle equipment that she would have been accustomed to, but instead rode either bare back or with a blanket only. It spoke highly of their skills as equestrians. Catherine was amazed by Jake's knowledge of all things related to horses and could well understand why he was terrified of her riding side saddle in country that she did not yet know when she had first come to Buena Vista.

Jake confided about the number of falls and bruises that he had received as a child learning the many difficult tricks. As a boy, he had thought nothing of those falls but thought in the light of day, he would not welcome that type of pain again.

*****

The next morning, Jake found the signal that he had been waiting for on the porch of the cabin as he gathered water for breakfast and washing. He knew that the signal meant that the US Marshal had arrived and that Jake and Catherine could now return to the English Rose. As much as he had loved their stay, he knew that it was time to return, as much needed to be done to combine the two ranches and to deal with the legal challenge that had been brought by Delaney and Carmichael. It was time for him to sit down with Catherine now and give her the full story of Delaney and Carmichael's treachery. When he heard Catherine start to stir in the bed chamber, he thought it best that they have their talk as soon as possible so that they could start back for the English Rose and the loose ends that they had left behind.

"Catherine love; once you are dressed, I have something that I need to discuss with you alright?" Jake called.

"What is it Jake?" Catherine asked worriedly. "Has something happened?"

"It has love; I have received the signal that I have been waiting on from the Judge that it is safe for us to return home," Jake said worriedly.

Catherine came to the outer room in her robe and slippers. She could tell that it was time for Jake to provide her with the rest of the story that he had withheld for as long as they had been on the mountain. She was ready to hear the long version of the story now.

"Catherine I want you to eat your breakfast before I start telling you the story," Jake said firmly.

"Is it so terrible then Jake that I won't want to eat? Is that what you are afraid of Jake?" Catherine asked worriedly.

"Come here darling girl and eat your breakfast. Don't start getting riled up when I haven't told you a thing yet alright?" Jake said with worry in his eyes. Catherine sat down at her place and ate her breakfast. She looked worriedly at Jake, but did as he had asked before she started asking questions that would probably annoy him. After she had finished her breakfast, he took her hand and proceeded to tell her the whole sordid tale about Delaney and Carmichael and what they had planned concerning Catherine. She was very quiet and didn't ask any questions until he had finished. He told her that he had just this morning received the signal that he had been waiting on that told him the US Marshal had arrived and that there was assistance for the local Sheriff in dealing with the charges and allegations that had circled around Delaney and Carmichael. He told her the sordid parts also about what they had planned for her and why.

"Jake, after what you and I have shared over the past few days; it makes me physically ill to think that someone would try to force another person to be intimate with them and not care a thing about them. I am so blessed Jake to have married my best friend and my guardian angel and the man that I love most in the world. You have looked after me since I first came to Buena Vista and you have looked out for me every day since we have been married. I am ready to face whatever we need to face Jake to bring those monsters to justice. You tell me what we need to do and I will do it," Catherine said earnestly.

"I knew that was what you would say Catherine. We can't live in fear. I brought you here until we could get the help we need to fight those two, but I will not live in fear in my own home. The valley is my home and has been for my entire life. We will reclaim it Catherine, but we need to stand together and with our friends to do so," Jake said adamantly.

"Will we go back today Jake?" Catherine asked.

"I think as soon as we get ready love we should get everything packed and get ready to go back," Jake said worriedly.

"I'll go get ready Jake. I won't be long I promise," Catherine replied smiling bravely.

Jake grabbed her hand as she stood then and pulled her over on his lap. "It will be alright Catherine; I promise it will be alright. We will do everything that we need to do to make it right Catherine," Jake said kissing her cheek and holding her tightly. She got up then and went back to the bed chamber to dress and to gather up her things to leave. Jake watched her go and thought that he would rather stay here in this cabin then anything in the world, but it was time to go back and fight along with the rest of the community to reclaim their valley.

When they had packed and were ready to set off, Jake suggested that they ride double until they got off of the mountain. The trail would be treacherous and he did not want anything to happen to her. Once they were back on Trinity land, Catherine could mount up and they would head back to the English Rose. Jake brought the horse to the steps again after all was loaded so that he could pull Catherine onto the saddle with him. She looked behind her at the magical cabin and at the lake and the totality of the clearing as if she wanted to memorize it all. It had been the most enchanting time of her life and she knew she would never forget. Best of all however, she was going home to the English Rose and would live there with the love of her life not just for five days, but for all of the days of their lives. Jake hugged her then around the waist and they set off with Catherine's horse and the pack horse following.

After travelling again for over an hour, Jake let out the same bird like call that he had done on their way to the cabin. He did so several times and heard the call returned. His friends from the tribe surrounded them again and Jake spoke to them and smiled and touched Catherine's cheek. They smiled also and patted Jake's leg. Catherine would ask him what he had said when they were back on the Trinity ranch. She hoped that he had thanked them for the lovely gifts which had been attached to the pack horse. She smiled at them and took their outstretched hands as they rode off. Catherine's eyes were swimming with tears again. She had not said a word all the way down to the foot of the mountain and Jake knew that she was processing everything that he had told her this morning. It was hard to leave the security of the mountain and the serenity as well. But they could not hide away; it was time to make their stand and Jake knew that they now had the assistance needed to make that stand.

When they were again on the Trinity ranch, Jake pulled the horses up to the ranch house so that he could check in with the crew. He opened the door so that Catherine could go in and rest while he checked on matters with the foreman for the ranch. He also wanted to hear all that had transpired since they were away so that he could be prepared for whatever they would find once they reached the English Rose. Catherine went into Jake's house and walked from room to room taking in the decidedly masculine house of the man that she loved. As he had told her, it was a Spartan affair. Jake would have a different life at the English Rose and she hoped that he would be happy there. She wondered if she should pack some of his clothes for him, then decided she would wait and see what he would need before starting to pack.

After a half hour or so, Jake came into the ranch house to find Catherine. He didn't want to tell her everything that he had been told by his foreman. He thought he had given her enough to think about this morning and he could tell by how quiet she had become on the trip down the mountain that she was still processing what he had told her this morning. He went over to her sitting on the large couch and gently touched her cheek "Are you doing alright sweetheart?" Jake asked tenderly.

"I am always doing alright when you are near Jake," Catherine said smiling bravely.

"Let's get you home then. I bet Ramon will want to spoil you with a homecoming meal; what do you think?" Jake said smiling.

"I bet he will want to spoil you too Jake. You are the new master of the house after all. He will probably want to make a special cake just for you," she said smiling.

"We both have a lot to get used to don't we darling?" Jake replied. "We will take it one day at a time Catherine. As long as I have you by my side; I don't need much else," Jake said smiling.

"Would you like me to help you pack anything for this evening?" Catherine asked.

"Why don't we come over tomorrow and get a few things. I will just grab a few clothes for now and be right back," Jake replied.

Catherine sat trying to get her head around the information that Jake had shared with her this morning. She was so glad that he hadn't told her the entire story on her wedding day or during their honeymoon for that matter. The time at the cabin had been so magical for them both. She was glad that she had decided to not let Delaney or Carmichael intrude upon their magical time together. Those two did not deserve to intrude upon anyone's happiest hours; least of all Jake and Catherine's. She was not sure how her Father would have dealt with this latest sordid behavior, but she was sure that he and Jake would have thought of something to make it right just as she, Jake and the Judge would now do.

Jake came back downstairs holding a small bag which she thought must hold all of his worldly goods considering how he teased her about her packing. He smiled at her then and she knew from that smile that they would be fine. Together they would face whatever they needed to face.

When Jake and Catherine came outside of the ranch house, she saw the Trinity crew saddled and ready for them to emerge. Catherine thought sadly that they needed an escort again now that they were back in the valley. After the blissful time in their sanctuary, she had to get her head around the fact that they needed an escort to ride from one ranch to the other so long as Delaney and Carmichael were still free and threatening the valley. The crew rode at a distance from Catherine and Jake so that they could still have their privacy Catherine assumed.

After they were back on horseback and setting off for the English Rose, Catherine asked Jake what he had said to his friends from the tribe. "They said that you were even more beautiful today than the day we headed to the cabin. They said that the mountain agreed with you and I told them that was so. I thanked them for the gifts also. We will do a thank you basket of food for them which I know they will appreciate. I have a special place that we leave messages for each other. That is how I received the message from the Judge this morning," Jake replied.

"I can't wait to go back Jake. Once all of this mess is straightened out and maybe after we get married again for the community; can we go back Jake and spend a week like we just did?" Catherine asked.

"Did you really enjoy it that much Catherine? I was worried that you were just going along to make me happy. Did you really enjoy the mountain love?" Jake asked smiling.

"Of course I did Jake. It was like something from Grimm's Fairy Tales and just magical. But of course, anywhere I go with you will be magical Jake," Catherine replied. Jake took her hand then and they rode on to the English Rose.

When they arrived back on the English Rose land, Catherine thought with fondness about the first time that Jake had taken her to her Father's resting place and onto the English Rose. Coming home this time was like coming home for the first time because it was the first time with her new husband. Together they would forge a new life and together they would combat the ugliness that had entered the valley once and for all. Ramon was out on the porch when they arrived as a rider had gone ahead to let the Rose crew know that Jake and Catherine were coming home. It would be good to see everyone even in the shadow of what lay ahead.

"Welcome home Miss Catherine and Mr. Jake. Did you have a good honeymoon?" Ramon asked smiling.

"It was wonderful Ramon; thank you so much. Thank you too for all of the wonderful food parcels. I think we had enough food for almost the entire week didn't we Jake?" Catherine said smiling.

"We did indeed Ramon. Thank you so much for everything especially the special cake. You know that is my favorite," Jake replied smiling.

"I do know that Mr. Jake; I have made one this afternoon when I heard that you were coming back. I will have dinner ready for you directly. The Trinity crew is welcome as well. I have prepared food for everyone," Ramon stated. The Trinity crew headed down to the bunkhouse to join the English Rose crew for dinner. They were all to be one big family now that the two ranches were joined in everything but name. Ramon went back inside to prepare for dinner and Jake took Catherine's hand as she dismounted. "I am going to carry you over this threshold Mrs. Nelson and then I am going to unpack the horses," Jake said smiling.

Catherine thought that this threshold was not as happy as the day she was carried over the cabin threshold, but that would change in due time. She knew that Jake was trying to keep up her spirits and she would not let him down. She went up to the room that would now be their room and took off her hat and smoothed her hair. She looked around the room that she had left as a bride and wondered if Jake would think it all too feminine and not be comfortable in it. She would ask him tonight once they had had dinner and gotten settled in. She knew that security would continue to be tight as long as these threats continued to swirl, but she felt safe here knowing the number of people who were around them and were on high alert for any actions from the Triple B ranch.

As she came downstairs, Jake was coming in the front door with the items from the pack horse. She saw the baby carrier and felt the tears start to well in her eyes. She wanted so badly to be back on their sacred mountain and back in her innocence before she knew all that had been threatened by Delaney and Carmichael. Today should have been a happy day for them in coming home and starting a new life. It didn't feel like that now and she needed to get herself together so that Jake would not see her upset. "I will take those things up to our room Jake," Catherine said smiling.

"That sounds nice Catherine; our room. I will go down and speak to the crew. I will be back in just a few minutes," Jake said smiling.

Catherine asked Ramon if she and Mr. Jake could have their baths and he told her that he was already heating the water. He knew that Miss Catherine liked to have a warm bath each night and thought that she probably needed it tonight after the ride back from their sanctuary. He would prepare a bath for Mr. Jake in Mr. Cameron's old room so that he could relax as well. He saw the tension on Miss Catherine's face and knew that she was happy to be home, but not happy to face what was ahead of them both. He said a quick prayer that all could be settled and things could get back to where they had been before all of this had begun.

Catherine placed her packed items back in her closet and unpacked the baby carrier, skirt, moccasins and blanket. She wanted them to have pride of place in their room so that they would be reminded everyday of the happiness that they had shared on the mountain.

Jake met with the two crews in the bunk house and outlined the protective security that they would continue to follow. He wanted the cattle for market brought into the home paddocks until this matter was settled so that there was additional support for the main house and extra protection for Catherine. He had been told about the hearing scheduled for the following week with the Circuit Court judge. He told the men that he would drive Catherine and himself in the surrey wagon, but wanted a protective detail as they went to town in case of trouble. He thanked both crews for working well together and thanked them too for keeping everything going well while Catherine and he were away.

When Jake returned to the house, he went up the porch stairs for the first time as the master of the house. As

Catherine had said, there were adjustments for both of them to make. As long as they did it together, everything would be fine. "Ramon, do you know where Miss Catherine is?" Jake asked as he came in the front door. He turned and closed, locked and bolted the door upon entry. Ramon saw the action and thought that Mr. Jake was doing security detail as he must have been doing since their wedding.

"She is upstairs Mr. Jake in your room," Ramon replied.

My room; Jake thought. That sounds so odd, but as long as Catherine is there; it will be fine with me. Once upstairs he walked along the corridor trying to decide which room was their room. He saw one door closed and thought that must be it. He knocked softly on the door and heard Catherine's voice. "Who is it?" Catherine called out.

"It's me love; it's Jake," he replied.

"Come in darling; the door is open," Catherine replied.

As he entered the room he realized that the room was nearly as large as the entire cabin on the mountain. The bed was as large which he thought a very good thing. He looked around the room but still couldn't find Catherine. "Where are you sweetheart?" Jake called out.

"I am over here behind the screen Jake," Catherine replied.

"Are you decent Catherine?" Jake responded.

"I am to you Jake, but not to everyone," Catherine answered.

Jake went up to the screen and saw that it sheltered the fireplace. A fire was going and in front of the fire was a small bathtub; the smallest that he had ever seen. He would have thought it was made for a child until he saw Catherine in the bathtub with scented water nearly to her neck. Her hair was up and she was relaxing in the scented water. "You look mighty pretty there sweetheart. I bet that feels good after a long ride," Jake said smiling. He knelt down so that he could be on eye level with Catherine. He stroked her cheek then and she leaned into his touch as was her custom.

"It does feel good Jake. Ramon has prepared a bath for you in Father's old room so that you can relax as well," Catherine said smiling.

"I was wondering when I saw this tub how I was going to manage. I think I could only use it as a footbath," Jake said laughing.

"That would probably be true Jake. Don't worry; Father's tub comfortably fit him so I know it will comfortably fit you as well. He planned it on the first floor in the event that he couldn't take stairs in the future. He thought of everything Jake. It is right off the library; Ramon will show you love," Catherine said smiling again.

"Alright then Catherine; I will go take a good soaking and give you a chance to finish your bath. I love you Catherine; everything will be fine love. You know that right?" Jake asked worriedly.

"I do know that Jake. As long as we are together; everything will be alright," Catherine replied. Jake kissed her then and left to find her Father's first floor bathroom. He did think of everything Jake thought. Imagine putting a room on the first floor just for baths. Cameron was a very smart man indeed. When he got to the bottom of the stairs, Ramon was waiting and showed him where he needed to go. As he entered the room, he found a large bathtub filled with steaming water, a robe, slippers and scented soap just like Catherine's, but for a man's taste instead. There was also a single bed against the wall that Jake figured was there in case of illness. Cameron had planned for his old age even if his chest had kept him from enjoying it. Catherine was right; he had a lot of getting used to in this house. He just didn't want Ramon and Catherine to treat him like a guest. He wanted to feel like this was his home now and that he was not just visiting. He would file that away to discuss with Catherine tomorrow. She had had enough to process today after he had told her the full story of their expedited wedding and honeymoon. He could see it in her face; the first time that he had ever seen her depressed since he knew her. He would have to get her spirits up tomorrow so that they could face what they needed to face now that they were back home.

Jake settled into the large tub and thanked Cameron again for his forethought. This was something that he could enjoy and get accustomed to. He thought then that Catherine had never complained that she didn't have her bath the whole time they were in the cabin. She had thanked him for the basin of warm water each evening and each morning and never said a word of complaint. She was definitely one of a kind; a real lady in every sense of the word. She could be pampered and petted with the best of them, but never complained when those things she was accustomed to were not around. She was serious when she said that she wanted to go back to the mountain. He could see it in her face when he saw her tears as he brought in the baby carrier. She had been happy there and a part of her just wanted to go back and be happy again. He knew how she felt. He had been on guard ever since they set foot back on the Trinity ranch and after talking with the men, he knew that they would need to keep up their guard until this whole sordid affair was at an end.

After he finished his bath, Jake went up to check on Catherine again. The door was closed again, but he knew which door to go to this time. When he knocked on the door, she called come in and he entered the room still fragrant from her lavender scented bath. She was seated at her dresser brushing her hair when he came in the room. She saw him in her Father's robe and smiled at the sight. "I think it fits you perfectly Jake. Ramon and I thought you would enjoy it after your bath. Did you like the bath Jake?" Catherine asked smiling.

"That was not something that I was used to sweetheart, but it was mighty comfortable. Are you feeling better since you had your bath? I bet you really missed that this past week sweetheart. You should have told me; I would have come up with something," Jake stated.

Catherine got up from her dressing table and put her arms around Jake's waist. "As long as we were together and we are safe Jake that is all that I care about. I wasn't always a princess you know. I had five brothers to grow up with and until I was in my teens, I got to tag along with them and do all sorts of things. Besides, don't you think your friends would laugh if we tied a bathtub onto a pack horse for one of our visits?" she said smiling.

"They would understand Catherine. They know that you come from a different world. They wouldn't judge you; except of course if they saw that bathing costume; that would raise a few eyebrows I think," Jake said grinning.

"I am feeling better and I think that you are feeling better now too. I have us set up in front of the fire with a tray for this evening so that we can stay in our room. Is that alright my love? I wanted us to be together for one more night before the world intruded again. Is that alright Jake?" Catherine asked earnestly.

"Of course it is Catherine. You have to promise me that you and Ramon aren't going to treat me like a guest after tonight. I live here now you know and I need to feel like I am family and not a guest," Jake said worriedly.

"We are always going to spoil you Jake just because we love you and are so glad that you are with us. That won't change; we just won't have a tray in front of the fire every night. Unless of course you want a tray in front of the fire and then we will do it every night," Catherine said smiling up at Jake.

"I don't want any special treatment Mrs. Nelson, but this is nice tonight love. Like you say, just one more night; just the two of us in a special place before the world intrudes again," Jake said smiling.

The two sat in front of the fire enjoying their dinner, talking about all that they had seen during the past week and what Jake wanted to accomplish with the joining of the two ranches. Catherine was so pleased to see him excited about the way forward. She wanted them to both focus on that in the days and weeks ahead. They needed to focus on the positive and on what mattered most to them and not on people who made it their business to bring hate and misery to everyone around them. After they had finished their dinner, Jake carried the large tray downstairs and Catherine started getting ready for bed. She wondered about the little things suddenly like which side of the bed that Jake would want to sleep on and if he would want a window open or not. She didn't usually sleep with an open window, but as long as Jake was with her, he would keep her warm so she wouldn't mind the fresh air. She turned down the bed then and blew out most of the candles in the room excepting the ones near the bed. She knew that Jake had made that request particularly when next they visited the cabin so it was foremost in her thoughts now.

When Jake returned to their room, the first thing she asked him was whether or not he slept with a window open when he slept at the Trinity ranch. "I do sleep with an open window, but I know how cold you get. I am fine with the windows closed," Jake replied smiling.

"As long as you are with me Jake; I won't be cold." Catherine opened the window farthest from the bed and pulled the shades on the remaining windows. It was strange because suddenly, she felt as if it was her wedding night again. She felt strange and new and nervous with Jake in their room together for the first time. She knew that she would get her head wrapped around it, but it hadn't happened yet. Jake as always sensed that something was bothering her. "Which side of the bed do you sleep on Jake?" Catherine asked worriedly.

"I usually sleep in the middle Catherine as I suspect you do as well. You have got to relax Catherine. You are acting more nervous than you did on our wedding night. Come here and talk to me sweetheart," Jake said tenderly.

"I just want to get everything right Jake. At the cabin it was temporary wasn't it my love? I just want to make sure that you have the windows the way that you want them and the candles the way you want them and whichever side of the bed that you need to sleep on because this isn't our honeymoon Jake; this is the rest of our lives," Catherine replied anxiously.

"Do you think that we have to make all of the decisions for the rest of our lives this evening my love? You are just tired and you are letting those snakes get to you. I won't have you upset anymore than you have already been by my explanations this morning Catherine. Come here and let me make you feel better. We will decide it as we go along Catherine. I told you, I will not have you and Ramon treating me like a guest at a hotel. If I want the window up, I can do that myself Catherine or blow out candles or any of the other things that you are worrying about," Jake replied smiling.

Catherine went over and sat on Jake's lap. "I just want you to be happy here Jake. I want to make you feel welcome and not like a guest in your new home," Catherine replied tenderly.

"I know you do, but you are running yourself ragged and we just got home. Now, do I see a summer nightgown under your dressing gown? I see I don't have to send home to Delaware for one of those after all. You didn't pack it because I told you to bring warm ones only didn't I and you always listen to everything that I say. That is a lot of responsibility for a man and you know I am not used to someone listening to everything I say. Sometimes even the crew disagrees with me Catherine and they work for me," Jake said laughing.

"You are just trying to make me laugh Jake," Catherine said smiling.

"I am just trying to make you laugh my love and I am about to get your mind off of windows, candles, trays, baths and sides of bed in very short order," Jake said smiling. He unhooked the fastening at the waist of Catherine's dressing gown and placed the dressing gown across the bottom of the bed. This nightgown had ribbons instead of tiny buttons as she had probably remembered his comment about the buttons on her chemise. It seemed that she filed away all of his comments so he needed to be careful going forward of his stray criticisms. Catherine placed her arms around his neck and leaned her head on his shoulder. She definitely needed him and needed his touch right now to chase away the demons of the day and the demons that she was imagining in her mind.

Catherine pushed Jake's robe open so that she could kiss his neck and the upper part of his chest. Jake leaned back against the tall head board of the bed. This was definitely something that they had not experienced in the cabin and he made a note of the fact that it was good back support going forward. He pulled Catherine towards him until she was straddling his lap. Slowly he began undoing the lavender ribbons that travelled the length of her nightgown. When he reached the last one, he parted the gown and placed his hands at her narrow waist. She untied his robe so that she could feel his chest against her own and rested her head against his chest. Jake slowly rubbed her back and placed his fingers beneath her chin so that he could tilt her head to kiss her full lips. Once he had begun kissing her, he felt her relax against him. He continued kissing her and mating his tongue with her own. She slowly placed her arms around his neck pulling him closer to her.

His hands travelled down her sides and came to stroke her back and bottom. He kissed her neck and his hands came to cup and caress her breasts. He raised her up then to caress and suckle her breasts. He heard the quick intake of breath and the sigh which he captured with a deep kiss. With the palm of his hand he caressed her abdomen and deeper making circles as he gently stroked. His hands then found and entered her inner recesses. Again he heard the soft intake of breath and the sigh that followed and captured them both with a deep kiss. Jake gently prepared Catherine for the lovemaking that was to follow. When she began to come apart in his arms, he raised her up and entered her gently at first and then with more and more intensity as they both neared their climax. The words of love and endearment that followed continued until they had both reached their climax. They clung to each other then until they were both able to hold a thought and regain their breath. Jake reached over to blow out the candle and lifted Catherine to his side. He pulled her up against him and she laid her head on his broad chest. He could feel the tears again, but knew that they were tears of release that Catherine cried each time that they made love. He no longer feared them, but understood they were just part of Catherine's gentle nature.

When at last she could speak, Catherine smiled into the darkness. "You told me that you were going to make me forget the candles and the window and the tray and the rest. You did a very good job of that Mr. Nelson. I didn't know that we could make love in that way," Catherine said smiling.

"We are just getting started Mrs. Nelson; have no fear of that. We are just getting started in so many ways love. We don't have to decide everything that we need for the next fifty years in the first month. Leave a few things to be decided as we go along. As long as you are by my side; everything else is just noise Catherine. It will all be decided as we go along. I will tell you what I like and you will tell me what you like and occasionally we will disagree, but we will sort it out in time," Jake said into the darkness. He held Catherine to him to both keep her warm and to remind himself that he was well and truly at the English Rose and that she was actually beside him as he had dreamt so many times over the past several months. His last thought was that they would face whatever may occur together and make it right again not only for them, but for everyone else in the valley.

CHAPTER TEN

The next morning Jake slept later than usual because of the window shades. He was used to the sun coming in and waking him up. He thought there would be some smiles from the men when he came out of the house this morning later than usual, but he could weather any teasing. As far as he was concerned, he was the luckiest man in New Mexico and maybe the whole country. Catherine was beside him as usual, keeping warm by her proximity to him. He got up and put down the window and then gathered the blanket from his native friends and placed it upon her. He knew from experience that she got cold when he got out of bed and would too quickly wake up when that happened. He grabbed his robe and slippers and went downstairs to wash and shave and greet the day. He thought that Ramon would have breakfast started and he would begin his day.

Catherine slept in recovering from the past day's activities, but mostly from the shock of information that Jake had relayed to her. When she awoke she knew that Jake would be up and about starting his work for the day. She hoped that she would see him at lunch and knew that she had mail and other tasks waiting for her in the library to complete. She got dressed and went downstairs to breakfast.

"Mr. Jake said to tell you that he would be home for lunch Miss Catherine. He asked that we stay close by the house this morning and every morning until the problem is resolved Miss Catherine," Ramon said earnestly. By the problem Catherine assumed he was talking about Delaney and needed no further explanation. She had her breakfast and went into the library to complete her tasks. As she expected, there were bills to take care of for the ranch and a letter from one of her brothers in answer to her previous letter home. She would have much more to tell them all in her next letter. She would invite them to come to visit next spring when hopefully everything would be sorted. After writing her brother and completing the bills, she sat down to update her diary. There had been many momentous events since last she had updated it and she knew that it would take quite some time to describe the time on the mountain and their return to the English Rose. The first Catherine had been such a vivid diarist that she wanted to leave a record for her ancestors of the second Catherine and her adventures in New Mexico. She hoped that she would have happy adventures to record going forward once the latest matter was resolved. Before she knew it her work was done and she heard a horse in the front yard. She looked out of the window cautiously when she heard the horse, but then saw the crew behind the first horseman and thought that Jake must be home for his lunch. Ramon had come to the front of the house when he heard the horseman as well. He smiled to say that Mr. Jake was home. She knew that the whole ranch was on high alert and hoped that state of affairs would change shortly as well.

Catherine opened the door when she saw it was Jake and stood on the porch waiting for him to come up the porch steps. When he saw her smile, his first thought was; I will be coming home to this beautiful woman each day for the rest of my life. I am indeed the luckiest man in New Mexico. "Hello Mrs. Nelson; what do we have for lunch today?" Jake said smiling. Once he reached her at the top of the stairs, he placed his hand around her waist as they walked into the house. He didn't want to kiss her out on the porch with the whole crew watching, but would definitely do so as soon as he had her in the house. He was as good as his word. When they entered the house and Jake closed the door, Catherine smiled up at him waiting for her kiss. She didn't have long to wait. He lifted her up and she put her arms around his neck. "I missed you this morning Catherine, but I had last night to think about all morning and tonight to look forward to. I think I probably didn't answer questions fast enough this morning. The crew will have to forgive me for a while. Every time I think of my beautiful wife, I lose track of what I was thinking before. It is becoming quite a problem," Jake said laughing.

"I had mail to go through this morning and a letter that I wrote to my brother. I will show you his letter after lunch. I asked if he and his family would like to visit next spring. I was hopeful that things would have settled down by then. I also updated my diary Mr. Nelson. There were quite a lot of updates to complete as it has been an eventful week," Catherine said smiling up at Jake. "We have lunch ready for you darling when you are ready to eat," Catherine stated.

"Let me go through and wash up and I will meet you in the dining room." He kissed the top of her head then and headed into Cameron's downstairs room to wash up. He somehow knew that there would be a basin of water waiting for him and soap. Between Catherine and Ramon, they think of everything. A man could get used to this treatment for sure.

When he reached the dining room, Catherine had laid a place for him at the end of the table in the place of honor. She was sitting next to his place with a smile on her face waiting for him to join her. Ramon was at the door waiting to set out a small feast for their lunch. If this keeps up, Jake thought, I will have to take a siesta each afternoon. Well, that wouldn't be such a bad thing so long as Catherine is taking a siesta as well. He smiled over at her then and she put her hand on top of his and gave it a squeeze. Yes, he thought, I am one happy man and no one is going to take this away from us, not ever.

"Tomorrow I think we should go into town and meet with Judge Wilkerson again Catherine. The Circuit Judge will be coming in next week and we need to see if anything further is needed from us in preparation for that hearing. I am sure there isn't, but I just want to double check. It would give us a chance to catch up on the latest that is underway with the US Marshal as well. He may want to speak to both of us Catherine," Jake said earnestly.

"Alright darling; I will be ready for whatever we need to do," Catherine replied smiling.

She is back, Jake thought smiling. She is ready for the fight and we will fight it together. Jake filled her in on the work that they had done that morning and how things were being handled with the two ranches working together and the two crews working in tandem. He was pleased with the work of the two ranches and had many plans of how they could do projects together.

"Don't forget Jake; you said that we would need to ride over today and pick up some of your things. I want you to be comfortable in bringing whatever things you would like over to the house. Maybe you would like to bring some of your books as well Jake. I am sure there are things that you would like to have around you here," Catherine said smiling.

"You mean other than you Catherine? There aren't things that I can think of more important than you and Ramon of course. Do you truly eat lunch like this every day or are you two just showing off?" Jake asked laughing.

"We weren't sure how much lunch you generally have Jake, so we thought we would make you some of your favorite things. You will need to give us a list so we can make them for upcoming lunches or dinners," she replied.

"If you two keep this up, I will have to walk to the Trinity each day rather than ride," Jake replied. "Understand I am not complaining, I am just letting you know that I might need a siesta after a lunch like this," Jake said with a wink. Catherine started to giggle when he made that comment and then stopped herself with a covering cough when Ramon came into the room to collect the dishes. Jake kissed her hand then after Ramon had left the room. Ramon in the kitchen thought how happy he was that Mr. Jake was here at last and that he and Miss Catherine made his life very happy indeed. We just all need to stick together to take out the scum of the valley and then everyone can return to happier days, he thought.

*****

The next day Jake and Catherine set off to meet with Judge Wilkerson. He knew his wife well enough to know that he needed to have the surrey wagon prepared for the trip because Catherine as always would dress for calling and not in her customary riding clothes. He was not disappointed when she appeared at the front door dressed in one of her *ten pound dresses* as Chet Stoner would call them and a hat which was the height of fashion, but did little to protect from sunstroke. She had her parasol in her hand as well as she knew that Jake would make comment otherwise. She smiled her mischievous smile at him then, waiting for him to make a comment. He only smiled and shook his head which she knew was his way of commenting without saying a word. He helped her into the surrey which was then circled with a contingent of four men as they set off for Buena Vista. Until Delaney and Carmichael could be taken into custody by the US Marshal, Jake was taking no chances. Catherine would have an escort with her at all times and that escort was armed as well. Jake would brook no argument and on this and many things, Catherine would not have made a comment. She knew that he only had her safety in mind when he made these arrangements and she certainly didn't want Jake or anyone from the two ranches to have to plan a rescue to the Triple B on her behalf.

When they reached town, Jake pulled up in front of the judge's office and the men dismounted and took their places on both sides of the door. This would be the protocol going forward in any instance in which Jake and Catherine were coming to town or beyond the confines of the English Rose. Hopefully this was a temporary precaution, but knowing Delaney and Carmichael, it would continue until the matter was settled once and for all.

Jake and Catherine went into the judge's office and asked to see him. They were immediately shown in. "Well now, how was the honeymoon Mr. and Mrs. Nelson? I see Catherine is dressed for calling as always and Jake I have never seen you looking so happy. In fact you both are looking awfully pleased with yourself so the marriage must be a good thing after all. I like to hear that because once I marry a couple, I like to see them stay married," Judge Wilkerson said smiling.

"You can make book on that Judge Wilkerson. This is one marriage that you won't have to worry about. I hear that there was quite a bit of activity last week in our absence Judge. First off, I wanted to ask about this hearing and whether or not there was anything further that you needed from us," Jake asked earnestly.

"No Jake; not a thing. We are ready to proceed and as I told you both, there is no question but this is a fishing expedition by Delaney and Carmichael, but as you know, that is what they do. They push and they push until someone pushes back once and for all. I know that you are aware of the visits that occurred last week to both ranches. I have met with the US Marshal and he is aware of that information. I have also had him meet separately with Ramon and with the foremen for the Trinity and the English Rose so that he could take down exactly what was said by Delaney in each instance. We also have disturbing information from the Triple B that the staff there has been questioned by Delaney as possible spies. The man is a menace and the quicker we can deal with him the better it will be for everyone. Your plan was a good one Jake and I would assume that you have men with you today as well," Judge Wilkerson stated.

"I do indeed Judge. We have four men with us from the English Rose and we will be escorted in this manner until this whole sorry business is over. I will not have Catherine frightened in her own home so we have taken precautions there as well," Jake said taking Catherine's hand and squeezing it. "Do you need me to meet with the Marshal as well?" Jake asked earnestly.

"At this point he is conducting his inquiries of all parties who have been threatened by Delaney and Carmichael. As I am sure you are aware, that makes for quite a long list at this point. The Marshal is working with the Sheriff and they have a list of all parties that they need to interview and have make a statement. He will have his work cut out for him, but he needs to tie up all loose ends and make his case as air tight as possible. I appreciate the extra precautions that you are taking and suggest that they continue for as long as Delaney and Carmichael are at liberty," Judge Wilkerson replied.

Catherine listened to the discussion in silence. She was not aware of all of the things that they had discussed and started to get the pang again in the bottom of her stomach that she had had ever since Jake had told her about the threats by Delaney against her. She wondered just how far Delaney would go to get what he wanted and then decided perhaps she didn't want to know that after all, at least not fully.

"The hearing will be next Wednesday and I will need you both to be there in case the Circuit Judge has any questions of you. I don't expect him to have any questions, but it is better to be prepared rather than have a delay that could result in the matter being continued. We want this behind us as quickly as possible," Judge Wilkerson stated.

"Thank you very much Judge for everything that you have done. If you need us for any reason, just send word and we will head into town," Jake replied.

"Likewise Jake and Catherine; should any additional threats be directed to either one of you, make sure you send someone into town for the Marshal and the Sheriff. They will put it all to rights in short order. Until next week, you two take care. Catherine I know that we will get this all sorted so don't lose hope," Judge Wilkerson stated.

"I most definitely will not Judge. Jake and I have decided that we would like to have a second wedding after all of this clears away and invite the whole town and the county. We hope that you will agree to marry us again and to have everyone join in our happiness," Catherine said smiling.

"It will be my pleasure Catherine. That is one of my happiest duties and I will be happy to do so for two of my favorite people. You just let me know when and we will get it onto the calendar," Judge Wilkerson stated smiling.

When they left the Judge's office, Catherine asked if she could go to the General Store again so that she could talk to Mrs. Downes about the fabric for her fall dresses. Jake walked down to the store with her and the crew from the English Rose followed along and sat on both sides of the store entrance while Jake and Catherine went inside. The fabric was brought up for Catherine's consideration a second time and the amount of fabric was decided upon. Catherine told Mrs. Downes that she would return when they could look at patterns and decide on the exact design of the dresses that they would make from the selected fabric. She didn't want to keep Jake any longer than necessary as she could tell that he was nervously circling the store and intimidating any customers who would harmlessly walk in Catherine's direction.

When they were again outside, Catherine took his hand and looked up at him with mischief in her eyes. "You know darling you can't give everyone who comes near me your look of murder. They could very easily be in the General Store just because they need to do business just like us," Catherine stated whispering.

"When all of this is over, I will take you shopping wherever you need to be taken. I just don't like people coming up to you when I don't know who they are or what they are up to," Jake replied earnestly. Jake kept hold of her hand and placed himself on the outside of the walkway closest to the street. He scanned every face and every rider as they proceeded back to the surrey. Catherine felt as though she was the Crown Jewels being taken for a walk in Buena

Vista. She saw that people eyed Jake and the men warily as they knew that all five were armed, but those who knew Jake also understood that he was doing what was necessary to keep Catherine safe. Word of their marriage had circulated in the small town and unfortunately, the reasons for the hasty marriage had circulated as well. It seemed that the entire valley was on alert; at least so it seemed from Catherine's perspective.

On their way back to the English Rose, Jake took a detour to the Trinity so that he could collect some of the things that they had discussed moving to his new residence when next they were out. The crew at the Trinity was obviously on high alert as they moved into the protective detail as soon as they saw Jake and Catherine in the surrey protected by the four crew members from the English Rose. Jake pulled up in front of the ranch house and went to Catherine's side to help her exit the surrey. She walked into the ranch house with Jake and told him that she would be happy to help him pack some items since they had the wagon to transport. Catherine walked from room to room hoping to remind Jake of some sentimental item that he would not want to leave behind. She spied a photo which she thought must be of his Mother and placed it in the stack of items that he was packing to bring to the English Rose

Her next foray was to the library. There were countless books there as he had told her that reading was his favorite thing to do especially in the winter months when there was precious little to do on the ranch except make sure that all of the animals were properly fed. She fingered some of the books on the shelves recognizing many of the classics that she herself had read and that she had seen in her Father's library. There were books about animal husbandry which she could understand considering Jake had been a rancher his entire adult life. There were also some unexpected books that she thought she would need to ask him about such as Gray's Anatomy. She had never seen this book before, but found some of the illustrations to be quite illuminating. Since her Mother had taught her rudimentary first aid and nursing to assist with the many injuries of her five brothers, she thought that this could have been a useful book indeed, but as an unmarried young woman, some of the material may have been considered inappropriate to say the least. Jake came upon her reading his Gray's Anatomy and smiled thinking that she may have more questions after a review of his book collection. To say it was varied was an understatement. It had been his source of entertainment and education in varied ways. Like the original Catherine and her husband Cameron, books were just one of the many things that bound Catherine and Jake. He wondered if their library would need to be expanded once all of his books were added to the collection.

"We needn't take all of my books this time love. We will move over so many on each of our visits. I assume that some of the titles you recognize and then there will be ones new to you as well such as the Gray's Anatomy in your hands," Jake said smiling.

"I think this would have been helpful to me when I was learning first aid from Mother, but I don't know if she would have allowed me to have one because of some of the illustrations," Catherine said blushing.

"Nothing is more important than education Catherine in all things," Jake said kissing the top of her head. "There are some other books there that might be of interest as well, but we will get them moved and then sorted in your Father's library," Jake continued.

By the time that they had concluded their cursory review, the surrey wagon was full behind Catherine and Jake and they set off for the English Rose and one of Ramon's excellent lunches.

*****

The next week, the same protocol was followed in the security detail to accompany Jake and Catherine to the Circuit Court hearing. Catherine had dressed very carefully for this event as she knew that the whole town would show up to the hearing and to hopefully hear Delaney and Carmichael put in their place. A contingent of the English Rose crew would remain behind for security purposes, but Ramon was also on horseback so that he could hear the outcome of the hearing. After the visitations by Delaney during Jake and Catherine's honeymoon, he had had his fill of Delaney and was glad that the courts would finally begin to rein him in.

The security detail, Jake, Catherine and Ramon set off for Buena Vista again in anticipation of the hearing. Catherine had been agitated again the previous night and Jake had done his best to get her mind off of the events of the day in his customary manner. He smiled at her as she had entered the surrey wagon that morning. "You sure do look mighty pretty Mrs. Nelson. You know that everything is going to be fine today right? The Marshal will be there, we have the security detail from the English Rose with us and Judge Wilkerson has it all in hand. We just have to be there for moral support. Don't worry; no one is letting you out of his sight today so don't give Delaney or Carmichael another thought," Jake said earnestly.

"I know Jake that everything you say is true. It is just the thought that someone would try to challenge everything that Father put in place after he worked so hard to make sure that all was done correctly. It is a slap in the face of Judge Wilkerson also and how exacting he is with all of his work," Catherine said anxiously.

"We will put this behind us Catherine and then we will start planning for the renewal of our vows. I want everyone in town to see the same beautiful bride that I saw and your Mother's beautiful dress. Besides, I am the luckiest man in the valley and I want everyone to know it," Jake said smiling.

"You say the sweetest things Jake Nelson," Catherine said smiling.

"I can't help but smile Mrs. Nelson. Whenever I get angry about Delaney and Carmichael I just look over at my beautiful wife sleeping like an angel and nothing else matters. Remember what I told you Catherine; it is you and me and all the rest of it is noise. The boys and I will keep you safe, so you just keep focused on today being over and us moving on with our lives in short order," Jake said smiling and squeezing her hand.

When they arrived in town it appeared to Catherine that the entire county had shown up from the look of the number of wagons on the street. Catherine noticed that Jake had gotten that same set to his jaw that he had the day of their wedding when he was fiercely devoted to spiriting Catherine away from the English Rose to their sacred mountain hideaway. She knew he was focused on the day ahead and on keeping her safe in light of Delaney and his crew's attendance at the hearing. It would be the first time that she had seen Delaney again since his unbidden visit to the English Rose. She noticed that Ramon had the same set to his jaw as Jake and thought that the atmosphere was going to be very tense indeed until this day was over.

Jake came to her side of the wagon and handed her down. She noticed that the members of the English Rose crew were directly behind him. Jake touched his hat to members of the crowd who were gathered outside of the courtroom. They all moved to let him pass with Catherine close by his side. He was holding her hand and then came to place his hand around her waist as they approached the waiting crowd of people. He was unsure if Delaney or his men were among the crowd waiting for the start of the hearing and was taking no chances.

Once inside, Jake took off his hat and looked for Judge Wilkerson. He was in the front of the courtroom in the well of the court. Jake and Catherine took a seat in the front row of the courtroom with Ramon on her right hand side and the members of the English Rose crew directly behind Jake and Catherine. Jake shook hands with members of the audience who were directly around them. Several congratulated him on his recent marriage. Catherine smiled at each who spoke to Jake and hoped that in short order she could invite them to the English Rose again for the renewal of their vows. As Jake had told her, keep focused on the happiness that will follow this day and not on this day itself which must be endured.

The Circuit Court judge entered the courtroom and the Sheriff stood at the side acting as his bailiff. He advised the courtroom to all rise. It was at this time that Catherine first spied Delaney and Carmichael on the opposite side of the courtroom. Because they were both so tall, they stood head and shoulders above the members of the audience near them. They both scowled in Catherine and Jake's direction and Catherine did her best to not make eye contact with them. This was not the case with Jake of course because as the tallest man in the courtroom he was able to quickly spy their location and provide them with one of his fiercest looks before turning forward in respect to the Circuit Court Judge who had just entered the well of the courtroom. Judge Wilkerson had told him that Circuit Judge Sanderson was a very fair judge and a man who was well schooled in the law. He would apply the law and only the law to this case. Judge Wilkerson did not expect a lengthy hearing and expected a ruling on the matter on the same day it was heard.

Judge Sanderson called the hearing to order and read the specifics of the matter. He then asked the attorney for Delaney and Carmichael to make his opening argument. The attorney for the two had come from Santé Fe and was not well known by those in the audience. Jake assumed he was one of those lawyers that Judge Wilkerson had warned against who took cases simply because they could and not on the merits of the case. By his presentation, it was abundantly clear that the Judge was correct. He stumbled through his presentation and offered nothing of substance to substantiate his claims. He seemed to believe his own hyperbole however, as he also seemed to get paid by the word for all of the talking that he did in defense of his petition.

Judge Wilkerson when next called to defend his brief was brief and to the point. He stated that he had completed all of the necessary paperwork for the sale of the ranch that was to become the English Rose. All processes had been done in compliance with territory law and Judge Wilkerson presented copies of all of the properly filed deeds on the sale. He explained that he had completed all of the necessary processes as an attorney before he was appointed as judge and that he had asked for a summary judgment on the matter on the merits of the case.

As predicted, Judge Sanderson was very direct and by the book on the matter. He summarized the arguments of both attorneys and in his application of the law, found that there was no doubt of the veracity of the English Rose brief. All had been done in accordance with the law and that the case before him was one that he would qualify as a nuisance case. He awarded in favor of the defendant and required the payment of all court costs by the Triple B plaintiffs Delaney and Carmichael. The case was dismissed by Judge Sanderson as he hit his gavel.

Jake leaned over and placed a kiss on Catherine's cheek and squeezed her hand. He told her that they would all stay in place and wait for the courtroom to clear out so that Delaney and Carmichael could hopefully be on the way to the saloon to drown their sorrows. The English Rose crew remained disciplined and in their seats as they watched Delaney and Carmichael leave the courtroom with the crew of the Triple B in their wake. Delaney again made eye contact with Jake as he left the courtroom. Catherine stubbornly refused to look in his direction. Jake squeezed her hand again and Catherine smiled bravely at him. After Delaney and Carmichael had left the courtroom, Judge Wilkerson turned in his chair and shook both Jake and Catherine's hands. "You two get some rest now. I know you were dreading this day, but all is well just as we said it would be. Our work continues however on the other matters. We have some very compelling statements that have been made thus far. It appears that the initial fear of the citizens to come forward has been addressed. People are coming forward in record numbers to put their complaints in the hands of the Marshal. It shouldn't be long now," Judge Wilkerson stated.

When at last they could stand to leave the courtroom, Catherine noticed a woman still seated in the back row of the courtroom. She was dressed very noticeably in a ruby red dress. She seemed to stare at Catherine and then smiled when Catherine noticed her stare and smiled seemingly in recognition. When they passed by the lady, Jake acknowledged her as did the other members of the English Rose crew. Catherine had no idea who she was, but thought that she would ask Jake once they were back in the surrey wagon. Jake took Catherine's hand again as soon as they left the courtroom and made their way through the waiting crowd. Again many people stopped Jake and shook his hand as he made his way back to the surrey wagon with Catherine in tow. The crew members patiently waited as Jake made his way through the welcoming crowd. Apparently news had spread quickly about Jake and Catherine's marriage and many people wanted to wish them both well in light of the verdict today.

When at last they reached the surrey wagon, Catherine noticed that the same lady had come beside her. "Mrs. Nelson, I would like to shake the hand of the lady who fought Delaney and Carmichael and won. My name is Ruby McGinnis and I am proud to meet you Mrs. Nelson. My best to you and to Jake as you set up housekeeping," Ruby stated.

"Thank you very much Miss McGinnis. I hope that things will start to calm down now, but we can only hope for the best. Thank you very much for your good wishes. It was very nice to meet you," Catherine replied smiling. Ruby acknowledged Jake again and Jake touched his hat as Ruby walked along the walkway down the street. Jake helped Catherine into the surrey wagon and watching that the crew and Ramon were again back in the saddle, they took off for the English Rose.

Once they were on the way back to the English Rose, Catherine asked Jake about Ruby McGinnis. "How do you know Miss McGinnis Jake? Does she run a business in town? I don't remember you introducing me to her before," Catherine asked.

"No love, you would not have met Ruby before because her business was not one that your Father would have frequented. Do you remember I took you to businesses that your Father did business with so that the owners could speak about your Father at the wake? Ruby would not have known your Father. She must have been very impressed with you to make a point of introducing herself to you. Ruby runs the local saloon Catherine and some of her staff has been hurt by Delaney in the past. It seems that he has a preference for women that he can spend limited time with and then abuse for their trouble. Delaney has many things to answer for love and Ruby is one of the persons who are trying to set things right by giving her statement to the Marshal. We may be coming at it from different angles, but we all have the same goal. She was very impressed no doubt with someone who could fight Delaney and win," Jake replied.

Catherine took in that information and had more questions of Jake and how he would know Ruby, but thought it best to leave those questions for another time. They had just won a victory against Delaney and Carmichael and she decided that she wanted to savor that victory hoping that it would be the first of many. It certainly appeared that people from all walks of life were lending their support to Jake and Catherine and that Delaney and Carmichael had much to answer for to the people of Buena Vista and the valley as a whole. Catherine hoped that their luck would continue to hold and that Delaney and Carmichael would soon be brought to justice.

"Jake, don't you think it would be nice to reward the crew for our good news today? Maybe we should do something special for luncheon or dinner. What do you think darling?" Catherine asked.

"I think that would be real nice Catherine. They have done an excellent job of watching out over you and of course moving all of the market cattle to the home paddocks is no small task. We usually reserve those paddocks for the new mothers and their calves, but we have done what was needed to keep everyone safe. I know that we are not out of the woods yet love, but we are one step closer. Each day that passes with more and more people coming forward brings us one step closer to those two ending their reign of terror on the county," Jake replied.

"I will talk with Ramon and we will put our heads together. I think it would be nice to invite the Trinity crew as well, although I know you have to stagger coverage to make sure that all is well there also," Catherine responded

"You are right Mrs. Nelson; you are learning the drill," Jake said smiling. "I was surprised that you didn't have more questions of me about Ruby darling, or are you saving those for later?" Jake asked grinning.

"I decided to savor our victory for now. I may have questions later on when we are alone," Catherine said with a mischievous smile.

"I will be ready for those questions. You remember when I used to mind your questions Catherine? They don't bother me much these days; it seems that few things bother me these days. I guess it is because I walk around with a fool grin on my face most times. I am not even bothered when I happen to sleep in and get teased about it by the crew. Few things bother me these days Catherine because my wife keeps me very happy indeed," Jake said grinning.

"That is my job my love; keeping you happy. Ramon and I work at it very hard you know. You are the center of our lives these days and we like it very much," Catherine said smiling.

*****

That evening after dinner and their evening baths, Jake came upstairs to their room and found Catherine at her dressing table as usual brushing her hair. He thought that no matter how many times he convinced himself that this woman was his wife, he would have to stop and take in that sight as he entered their room. He wondered if she would ask her questions of him now about Ruby. He had thought about it quite a bit on the way home and considered how he would answer her questions. He didn't want to lie and he didn't want to upset her. He just needed to be honest in his approach and help her to understand his life before she arrived in Buena Vista. He would wait until she broached the issue, however and not rush into something unwarranted.

Jake took off his robe and got under the covers waiting for Catherine to finish her evening preparations. She opened the farthest window and pulled each of the blinds, blowing out each of the candles excepting the ones closest to the bed. She smiled at him then as she took off her dressing gown and got into bed. As was customary, she snuggled next to him and placed her head on his chest. This time he blew out the candles as he thought perhaps she would be more comfortable asking about Ruby in the comfort of the darkness. It turned out that his guess was correct.

"Jake, you don't have to answer this question if you don't want to because I know it was before I came here and before you knew me, but I was just wondering; did you and Ruby have a relationship in the past?" Catherine asked quietly.

"We did love. Ruby didn't always run a saloon, but she worked in one and she had a real good head for business so she was set up in her present location by one of her customers. She has ladies who work for her and they entertain men at her saloon. I guess it started when there were very few women in this territory. It wasn't like back home in Delaware when people could go to dances and church socials and meet people and court. There were very few women other than wives in the area when I was growing up. Young boys became men when they went to places like Ruby's. Not all the men who go there go for that reason of course. Some just go to drink and spend time with a lady before returning to their ranch. Some just want someone to talk to. I can tell you Catherine that you are very smart in saying that it was before I met you and before you came to Buena Vista. From the time that you got off that train, there hasn't been anyone else in my life and I don't plan on there ever being anyone in my life again. We are each the sum total of our life experience Catherine and she was one of mine. Does that answer your questions?" Jake asked tenderly.

"Did you love her Jake?" Catherine asked quietly.

"I don't think I knew what love was Catherine until I met you darling. I am not apologizing for it, but I will tell you that sometimes men sow their wild oats. It is not something that we are proud of, but we do it nevertheless. Ruby was part of that time in my life. I think she realizes how special you are to me and I think that she respects you for what you have tried to do here at the English Rose and in the community. She would not have come to you as she did today and said what she did if she didn't respect you," Jake replied.

"Thank you for telling me Jake. I didn't mean to pry it is just that I thought there must be something there but I wasn't sure," Catherine said quietly.

"Like I said love; from the moment that you stepped off that train, that was it for me. You were like a thunderbolt when you walked into my life and nothing has been the same since. I might have fought against it at the time, but nothing has been the same Catherine and nothing ever will be again. I have never wanted another woman the way that I want you and I have never loved another woman the way that I love you. You are the woman that I want to be with for the rest of my life and the woman that I want to have children with Catherine. I think that pretty much sums it up, but if you have more questions, you just let me know because I don't want you stewing over this and worrying yourself. You have had enough to worry about ever since Delaney and Carmichael entered your life; you sure don't need something else to bother you," Jake said kissing the top of her head.

"Thank you for telling me Jake. I would never pry about your life in the past because it was before you met me. I just wondered because she looked at you in a special way and well, I know you are the most handsome man in any room that you enter but I thought there was something special there. You were very respectful of her and didn't say anything that would make me think differently, but it was just something that I picked up on I guess woman to woman," Catherine stated.

"I think that is a very smart way to look at it Catherine, but thank you for the compliment. I don't think you had ever told me before that I was the most handsome man in any room that I enter. That is really something to be told by my beautiful wife. I thought people just looked at us because they were looking at you and how beautiful you are. Now, unless you have any other questions Mrs. Nelson, I would like to celebrate our victory today with a very special night that I have planned for my beautiful wife. How does that sound to you darling?" Jake said into the darkness.

"I think that sounds very good indeed Mr. Nelson. There is nothing that I love more than your special nights and special locations like the mountain and the cabin. I can't wait to go back there Jake for a variety of reasons," Catherine said grinning.

"I can't wait to take you back there Catherine. I just have to figure out how to tie a bathtub onto the back of a pack horse," Jake said laughing. Catherine laughed then also and the discussion was behind them. It was not something that Catherine planned on bringing up again and Jake was glad that he had been honest with her. He didn't want it to fester and he knew if she had not asked, he would have had to come up with a way of making it known so that she didn't sit around and worry about other women. As far as he was concerned, no other woman existed as soon as Catherine McCullum came on the scene.

CHAPTER ELEVEN

The next day, Catherine and Ramon planned their luncheon to thank the members of the Trinity and English Rose ranches for their diligence over the past weeks in keeping Catherine safe and in maintaining security for the main house. A half beef was placed on the barbeque and tables were set out for a late summer picnic. Catherine knew that she needed to celebrate their victory even if diligence was still the order of the day. She could tell from Jake's face each time that he saw horsemen approach the ranch that his security concerns had not abated. If anything, she thought he was being even more careful because he assumed that Delaney and Carmichael would be planning their next attack. Catherine and Jake had pushed back on two counts; keeping Catherine away from Delaney and beating him in court. He would most definitely retaliate, but Jake just didn't know how and in what manner. Until those two were behind bars, Jake would keep up his guard and keep up the guard of both crews. He relented briefly for today's celebration because like Catherine, he wanted to thank the men for their great work.

Ramon had outdone himself with all of the picnic fixings of cole slaw, potato salad, baked beans and corn bread. It was a feast and they were all planning on enjoying themselves. Ramon had even made some of Jake's favorite special cake just to make sure that he knew he was being thought of by Catherine. A reminder was not really needed because she continued to see to his every need as though he was a guest in the house and not its new master. He had tried to convince her otherwise, but she would not be swayed. As she told him, he was the center of her life and she wanted him to know that each and every day. He had never been so cherished in his life. His Father was a good man, but he had never had the knack of Mothering and as a man who lost his Mother at birth, this was a rare experience indeed. Jake shook his head every day and just remembered to thank God for Catherine and the change that she had made in his life.

Jake and the men came in at lunch time with Jake as usual leading the way. Catherine had dressed carefully for the luncheon in the lavender dress that she had worn the night that Jake had first stayed for dinner. She wondered if he would remember because she certainly did. It was the first time that she thought that he actually cared for her and the first day that he had kissed her. It was a very important day for sure right up there with the day that Jake asked her to marry him. So many blessings to celebrate on one day but all of them began and ended with Jake.

As he came into the house to wash up for luncheon, he saw her coming down the steps in her lavender dress. He smiled up at her then and remembered fondly the first time that he had seen her wear that particular dress. It was the first time that he saw her in a dress that didn't weigh ten pounds as Chet Stoner and he had teased and he thought that night that she looked like a woman who was being courted. She definitely was being courted and to this day he continued to court his wife as he wanted her to experience what he would have liked to continue had Delaney and Carmichael not intervened.

"You sure do look pretty there Mrs. Nelson. I remember that dress very well. I thought when I first saw you in that dress that you looked like a woman who was being courted. You still look like a woman that is being courted," Jake said grinning.

"Have you had a chance to read my great-great-great Grandmother's diary yet Jake?" Catherine said grinning.

"I have not my love; there have been a few other pressing matters that have taken my time," Jake responded smiling with one eyebrow which rose like a question mark.

"Well, when you do have a chance to read it, you will find that my great-great-great Grandfather used to come home every day for luncheon and because his Catherine was so tiny, she would meet him on the third step of their staircase each day. They would embrace and kiss and he would swing her off of the step as they went into luncheon. I thought that was a very beautiful thing and so did she because she wrote about it in her diary. Don't you think that is a very beautiful tradition?" Catherine said mischievously.

"Are you suggesting that you would like to start that tradition today Mrs. Nelson? Because if you are, I would be open to that suggestion," Jake said laughing. Catherine put her arms around his neck then and he kissed her very deeply and very intensely and swung her off of the step when she least expected it. "And that Mrs. Nelson is how traditions begin. If you have any others you would like to suggest, you just let me know and I will be happy to oblige ma'am," Jake said swatting her bottom as he went on to wash up for luncheon. Catherine grinned to herself and went out to the kitchen to check on Ramon and the preparations for luncheon.

When everyone had washed up and gathered for the feast, Jake rose and thanked everyone present for the security that they had done for the English Rose and for his personal English Rose as he said smiling at Catherine. He asked that all remain vigilant until the whole matter was resolved once and for all and asked that everyone enjoy themselves with the wonderful meal provided by Ramon. Catherine smiled happily at Jake content that he was relaxing at least for a few hours in the constant security task that he had set for himself since the day of their wedding.

The picnic was a success and enjoyed by everyone present. Jake made the comment that after such a meal a siesta was in order. The men shouted and threw their hats into the air and Jake took Catherine's hand and went into the house; whether he was teased or not, he didn't really care at this moment in time. As they entered the house, Jake kept right on walking with Catherine's hand in his own as they mounted the stairs to their room. Catherine started to smile and then blush when she realized that the whole crew would have a pretty good idea what was occurring when they went upstairs for their siesta. She then decided that she didn't really care at this moment because after all, she was a married lady and as Jake had told her, whatever they did was between the two of them and no one else really needed to be concerned.

When they reached their room, Jake closed the door behind them and came up behind Catherine. Slowly he undid her dress and started to kiss her back as he did so. The chills started down her spine and Jake could feel them as he kissed her and brought his hands around her waist. He sat down on the bed then and helped Catherine out of her dress, placing it on the bedside chair. Jake untied her petticoats and let them drop to the floor. Next he untied the ribbons to her corset shaking his head and smiling as he did so. He didn't have to say a word to Catherine; that head shake told her all that he was thinking about her ever present corset. She stood in front of him with only her chemise remaining. He undid the pins on her hair and it gently fell about her shoulders and back. He worked his fingers through her hair and pulled her down on his chest across the bed.

Catherine started to unbutton his shirt then and kissed the exposed skin as she did so. Jake lay across the bed and closed his eyes as Catherine kissed and caressed his neck and chest. She pulled the shirt from his trousers and began to extend her kisses down his chest to his abdomen. When she reached the deep v at the base of his abdomen, she heard a deep growl coming from his throat. He rose then and took off his boots and his trousers and rejoined her across the bed. He made short work of the chemise and began kissing and caressing her neck, breasts and abdomen. Catherine moved restlessly against him as she caressed his shoulders, his back and his arms. She loved to feel the strength of his body against her own and could not seem to get close enough to drink in his warmth and his scent.

Jake could take no more and began to prepare her for the lovemaking to follow. Catherine sighed and Jake captured that sigh with a deep kiss, mating his tongue with her own, Jake continued his exquisite torture of Catherine until she began to cry and call out Jake's name. At that time he entered her and cried out his love for her. The two forgot all concerns about siestas, the teasing of the crew below and anything but their love for one another. When at last Jake had met his climax he collapsed into Catherine's neck inhaling her lavender scent and kissing her with words of endearment only for her ears. He rolled to his side and she lay on the bed looking into his eyes and brushing the hair from his forehead. She placed her head on his chest then and he felt the warm tears that Catherine always cried when they made love. Never had Jake felt anything like his love for Catherine each and every time that they made love. It was the greatest joy that he had ever experienced and he reached out to kiss her forehead, her eyes and lastly her red and swollen lips. No words were needed. They held each other more in love with each passing day and not really concerned about who knew it. The picnic had been a great success for everyone and the siesta was just the topping of that event.

*****

The next day the crew led by Jake went over to the Trinity ranch first thing to bring over more of Jake's possessions. He felt more and more comfortable each day in sharing all aspects of his life with Catherine. He wanted to make sure that all of his special things were brought to the English Rose prior to bad weather setting in this autumn. He had seen many rough winters in the valley and knew that it was time to start preparing for autumn. He smiled when he thought of the days that Catherine and he would spend in the library reading as the snow came down this winter. There were also those siestas to look forward to. He knew that he was smiling like a fool again, but really didn't care. He was happy and he wasn't shy about anyone knowing it. He somehow knew that the crew knew that as well because there had been no comment about the siesta yesterday and the fact that the day's work had ended with lunch. Everyone deserves an afternoon off occasionally. He couldn't believe he was thinking that either, but he was glad of the change in his life and thought the crew was probably relieved as well as he used to be a dawn to dusk taskmaster.

After the wagon had been filled with some of his keepsakes, he checked on mail and loaded up anything that needed to be taken care of so that he could review it in the library at the English Rose. He was not comfortable having the crew out and exposed until the Delaney menace was addressed. Judge Wilkerson had assured them that all was in hand and he certainly hoped that was the case. The crew mounted and headed back to the English Rose with Jake leading the way. On his way back past the oasis, he thought about the first time that he had brought Catherine here and the day of course when he first kissed her and first let his feelings for her be known. They had come a long way in a very short time and he thanked Cameron for setting the wheels in motion to assure this happy conclusion.

As they entered the English Rose land, Jake heard the first shot. He thought at first that someone was out hunting and putting down meat for the autumn to come. He thought little of it at the time other than the fact that he didn't want anyone poaching on the English Rose and endangering the crew or cattle. The second and third shot was not an aberration and the shots were getting closer to the wagon and the men by the sound of the echo. He brought up the horses into a fast gallop in the event that he and the crew was the target of the shots. The crew circled the wagon then with the same fear in mind. The next shots that came spooked the horses and they reared in fear. Jake was able to calm them and keep them in a gallop heading closer and closer to the ranch house. His only thought then was to get to Catherine, to see Catherine, to not die on his own ranch a mile from the love of his life. The wagon continued to gain speed as he urged the horses on. The fear showed in their eyes. He could tell that he needed to keep them calm or they would break for the home paddocks and he would lose control completely.

By the fourth shot, the horses were in a dead run. He was holding onto the reins with all of his might and skill and trying his best to calm the horses. The horses were lathered and the fear was apparent in their eyes and in the eyes of the crew's horses as well. They all did their best to keep the horses calm, but shots continued coming at closer and closer intervals, causing the crew's horses to rear and they were doing their best to keep them under control. At the dead run in which the wagon was rolling, all was well and the ranch house was in view. Jake kept telling himself, Catherine is near. I just need to get to her and all will be well. At that moment, the axle of the wagon broke and Jake was pulled from the wagon as it rolled to the side. Jake continued to roll and the crew members averted running over him as their horses continued in a dead run. They made a circle then and doubled back, jumping from their horses and checking on Jake's condition. One of the riders rode ahead and went for another wagon to bring Jake back to the house. None could face the thought of having to tell Miss Catherine that Jake had been hurt or worse still could be dead or dying.

The rider who rode on went quickly to the shed, hitched up another wagon and brought it at a dead run to Jake's side. The rest of the crew had taken defensive action circling Jake and making sure that they could shoot in whatever direction was needed to hit the unknown and unseen assailant. They all thought as they checked on Jake and tended to his injuries that they did not want to face Miss Catherine and tell her that her husband was dead. They had all seen Jake and Miss

Catherine yesterday and the fact that they couldn't keep their eyes off one another. The thought of that woman becoming a widow in front of their eyes was something that none of them could face. Jake was unconscious, but was still breathing when they could reach him. The foreman for the English Rose checked on Jake first and heard his breathing continue shallow but constant. The men lifted him carefully and placed him in the second wagon. They all dreaded the news that they needed to break when they arrived at the house.

Miss Catherine came to the door as she always did waiting for Jake to join her and Ramon in the house for luncheon. Since Jake was always the first one in the yard either on horseback or in the wagon, she looked confused that she didn't see him. She looked from one face to the other and couldn't find him. Jim Eaton came up to Catherine then and told her that they needed to carry Jake into the house. The wagon had a broken axle and Jake had been thrown from the wagon. He didn't yet tell her about the shots that had been fired at them that had caused the dead run to the ranch house. Catherine came to the side of the wagon and saw Jake lying unconscious. She didn't faint as they thought she might do. Her face said it all however as she looked as though her eyes were deceiving her. "Please lift him very carefully. We will place him in Father's downstairs room. Will one of you please go for the doctor and tell him that it is an emergency? Please be very careful with him until we can determine the extent of his injuries," Catherine said slowly. It was evident that she was trying to keep herself very calm as she figured out what to do next.

Ramon came to the screen door then and she called to him for hot water. The men gingerly lifted Jake from the wagon and carried him the short distance to the porch steps. Catherine went ahead of them and held the door for them and then led the way back to her Father's downstairs bedroom. She pulled back the covers as they tenderly laid Jake on the bed. Catherine then ran upstairs for her medical bag and was glad that in her endless suite of luggage upon her arrival, she had the sense to pack an entire emergency kit for just such a circumstance. She could not get her head around the fact that Jake was lying unconscious in her Father's downstairs bedroom. She knew that she needed to keep calm or else she would start to scream and possibly faint as she had done when she heard the news of her Father's death. She knew that she couldn't do either, but needed to tend to her husband until the doctor arrived.

Ramon came running with hot water and the men scattered to the library. They had not told her about the gun shots and would need to report all to the Sheriff and to the Marshal. They decided they had better leave the wagon as it was so that the Sheriff and Marshal could both see what had occurred and make note of the circumstances. They knew this was no accident, but for now, just needed to know how to support Miss Catherine.

Catherine raced to Jake's side and asked Ramon to get a pad of paper. She wanted to do an inventory of Jake's condition so that she could have that information ready for the doctor when he arrived. She started with his head and looked for the signs that she expected of a concussion. His face was bleeding on the left side so she carefully washed the left side of his face and saw the cause of the bleeding in his scalp area. As she washed the area, she saw that there was no new bleeding and thought that was a good sign. She washed the area with witch-hazel to avoid infection. She carefully checked on both sides of his face and then started to work towards his upper chest. She slowly unbuttoned his buttons and tried not to think of the day before when she had lovingly done so during their siesta lovemaking. She told herself she could not think about that now because she needed to focus on his possible injuries. She carefully removed his shirt and saw the bruising that was already starting on the left side of his rib area and arm. She had a liniment mixture in her emergency bag and started to apply that to try to draw out the soreness. She could not feel any breaks in the ribs which she thought was a very good thing. She checked both arms for breaks and then slowly with the help of Ramon moved him to his side so that she could see if there were any abrasions on his back.

So far so good Catherine; she thought. You have not found any breaks just this concussion and the fact that he has not yet come around from his fall. She checked both legs then and could find no break there either. She knew that he would be very sore when he did regain consciousness, but thanked the Lord that there were no visible injuries such as breaks that would need to be addressed.

She felt his pulse then and took readings to provide to the doctor. She looked up at Ramon as if to say, what should I do now?

"Miss Catherine, I know you have checked Mr. Jake for any broken bones. It is a good thing that we have not found any breaks. He is a strong man Miss Catherine. The injury to his head will take some time, but he will be fine, I just know it," Ramon said emphatically.

Shortly thereafter the doctor arrived and with him the Sheriff and the Marshal. Catherine had not been told the circumstances of the accident as she was too busy assessing Jake's condition. She would ask later how everything came to happen, but the fear nagging at the back of her mind told her that this was no accident and that her husband was just the latest victim of the scourge of the valley. "Mrs. Nelson, I see that you have evaluated Jake for his injuries while you were waiting for me. What have you found so far?" Dr. Martin asked.

Catherine provided him with the inventory that she had found. He went through and did a follow up to her initial assessment. He found her notes to be very thorough and complete. She would be a valuable resource for him as he treated Jake because unless he missed his guess, Jake's concussion could result in an extended state of unconsciousness and he would need Catherine's strong hand in the house to keep the patient calm and comfortable until the fog of concussion cleared. Unfortunately he could not advise her how long that would take. Only God knew that answer. He needed to make sure that he kept Catherine calm and she could keep her patient cared for. He did not think that she knew the reason for the injury yet and was unsure how much the men would tell her, but he had heard the rumors like the rest of the town and had a good idea who was behind the injuries and this accident which was not an accident at all.

"Mrs. Nelson, you have done an excellent job of assessing Jake's injuries. I see that you have a full emergency medical bag. I will give you my recommendations of what we need to do to keep Jake comfortable. The concussion will have caused his unconscious state. We will not know how long that will last. We need to keep him warm and comfortable as I know you will do and we will take it one day at a time," Dr. Martin stated smiling at Catherine.

"Can he hear us Dr. Martin?" Catherine asked anxiously.

"We don't know Mrs. Nelson. My bet is on the fact that he can hear us or at least a portion of what we say. I would keep talking to him to encourage his recovery. If you want to read to him that would be fine as well. It is good for both him and for you to help him with his recovery. Like I said, I will be here every day until we have him back on his feet. He is going to be sore on the left side of his body for sure where he fell from the wagon, but other than that, I do not see any broken bones only the concussion that we need concern ourselves about," Dr. Martin said earnestly.

"Thank you very much Dr. Martin. I will not leave his side until he is well. Ramon and I will take care of him and we will see him through this trial," Catherine said earnestly.

"That is all well and good Mrs. Nelson, but you cannot get down yourself. You have two ranches to say grace over along with some very good people of course. You need to take care of yourself as well and need to promise me that you will do that very thing," Dr. Martin said earnestly.

"I promise Dr. Martin. All that matters is Jake's recovery. I can run the ranches from my Father's library right next door if needs be until Jake is better and back with us," Catherine said smiling bravely. Ramon had stayed at Catherine's side throughout the initial assessment and the assessment by Dr. Martin. He would have the information to share with the crew once the doctor had left. He also needed to understand why the Sheriff and the Marshal were here so that he could break any additional news to Miss Catherine as well. He thought how happy Catherine and Jake had been only yesterday and now this has to happen. He knew in his heart this was no accident because Jake was too good a horseman. He prayed that this trial would soon be over for Miss Catherine.

"Ramon, I will need to have a bed moved into this room so that I can be with Jake until he recovers. I will take my meals here also. I will need to have all of the mail, bills and payroll from the Trinity ranch moved over because I need to make sure that everything is handled while Jake is recovering. If you will be so kind to ask the two foremen to meet with me, I will meet with then in Father's library so we can establish what to do going forward. I don't want anything to fall through the cracks while Jake is recovering." She looked behind her to Jake lying on the campaign bed in her Father's downstairs bedroom. She thought then that her Father would have never visualized the room being needed by Jake, but thank the Lord her Father had been an excellent planner and had prepared for all possible outcomes.

Catherine pulled up a chair then and held Jake's hand. "I don't know if you can hear me my love but you have had an accident and been thrown from the wagon. I don't know the details yet, but I am sure that I will have them soon enough. The doctor has been here to see you and concurs with my assessment. We just need to deal with this concussion and get you back on your feet. Please come back to me Jake. I need you every day. I love you darling," Catherine said with tears forming behind her eyes. It was the first time that she had allowed herself to cry since seeing Jake lying in the wagon. She didn't want to upset the crew members and she certainly didn't want to faint as she had when she heard of her Father's death. We will take it one day at a time and like the doctor said, he is a strong, healthy man; he will come around and everything will be fine, Catherine thought.

She sat down with a pad then and started her chart on Jake's condition. She would make a list of everything that she needed moved to this room so that she could stay here until Jake was better. She would work out of her Father's library next door and between the two rooms, could keep an eye on the ranch and everything that needed to be done as well as taking care of Jake. Thank God for Ramon who she knew would be her right hand man.

Ramon was back at her side in a few minutes. She gave him her list of things that she needed to be moved into her Father's alternate bedroom. "Miss Catherine, the Sheriff and the Marshal need to talk to you. They have been outside talking to the crew so that they could tell them what happened. It was not an accident Miss Catherine. Mr. Jake was being shot at when they made a run for the house. The wagon axle broke because of the speed of trying to return to the ranch house Miss Catherine; that and keeping the horses under control as they reared up in response to the gunshots. The crew members are loading up the items that Mr. Jake packed this morning to bring here. They will have them in just a few minutes and then we will get them going on moving things into Mr. Cameron's downstairs bedroom," Ramon said anxiously.

"Thank you Ramon. I feared that this wasn't an accident, but I just didn't know for sure. Did they see whoever was firing at them Ramon?" Catherine asked quietly.

"They did not see Miss Catherine. They were trying so hard to keep the horses under control. If it had not been Mr. Jake driving the wagon, anything could have happened," Ramon replied.

"Thank you Ramon. I will talk to the Sheriff and the Marshal as soon as they are ready for me. I will sit here with Jake until the crew and the Sheriff are ready for me," Catherine replied. She folded the sheet back and tucked in the blanket. She had to keep finding things to keep her hands busy because she could not get her head around the fact that her husband was lying on this bed unconscious and that he had been put there by the same men who had terrorized the entire valley.

In a moment Ramon was again at her side and told her that the Sheriff and the Marshal were ready to see her. She got up and went out on the porch to greet the two men.

"Sheriff, Marshal; won't you come into my Father's library? Thank you so much for coming so quickly. I believe from what I have been told that this was no accident. I understand that my husband's wagon was being shot at as well as the crew from the English Rose who were with him," Catherine stated earnestly.

"Yes ma'am; that is true. We have statements from each of the crew members and we are trying to find the location of the shooter. We know that you and your husband have been subject to some serious threats; you even more than your husband Mrs. Nelson. Was there any type of written threat that preceded this attack?" Sheriff Will asked.

"No Sheriff; no written threats. The threats that have been received have been verbal and have been directed to the crews both here and at the Trinity ranch. We of course had the nuisance lawsuit which has been resolved. I know that you have been collecting statements from a number of other parties in the valley and I will certainly share anything that I receive. I am just going to concentrate on getting my husband better and of course on running the two ranches until he is back on his feet. I don't think that any of us will be travelling anywhere going forward until we can find out who is behind this Sheriff, because we don't want to endanger anyone else on either ranch," Catherine said earnestly.

"Thank you Mrs. Nelson. I want you to promise me that you will send one of the crew members to town if there is any threat here at the English Rose. I know from talking to Judge Wilkerson that you and Jake took Delaney at his word of what he threatened you with and we all take that threat seriously. Jake has done a great job of keeping both ranches safe and keeping you safe Mrs. Nelson. I will do everything in my power to protect you until this business ends once and for all," Sheriff Will stated.

"Thank you again Sheriff and Marshal," Catherine replied.

"Good day ma'am. We will all be praying for Jake, but we will also keep his injury under wraps Mrs. Nelson. We don't want anyone to get the wrong idea about what happened here today," Sheriff Will stated.

The crew members were the next to ask to see Catherine. They had gathered the books and other items that Jake had packed this morning and had them ready to place in the library. Catherine thought that it now seemed like such an innocent thing; moving things from one house to the other. But even the simplest things were not simple so long as this menace was active in the valley. She thought that she would surprise Jake by having his books shelved with her Father's when he woke up. She would put that on her list of things to do to keep her hands busy while Jake was recovering.

"Miss Catherine, we have Jake's items here that we gathered up from the wagon. We want you to know Miss Catherine that this was no accident. We were shot at and Jake was trying like the devil to get back here in one piece. If that axle hadn't broken, he would have made it too. He kept the horses calm and it took a horse whisperer to do that ma'am. Those horses were terrified; you could see it in their eyes. They were rearing and carrying on, but Jake kept them calm.

He will be fine in no time Miss Catherine we just know it. You have to know it too and keep faith that everything will be fine," Jim Eaton stated.

"Don't worry Mr. Eaton; I know that everything will be fine. I just have to get Jake back on his feet. Until then, whatever you need to discuss with me or any of the men from the Trinity need to discuss with me; just let me know. I will take care of all of the mail and bills from the Trinity as well and of course payroll. I will need the information whenever it can be transferred and I will take care of everything from here. If you can let me know what is being taken care of on both ranches I will keep a list for Jake so that he will know everything that had been done while he recovers," Catherine said quietly.

"Yes ma'am; don't worry about anything. We will take care of the outside and you keep focused on taking care of Jake. He sure thinks the world of you Miss Catherine and we won't let him down or you either," Jim Eaton stated.

"Thank you Mr. Eaton. I appreciate that very much. Like I said, just let me know what you need and I will be happy to help," Catherine replied.

Once all of the parties had left, Catherine went back into her Father's downstairs bedroom and sat in the chair next to Jake. She took his hand and saw the abrasions on his left side from his fall and from the rolling that took place after the axle had broken. She lifted his hand to her face and the tears started falling. She had kept strong for Ramon, Dr. Martin, the Sheriff, and the Marshal and now for the crew, but she couldn't keep strong any longer. She needed time to process what had just occurred and she needed time with just her and Jake so that she could let him know that he was not alone within his concussed mind. She didn't know if he could hear her, but she was going to keep talking to him. She thought she would pull her great-great-great Grandmother's diary from the library to read to him. He had teased that he had not had time to read it, so she would read it to him. Even the racy parts when she described her love for great-great-great Grandfather Cameron. She thought Jake would actually enjoy the racy parts once he was awake to take them all in. She would also shelve each of Jake's books so that he could see that they had been added to the English Rose library. Lastly she would bring in flowers from the garden so that he had them each and every day that he was recovering.

CHAPTER TWELVE

The next morning, Catherine woke in her Father's downstairs bedroom and she could not at first get her bearings as to where she was. The crew had moved the leather couch from the library into the room and Ramon had made it up as a bed for her. She told Ramon that she would not leave the room except to work in the library until Jake was better. As soon as she could gather herself together, she sat up and looked over at Jake. He was still appearing to sleep peacefully. As soon as she could get herself up and dressed, she would check him out again and take his vitals so that she had that information for the doctor when he visited. She put on her dressing gown and told Ramon that she was going upstairs to get ready. She asked if Ramon would sit with Jake while she was dressing.

"Miss Catherine, let me bathe and shave Mr. Jake while you are dressing. You cannot do everything Miss Catherine. Let me take care of this for you while you get yourself dressed and ready for the day," Ramon asked urgently.

"Thank you so much Ramon. I know I can't do everything and you are right, I have to ask for some help. Thank you again. I will go upstairs and get ready and then have some breakfast while you give Jake his bath and his shave," Catherine said.

Catherine got dressed and ready and then came downstairs to try to eat some breakfast. Just the thought of food was something that she had to fight, but she also knew if she was going to keep going that she had to eat something. She managed to choke down a little food and tea and then went back into the library to see if there was any mail or bills or any other project that she needed to address. Ramon came out then and said that he had given Mr. Jake his bath and shave and they could now take his vitals for the doctor.

Catherine came back into the downstairs bedroom and reviewed each of the areas that had been injured by the accident. She cleaned the wound on his head with witch-hazel again and saw that overnight the whole left side of his face had become bruised and blackened by the fall. She then reviewed the bruising on the arm, ribs and leg. Just as she had expected, the bruising had become a deep black color there as well. She placed more liniment over the area to draw out the soreness. She thought they would see all colors of the rainbow before his recovery was over. She checked the abrasions on his hands and placed witch-hazel over those abrasions as well. His breathing was steady and his pulse was at a normal rate as well. Only the concussion remained and the period of unconsciousness which she knew could drag on for an interminable time period. She placed water on a sponge so that his mouth would not dry out and then lotion on his mouth so that his lips would not dry out. She remembered telling him once that she thought he had the most beautiful mouth. She remembered so many things about their time together and wanted him to just open his eyes so that she could tell him again. Each time she thought of those special times between them, the tears would form again behind her eyes. She fought through it and would continue doing what needed to be done for Jake and for everyone on the two ranches. Just keep going she told herself.

*****

The days that followed became a routine of Jake's care, care for the ranch, the daily visit by the doctor and the visit of the two foremen who gave a rundown on each project that was undertaken and was completed on Jake's master list. It seemed that he had a master list for the Trinity with all of the annual tasks and that master list she had transferred to the English Rose also so that they would be equally prepared for autumn and for the winter that would follow. After lunch she gathered flowers for his room and then took down her great-great-great Grandmother's diary so that she could sit and read to Jake. There were parts that she had forgotten as well, as there had been some time that had elapsed since she had last read it. She remembered her Mother taking it away from her when she was little because she assumed she didn't want her to read the racy parts and ask her Mother what they meant. It had disappeared from the library at home for a period of time, but then her Father must have put it back as he knew that his daughter was curious about all things that related to her ancestor who she so closely resembled.

Catherine found that the days were not the problem. The days were filled with one activity after another and one thing after another that required her attention. The nights were the problem. When she was alone in the room with Jake and could hear his breathing, but didn't know how far away he might be, that was the desperate time. Then her mind would not stop as it took her to the worst case scenario of his injury and robbed her of her sleep. It was at that time that she rolled herself into a ball on the couch and tried to think back to the days when she first arrived in New Mexico and Jake had taught her to shoot and had taken her to the oasis and kissed her for the first time. She ran her mind over these images so many times that it became a ritual to help her find sleep. Each day began and ended with Jake and the images of Jake that she wanted to keep in her mind not the bruised and battered Jake that lie so quietly on the campaign bed; so near yet so very far away from her now. *Come back to me Jake.* She said it each morning when she tended to his injuries and she said it each night as she kissed him before blowing out the candle and trying to sleep. *Come back to me my love.*

*****

"Where am I and why can't I move?" Jake asked himself. "I feel so sleepy and I want to wake up, but I just can't. I can feel Catherine's hands on me; she is at my head and then my ribs that are so sore. They are as sore as when I fell from horses as a boy as I tried to learn trick riding. Whatever she puts there eases the soreness that is for sure. She has angel hands along with her angel face. I feel her there and I want to reach out and touch her, but I can't seem to wake up. I have to remember what took place before I was brought here wherever here is. I know I must be in the house because Catherine is here. She is reading to me and talking to me and then the doctor comes and Ramon moves me helping Catherine. I want so badly to cry out to her, to touch her, to see her face, but I can't move and I don't know why."

"I remember now; I was coming home from the Trinity and I had the wagon full and I heard shots and I was trying to get home to Catherine. I could see the house in the distance and I kept trying to get home to Catherine. I can hear her now crying and all I want to do is hold her and make her stop crying. These are not her happy tears after we make love. These are tears of pain and I can't help her. I need to rest again because I have remembered a lot of things all at once and I am very tired suddenly."

*****

"Well Mrs. Nelson, how is our patient today?" Dr. Martin called out from the front porch as Catherine moved to greet him.

"He is about the same doctor. The bruises are becoming lighter in shade. I predicted we would see all colors of the rainbow and we definitely have. Do you have any idea when he might wake up Doctor?" Catherine asked anxiously.

"No Mrs. Nelson, like I told you before, each patient reacts differently. I will keep checking his reflexes. Are you reading to him as we talked about?" Dr. Martin asked intently.

"I read to him and Ramon bathes and shaves him daily and we move him so that he is not in one place all day and all night," Catherine said quietly.

"I think you and Ramon are about the best nursing team that a man could have Catherine," Dr. Martin replied. Catherine stayed at his side as Dr. Martin gave Jake his daily examination. "The wound on the head has definitely improved and the bruising of the ribs has definitely improved as well," Dr. Martin stated. Catherine smiled then bravely, pleased at the fact that Jake was being so well taken care of and that the doctor had noticed the care given. "Catherine, you are the one that I am worried about now. Are you eating every meal? You look as though you have lost ten pounds and you didn't have ten pounds to lose. I need you to make sure that you are eating every meal. You can't take care of Jake and two ranches if you are not taking care of yourself. Sit down here and let me take your vitals next," Dr. Martin asked.

"I am fine Doctor. I am just worried about Jake. I don't seem to have any appetite. I know that I need to eat but I just can't get past a few bites of food at each meal. I am trying to eat snacks in between so that I can get in some food. I know it is important Dr. Martin I just don't seem to be able to eat," Catherine said quietly.

"I am bringing a tonic for you tomorrow Catherine. Promise me you will keep trying to eat something whatever it may be. I can't have you both down because then poor Ramon will be worked off his feet," Dr. Martin said. He was trying to say anything to get the poor girl to smile. "Are you even leaving this room Catherine?" Dr. Martin asked.

"Oh yes, I work out of the library to meet with the crew members and I go outside and pick flowers for Jake and I go upstairs to change my clothes," Catherine said smiling briefly.

"My prescription is tonic that I will bring for you tomorrow and going outside even if only to sit on the porch Catherine. Promise me you will try to eat and go out on the porch to sit," Dr. Martin said intently.

"I promise Dr. Martin; I will do both things. Is there anything else that we need to do for Jake, Dr. Martin?" Catherine said anxiously.

"No Catherine; he is getting the best of care from both you and from Ramon. His good health and strength will pull him through this; you must have faith that it will occur."

"I do Dr. Martin. I just want to make sure there isn't something that I should be doing that I am not doing already. Thank you again for checking on Jake and asking about me," Catherine said smiling. Catherine saw the doctor out and then went upstairs to find a vest to put over her blouse and a belt as well. If the weight loss was so very evident, she must try to cover it in case Jake were to wake up and see that she was falling away in front of him. He would be doubly upset by that and she didn't want anything to upset him when he finally woke up at last.

*****

"I heard the doctor with Catherine. He thinks that I am healthy and will come out of this, whatever this is. If only I could open my eyes, I think that Catherine would stop crying at night. That's right, I remember now the wagon fell over when I was trying to reach the house. That must be why I hurt so on my left side. Catherine is taking care of that with whatever she puts on me. I can feel her angel hands on me as she tries to take care of me and asks me to wake up. I hear her telling me to come back to her. Where am I and why can't I come back to her? I must come back to her if only to stop her tears. I have always stopped her tears until now. I can't be the cause of those tears. I feel stronger now maybe I am coming back. I just need to rest. Maybe tomorrow I can come back and hold Catherine again. Goodnight my love. I am trying to come back to you as you asked."

*****

Catherine began each day checking her chart prepared for Jake's injury, recording the number of days since the injury and recording all of Jake's vitals. She and Ramon pray each morning now and each evening at Jake's bedside. They do so after he is given his daily bath and shave and his vitals are taken. They pray because they do not know what else to do. Everything asked of them has been done and they know that Jake is healthy and fit; he just needs to come back from his concussed world. All is well with both ranches. Catherine knows that he will be pleased by that as he likes everything done properly on the ranches. The men have been wonderful and have done as Mr. Eaton promised; they have taken care of the outside while Catherine takes care of Jake and takes care of the inside.

Catherine continued her reading to Jake. She began reading novels to him that she found among some of Jake's books. She thought he would enjoy those as well. She is taken to sitting out on the porch as Dr. Martin advised even though she times the period away from Jake. She does not want him to wake up and she not be beside him. She has Ramon sit with him while she is on the porch in case he would awaken and not see one of them as he comes out of his concussed state. She found at first that she was frightened to even go outside after the episode with Jake and the men but, she knew that she cannot live with such fear and must go outside if only for her own health and her own sanity. Her appetite had still not returned so she hid her shrinking body with a vest and a belt on her skirt in the hope that the doctor will not comment. He has brought a tonic, but the tonic did no more for her appetite than Catherine's continued efforts to force herself to eat if only to stay strong for Jake.

Jake's wounds continue to improve and the bruising has gone through all of the colors of the rainbow just as she anticipated. It is bright yellow now like the yellow flowers that she collected for his room. Today when she treated his wounds she thought she felt him tighten his hand around her fingers. She was afraid to say anything to Ramon because she was afraid that she had just imagined it because she wanted it to happen so badly. The next day, she felt the same thing and thought that she would tell Dr. Martin because two days in a row must mean something. He will tell me that it is just a muscle spasm, but I know that it means something, Catherine thought. Catherine took her lotion then and started to massage his arms and his legs hoping against hope that the massage might bring him closer to the surface, closer to coming back to her.

By the third day of his improvement, his hand was definitely curving around her fingers as she treated the abrasions and massaged her lotion into the arms, hands and legs. She looked at his face anxiously each time that she felt it and continued talking to him to encourage him to return to her and to the people that they loved. Dr. Martin continued to say it was just a muscle spasm, but she knew differently. She knew it was a sign from Jake and she would not give up on that sign.

On the fourth day of his improvement, Jake's hand pressed hers while she placed lotion on his arms and legs. She talked to him and asked him to press her hand if he could understand her. He doesn't at first, but then the hand pressed hers and she was convinced that he was coming back to her. She told Ramon this time because she did not want to keep this hope to herself only. Ramon could see the tears in her eyes and knows that she has been trying to hold in her grief for the full two weeks that Jake had been in a concussed state. He prayed for Jake's sake and for hers because he does not know how much more Miss Catherine can endure. He knows that she is much stronger than anyone else realizes, but he also knows that she is very close to the end of her strength. He has seen her fall away and adds her favorite dishes to the menu each day hoping that he can encourage her to eat. He brings her snacks during the day and she tries to eat those as well because he knows she is trying to stay strong for Jake and for everyone on both ranches.

On the fifth day of his ongoing improvement, Catherine continued her massage and Jake took her hand and held it. She bent over the bed then praying with her head down on the bed. Jake's eyes opened for the first time in over two weeks and he saw Catherine knelt at his bedside in prayer. His hand reached out and touched her head. His fingers stroked the silken hair that he so loved to touch. Catherine at first thought that she was imagining the touch that she had dreamt of for so long. She looked up and saw Jake smiling at her, his eyes open for the first time. Catherine called then for Ramon who came running. She wanted another witness to what her eyes were seeing. Ramon saw Jake's eyes open and fell to his knees in prayer beside Miss Catherine. He raised himself up then and said that he would go for the doctor and bring him back to the ranch.

Catherine sat looking at Jake who was smiling at her now. "I knew that you would come back to me Jake. I knew that you would come back to us all. I have prayed for so long that you would and you have," Catherine said through tears. She went over to the table and wet the sponge to moisten his lips and placed lotion on his mouth again. "What can I get for you my love? Do you need water? Are you thirsty?" Jake nodded his head yes and she got a cup of water and a spoon so that she could give him a little bit at a time since he was lying down. She didn't want him to choke. Jake drank in her face with his eyes and placed his hand on her cheek. She leaned into his touch as she had done so many times. He noticed that her face was thinner and he saw the dark stains under her eyes. He said nothing until later but made a note of that fact. "I must tell Catherine that she needs to rest," he said to himself. "When I can talk again, I must tell Catherine that she needs to rest."

Within no time at all, Ramon returned with the doctor. They found Catherine still beside the bed holding Jake's hand. He had closed his eyes again, but only for a moment. As soon as he heard Dr. Martin's voice, he opened his eyes and smiled at him as well. Catherine rose then to greet Dr. Martin, but would not let go of Jake's hand. "Catherine, may I sit down for a moment and check on our patient? I promise I will give you his hand as soon as I am done," Dr. Martin said smiling.

"Of course Dr. Martin; I am sorry, I just have trouble getting my head wrapped around it. I told you that it wasn't a muscle spasm. The past two days, he has wrapped his hand around mine when I was massaging his arms and legs. I knew that he was trying to come back to me Dr. Martin and he has. Here are his vitals and I have given him a half cup of water with a spoon because he said he was thirsty. I didn't want him to choke. I am sorry Dr. Martin that I can't stop talking but I am just so excited. Ramon and I are so very excited to see him awake at last," Catherine said smiling.

Jake looked up at Dr. Martin with a smile and a wink. "I know what you are going to say Jake Nelson; you are going to say that I can't stop talking and you are right," Catherine said smiling. Dr. Martin shook his head then at the banter of this brave woman who had sat vigil at Jake's bedside. If ever he had seen devotion of one person to another, she had certainly provided it. He thought about the long days of worry and the fact that he had watched her continue to fall away. Ramon and he had discussed it and tried to come up with some way for them both to get Catherine to eat again. He knew that she would only eat when Jake got better, but what if he had never come out of the extended concussed state? He had seen others who were not so lucky, but he couldn't tell Catherine that because hope was the only thing that she was holding onto; that and Jake's hand.

"Well Jake, Catherine, Ramon; I think our patient is doing wonderfully well. I knew that his good health and strength would bring him back and so it has. Now Jake, you are going to want to move and I understand that. Ramon and the boys will need to help you to come to a sitting position, but very slowly as you will be light headed until you can move about. Also you will want to eat everything in sight, but you need to start with only very limited items like broth until your stomach gets used to food again. Catherine he will need to eat about six times a day until he gets used to food again. I know that you and Ramon will see to that. His voice will be weak at first because it hasn't been used and as you said, he will need water as he is dehydrated from the long time in the concussed state. Now get plenty of rest Jake and come back slowly. I will check on you each day as I know that you are in the best of hands with Catherine and Ramon," Dr. Martin stated.

"Thank you so much Dr. Martin. We will follow each and every one of your instructions," Catherine said smiling. "I will walk out with Dr. Martin and be right back Jake," Catherine said smiling. Catherine walked to the front porch with Dr. Martin then to see him on his horse and away.

"Catherine I didn't say anything in front of Jake as I don't want him to worry. It is not just Jake that I have been worried about. You have to promise me that you will start to focus on eating again. I know that Jake will notice and he will start to be worried about you next and we don't need that. Do you promise me that you will take care of yourself?" Dr. Martin asked.

"I do promise Dr. Martin. It is exactly as you told Jake; I have tried eating and now I am doing everything possible to eat but my stomach has rebelled. I think I just need to come back slowly. I will be better now that he is getting better. I will want to eat because this terrible worry has being lifted. Thank you so much Dr. Martin and I will continue to monitor to make sure that he doesn't do too much going forward. Would you be so kind to advise the Sheriff and the Marshal of his improvement also? I know that they have kept this all very quiet because of the threat, but I know that they will want to know and possibly also want to talk with him when he is stronger," Catherine said smiling. She remained on the porch as Dr. Martin rode away. As she turned back to the house, it was with the joy that things were going to get better. Jake would improve each and every day. They would work with him to make sure that he didn't do too much and he would get stronger with their care.

Catherine returned then to Jake's room. It was now Jake's room in her mind and not her Father's extra bedroom. She thought then that everything that they would need to help Jake get better was in this room. His bed was here and she would continue to sleep in this room until he could join her again upstairs. The large bath was here as she knew that Jake would not want a sponge bath much longer. He would not want Ramon and her to continue looking after him even though they would do so for as long as he needed. The table was here that she had used to take her meals even though she had eaten precious little since Jake was carried into the house. Everything that was needed was in this room. Soon he would be able to branch out to the library and from there to the dining room and then back upstairs. He could even sit on the porch and they could both take in the wonderful breeze and Jake could talk to the men and see the cattle and the horses and everything that he loved outside of this house.

CHAPTER THIRTEEN

By the next day, Jake was beginning to speak again and he asked if he could be raised up. Ramon and the boys from the crew came in and raised him slowly to a sitting position. Catherine was not sure that this was a good thing, but she wanted him to do as much as he could each day. She sat by him all of the time until he made her go out on the porch. It seemed that the doctor had been talking to him about that and she hoped that he hadn't told Jake more about her weight loss. She hoped that she could rectify that before Jake noticed.

"Catherine you cannot sit in this room with me every hour of the day. You must go outside for your own good," Jake said sternly, but then smiled to relieve his order. He found he couldn't be stern with Catherine because he wanted her with him as much as she wanted to be with him. He couldn't get enough of looking at her after so much time away. He worried about her thin face and the dark stains under her eyes. Dr. Martin told him that she would be fine now that he was getting better. He told Jake about the tonic as well and asked that Jake make sure that she took the tonic whenever he could encourage her to do so.

Ramon and Catherine worked with Jake to try to have him move about his room first and then into the library. The massages that Catherine had given him had been good for his muscles. He just needed to get his strength back by moving from one room to the other. He found that he got tired so easily which was frustrating to him. The good healthy broth that Ramon made for him was helpful in getting his appetite back in place. In short order he was asking for some real food and Dr. Martin gave them a list of items to tempt his appetite back and to tempt Catherine's back as well although he would not admit that fact yet to Jake. She took her bath in the upstairs room each night and dressed for bed there as well so that Jake would not see the amount of weight that she had lost. The vest that she wore over her blouse and the belt at her waist helped to hide the fact that she had fallen away considerably. She was doing her best to hide that fact from Jake.

The camouflage was becoming harder and harder for her to achieve however, because as Jake became stronger, he found that he wanted nothing so much as to be with Catherine again as her husband and not as her patient. At first it was in small ways when he would grab her hand as she took his vitals or when she continued to massage lotion on his arms and legs. Later when he was able to move about the room and then into the library, he would ask her to sit next to him when she was telling him about something about the ranches and he would steal a kiss and linger in the hope that she would take his hand and lead him back into his room for the long awaited reunion. He finally asked Catherine to go out on the porch one day while Dr. Martin was visiting just to make sure that he was ready for a return to his normal activities. Dr. Martin had assured him that he was healthy and ready for everything that he had done before the injury except for riding or driving the wagon. He wanted him to wait for any physical activity of that sort until he had had at least two more weeks of therapy in the house. Then they would reevaluate.

"What I really need to know Dr. Martin is if I am ready to be a husband to my wife again? I know I want to and have wanted to ever since I woke up, but I think Catherine is afraid that she will injure me again. I just want to make sure that I can assure her that everything is fine in that department," Jake said anxiously.

"You are fine in that department Jake. Just give her time because she has been so traumatized by your injury that I think she just needs to assure herself that you are well enough again to be . . . well, intimate again. Do you want me to talk to her Jake?" Dr. Martin asked anxiously.

"No Dr. Martin; as long as you are telling me that everything is fine in that department, that is good enough for me. I just need to make sure that she understands she doesn't need to be my nurse anymore. I am getting stronger by the day and I need things to return to normal," Jake said smiling.

That night, Jake was thinking of the right way to broach the subject to Catherine. She was busily moving about the room checking on everything that Jake would need from food to drink to his nightly bath. "Do you want me to ask Ramon to come in and help you into the bathtub Jake?" Catherine asked. She was continuing the regular routine that they had established since Jake had returned to them from his concussion.

"No Catherine, Dr. Martin doesn't think that I need any help in the bath anymore. In fact he thinks that I can return to everything that I did before the injury except for riding and wagon driving of course. We need to wait for those two things for about two more weeks. He says that I am well enough for everything that I did before the injury Catherine. You know that I am not bruised anymore. You know that you won't hurt me right?" he asked watching her intently.

"Of course Jake, I have been checking your injury daily and your bruising isn't multi-colored anymore. You have been doing so well darling. In no time you will be doing everything that you did before," Catherine said smiling.

"I need you to understand something then Catherine; I need you to understand that you need to stop treating me like a patient and start treating me like your husband again. The good Lord knows that no one is more grateful for how well you have looked after me honey, but I need you as a husband Catherine in the worst way. I watch you every day as you go about checking on me and making sure that you are feeding me and giving me something to drink and all of the rest, but I need you Catherine and not as my nurse. Can you do that for me Catherine because I need you very much honey?" Jake said smiling at her.

Catherine looked at him then with worry but with understanding. "Did you ask Dr. Martin when he was here Jake? Is that why you asked me to step out on the porch?" she asked worriedly.

"That is the exact reason Catherine. I couldn't have you thinking that you were going to hurt me in some way because as you said yourself, I am not even bruised anymore and I have been moving about the room and the library and even into the dining room without any problem. You need to stop fussing over me Catherine and start treating me like your husband again," Jake said with far more anger than he had wished.

Catherine bit her lip then and tried to consider what to do. Jake moved from the bed and took off his robe and got into the large bathtub all on his own. Catherine knew that he was right in what he was saying, but she was also worried that he would see for the first time just how much weight she had lost and then he would be worried about that as well. She couldn't have him think that she didn't want to be with him again as his wife because she wanted that more than anything. She just didn't want him to see her so thin and start to worry about that as well. As she looked at him again, he held out his hand to her and she knew what she needed to do.

She slowly walked over to the door and locked it so that Ramon would not be worried about the two of them and whether they needed anything. She went over to the table where she had kept her things during Jake's recovery and pinned up her hair as she always did before she took a bath. She started to slowly undress and place her things on the adjacent chair. As soon as she removed her vest, Jake saw the belt around her skirt. He had never remembered seeing her wear a belt before and wondered why she was wearing a vest and a belt. She took off her blouse then and her skirt and he saw the ever present corset. He smiled when he saw it but only for a moment because the corset showed a significantly smaller waist. He had always thought that she had the tiniest waist that he had ever seen, but he did not remember it being that small. He noticed that she kept on her chemise when she turned and moved back towards the bathtub. She smiled at him shyly as if they were again making love for the first time. He knew that something was not right but he didn't know what at that point.

She waited until she returned to the bathtub and then unbuttoned the chemise right before slipping into the bath directly in front of him. That was when he saw it; as she sat down in front of him he saw that he could nearly count every rib and could see her shoulder blades on her back as she sat down in front of him. She took the soap then and the sponge and started to soap the sponge to wash Jake's arm. He grabbed her wrist then and saw how tiny it had become. His left arm came around her chest and drew her to him so that her back was resting on his chest. He closed his eyes for a moment drinking in the feel of her so close to him at last. He could feel her tense and then gradually she relaxed into his embrace. She turned her head to the side so that her cheek was resting against his chest.

"I have missed you so much Catherine. You are right in front of me everyday taking care of me and I don't want you to think that I don't appreciate it because I do honey, but I am worried about you now. Is that why you didn't want me to make love to you because I would see how you have fallen away?" Jake asked worriedly.

"I kept hoping that I would get my appetite back and that I could correct the weight loss before you saw it Jake. I knew that you would be worried and I didn't want you to worry about anything. I will be fine now Jake because I know that you are improving. So long as you are well again Jake I will start eating again. It was just the worry you see; I just couldn't eat. Ramon tried all of my favorites and I even ate between meals, but it just didn't seem to help," Catherine said quietly.

"We have both been through a test Catherine, but we are coming out of it on the other side. You know that I told you as long as I have you and you have me all the rest is just noise. Well that is true Catherine for us both. The whole time that I was fighting my way back to you I could hear you talking to me. I could hear you asking me to come back to you. When I did come back to you, I was afraid that you only thought of me as your patient and not as your husband. I am sorry that I was cross with you after all that you have done for me. I just couldn't understand why you didn't want to be with me again. You can't keep things like this from me Catherine because they will always come out anyway and besides, I wouldn't have you grieving like this for me for anything," Jake said tenderly. "You turn around to me this minute and let me see your beautiful face." Jake pulled her onto his lap and held her to his chest. He placed his hands on either side of her face and looked into her eyes intently. He could still see dark stains under her eyes, but they were better now than they had been. As for the rest, he would take care of that in short order. "You just need to gain your winter weight Catherine and then you will be fine and dandy," Jake said grinning.

"What is winter weight Jake?" Catherine asked frowning.

"That is what we put on the cattle for the winter to make sure that they make it through the cold and snow alright," Jake said grinning.

"Did you just tell me that you are going to put winter weight on me like you would the cattle?" Catherine said wide eyed.

"Yep, that is what I said Mrs. Nelson; winter weight is the solution to this problem," Jake said laughing.

"Now you see why I didn't want you to know about it? I knew you would start watching everything that I eat and need to comment about it and make comments like *winter weight*," Catherine said working herself up into a full head of steam.

"And what have you been doing Mrs. Nelson but commenting on how much water I drink and how much food I eat and how much exercise and whether or not I have had my massage for the day," Jake said smiling.

"Are you saying that you don't like your massage?" Catherine replied with mischief in her eyes.

"I like my massage just fine thank you very much. I like it when you touch me Catherine which is why I needed to encourage you into this bathtub so that you would touch me again and not just as your patient," he said looking intently at her. She bent her neck then and leaned her cheek into his hand.

"I have so missed you touching me, Jake. I would lie on the couch every night and think about how close you were to me and yet so far away. I don't want you to be cross with me Jake. I just want you to love me," she said softly. Jake ran his thumb across her lips then and kissed her intensely. There was no more talking then as there was no need. Both had told the other what they needed to hear. Despite the fact that they had been together non-stop for three weeks, there had been a divide. Two weeks of that divide had been Jake's injuries and his concussion. One week of that divide had been Catherine's fear of hurting Jake and her fear of his seeing what grief had done to her. That divide had been crossed and more than any other care that she had given to him, he needed to feel Catherine the woman and not Catherine the nurse coming to him and loving him so that he knew he was back on the road to his normal life.

Jake kissed her passionately then and Catherine placed her arms around his neck as she had always done. She wasn't worried about his side any more. She knew how slight she was now and that she would do no harm to his injuries. She knew that he needed her and she needed him just as badly to chase away the memories of those lonely nights when they were together but yet apart. Jake drank in her neck and lifted her so that he could kiss and caress her breasts. She was not quiet in her delight of that feeling. She clung to him and called out to him. His growl was as loud as a wolf and he felt as free as a wolf to express his need to Catherine. She laughed then when she heard his growl because she knew that her husband was back on the road to recovery. If he was getting better, she would be better as well. Jake's lovemaking for Catherine was not tame and was not gentle. He tried to slow himself, but knew it was useless. He needed Catherine as much as he needed the water that she brought to him and the food he ate. He needed to drink in her love and to inhale her lavender scent to convince himself that he was well and truly back among the living and not just dreaming of holding her. He told himself that the next time they made love he would be gentle as he always tried to be with Catherine, but this time, he would have to apologize because he could not be gentle after being away from her in his concussed mind.

When he reached his climax, she heard the roar beside her ear and smiled at the thought that her husband had indeed returned to her in both body and spirit. She smiled and cried the happy tears that Jake so loved. He wiped away the happy tears and kissed her until her mouth was red and swollen.

When at last they were able to pull themselves away from the need to hold each other and the water in the bathtub had cooled considerably, Jake got out of the bathtub and helped Catherine out as well. He pulled up the towel to wrap her and she was swallowed by the large towels always used by Jake. He wrapped his robe around himself and around Catherine. "Just so you know Mrs. Nelson, you are not sleeping on that couch tonight. You are sleeping with me and that is final," Jake said grinning and kissing the top of her head.

"But Jake it is only a campaign bed; it is only meant for one person not two," Catherine replied worriedly.

"Well since we are only one and a half persons at this point in time, we will be just fine. You slept on my chest when we were at the cabin remember?" Jake said grinning.

"I do remember Jake, but that was before you had your injury and you need your rest," Catherine said earnestly.

"I can only rest when you are with me Catherine and you can only rest when you know that I am alright. I think this is a good solution until tomorrow. Tomorrow I will ask the boys to help me upstairs for the first time and then everything will be back to normal and we won't have to figure out ways for my nurse to be with me while I sleep. Don't worry, I won't tell the doctor," Jake said laughing.

"You said you checked with Dr. Martin?" Catherine said eyes widening.

"I did check with Dr. Martin, Catherine; I am teasing you. Stop being so serious and go to sleep with your husband for a change," Jake said stretching out on the campaign bed. "Come here my love so that I can truly sleep for the first time in three weeks. I can't sleep without my love beside me you know," Jake said kissing Catherine on the top of her head. Before she could barely settle, she was asleep and he was kissing the top of her head and pulling the blankets up on them both.

CHAPTER FOURTEEN

The next day true as his word, Jake asked the crew to stand beside him as he practiced taking the stairs. After two trips up and down, he thought that he would be able to make them on his own. On his second trip down the steps he grinned and winked at Catherine who was monitoring the progress. She knew by the wink that he would be leaving the downstairs bedroom except to bathe each night. She was relieved to see that one more thing in their life was getting back to normal. After his daily exercise, Catherine sat down with him in the library so that she could continue to fill him in on the work that had been done during his recovery.

"I have a list Jake of everything that was done during your recovery. We took the master list from the Trinity and applied it to the English Rose as well so that we could start preparing for the autumn and for the winter to follow. I hope you are pleased Jake because both crews worked so very hard. Jim Eaton told me on the day of your injury that they would take care of the outside while I took care of you and the inside. I have here the records for all of the bills that I have taken care of for both ranches and the payroll for both. I thought if it was alright with you I could keep doing that for both ranches so that you didn't have that to worry about as well as the ranch work. My great-great-great Grandmother used to do all of the accounts for her husband's shipbuilding business and that way they had more time for each other. What do you think of that idea Jake?" Catherine said smiling.

"I think that sounds like a fine idea Catherine and it means we can work the ranches together which is what we should be doing. I just want you to promise me that you won't do too much and get yourself down," Jake said looking at her intently.

"I won't Jake. I promise I will take care of myself and you and the accounts for the ranch. It won't be a problem you will see," Catherine replied.

"And what about the babies Catherine; what about when the babies start coming; have you thought about that love?" Jake asked smiling.

"Of course I have Jake I will have the baby carrier just here," she pointed beside the desk, "and the baby can nap while I do the accounts and the payroll. When he is older, I can have him play in the downstairs bedroom which I can make into a downstairs play room when it is not needed as a recovery room of course," Catherine replied smiling.

"So we are having a boy are we? How have you made that decision Catherine?" Jake said grinning.

"Well, you were a boy and the first in your family and my Mother had five sons before me so I think there is a good chance Jake," Catherine responded.

"Maybe you won't have to worry about winter weight after all Catherine. Maybe we can count on baby weight. What do you think?" Jake said laughing.

"I think we will wait and see Jake and in the mean time, I will take my tonic as you have been instructed to watch me do every day and I will work on getting my appetite back because something tells me you will be watching my vest and my belt to see if they disappear anytime soon," Catherine replied smiling mischievously.

"You are correct about that Mrs. Nelson and don't forget that I will be watching very closely. I need to give my report to Dr. Martin when he comes to visit me," Jake replied frowning.

"You needn't frown at me like that Jake Nelson. If you are trying to intimidate me you are just wasting your time. I will eat properly and take care of myself because it is just good sense isn't it; like wearing my hat in the sun and riding astride and learning how to shoot. That reminds me Jake; when you are able to ride again, we will need to take a trip to the oasis again so that I can practice my shooting. I haven't done it in so long that I might have forgotten how. You may have to teach me again Jake darling," Catherine said smiling her best dimpled smile.

"I know when you call me Jake darling that you are trying to curl me around your little finger. Well let me tell you one thing Mrs. Nelson . . . it works every time," Jake said laughing and kissing Catherine.

While they talked in the library, they saw a wagon pull up and two horsemen. Catherine looked at Jake worriedly until they saw that the wagon was driven by Judge Wilkerson and the two horsemen were the Sheriff and the Marshal. Catherine went to the door to greet all three men.

"Come in gentlemen; it is so wonderful to see all three of you. Won't you come through to the library? Jake is up and doing well after his exercise this morning. Please come in," Catherine said in greeting.

Judge Wilkerson, Sheriff Will and Marshal Jones came into the library. Jake rose then and shook hands with all three men. "Please come in and sit down gentlemen. Can I get you anything to eat or drink?" Catherine asked.

"You gentlemen will want to have a piece of Ramon's special cake. I can speak highly for it. That cake and Catherine's smiles are two of the best things about the English Rose," Jake said grinning.

"Thank you Jake very much for the offer; but maybe we will have something later. We are all so glad to see you up and about again. We know that you have had the best of care. Dr. Martin tells us that Catherine was your round the clock nurse and she has done a wonderful job of getting you back on your feet again," Judge Wilkerson said smiling.

"That is for sure Judge. No man could have better care than I have had through all of this. I know that you three are very busy men and are not just here for a social call. I reckon you want me to tell you what I remember about the day of the accident which was not an accident of course," Jake replied.

"We do indeed Jake, but we also have a plan that we want to discuss with you. We know you may have reservations, but we think it is a sound plan. Sheriff Will, Marshal Jones; I will let you discuss the plan," Judge Wilkerson stated.

"Thank you Judge Wilkerson. Jake, Catherine, we all know that Delaney was behind the shooting that resulted in Jake's accident. We have witnesses that say he was away from the Triple B on that day and no other alibi as to his whereabouts. If he didn't do the shooting himself, he was behind it. We have all been very careful to not relay information on Jake's condition. The only people who know that he has recovered are Dr. Martin, the people in this room and your closest staff persons Ramon, Jim Eaton and maybe one or two others. No one else has that information. We have done so purposely because we did not want Catherine to be vulnerable while Jake was recovering. We know that Catherine has had her hands full taking care of Jake and keeping both ranches running."

"We think that perhaps the way to end this thing once and for all is to put about the story that Jake has succumbed to his injuries. There can even be a mock funeral here at the ranch or the oasis. It is a web we are weaving for Delaney and we think it will work. If we have men posted here at the ranch, we know that Delaney will come if only to gloat or to make another run at Catherine. This is the part that Jake may object to. In addition to having to pretend that Jake is dead, Catherine will need to be willing to serve as the lure to Delaney and the ranch. We think that he is arrogant enough that he will gloat over what he has done and we will have the evidence that we need once and for all to put him away. That evidence combined with the statements from others across the valley will be sufficient evidence to end this Jake. What he did to you was attempted murder and but for your skill, your good health and Catherine's nursing, it could have been murder Jake. Not everyone could have kept those horses under control and survived the roll of that wagon," Sheriff Will stated.

"We have gone at Delaney directly Jake and of course he has denied the shooting. We saw the look on his face however when we said that Jake had been wounded and was not expected to recover. There was a queer smile there Jake so we know he is behind it. We just need his confession which we believe he will give to Catherine. Catherine has been his obsession from the beginning because if not her personally, her coupled with the English Rose and now of course the Trinity as well will be sufficient reason to make him stupid enough to have another go," Marshal Jones stated.

Jake looked very thoughtful for a moment. He knew that Delaney was behind the attack on him and his crew. He knew that they would never be safe again in the valley if Delaney was not stopped once and for all. The terror that he felt was in using Catherine as bait to bring the man to justice. He looked at her intently trying to decide what to do next. Catherine helped him make the decision. She looked at him then as if they were the only two people in the room and she slowly shook her head yes. She was a lot tougher than people ever thought. It was her one secret weapon. When they looked at her tiny frame and her angelic face, they thought she would faint with each new challenge. Jake knew from experience that she was a lot stronger than people ever expected or would ever know. Only he and Ramon knew the steel that was in that spine.

"Alright Marshal; I will agree to your plan assuming that there will be men stationed at the ranch. I will not agree otherwise. Our men are armed and have been so since the first threats on Catherine. They are not gunmen however and it is not fair to make them assassins to bring this man to justice. I will agree so long as there are men who will help us protect Catherine and keep her safe. We need to end this for all of our sakes because we will never be safe in the valley again until this ends once and for all," Jake said heatedly.

"We will make all of the arrangements Jake. I will have men stationed here tomorrow who will look like new hands to the ranch for all purposes. Catherine we will need you to go through the appearance of a funeral for Jake. It might be best that it be done at the oasis so that the word will get back to Delaney that Jake has succumbed to his injuries. If the funeral is here at the ranch, no one will know except the ranch hands. If Delaney is having the oasis watched as I suspect he is, he will see the funeral and knowing him as we do, the trap will be set. Are you up for that Catherine? I know it is more worry being placed on you when you have endured more than any one person should have to do?" Judge Wilkerson asked anxiously.

"I will be ready Judge Wilkerson. I have found myself afraid to sit on my own porch. I can't live my life like that. I can't be terrified each and every time that I see Jake ride away from here that he may not come back or he may be maimed or injured for life. This must end for our sakes and for everyone else in the valley that has been hurt as well by this man and his evil," Catherine replied.

"Alright then; the new men will arrive in the morning. If we can plan the funeral for tomorrow morning as well, we will all ride out to the oasis around 11:00 and then back to the English Rose. It will appear to anyone watching like a wake and like we are getting more information from you Catherine to make the case. I expect Delaney will not be far behind once he believes Jake is out of the way. It will be all that he needs to press his case again with Catherine or try to intimidate her again at the very least," Sheriff Will stated.

"We will leave you both then until the morning. Jake, you will need to keep yourself scarce for the next few days, but if it allows you to keep up your therapy and end this madness once and for all, I know that you will be up for it," Judge Wilkerson replied.

After they had left, Catherine went to the window and looked out. Jake came behind her and placed his hands around her waist. "It will be alright honey; the deputy marshals will be here on the place and you can rest assured if that snake reappears, I will have my rifle on him from the upstairs window. If he as much as moves a muscle towards you, he will be mine Catherine. Not only for what he did to me and to you, but for everyone else who lives in the valley and lives in fear of what he may try to do next," Jake said heatedly.

"We will get through this Jake. Like you said, we have been tested and tried and we have not been found wanting. As long as you are getting better Jake, I can face whatever comes our way. I said when you asked me to marry you that as long as you were standing next to me, I could face whatever may occur and I continue to say that," Catherine said earnestly. Jake tightened his grip around Catherine and kissed her neck and cheek. How did I get so lucky to have been given this treasure Jake asked himself? He redoubled his commitment to keep her safe and to keep everyone on the two ranches safe as well.

CHAPTER FIFTEEN

The next day Catherine dressed in black from head to toe including a black veil. Jake looked at her and said it was like someone was walking over his grave and it was not a good feeling. "Did you have that outfit in your endless suite of luggage also darling? I have to admit, you packed for everything that you could possibly need. I couldn't believe that one of those bags had medical supplies until you needed them and showed them to me," Jake asked from the bed.

"I had to plan for all eventualities Jake. I didn't know what kind of medical care would be here so I thought if I brought one of everything I would need, I would be prepared and hopefully not need it. As it was, I was glad to have all of my lotions and potions if only to help you on the road to recovery," Catherine said smiling. "I hate that you will be cooped up here while we are at the oasis, but I guess it is a small thing to bring about what we hope to accomplish," Catherine said smiling bravely.

"Come here and let me kiss the most beautiful widow in New Mexico," Jake said smiling. "It will all be over soon my love, don't worry," Jake said earnestly.

Catherine went downstairs then to meet the wagon and the impromptu coffin that had been fashioned by Jim Eaton yesterday afternoon. It gave her chills to think how close this whole scenario was to the reality of the injury, but she knew they had to keep up the façade in order to fool Delaney and make the day more convincing. Jim Eaton drove the surrey wagon that carried Catherine to the oasis and Ramon drove the wagon that carried the coffin meant to house Jake. The deputy marshals posing as hands rode alongside Catherine and Jim Eaton to provide coverage as well as to serve as pall bearers once they reached the oasis site.

When they reached the oasis, Judge Wilkerson, Sheriff Will and Marshal Jones were all assembled next to Cameron McCullum's gravesite. It was surreal to Catherine when she thought that they were going through this charade to prove to a mad man that he had been successful in killing her husband. It was made even more surreal by the fact that he had come very close to accomplishing his goal. She thought then about what she would have done here at the English Rose all alone. It gave her chills and she put it to the back of her mind. She looked to Judge Wilkerson who she knew would say a few words about Jake. His words were kindness itself and Catherine smiled bravely at the regard that her husband was held in by the valley as a whole. She would remember to remind Judge Wilkerson when next they met that Jake would like to renew their wedding vows again once all the dust had settled and they had their lives back. He wanted them to start anew and be able to share their happiness with the entire community. She knew she needed to look forward to happier days until the madness of her current life was behind her.

After a shaking of hands all around, Catherine took her place in the surrey wagon again and they all returned to the English Rose. Ramon had prepared a luncheon for them all and for Jake who would have the dubious distinction of attending his own funeral luncheon. At least Catherine could seek comfort in the fact that she would be able to see Jake in the flesh as soon as she re-entered their private world again. She went upstairs as soon as she returned to the house and took off the veil that covered her from head to waist. At least if she was going to wear mourning for a while, she would not wear a veil. It was morbid enough to wear black to lure a mad man to her home, but she was not wearing a full length black veil to sit and have lunch with her husband and his friends.

During the luncheon the plan was again re-enforced. Sheriff Will asked that a rider be sent to him as soon as Delaney showed up on the English Rose. They wanted to make sure that the deputy marshals had all of the support they needed in case Delaney came with multiple men. Jake sat at the head of the table taking in the discussion and squeezing Catherine's hand whenever she looked distracted by the conversation around her. On those moments, it was as if they were in the library yesterday when the plan was first discussed. They were the only two at the table and their smiles for one another kept them going. Judge Wilkerson saw it and thought again the wisdom of urging Jake to marry his English Rose. He knew that they would be happy together. He knew that they had already had their share of trials, but through each one they would stand together and that was all anyone could ask for from their partner in life.

"Well Jake, it was a real nice funeral," Judge Wilkerson said at last. "The best part about it is that I get to come here and have lunch with you afterwards. Like we said weeks ago, this is all going to be sorted and we will go back to living the lives that we were meant to live."

"You are right about that Judge Wilkerson. When this is all over, Catherine and I would like to renew our vows and invite the whole community like we did for Cameron's wake. We want everyone to share in our happiness once we can do so openly again. I want to thank all of you for sticking together to get this business behind us once and for all. We will make it right and then we all have a lot of living to look forward to. Speaking as one who has escaped the grave and lived through his own funeral, I have a whole lot more living to do. Isn't that right Catherine?" Jake said grinning.

"That is right Jake. Thank you all for helping rid the valley of the snakes that are destroying paradise," Catherine said smiling bravely.

After their company had left, Catherine walked over to the library. She asked Jake if he remembered any of the diary passages that she had read him of her great-great-great Grandmother Catherine. "I remember words here and there Catherine, but not all of it. I would hear bits and pieces. I remember hearing your voice and it was like a welcome hum, but the words didn't always register. It was just the fact that I knew that you were there and that you kept telling me to come back to you that I heard the most. I heard that over and over again Catherine and I swore that I would come back to you if only to see those beautiful eyes and that beautiful smile. I won't let anything happen to you Catherine, you know that right? When that man sets foot on this ranch and I know that he will, he is mine Catherine. This ends the day he steps foot on this ranch." Jake held her to him then and his jaw had the same set to it as the day that they were married and he spirited her away to the magical mountain. When all of this was said and done, he would spirit her away again and they would rest in the peace of the mountain paradise far away from the pressures of life.

*****

Catherine decided that the worst part of this plan was the waiting. She woke the next day and quickly looked beside her to find Jake resting comfortably. One advantage of his feigned death was that he couldn't be up and about before she awoke. She didn't want to wake up alone in this huge bed for a very long time to come. She kept waking up in the middle of the night and placing her hand on Jake to make sure that he was well and truly there and that she had not dreamt of his recovery. She knew that she was still traumatized by his injury and it made waiting for Delaney all the worse. "I am right here Catherine. You don't have to feel for me, I am right here honey and everything is alright. You just keep telling yourself that and you will eventually believe it," Jake said lying still with his eyes closed. "I was just playing possum waiting for you to wake up again and to see if I was still lying here next to you. I think you were more spooked by that fake funeral yesterday than I was and I was the corpse," Jake said grinning.

"Jake Nelson, I cannot believe you just said that to me," Catherine said crossly.

"I am trying to make you laugh again Catherine because you are going to wear yourself out worrying if you don't stop. Do I need to make you forget all of this nonsense one more time?" Jake said with a wink.

Catherine lay down again then with her head on his chest. "I will be fine Jake. I just have to remind myself enough times that you are alright and like you said, I will finally believe it. I do like it when you make me forget the nonsense, just so you know darling Jake," Catherine said smiling.

"So I am darling Jake again am I? I sure am glad to hear that Catherine. I like it when you call me darling Jake. It usually means you are going to try to wrap me around your little finger. God help me if we have a baby girl. She will have me wrapped as soon as she is born. She will take one look at me with dark blue eyes and dimples and a smile that will melt January snow and I will be wrapped for the rest of my life. Just like her Mama did when she got off that train," Jake said smiling.

"Are you telling me darling Jake that you were in love with me the whole time that you were trying to make me go back home? That hardly seems fair Jake. What if I had finally changed my mind and gone home? Then what would you have done?" she said gazing up at Jake.

"I would have gotten on that train and brought you back. Just so you know, if you ever get any idea of getting back on that train without me Catherine, I will always bring you back. A promise is a promise darling and you made one downstairs in the library and I am going to hold you to it. That is a promise also," Jake said kissing Catherine intensely.

When Catherine got up and got dressed, she looked again at the black mourning that she would be wearing so long as this charade continued. It gave her the chills to see it hanging in her closet much less wearing it. It would all be worthwhile she decided so long as the worry of the past month was behind them. After dressing and breakfast she went into the library and prepared to work on the accounts for the ranches. She knew that doing accounts always calmed her mind and she needed something for the next few days to calm her mind.

By lunchtime the accounts were done and she went to the kitchen to prepare a lunch tray for herself and Jake and take it upstairs to their room where they could have lunch in front of the fireplace. They decided since he was meant to be the late Jake Nelson, it would not do for him to be seen in the downstairs rooms until the trap was set. He would have the entire upstairs to continue his exercise and the steps in the evening when he came down to take his bath before bed. It was a strange existence for a man who was always up and out each morning, but a necessary part of the charade.

As she carried the tray up to their room, she heard horse's hooves in the front drive. Jake came to the upstairs landing, rifle in hand and motioned to Catherine to take the tray back to the kitchen. The horseman that they had waited for was arriving on the English Rose. Ramon was out the back door to find Jim Eaton and have him notify the Sheriff and the Marshal. The trap had been sprung and the intended was on his way into it. Catherine heard the horse stop in the front yard. She heard the horse tied up and she waited for the call to the house.

"Catherine McCullum, are you in the house? If so, I would have words with you," Angus Delaney arrogantly shouted into the house.

Catherine squared her shoulders and went out on the front porch, the screen door slamming behind her. "My name is Catherine Nelson now. What do you want Mr. Delaney?" Catherine replied.

"Well I figured you would be returning to your maiden name now that old Jake is toes up in the oasis," Delaney responded.

"No sir. I was proud of my husband and his name and I will continue to be Mrs. Nelson," Catherine replied.

"Well that is why I am here Catherine. I am here to make a proposal to you and I thought to get it out in the open before anyone else comes marching up your porch steps. A fine looking woman like you could have her pick of any man so I wanted to make sure you had the best. I told old Jake that when you were courting so now I am here to make that known to you as well. I am the best man in the valley Catherine and I came to make an offer of marriage to you. As I see it, if you marry me, the Triple B, Trinity and the English Rose will all be united. We can buy any ranches that lie between and you and I can own half of the county. How does that sound to you Catherine?" Delaney shouted mockingly.

"Thank you for the offer Mr. Delaney, but it is not my intention to remarry," Catherine replied.

"You are a young woman Catherine and sooner or later your bed is going to grow cold. Like I told you, I am the best man in the valley and you will soon find that out when we are married Catherine," Delaney responded.

"Again Mr. Delaney, thank you for the offer, but I must decline. I cannot believe that you would have the nerve to show your face here the day after my husband's funeral. Do you actually believe that everyone in the valley is so in love with you that they will fall at your feet when you offer marriage?" Catherine said heatedly.

"Not everyone Catherine; only you. You see, I planned on courting you before you got hooked up with old Jake. You are the reason that he is dead Catherine. You wouldn't see the sense of marrying the best man in the valley and instead married old Jake. He didn't see what was coming, but I made sure that I would have him out of the way. I always get what I want Catherine and I will have you," Delaney hissed.

"You don't want me Mr. Delaney, you never did. You want the English Rose and the oasis and now of course you want the Trinity as well because the Trinity came to me when

Jake died. Just so you know Mr. Delaney, you will not have me or the English Rose or the Trinity. The only man who will have all three is my son. When he is born, he will be raised to be a rancher like his Father was and he will be taught to respect the land like his Father did and he will be taught that the protected land will take care of those who protect it. That is a lesson that you will never learn Mr. Delaney and that is why the English Rose and the Trinity will never be yours," Catherine said.

"So what I am hearing is that old Jake left you pregnant? Is that what you are telling me? Catherine you alone are vulnerable. You with a baby are twice as vulnerable. If I could get at Jake what makes you think that I can't get at you and more importantly, what makes you think that I can't get at your baby? You marry me and I will offer you protection. If you want to go back home to Delaware, I don't really care, but you will marry me or conversely, you will sell the English Rose to me as well as the Trinity and then you can go back home and raise old Jake's son in whatever way you see fit Catherine," Delaney shouted.

"Mr. Delaney, were you the last man on earth and I the last woman, I would never marry you. You have just admitted to me that you killed my husband, the Father of my unborn child. On what possible conditions would I marry you or have any connection with you whatsoever?" Catherine replied.

"You will marry me Catherine because you will not have a choice. I planned on dragging you out of this house before you married Jake. He foiled that plan. He is not here to foil the next one. Do you think that the men you hire will protect you? Without Jake's oversight, they will run to work for me because they know if they don't they will be out of a job when you lose this ranch and make no mistake, you will lose this ranch. I will see to that. I will kill every head of cattle on this ranch if I have to in order to change your mind and then I will come for you Catherine and then I will come for your baby. I will never stop Catherine because I don't stop until I have what I want and I have already made it clear that I want you. I want you because you were so proud and uppity the first time that I came here. You made me sit on the front porch and would not even invite me in for conversation. I came here to court you real and proper, but it won't be that way the next time Catherine. I will come for you when you least expect it and I will drag you back to the Triple B and I will do things to you that I usually reserve for the women at Ruby's. When I am done with you, you will beg me to let you go home to Delaware and explain to your family about your New Mexico adventure," Delaney shouted.

"You are mad Delaney and you are a murderer. You must live with the burden of your sin and no one else." Catherine turned to leave the porch then as she thought that she could truly not listen to one more word from this man. She saw the deputy marshals closing in on Delaney and she knew that she had to get inside before this depraved man said one more thing to her that she could not erase from her mind.

"Don't you turn your back on me Catherine McCullum; not ever. I will show you when we are married what I do to uppity women. I will show you as I have shown others." At that moment, Delaney pulled a revolver from his gun belt. Catherine had turned towards the door and had not seen the action. Jake in the upstairs window saw the action and knocked out the glass to shoot Delaney where he stood. The shot came, but it came from a completely different direction. Jake scanned the yard looking for the shooter. The next shot rang out as Delaney went down to his knees. The shots continued and the shooter came into view. A woman dressed all in black came into view. She wore a veil that covered her head and went to her waist. It was so like the veil that Catherine had worn the day before that Jake thought he was seeing an apparition. He ran down the stairs then with only one thought in mind. He had to get to Catherine. He had to make sure that she did not see Delaney die in front of her eyes in her own front yard. It was a vision that she would never get out of her head and he had to make sure that she didn't see it.

Catherine had turned and placed her hands over her ears when she heard the shots ring out. She thought for sure that Jake had killed Delaney then as he had promised her he would do. She didn't want to see that in front of her and she did not turn because she knew that Jake would take care of whatever needed to be taken care of just as he had promised her he would do. When Jake came to the bottom of the steps, he saw Catherine turned towards him with her eyes shut and her hands over her ears. He called her name then and she looked up at him with tears streaming down her face. "Catherine, Catherine, it is over baby girl. It is over," Jake called out. The apparition in the yard turned then also. Delaney was on the ground, dead from the first shot that had rang out. The apparition had seen to that. She turned then and looked up at the porch when she heard Jake's voice. She lifted the veil and Jake saw Ruby McGinnis standing over Delaney's body, her gun in her hand emptied into him. He saw too that the one side of Ruby's face was blackened as if she had been pistol whipped. It looked very much like his own face had looked as Catherine had described it to him after his accident. Jake did not have to kill Delaney after all; another of his victims had done it for him.

Jake came out on the porch then and held Catherine to his chest. "Catherine honey, don't turn around. I don't want you to see Delaney. He is dead honey, but I don't want you to see that and have that image in your mind. I have you Catherine, don't turn around," Jake said firmly.

"I won't Jake. I don't want to see that. I don't want to see Delaney dead in my own front yard. I remember you telling me that you needed to teach me how to shoot Jake because someday there might be something in my own front yard that I would have to shoot. I just never thought it would be a person and I never thought a person could be so vile and so evil Jake until I met Delaney," Catherine said wide eyed.

"You go inside now and go upstairs to our room. I will come and get you when this is all over, alright? You go now and lie down on the bed and try to get all of this out of your mind," Jake said holding Catherine to his chest.

"Alright Jake; I will go upstairs as you say," Catherine said. He could tell from her face that she was in shock and could not grasp what had really happened. There was a part of her that understood, but the rest of her was numb from the whole experience. Jake called then to Ramon and asked him to take Miss Catherine up to their room and to have one of the boys go after Dr. Martin. Ramon put his hand around her waist then and helped her to the upstairs room.

Jake went into the yard as the deputy marshals had circled Delaney's body and had started to question Ruby McGinnis. "If you men need to come into the library to talk to Ruby, that will be just fine. I suspect that Ruby will be in the same state of shock as Catherine right about now," Jake said looking intently at Ruby. She had dropped her veil again as she did not want Jake to see the bruising on her face. She looked at him as if she had seen a ghost and in the charade that they had played out, he would be the apparition and not Ruby.

Sheriff Will, Marshal Jones and Ruby McGinnis came into the library then and sat down. She persisted in keeping her veil over her face as she did not want Jake to see what Delaney had done to her. Jake poured a glass of whiskey for Ruby and she started to talk. "I saw Jim Eaton pass by the oasis this morning while I was visiting Jake's grave. I thought he might be coming into town looking for the Marshal and for Sheriff Will. I had given them my statement about the latest visit by Delaney. He came into the saloon yesterday hooting and hollering about how he had killed Jake and how he was coming after Catherine today. I told him that he was a mad man and that Catherine would never allow the man who had killed her husband anywhere near her. He told me it was none of my affair and then he started beating me with his fists. He said that no one would tell him what he could or couldn't have and least of all a whore. He said that his Mother had been a whore when she had slept with his Father all the while married to another man and that all women were whores and he would make sure that he made every woman suffer for it. I asked him then if he hated every woman or just me. He hit me more for my troubles. When I saw Jim Eaton race into town today, I said to myself, Delaney is going after Catherine and she is defenseless now that Jake is dead. That is when I continued on to the English Rose. I hid my surrey behind the house and I waited for Delaney's next move. I thought I would just watch and wait to see what would happen. When he pulled the gun and I saw that Catherine had turned her back I thought, he is going to shoot her in the back and there is no one here to protect her. That is when I fired the first shot. When I saw him fall, I decided to end it and to take him out like the rabid dog that he was. If you need to arrest me for it Sheriff Will, then I am ready to be arrested. I had to end it don't you see because that man was never going to stop until he hurt someone else and maybe killed them," Ruby said heatedly.

"No one is going to arrest you Ruby. You defended Catherine. We all saw it. You defended her because Delaney was going to cold bloodedly shoot her in the back. We didn't know until today Jake that Catherine was pregnant. He would have shot her and the baby and he would have had three murders on his hands along with all of the assaults that we have statements for. Ruby is just the most recent of the assaults. We have him on the threats to the ranchers who he has bought out along with Carmichael of course. My deputy marshals are going to pick up Carmichael right now as we don't want him to try to sneak away. It is over Jake. The nightmare is over. If it hadn't been for you and for Catherine willing to see this thing through, there is no telling how many more people would have gotten hurt in the process," Marshal Jones stated.

"Jake could we see Catherine for a few minutes so that we can take down her statement as well?" Sheriff Will stated.

"I am not sure how she is going to be Sheriff. Let me go check on her and then I can let you know. I think that she is in shock. Ramon is with her and I have sent for the doctor. He may need to give her something to help her through this and to help her sleep. Ruby you might need to be checked out also. Has Dr. Martin tended to your face from Delaney's visit?" Jake asked anxiously.

"I tended it myself Jake because I was too ashamed for anyone else to see what he had done other than the Marshal and the Sheriff. They had to see it so that it could be part of the record against that scum," Ruby said heatedly. She was starting to cry now which Jake thought was a good sign. If she was starting to cry, she was starting to come back to the realization of what had happened to her and to what had just occurred in their front yard. He left her in the care of Sheriff Will and Marshal Jones and went upstairs to check on Catherine.

Jake found Catherine lying on the bed as he had told her to do. He motioned then to Ramon who went back downstairs to assist Ruby. Catherine's face was white as a sheet and her face was turned to the window staring in front of her. She turned towards the door when she heard Jake come in. Jake went to the side of the bed to comfort her. She sat up then and Jake put his arms around her. She placed her head on his shoulder and just held onto him for dear life. "Catherine honey, the Sheriff and Marshal would like to talk to you for a few moments. Do you think that you can come downstairs honey? I promise they won't keep you for long, they just need to ask you a few questions and then it will be all over," Jake said tenderly.

"Have they taken Delaney away Jake? Is he still in the front yard? I don't want to see that Jake. I don't want to see him dead even if he did deserve it many times over," Catherine said wide eyed with shock.

"I won't let you see that Catherine. I told you I wouldn't let you see that and I always keep my promises don't I?" Jake said tenderly. "Dr. Martin will be coming to see you in just a few minutes and I will ask him to give you something to help you sleep. I want you to rest Catherine. I didn't know that you were pregnant honey. You hadn't told me that," Jake said holding and soothing Catherine.

"I don't know that I am pregnant Jake. I just didn't know what to say to the man, so I kept trying to think of things to say to him. I thought of that because of our conversation from the other day when you asked me what would happen when the babies came. I had thought about that ever since and I started to think how I would raise our son to be a rancher just like you and to love the land and protect it just as you have done. I just started to tell him that because I knew I had to keep him talking, but I just didn't know what to say to a mad man," Catherine said through tear stained eyes.

"I know honey, I know. You did such a wonderful job of keeping this all going. I heard every word Catherine and I didn't know how you kept so calm. I wanted to break out the window when I first saw him get off his horse, but I kept saying, no Jake, don't do it; don't kill the man in cold blood. Let him talk and it will all come out and the Marshal will have all of the evidence that they need to see the man hanged," Jake said heatedly.

"Jake who did shoot Delaney? I heard the first shot and then I heard the shots coming closer and closer to him so I knew that it wasn't you because you were upstairs. I heard the window being broken so I assumed that you were getting ready to shoot," Catherine said worriedly.

"It was Ruby darling; Ruby has been beaten so badly by that monster that she won't take off her veil. I saw this woman coming from the back of the house and she was dressed like you were yesterday. I thought I was seeing things and then she was standing over him . . . and the shots were from her gun Catherine. She came to help you because she thought that I was dead and that you were here alone and helpless," Jake said tenderly.

"I must thank her Jake. I had no idea because I had turned my back on him Jake. I couldn't listen to anymore of his vile talk. I had turned and then I heard the first shot and I thought, Jake is taking care of it just as he promised and I didn't want to see anymore. I didn't want to see him die in my own front yard and not get that image out of mind ever again," Catherine said staring in front of her.

"Sweetheart, can you come with me for a few minutes and talk to the Sheriff and to the Marshal?" Jake said worriedly.

"Alright Jake; I can come with you," Catherine said with her eyes blank. Jake took her hand and held it as they went down the stairs. Catherine kept looking in front of her as though she was trying to see, but couldn't quite focus. Jake kept hold of her hand which was very cold. He noted that she wasn't shaking, but she was definitely still in shock. As they turned to go into the library, he felt her grip loosen and he saw that she was going to faint. He quickly grabbed her and lifted her into his arms as he had the very first day they had met when he had told her that her Father had died. He carried her back to her Father's downstairs bedroom and closed the door. The Sheriff, Marshal Jones and Ruby all stood and watched as the door closed. They knew that something had happened, but were not quite sure what. Within the space of just a few minutes, Dr. Martin arrived at the house. He had come in a dead run when Jim Eaton had told him what had happened. He needed to make sure that Catherine had something to help her sleep in case she did not already have something in her vast medical bag. He knew that she was the one that needed looking after this time and from what Jim Eaton had told him, she would need help for sometime afterwards getting over this event. When he came up on the porch stairs, Sheriff Will and Marshal Jones were standing waiting for him.

"Jake has just carried her into the back bedroom Doc. She fainted when she came around the corner. She was white as a sheet Doc. I don't know what has happened, but we fear the worse. We think she was pregnant Doc," Sheriff Will said hurriedly. Ramon heard that statement as he came up behind the Sheriff and the Marshal and his face quickly drained of color as well. Perhaps he thought, she had not known herself.

Dr. Martin went quickly to the back bedroom that he knew so well from his many visits to Jake during his recovery. That Catherine was now the patient was too much to bear even for him. He knocked quickly at the door and Jake called for him to come in. Jake was seated on a chair next to Catherine who was still unconscious. He was holding her hand and was trying to bring warmth back into it. When he looked up, Dr. Martin thought his face was the very definition of grief. Never had he seen two people more in love than these two and they had suffered for that love much too much for two people married for only two months.

"Jake, tell me what happened while I examine Catherine. Jim Eaton has told me about Delaney and the rest. Tell me what happened with Catherine," Dr. Martin said to get Jake talking and thinking again.

"I had gone up to get her from our room, as Sheriff Will and Marshal Jones said that they needed to talk to her about everything that happened for their records. I went upstairs to get her and she was lying across the bed like I told her to do and she was just staring out the window. I took her hand then and it felt like ice Doc. I started to rub warmth back into it and just talk to her for a bit to try to get her mind off of what had just happened. She had told Delaney that she was pregnant, but I didn't know if she really was pregnant so I asked her. She said that she had said it because she didn't know what else to say to a mad man to keep him talking." Jake stopped then and looked at Dr. Martin as if he was still trying to reconcile all that had happened and the fact that his wife was lying in front of him unconscious. "She said that she would come down with me and we came down the steps. I was holding her hand and I felt it go limp and I looked at her and she was fainting. I carried her back here and she has been out ever since. She is white as a sheet and so cold that I think she is in shock. That is why I wrapped her in the blankets," Jake said finishing. His eyes were staring but not comprehending the sight in front of him.

"Alright Jake; do you want to stay while I examine her further or do you need to leave? You look pretty bad yourself Jake. I don't want you fainting on me," Dr. Martin asked anxiously.

"No Dr. Martin; I want to stay. If Catherine could face seeing me injured I definitely want to be here for her," Jake said earnestly.

Dr. Martin continued his examination and when he reached her lower abdomen, he heard Catherine moan. "It is just as I thought Jake. I think she has had a miscarriage. I don't think that she even knew that she was pregnant. There has been so much that I am sure she just lost track. It is very common especially with first time Mothers. You mustn't worry though Jake; you and Catherine are young, strong and healthy people. She will rebound quickly and you can try again in no time. We just need to make sure that we keep her warm and that she gets plenty of rest. I brought laudanum with me Jake as I thought that she would need it to sleep after what she has been through. She will need it Jake because I need her to sleep until she is strong enough to hear this latest news. I am going to sit her up a little so that I can get this dose into her and then she will sleep. From the look of you Jake you need sleep as well. Don't forget you are still in recovery yourself Jake. You don't need to get down. Like I told Catherine, I can't have you both down or Ramon will be run off his feet," Dr. Martin said. He waited for the smile that he thought would come with that comment, but there would be no smile today. Jake was as bereft as Catherine but Jake was still conscious and was feeling the pain of yet one more attack by Delaney. It was the last attack against Jake and Catherine and perhaps the cruelest of all.

"He told Catherine that he would come for her and then he would come for her baby. He did come for her baby even after he died," Jake said woodenly. Now he was staring straight in front of him as if the shock had somehow entered his body from Catherine's. Watching the two of them, Dr. Martin felt as if someone had walked over his grave. He knew that both patients needed rest and he knew that the comfort that they would receive would be from each other. He had seen that when Catherine grieved during Jake's accident and now saw the same look on Jake's face.

"Jake, I am coming out again tomorrow to check on you both. I need you to get some rest and Catherine of course will rest. Do you want me to leave something behind for you now Jake?" Dr. Martin asked anxiously.

"No Dr. Martin; thank you though. I just need to watch out after Catherine. That is what I need to do now. I don't want her to wake up in this room and think about everything that has happened. I am going to carry her upstairs to our room and I will keep her warm and make sure that she sleeps just like you said. Thank you Dr. Martin; we will see you again tomorrow," Jake said without emotion. Dr. Martin opened the door for him and Jake having wrapped Catherine tenderly in the blankets again carried her out of the door. Sheriff Will, Marshal Jones and Ruby watched as he carried her up the stairs saying not a word to anyone and looking in front of him as if he had to reach their room and the refuge that it would bring to them both.

Sheriff Will, Marshal Jones and Ruby then turned their attention to Dr. Martin. He shook his head slowly and told them that Catherine had miscarried. Ruby looked at Dr. Martin and her hands started to form into fists. "Delaney has yet another victim to answer for Dr. Martin. Even after death he has yet another victim and this may be the worst one of all. An innocent baby and the impact that it will have on Jake and Catherine," Ruby said heatedly.

"Dr. Martin, will you take a look at Ruby here while you are visiting. She was beaten something fierce by Delaney yesterday and she was too embarrassed to come to you to be seen about it," Marshal Jones said worriedly.

"Of course Marshal; Ruby, why don't you come back into the back bedroom and let me look you over. You have had a terrible shock today also. I can't have the whole town going down over that bastard. Sorry for my language Ruby, but the man has a lot to answer for and today the fires of hell must be running especially hot knowing that he is on the way," Dr. Martin said bitterly. Sheriff Will made a grunting noise as if he was definitely agreeing with the last comment. He knew that Catherine was in no position to be questioned today so thought that he and Marshal Jones would just need to return back to town.

"I am going to stay Sheriff and make sure that Miss Ruby is alright. I can drive her back into town and tie my horse to the back of her wagon. After the beating and now the shooting, I don't think she needs to go back into town by herself Sheriff. I will stay and make sure that she is well enough to travel. Jake may need something also from the look of him. I never saw anyone look so lost in all my life. Those two sure have been through enough," Marshal Jones said shaking his head.

*****

When Jake reached their room, he carried Catherine over to the rocking chair by the fireplace. He knew that she would sleep. He knew also that physically she would recover quickly. Like the Doc had said, they were young, fit and healthy. They could have another baby on the way in no time. The wound that he worried about was the mental wound of this one last cruel attack by Delaney. He knew that Catherine would grieve for their lost baby as he was grieving now not only for the baby, but for Catherine and how she would be affected. He knew that he needed to be the strong one this time and nurse her back so that she would not carry this grief forward, but would leave it behind with the whole sorry affair that was Angus Delaney.

He rocked Catherine then as he would rock a baby. He sang to her a native song that he had heard the medicine man sing to the afflicted of the tribe. The song was sung to bring about the healing of the patient. The healing that was needed now was healing of the mind and of the heart in Catherine's case. It made no difference to him. If he were on the mountain, he would have the medicine man sing to Catherine to bring joy back to her mind and to her heart. That is what he sang for and for the healing of his own heart. If Catherine suffered, he suffered as well. Although they should have felt the relief that the whole sorry affair with Delaney was behind them, he had left them with one more piece of grief; one more hurt that was perhaps the worst hurt of all.

Ramon came up the stairs shortly thereafter to see if Jake and Catherine needed anything. He saw Jake holding Catherine and rocking her in the chair as he would rock a baby. He heard the song of the native people and the tears formed in his eyes. Never had he seen such devotion of two people to one another. He knew that their nightmare had ended this day, but that one more cruel attack had been in Delaney's quiver and that attack was now resonating with two people that he cared about most in the world.

CHAPTER SIXTEEN

Jake held Catherine most of the night in the chair. When he felt himself finally able to doze, he carried her to the bed and laid her carefully next to him. He wanted to be with her when she awoke. He did not want her to wake on her own and try to understand what had happened to her. By mid morning the next day, he finally awoke, stiff from sleeping in one position through the night; he could feel the pain from his injuries after the fitful night's sleep. He looked down at Catherine who was still peacefully sleeping. He kissed the top of her head as he had done throughout the night as he sang his song of healing to her. He would do so again today and as many days as it would take until he could see her smiling eyes again, full of mischief and love as they had smiled at him so many times in the past.

Shortly after his waking, he saw Catherine's eyes start to flutter. She looked up at him then and brought her hand out of the blanket to smooth the hair over his eyebrow. He wanting nothing more but to wait to tell her the news that she would need to hear, knowing the reaction that she would have once she learned the truth.

"Jake have I slept here all night? The last thing I remember was walking downstairs to meet with the Sheriff and the Marshal. I don't remember anything else Jake. What has happened now?" Catherine asked wide eyed.

"Yesterday when we went downstairs to meet with the Sheriff and the Marshal, you fainted when we reached the bottom of the steps. I took you back to the back bedroom and Dr. Martin came to check you out honey. It seems that you were pregnant Catherine. You had a miscarriage honey, when you fainted yesterday. I am so sorry Catherine. Dr. Martin said that it was just all of the shock. Too much shock at one time Catherine," Jake said tenderly. Catherine had started to softly cry as he had told her what had happened. As always, Jake could bear anything but her tears. She held onto him then and he placed his arms around her so that she could cry and grieve one more time.

"Dr. Martin said to tell you that we are both young and healthy and fit and that we can try again for a baby honey. You mustn't worry about that at all. You just need to get yourself strong again and I need to do the same. We will nurse each other until this whole sorry affair is behind us. We will have the round up Catherine and then I will ask Judge Wilkerson to marry us again just as we planned and then I am going to take you up into the mountains again. We will probably have snow in the mountains by October, but it won't matter. I will keep a big fire going and I will keep you warm and the mountains will heal us both Catherine, the mountains will heal our heart and our soul and we will be whole again. You keep holding onto that Catherine and keep holding onto the fact that I love you with all my heart. We have been tested and tried honey just like you said and we have not been found wanting. We will put this whole sorry mess behind us and after as many trials as we have had in the past two months, we won't have another test again for the next fifty years," Jake said holding Catherine tenderly.

Catherine listened to everything that Jake said to her and she said not a word. She just held onto him and listened to his words. Just the sound of his voice was a comfort to her. He started to sing to her again and she held onto him as he did so. She didn't know what the words meant, but she knew that they were comforting. She closed her eyes again as if she was hearing a lullaby. Jake kissed the top of her head and kept singing to her until she fell asleep again. He felt the tears in his eyes and knew that he was not a man who cried. He knew that he needed to feel her next to him as much as she needed him to hold her. Tested and tried and not found wanting indeed.

*****

Jake and Catherine lay holding one another most of the day. By dusk, Catherine woke again to find Jake lying next to her watching for her wakefulness. He smiled down at her again and she looked at him and shifted the hair from above his eyebrows. He kissed her hand as it moved past him and she smiled up at him. It was her first smile for two days and he thanked the Lord for it. "Catherine, I need to feed you honey. You haven't had anything to eat since yesterday morning and neither have I. We both need to eat or we will blow away," Jake said smiling.

"I know Jake. I want to take a bath also. Could I take my bath before we eat supper?" Catherine asked. "If you need to go ahead and eat I understand. I just want to take off these clothes and take a bath Jake," Catherine said anxiously.

"I will get up and ask Ramon to start heating some water. I think it would do us both good. Do you want to take your bath here honey? I can help you to make sure that you aren't too light headed," Jake said worriedly.

"I will be fine Jake. You go ahead and have your bath and I will be fine," Catherine said shyly.

"I am not leaving your side Mrs. Nelson. Don't go getting bashful on me. You stayed with me for three solid weeks when I had my accident and I am not leaving your side until you are strong and back on the mend," Jake said earnestly.

"Just stay with me until I sit up for the first time and then I will be fine. I just want to take off these clothes Jake. I don't ever want to have to wear these mourning clothes again Jake. It gave me the chills yesterday and I just want to burn these clothes rather than wear them again," Catherine said quietly.

Jake came to her side of the bed and sat with her as she slowly sat up. He helped her unwrap from the blanket that he had wrapped her in. "I am going to get Ramon started on the hot water. You sit here now until I get back," Jake said anxiously.

Catherine waited until Jake had left the room and then started to undress from the mourning clothes that she had worn for three days. She took off everything then from behind her dressing screen and placed her dressing gown around her. She had not looked in the mirror because she did not want to see the dark stains under her eyes that she knew would be there. She knew that Jake would hover and worry and she could understand his worry because she had felt it during his recovery. She knew that she needed to be strong so that Jake could see that she was gradually getting better. If he saw that, he would stop worrying as well and they could both start to get back to normal.

He was back up the steps in no time looking around the room for Catherine. "Honey, are you alright? I thought I told you to stay put until I got back," Jake said worriedly.

"I am here behind the screen Jake. I just had to get off those clothes Jake. I just needed to get them off so that I wouldn't look at them and think things that I don't want to think about right now," Catherine said quietly.

"Alright honey. I am staying right here until you are finished your bath. Then you can rest while I take my bath and then we will try some supper for us both," Jake said tenderly.

"Alright Jake; you can talk to me while I take my bath. Jake, they are not going to charge Ruby for yesterday are they?" Catherine asked worriedly. "If they are going to charge her, we have to help her Jake. If it hadn't been for her, I may not be standing here or you would have had to kill him and then you would have that death on your conscience," Catherine said worriedly.

"I don't think any of us would have had that death on our conscience darling. If you had had a gun in your hand, you might have been tempted yourself. No darling, they won't charge Ruby. They know that she was trying to protect you because she thought along with everyone else that I was dead. Along with that, the beating that she took at Delaney's hands alone would have been reason enough to do what she did," Jake replied.

"Did Dr. Martin see her when he was here yesterday Jake?" Catherine asked.

"I am not sure Catherine. I carried you upstairs after Dr. Martin had finished his examination. I know the doctor was still here and that Ruby was still here along with the Sheriff and Marshal Jones. We will need to ask Ramon I expect. He will know what all took place after I brought you back upstairs," Jake replied. He thought about carrying Catherine back upstairs and about the grieving that he had done before she awoke. They would talk about that again, but he just didn't want to talk about it now unless Catherine asked of course. Ramon came to the door then with her hot water and Jake smiled and took the containers to fill her bath tub. He smiled when he filled the smallest bathtub that he had ever seen, but it was all she needed. He knew that she needed her privacy now and he would wait on the other side of the screen until she was done her bath. "There you go honey. I will wait on the bed for you and keep talking to you. You tell me if you get dizzy again and bath or no bath, I am coming to get you," Jake said kissing her on the top of her head again. She looked so lost sitting on the chair, but she smiled at him each time that he touched her or spoke to her. He knew she was trying and he knew how hard she was trying for his sake.

"Jake, tell me again about the roundup and bringing the cattle to the rail head. When will that happen again Jake?" Catherine asked. He knew that she was trying to look forward and anywhere but where they stood currently. She was doing as he asked last night; to look forward to what they would share and to not dwell on what they had lost.

"We have most of the market cattle herded into the home paddocks already Catherine. If you remember, we did that when the threat of Delaney was at its worst. We will take the cattle from here down to the rail head and they will be shipped from there. That usually happens the third week in October. Once October hits, we can have all sorts of weather, so we get the cattle that we plan to sell moved out before the bad weather hits. That is when we have the parties that I told you about Catherine," Jake replied.

"Jake do you think it would be too much for us to host this year's party? If we did that, then we could have the community here and then Judge Wilkerson could do the vow renewal that we talked about. What do you think Jake?" Catherine asked.

"I think that sounds like a real nice idea Catherine, but you have to promise me that you aren't going to overdo. We both have had a rough time of it honey and no one would blame us if we passed on the party this year," Jake responded.

"I know Jake but I think it would also be a good thing for us both because we can say to everyone; the worst is over and we have come through it all and everyone would be able to see how much better you are doing. There are probably a lot of people who will believe that you died Jake and well, it would confirm that you are alive and kicking if not as high as you would like. I am glad that the cattle are in the home paddocks because I am sure you like to supervise that and you won't have to worry so much now that it is already done," Catherine replied quietly.

"You mean I won't have to work so hard because you are still worried about me right?" Jake said smiling.

"Well there is that also Jake. You know I only worry about you because I love you right?" Catherine responded.

"I do know that honey. And that is why I worry about you also. Are you about ready to finish up your bath Mrs. Nelson? I need to get you fed as soon as you are ready," Jake called out. Catherine came from behind the screen then in her dressing gown. She still had the dark stains under her eyes, but at least he knew that she was more relaxed after taking her bath and getting rid of the mourning clothes that she swore she would burn given the first chance.

"Jake, do you mind if I come down with you and sit in the library while you take your bath? I don't think I am ready to be alone just yet," Catherine asked shyly.

"Of course honey. You can talk to me while I take my bath like I talked to you. We have a lot to plan Catherine and we need to keep looking forward to all that we will share together. After the round up and the party, don't forget, I am taking you back to the mountain again. That will be like our second honeymoon. We need to go while the weather is still fit. Then we have Christmas to plan for and the winter will be on us and we can have a good long rest over the winter. We can read all winter and plan for the spring and the visit by your brothers. I can't wait to meet them Catherine and meet all of your family," Jake said. He thought then how odd it was for him to be the talkative one. He usually listened while Catherine talked, but he knew for her sake he needed to keep talking and keep her looking forward.

He held her hand then as they went downstairs and into the library. She sat down on the couch as he went in to take his bath in the downstairs bedroom. "Jake we need to find a way to thank Ruby for what she did for us. Do you think that I could send her a note once we are able to go into town again?" Catherine asked.

"We will take care of all of that honey, don't you worry. We will take it one day at a time. Today you came downstairs for the first time and we will see how you do after you have your dinner. One step at a time darling and we will both get mended and back in step again," Jake replied. After his bath, they went back upstairs and had a tray in front of the fire like they did on their first night back from their honeymoon. Jake felt like they needed to rewind the clock and start over again. So much had happened in such a short time and they needed to get their heads wrapped around it and heal from the pain of the past month. That night when they went to bed, Jake pulled Catherine over to hold her as he had done the past two days. He sang to her again and he wished with all of his heart that the words would start to do their work; that her heart and her mind could be healed from the heartbreak of the past month.

CHAPTER SEVENTEEN

The next day, Dr. Martin came out to check on his two patients. Ramon had gotten word to him that Catherine had slept most of the day before, so there was no need to come out and check on a sleeping patient. She needed sleep more than anything else to heal her body and to heal her mind. When he arrived, Jake met him out on the porch. "How is she doing Jake?" Dr. Martin asked.

"She is moving slowly, but she is determined to keep moving. I know that she is doing it because she doesn't want me to worry. She is not herself yet, but that is only to be expected. I know that I should send her back home to Delaware to rest Doc, but I just can't do it. I don't know how it happened because I spent a lot of my life alone, but I can't live without her Doc. That is the plain and simple fact. I can't send her home because I will grieve for her the way that she grieved for me when I was concussed," Jake said looking in front of him at the activities of the men.

"I know Jake. Everyone sees it; you two are two sides of a whole. What you and Catherine have is the kind or partnership that other people only dream of. Catherine is a strong, healthy, young woman. She will come back from this Jake. Her love for you will ensure that happens. You just need to keep making sure that she eats well and takes her tonic and she will come around in no time," Dr. Martin stated.

"I know Doc, you are right. I keep telling her to look forward to all of the things that will happen in October and most especially to the fact that she and I will do a vow renewal with Judge Wilkerson. It was a private wedding with few witnesses when we got married the first time, but she wants to host the cattle drive party this year and we will do our vow renewal then," Jake replied softly.

"Just make sure that she doesn't overdo Jake and that might just be the best medicine for you both. I will go in and see her now and check on how she is doing," Dr. Martin responded.

Dr. Martin found Catherine sitting in the library. He thought she still looked very pale, but that was to be expected. She had still not gained as much weight back as he had hoped, but that was to be expected as well considering the strain of the past week. "Catherine, how are you doing today?" Dr. Martin asked cheerfully.

"I think I am doing much better Dr. Martin. Jake fusses but I really can't complain because I worry about him as well," Catherine said smiling.

"Let me check you out and you can ask me any questions that you need to ask while I am examining you. Let's go back to Jake's old room while I check you out," Dr. Martin stated.

Catherine lay down on the campaign bed that her Father had included in his design for the first floor. She found it hard to believe that this room would have so much use, but it had certainly served its purpose in the past month. "Dr. Martin, how is Ruby McGinnis doing? Have you seen her since the day here at the ranch?" Catherine asked.

"She is doing very well all things considered Catherine. I think that Marshal Jones has been very solicitous to her since all of this has happened. I think that has helped her recovery quite a bit," Dr. Martin said smiling. Catherine smiled then also.

"It is wonderful to have someone special in your life. It makes all of the difference in the world. Dr. Martin, how soon do you suppose that Jake and I can get back to our normal life again? I mean how soon can we be together in, well . . . an intimate way?" Catherine asked shyly.

"I would give that at least another week Catherine. I will keep checking on you and we will decide from there. You need to give yourself some time Catherine. You have both been through a lot. I know you want to get your old life back and we will make sure that happens sooner than later. I will tell Ruby that you asked about her. I think you are both the bravest women in the valley and there are many who will agree with that. You keep doing well Catherine but don't overdo. You know that Jake will be watching your every move and we don't want to worry him do we?" Dr. Martin asked watching Catherine intently.

"No Dr. Martin; I will be very careful because I know he worries so. I just need to start doing things again. If I am not doing things, my mind just starts to wander and I don't want to look back Dr. Martin, I want to look forward," Catherine said quietly.

"You need to take it slow, but you need to get back to your old routine. Do you want me to talk to Jake about that? I know he worries, but I also know you need to get back to normal again just like Jake did after the attack," Dr. Martin said earnestly.

"I will try to help him understand Dr. Martin. I know he will see reason since he has just been through that process himself," Catherine replied.

When Dr. Martin went out on the porch, Jake was sitting watching the men at their work. Dr. Martin thought it a very good thing that Jake was outside. For a man as active as Jake, being cooped up in the house was not a good thing. He needed to help him understand that the same was true of Catherine. "So how does she seem to you Doc? Is she on the mend?" Jake asked anxiously.

"She is indeed on the mend. Don't be surprised if she asks to go back to some of her normal duties. She needs to keep her mind occupied Jake. I know you understand that. You need to get her out on the porch again which I know will bring back bad memories, but you need to coax her into it. Another good thing will be walks around the property. The weather will be cooling here shortly and walking will do her good. Next week you will be off restrictions for driving and riding. Maybe you can take her out to the oasis or over to the Trinity and then back into town; it will do her a powerful bit of good Jake. She needs to see that normalcy is returning to her life when so much has been out of control for so long. Just keep an eye out that she doesn't do too much too soon. I know I can count on you for that. You will watch out for her the way that she took care of you Jake. You are both very lucky to have each other in that way. Well Jake, you take care and I will see you again next week. Don't hesitate to have one of the boys send for me if you need me beforehand," Dr. Martin stated.

Jake went back into the house then and found Catherine sitting at her desk in the library. He frowned when he saw her there, but then remembered what Dr. Martin had told him. "Are you going to do some of the accounts darling? You won't do too much will you? Just take it easy getting back into the routine," Jake said worriedly.

"Don't worry Jake; I am just checking on the bills for both ranches and I need to get ready for our next payroll to make sure that everything is in hand. I won't be long darling, don't worry. You can read while I work so you can watch out for me," Catherine said with a brief smile.

Jake thought to himself then she is trying just like the Doc said. Don't hover but just stay close by in case she needs you.

Thus began the dance of oversight, one for the other. It was in an unspoken fashion from that time forward. A raised brow from Jake over his book meant "*Catherine are you alright and are you doing too much?*" The answering smile back from Catherine meant "*I am fine Jake, don't worry; I am just trying to get back to normal as you have done.*" At dinner Jake would cover her hand and squeeze it as they sat side by side. The squeeze meant "*I love you Catherine and I am thinking about you every moment.* Her pat of his hand afterward meant "*I know Jake; I love you too and everything that you do for me.*"

Jake found coaxing her onto the porch again was a bit of a stretch. He knew that she needed to get out of the house and needed to get outside to get some fresh air just as she had when confined inside during his recovery. Standing on that porch again meant that she was confronting the day of Delaney's final attack and the loss of their baby shortly thereafter. The first time that he suggested it, her eyes widened and she started to go very pale again. Ramon was the answer in that case as he suggested to them both that he would serve lunch out on the porch so that they could enjoy the wonderful late September weather. He moved the tables and chairs to the right side of the porch so that the view would be different. Jake had made sure that any blood stains left from Delaney's death were washed away as soon as his body had been removed. He wanted no visible reminders to Catherine even though the events of that day were burned into both of their memories forever.

Jake held Catherine's hand while they left the house for the porch. He seated her comfortably in the new placement of chairs and then started telling her about all that was going on during the days leading up to the cattle round up. As the talkative one again, he was taking the fear of what had occurred and focusing on what was happening in the here and now and in the near future with the drive to the railhead. That gave him the opening to talk about the party and the vow renewal. "Next week Catherine I will be able to drive the wagon again. Dr. Martin says the restrictions can be lifted then from the concussion. How about we go into town and talk to Judge Wilkerson about a date for the vow renewal? Then we can invite everyone to the party and we can start planning for it," Jake said smiling.

Catherine's eyes lit up at that news. "It would be wonderful to go into town Jake. I need to pick up my material from the General Store. I had said that I would select patterns with Mrs. Downes, but what with everything that has happened, I haven't been able to go back," Catherine replied smiling.

"Well we will plan on that for sure Catherine. You will need some autumn clothes in short order and hopefully they won't be ten pound dresses either. You know what Chet Stoner would say about that," Jake said grinning.

"I know what you and Chet Stoner say about the ten pound dresses Jake. I will try for something simpler to wear while I am working in the library," Catherine said smiling.

The luncheon on the front porch was a success but like every day since her miscarriage, Jake made sure that Catherine was in their room and taking a nap after lunch. He secured this agreement by taking a siesta with her. It was part of his recovery, but more importantly, part of his role as guardian of her health going forward. Both secured improvement in their recovery and both could say that they were honestly taking care of the other.

By the first week in October, Jake was able to drive the wagon again. He was anxious to be at the reins and rigged the surrey wagon himself for a visit into town. Catherine fretted that every dress she put on was too big, but Jake just smiled and said that she looked beautiful in everything that she tried on. He was just glad to see her excited again about going into town and about the next step forward in both of their recoveries.

Their first stop was Judge Wilkerson to find out his schedule and set a date for the round up party and the vow renewal that would kick off the party. As always, they were shown directly into the judge's offices upon arrival. "Well, it sure is good to see both of you up and about again. I bet you are here to ask me about the vow renewal and my schedule. Well it looks like the third week in October would be best if you want to do a party and a vow renewal. How about the 16th of October? How does that look to both of you?" Judge Wilkerson said smiling.

"That sounds just fine Judge. We will let everyone know and plan for that accordingly," Jake said smiling.

"Judge Wilkerson, I have a note here for Ruby McGinnis. Would you be so kind to make sure that she receives it? I want to make sure to thank her for her kindness to me on the day that Delaney came to the ranch. It was wonderfully considerate of her to look out for me as she did and I want her to know how much I appreciate it," Catherine said quietly.

"I will sure make certain that she receives this note Catherine. I know that she will be very happy to know that you are on the mend and doing much better. Thank you both for coming in and I will see you on the 16th of October if not before," Judge Wilkerson said as he showed them out of his office.

"Jake, do you want us to go about asking everyone if they want to come to the party now that we have a date selected?" Catherine asked.

"I think we should do one more stop at the General Store and call it a day for today Mrs. Nelson. This is your first time in town and I don't want you to wear out," Jake said smiling. He took her down to the General Store and waited as she picked out patterns for the dresses that Mrs. Downes would make for her. Like many people, Mrs. Downes had heard the stories. She saw how much weight that Catherine had lost in the process and was just glad to see her up and about and looking forward to the future. With their business completed, Jake took her back to the surrey wagon and they headed towards home.

"Jake, do you think we could stop at the oasis on the way home? I would like to stop off and see Father's grave as we go by," Catherine asked.

"Of course honey. We won't stay long though because I want to get you back for lunch and your daily siesta," he said smiling. Jake pulled the surrey wagon next to Cameron McCullum's grave just as he had done the first time that he had travelled to the English Rose with Catherine. He helped her from the wagon and held her hand just as he had done that first day. He watched her face very closely to see how she was doing and whether or not she was wearing herself out.

"Jake, has the coffin that we buried next to Father been removed? I just want everything returned to normal here again," Catherine asked quietly.

"Of course honey; I had the boys take care of that right away. Everything is being returned to normal everywhere honey, you will see," Jake said smiling. He pulled her into his arms then and she looked up at him with the same misty eye passion that he had seen the first time that he kissed her right here at the oasis. He pulled her up off her feet then and she put her arms around his neck. He kissed her very gently and she clung to him as if she did not want him to ever stop. All too quickly for Catherine, he released her back to her feet. "I have to get you home now honey and get your lunch. Ramon will be waiting for us," Jake said.

"Of course Jake; I don't want to keep him waiting," Catherine replied quietly. He took her hand and helped her back into the surrey wagon and then returned home.

When they took their siesta after lunch, Catherine put on one of her summer nightgowns, the one with the lavender ribbons. Jake noticed it right away and remembered the first time that he had seen her wear it. He smiled at the memory and remembered it again when Catherine put her arms around him as they settled in for their nap. He was starting to think that Catherine might need him as much as he needed her during his recovery. He needed to check in about this turn of events with Dr. Martin before he did something that could possibly hurt her. He needed to make sure that she was ready for their return to intimacy. He had a good idea that return to normalcy might be just the thing to get both of them back to their normal lives, but needed to be sure before they progressed.

The next day was Dr. Martin's day for a visit to the ranch. Jake met him on the porch as had become their practice. "So how is our patient doing today Jake?" Dr. Martin called out from the buggy.

"Well Doc, I have done everything that you suggested. We started having lunch out on the porch again and yesterday we took a trip into town. It felt good to be able to drive the wagon again and it felt especially good to get Catherine out and about again. There is one thing that I needed to ask you before you go in. I know that everyone is different and you can't just say that what works for one will work for everyone but . . . well I was wondering Doc if, well if Catherine and I could return to being together in every sense of the word. What I mean is . . . ."

"You need to know if you and Catherine can be intimate again. Is that about it Jake?" Dr. Martin asked.

"That is right on the money Doc. I don't know if Catherine has mentioned it yet, but I have a feeling she might so I thought I would get it out of the way right off the top Doc," Jake said anxiously.

"She did mention it Jake on my first visit after her miscarriage. I think she was trying to figure out what was normal and needed some direction. I will talk with her again today and something tells me that you are both ready since you both are seeking the word from me. You are right Jake, everyone is different. Catherine was very early in her pregnancy when she miscarried so that is but one factor. I need to assess if her grieving has improved and some physical factors as well. I will let you know Jake before I leave," Dr. Martin replied smiling.

When he went inside, Dr. Martin found Catherine at her desk where she was usually found this time of day. "So how is my favorite patient doing?" Dr. Martin said smiling.

"I am doing very well Dr. Martin. Jake has taken very good care of me indeed. We went into town for the first time yesterday and we have the annual party for the cattle round up and our vow renewal planned for the 16th of October," Catherine said smiling.

"Well that is good to hear. I know you will both look forward to that as will the whole community. It looks like life is getting back to normal in many ways. Let's check you out Catherine and maybe this will be our last visit for a while," Dr. Martin replied smiling.

They went back to Jake's recovery room and Catherine sat smiling as Dr. Martin asked her questions. She inquired again about Ruby who the doctor said was recovering well. "Dr. Martin, I have a question to ask you that I asked on your first visit. Dr. Martin, when will it be alright for Jake and I to resume our usual . . . well, married life, I mean . . ."

"When can you and Jake resume the intimate side of your marriage?" Dr. Martin offered. As was frequently the case with these two, they were of one accord on most issues and just wanted to make sure that the other was not hurt by whatever steps needed to occur next.

"Are you having any pain from the miscarriage?" Dr. Martin asked.

"No Dr. Martin. I have been resting like you suggested and I have gotten my appetite back some so I am feeling much better. I am going out on the porch because Jake insisted and like I said, yesterday we went into town again and it felt like life was getting back to normal. I don't want to do anything prematurely, but I certainly feel fit again Dr. Martin," Catherine said smiling.

"Well I think you are right on target for your recovery and Jake has certainly returned to his old active self. I think if you are both of one accord Catherine, you can return to *all* of your old activities as soon as you are both ready," Dr. Martin said smiling. "Unless you need me any further, I can safely say that I can release you from care as of today," Dr. Martin said smiling.

"Thank you so much Dr. Martin. That is good news indeed. I hope that you and your wife can join us on the 16th of October. Ramon is bound to outdo himself as he always does such a wonderful job with the refreshments. Thank you again Dr. Martin," Catherine said with eyes shining.

As Dr. Martin gathered his kit to leave, he shook his head at the couple who had weathered so many trials so early on in their marriage. He thought Jake was correct in his plans to restart their life together. So much had happened in such a short time to them and yet, they were more in love today than they had been two months ago. Tested and tried and not found wanting as Catherine had so frequently said to him. Tested and tried indeed.

*****

That night Catherine decided she would emphasize to Jake as discreetly as she could that she was ready to resume their intimate relationship. She understood now how important it had been to Jake for him to feel that his injury was behind him to the extent that Catherine and he could resume intimacy. Catherine realized that she did not want Jake to continue to see her as wounded and in need of recovery, but instead ready to restart her life. She knew that she could never completely forget the past month and its impact to both she and Jake, but she also knew that she didn't want to dwell in that state. She wanted to demonstrate to Jake and to the world as a whole that she had survived and now thrived again as she had before the whole Delaney business had begun. Most of all she wanted to return to her husband and for him to see her as whole and not as wounded. She knew that she had not recovered the weight that she had lost during Jake's recovery, but at least the dark stains had gone from beneath her eyes and her skin had regained its luster. She had roses in her cheeks and she knew when Jake had kissed her the day before that she did not want him to stop. She just had to convince him that everything was alright and that he wasn't going to somehow hurt her. She remembered when she felt the same after Jake's accident and clearly understood the torture that he had felt in not being able to touch her and to feel her in his arms. She wanted her husband now more than anything and she needed to make Jake understand it in the only way that she knew how.

After dinner and her bath she sat at her dressing table and brushed her hair as she had on so many occasions. She had on her summer nightgown with the lavender ribbons again with her dressing gown over top. Although she had worn it yesterday, Jake had not seemed to remember or to comment if he had remembered. She needed to make sure that she was more direct about the matter tonight. She opened the farthest window from the bed, pulled the shades and blew out all of the candles except for the ones closest to the bed. Jake came in then in her Father's robe and she smiled her best smile with the deepest dimples as he came into the room. Somehow she needed to make him understand just how much she needed him and his touch.

*****

"Catherine has on her lavender ribbon gown again," Jake thought as he came into the room. "She has that smile that would melt a January snow. Dr. Martin says that everything is alright between us, but I still need to make sure that Catherine is ready. I will need to look for a sign from her and make sure that she is ready for us to be intimate again. I wonder how she is going to let me know?" Jake wondered.

*****

As Jake came to bed, he took off his robe and blew out the candles next to the bed. Catherine was worried at first because she thought he liked the candles lit when they made love. Maybe he doesn't understand that I want to make love she thought. I am going to have to try to make him understand. She took off her dressing gown and coming to bed laid her head on Jake's chest with her hand around his waist. He kissed her on the top of her head as he had been doing the past two weeks. She knew that no one could have been more considerate or more kind and she knew that she loved him so much for his understanding of her quiet and her tears over the past two weeks. She loved him so much for everything that he had done for her and yet . . . she needed him to love her again as a woman.

"Jake, could I have your hand please?" Catherine said quietly.

"Which hand honey?" Jake asked anxiously.

"Your left one I think," Catherine replied quietly.

"Do you need me to check you for a fever honey?" Jake asked worriedly. He placed his hand on her forehead then and she felt normal and cool to the touch.

"No darling; I don't need you to check me for a fever," Catherine replied quietly.

Jake turned to his right side then and placed his left hand in her two small hands. She lifted his hand then and placed it to her lips. She then placed his hand on the right side of her face and leaned into the hand as she had done so many times before. With her own hand, which she placed palm down, she felt for his mouth and pressed it against his lips. He kissed her hand and she rubbed her thumb against his lips as he had down to her so many times in the past. In the dark she felt for him and then placed a passionate kiss on his lips. As she felt him move towards her, she parted her lips and placed her tongue at the tip of his lips. He groaned then deep within his throat and his hands left her face and came around her waist. He pulled away for a moment temporarily surprised and concerned.

"Catherine honey, did you speak with Dr. Martin today? Did he say that you were alright sweetheart?" Jake asked anxiously.

"He did say that Jake," Catherine was now kissing his neck and into the shoulder blade. Jake was trying to concentrate, but found that his concentration was quickly melting away.

"Catherine, are you sure that you are alright honey? I am not going to hurt you am I?" Jake asked worriedly.

"You will not hurt me Jake and nor will I hurt you. I couldn't hurt you darling because you told me that when you started to improve from your accident. I am telling you the same now. Do you understand Jake? When you kissed me yesterday, I didn't want you to stop. I wanted you so badly Jake and I wanted you to want me and not to see me as somehow . . . wounded," Catherine said quietly.

"Is that what you thought honey? I just didn't want to hurt you and I wasn't sure when you would be ready for me to show you how much I love you. You have been through so very much sweetheart that I just didn't want to hurt you. Every time I held you through the night, I thought about when we would be together again, but I just didn't want to hurry you until you were ready," Jake replied tenderly.

"I know darling Jake. I know so well because I felt the same way when you were injured. I just decided that I had to show you rather than tell you," Catherine said quietly. Catherine found his lips again in the dark and kissed him deeply. He felt her pulling him towards her as if she couldn't get close enough to him and to his warmth. It was the last thought that he had before he started to untie her lavender ribbons as he had done in the past and drink in her lavender scent as he had done for the first time on their wedding night. Her silken skin felt warm to the touch for the first time in recent memory. She was showing him with every fiber of her being how much she wanted him.

Jake moved her to her back then and began ravishing her neck, breasts and abdomen with his lips and his hands. He kept telling her over and over that he had missed her so much. She was a constant presence for two solid weeks while he watched over her and took care of her and yet she was miles away in her grief and in her recovery. He told himself that it was enough that he could hold her every night and know that she was getting better. It had been enough until yesterday when he had kissed her for the first time not on the head in a paternal way, but on her beautiful full lips and she had answered that kiss with the promise of so much more. Her eyes had told him that she wanted him and he thought he was right, but he just didn't want to press her, he wanted her to be ready.

Remembering that kiss and how it had affected him, Jake returned to Catherine's mouth and kissed her intensely. He mated his tongue with hers and she moaned and held him around the shoulders, kneading the muscles in his back and upper arms. "Catherine, I want you so badly. Are you ready for me Catherine?" Jake asked anxiously in the dark.

"I want you Jake, so very badly. Please love me Jake," Catherine said quietly.

It was all the confirmation that he needed. His hands moved from her abdomen that he had gently kissed and caressed and quickly entered her intimacy. His touch was light at first, but more pressing as he felt the need in him arise. Catherine began to come apart in his arms and cried for him. He entered her then and felt as if his heart would burst. His need for her overpowered all thoughts and all concerns. He had returned to his love, his other half and the roar that he released was the same wolf sound that he had made when they had returned to each other after his accident. He called her name when he reached his climax and he felt the tears that Catherine always cried after they made love. He knew that he was home and she was home and they had somehow remained strong and together through the worst trials that any two people could experience. Their long nightmare had ended and they were at peace yet again.

CHAPTER EIGHTEEN

Jake's last thought before falling asleep was that he would make love to Catherine again in the morning so that he could see her shining eyes. He woke with that same thought foremost in his mind. Catherine was lying across his broad chest as she had done on their wedding night. He was lying in bed thinking of all that had come before and all that would come again. They had weathered the storm together and together they could face anything. Catherine started to move then and he remembered the sweet torture of her moving against him in the morning. He could take that torture if it meant that Catherine was back in his arms and that their nightmare of the past two months was coming to an end. She moved then slowly as if she would roll to her side and he quickly stopped the motion.

"Just where do you think that you are going Mrs. Nelson? You are in an awfully precarious position you know just in case you hadn't realized it," Jake said with his eyes closed. His arms had come around her waist then tightly and she started to giggle. He hadn't heard that giggle in so long that it was music to his ears. He pulled her up towards him so that she was at eye level and opened one eye to look at her.

"Were you playing possum then Jake? I thought you were still asleep," Catherine said with mischief in her eyes.

"So you thought you would just sneak away while I was sleeping? Is that what you thought? You have a lot to answer for if you thought you could get away that easily," Jake said grinning.

"I wasn't going anywhere Jake, honestly I wasn't. I thought you just might need to shift position that's all. After all, I have been lying here all night," she continued with the same look of mischief.

"Have you been lying there all night? I hadn't noticed since you are so slight these days," Jake said grinning.

"You hadn't noticed at all Jake?" she asked innocently enough, but with the look of mischief extending to her lips now.

"Oh I noticed alright. I noticed plenty Mrs. Nelson. You are going to wear me out. You are killing me woman!" Jake said laughing. Catherine's last conscious thought after that statement was that Jake did not seem to be worn out at all as he very healthily demonstrated.

After breakfast, Catherine sat down to her accounts and payroll. A note had come to her from Ruby McGinnis after breakfast. In the note she asked Catherine if she would meet with her at the oasis on the following day. Catherine showed it to Jake and asked if he was alright with her riding out to meet with Ruby at the oasis.

"Mrs. Nelson, what are my three rules to you at all times?" Jake asked with his hands on his hips.

"Rule #1; always wear a good hat in the sun to keep from having sunstroke," Catherine replied dutifully. "Rule #2; always ride astride and never ride side saddle," she continued. Rule #3; don't ride out alone," Catherine said answering his stare with a smile and another look of mischief.

"That's right and don't you ever forget them. I am taking you to the oasis tomorrow. I will be discreet while you meet with Ruby, but you are not going alone anywhere. Have you got that Mrs. Nelson?" he said with his most intimidating stare and his hands on his hips.

"You needn't try to intimidate me Jake Nelson. It won't work you know and it never did. I will be honored for you to drive me to the oasis tomorrow because I know you are only doing so because you watch out for me all the time and I love you for it so you can stop staring a whole through me right this minute, Jake darling," Catherine said grinning up at him.

"So I am Jake darling again am I?" Jake said with one eyebrow raised.

"You are always Jake darling to me," Catherine said with her deep dimpled smile.

"Just you make sure you remember those rules Mrs. Nelson and don't try wrapping me around your little finger with that smile of yours. It won't work you know," he said grinning. For her troubles, he swatted her on the bottom as he left the room. Catherine started giggling again because it seemed that she had started the day giggling and would giggle all day long. Jake thought to himself that giggle was worth all of the tea in China to hear again.

When Catherine had finished her accounts for the day, Ramon had lunch prepared for them on the porch again. They were counting down the last days of September and as trying as the month had been, they had much to look forward to with the cooling weather, the cattle drive and the planned party and vow renewal. When they sat down to luncheon on the porch, Jake took Catherine's hand again. It was a continuation of their unspoken dance of concern which had begun with Catherine's miscarriage. "You know that you could have told me Catherine. You could have told me that you needed me just as I told you," Jake said looking intently at her.

"Oh I couldn't tell you Jake. I could show you, but I couldn't tell you Jake," Catherine said blushing.

"I don't see why not honey? It is the most natural thing in the world. Why just look at all of the animals on this ranch; how do you think they all got here honey? It is the most natural thing in the world. It is what keeps the world spinning on you know?" Jake said smiling.

"Jake, are you going to tell me another story about horses and being frisky as the weather starts to cool?" Catherine said with mischief in her eyes again.

"Well honey it is true all the same. The mare just gives the stallion one look and then he just knows honey. Maybe you should work on a look since you have trouble telling me and I can't read your mind. That is just the ticket honey, you need to work on a look and I will know every time that I see that look going forward," Jake said grinning. Catherine had been turning redder as the conversation continued and Jake was enjoying that fact as well. Teasing Catherine was one of the great joys in his life and not being able to do so over the past month had been a great strain. He was recovering from that deficit in great measure today. If they had their banter back, they were just about back to normal in every way, he thought.

*****

The next morning, Jake and Catherine set off for the oasis. As he saw Ruby's surrey wagon near the grave of Cameron McCullum, he pulled up beside the wagon and helped Catherine out. He tipped his hat to Ruby then and moved the wagon to the other side of the oasis. He wanted to give them their privacy, but as he had told Catherine the day before, she was not riding out alone. He had had enough worry in the past month to last him the rest of his life. He would not risk anything happening to her ever again.

Ruby smiled when she saw Jake driving the surrey. She knew what was in his heart and she knew the reason. Catherine smiled on seeing Ruby and looked a trifle embarrassed as well. "It is so good to see you Ruby. I am glad that you got my note. I wanted to come visit you when we were next in town. I was surprised that you wanted to meet me here," Catherine said smiling.

"I see that Jake is still hovering close by Catherine. That is to be expected. You two have been through a lot and I don't blame him for not wanting to tempt fate. As for you meeting with me in town, well Catherine, I appreciate it, but that wouldn't be proper. I doubt you have ever been in a saloon in your life and well, Jake probably wouldn't like that either," Ruby said smiling.

"Fiddlesticks Ruby, how do I properly thank someone for saving my life? I know that Jake was at the upstairs window ready to strike, but you had no way of knowing that. No one knew except for the Sheriff, Marshal Jones and Judge Wilkerson. Anyway, I am proud to thank the lady who saved me on the darkest day of my life. How are your injuries Ruby? Has Dr. Martin been taking care of them for you?" Catherine asked anxiously.

"He has been taking care of me Catherine and like you I am trying to get my life back to normal again. You may have heard that Marshal Jones and I are keeping company now and he is a real good man. I think that he will be staying now because we are becoming a bigger community. There is talk of more businesses coming to Buena Vista so I guess we warrant a full time Marshal now," Ruby stated.

"There is something else that I wanted to tell you Catherine while we are together. First off, I wanted to tell you about Consuela who worked for Delaney and Carmichael. He has probably been too shy to say anything to you, but Ramon and Consuela are sweethearts. She was the source of all of the information that was coming out of the Triple B Catherine. They didn't know she spoke English so they thought they were safe talking in front of her about all of their plans. What they didn't know was that she was the source of information to the Sheriff and Judge and she is the reason that we knew about all of Delaney's plans before he had a chance to carry them out. Anyway, now that Delaney is dead and Carmichael in jail ready to be hanged, well, Consuela is out of work. I thought of bringing her to work in the saloon, but I didn't know if Ramon would approve of that idea. Then I thought of you Catherine. I knew how you would feel about someone who risked her life to help you and Jake and well, I thought I would tell you because I figure you might want to hire her on," Ruby stated.

"Of course Ruby; there is no question that we would want to hire her on. Well hopefully she and Ramon could get married that way. Oh thank you so much for telling me Ruby. I agree that Ramon was probably too shy to want to ask me, but that would be just the thing Ruby. Thank you again," Catherine replied smiling.

"The other thing that I wanted to tell you Catherine is I know that you have a good man in Jake. I am sure that everyone has told you the same. You keep holding onto a good hand Catherine whether it is in cards or in life. Don't let what has happened to you color your future. Don't look back Catherine. I certainly am not going to do so and I think you have the same amount of grit. You wouldn't have survived here since May if you didn't have that grit Catherine. Keep looking forward and keep holding onto a good hand. I know I plan on holding onto a good hand with Marshal Jones and I hope that you will do the same," Ruby said smiling.

"I plan on doing that very thing Ruby. Thank you again for telling me about Consuela and for all of your kindness. It is something that I won't forget Ruby," Catherine said smiling

Ruby motioned over to Jake then and he brought up the surrey wagon for Catherine. "You take good care of her Jake. She is one special lady," Ruby said smiling.

"I will do just that Ruby. You take care of yourself also," Jake said tipping his hat once more.

Jake had decided while they were out that they would ride on over to the Trinity ranch today. He had not been there since the day of his injury and he wanted to pack some more things to bring over to the English Rose. With the weather turning cooler, he knew that they needed to start planning for late autumn and winter around the corner. They would not have so many beautiful days as this one and he planned on taking advantage of it. He was also wondering how much Catherine would tell him of her conversation with Ruby. He wouldn't pry, but would just wait for her to tell him.

"Jake, Ruby told me something that I think you need to know about. It seems that the source of information coming out of the Triple B on all of the plans by Delaney and Carmichael was Ramon's sweetheart Consuela. They didn't know that she could speak English so they freely spoke in front of her. She risked her life Jake to get information out of the Triple B to the Sheriff and to Judge Wilkerson. If we hadn't received that information Jake we might not both be here. Since Delaney is dead and Carmichael in jail, Consuela is out of work. Ruby was going to hire her at the saloon, but she didn't think that Ramon would care for that. Oh Jake, I was thinking that we could hire her and then maybe Ramon and she could get married. Don't you think that is a good idea Jake?" Catherine said anxiously.

"I think that is a fine idea honey. I think Consuela, you and Ruby are the bravest three women that I know. Those bastards were so arrogant that it never occurred to them that a woman was helping to bring about their downfall. It was an insult that they thought she couldn't speak English, but then again, why would we be surprised by anything that they did. Consuela can help you out with all of your lady things that Ramon doesn't need to deal with," Jake said earnestly.

"What lady things would those be?" Catherine asked innocently but with mischief in her eyes.

"Well you know honey, lady things like washing out those things you are always wearing that you don't need to wear," Jake said pointedly.

"Oh do you mean my corset Jake darling?" Catherine said mischievously.

"That and helping with other chores related to lady things. Don't give me that look Catherine you know what I mean or do I have to spell it out for you?" he asked pointedly.

"No Jake darling. I think I understand *lady things* well enough. It covers a wide variety of items," Catherine said smiling.

"We can build them a cabin honey and then I can have you all to myself in the house at night. You know you can get a little loud in the boudoir so we won't have to worry about that anymore," Jake said laughing.

"Did you just say *boudoir* and did you just say that I get noisy?" Catherine said shocked. "Where did you learn the word boudoir pray and why on earth would you say that I was noisy or do I have to remind you about wolf calls Mr. Nelson?" Catherine said grinning.

"I learned the word boudoir from *your* novels honey after I had read all of my own while I was recovering. Where did you get some of those books Catherine and what kind of ideas have they been putting into your head?" Jake said winking. "Besides, wolf calls are just a natural thing just like the look from the mare to the stallion that I told you about yesterday honey. Have you mastered a look yet just so I know going forward?" Jake said grinning.

"I have not Jake Nelson and you know that. You are just trying to make me blush again," Catherine said primly.

"I know honey. I have missed teasing you and I have especially missed making you blush. I have never seen anyone that can blush like you honey. It is one of my favorite things to do. I have a list of those just so you know," Jake said winking.

By the time their banter had worn its way through, they had arrived at the Trinity ranch. The hands at the Trinity welcomed them both. It had been a long time since the boss had been able to ride out and they had not seen Miss Catherine since the day of the celebration party at the English Rose. That had been before Jake's injury and Delaney's final attack. Much had happened in one month's time and they were glad to see Jake and Catherine out and about again. Jake told Catherine to go in and rest in the house and he would walk around with the foreman and get updated on the current work.

Catherine went inside and started to gather some more of Jake's books for transfer to the English Rose. She felt as if she and Jake had definitely turned the corner. They had their old banter back and she was happier than she had been since returning from their honeymoon. Thinking of the honeymoon made her think of their native friends and she made a note to make a special basket of treats to bring with her when they next went to the mountain cabin. Jake and Ruby were both right; they needed to look forward to all of the happiness that was to come and not look back. The pain of the past would not go away, but neither did it need to cloud the happiness of the future.

Catherine had a stack of books packed in the boxes that Jake had stashed in the back of the surrey wagon. She would add these books to the library at home when they returned to the English Rose. She wondered then what other items that Jake might wish to bring with him. She hadn't seen winter clothes on their earlier packing trips, so she would mention those when he came in from the fields. She knew that he was so happy to be free of his restrictions and to be able to move about again. She could tell that was but one of the reasons for his high spirits the past day or so. Other reasons made her smile to herself and probably blush as well although she wasn't close by a mirror to see. Jake would definitely notice however as he always did notice. She would have to start working on a look to give him and then she guessed she would have to tell him that was the look so that he knew going forward. She covered her face with her hands and felt her cheeks were burning so she knew she was blushing again.

Jake picked that moment to come into the ranch house and she tried to regain her composure before he saw the blush. It was too late of course, because he saw the blush as soon as he entered the house. "So are you looking for more racy novels Mrs. Nelson? Just so you know, I don't have racy novels in my particular book selections, but I suppose you know that from the titles that you have been packing," Jake said with a wink. "Boudoir indeed Mrs. Nelson," Jake said laughing. "Do you want to come upstairs and help me pack my winter clothes?" Jake stated.

"I was just going to ask you about those Jake so yes, I will come up and help you," Catherine said trying in vain to regain her composure. Catherine followed Jake up the stairs and he turned into the large master room which she assumed was his room before they were married. The room was very masculine and very Spartan just as he had told her. He opened the closet and began handing her winter clothes to be folded and placed in the boxes that he had brought with them. Before they were finished, two boxes were full of winter items along with the boxes of books below. They would have a good load of items to place in the surrey wagon and few things would remain that would need to be moved back to the English Rose. Jake sat on the bed as Catherine folded each item and carefully placed it in the available boxes. "I think that is everything for now darling unless there are any other items that you want to pack for the day," Catherine said smiling.

"You know I love to tease you Catherine, but I also need to tell you something serious while we are here. I did a lot of dreaming about you in this room Catherine. I dreamt of what it would be like to fall in love with you and to have you fall in love with me and I dreamt of what it would be like to marry you and be able to talk and laugh with you every day and hold you every night. Whatever dreams that I had honey; they were nothing like the reality has been. To hear you laugh again this week has been like music to me honey. I have been so happy to hear it and I know you have been happy to laugh again. You know I love teasing you, but most of all I love seeing you happy again Catherine. It means the world to me," Jake said smiling.

Catherine listened to him and the tears came to her eyes again. "These are happy tears Jake Nelson so don't start worrying again. I know you love to tease me and I know you and Mr. Stoner told me long ago that you only tease people you like. I know you love teasing me because you love me and you love to laugh as much as I love to see you laugh and laugh with you. We have been through so much over the past two months and it is so wonderful to feel that freedom again to laugh and not have to look over our shoulder or be worried that someone is coming for us. I don't know how we survived it, but we did. We survived it together. I am not naïve enough to believe that we won't have any other challenges Jake. Every generation has challenges. If you have read my great–great-great Grandmother's diary you know that they faced the War of 1812 and bombardment of their own home town. We may face drought or too much rain or any other type of challenge going forward. I just know if you are by my side, I can face anything Jake and somehow we will find a way to laugh again when whatever challenge we face is behind us," Catherine said smiling.

"Come here honey," Jake said smiling. Catherine went over to stand in front of him then. "You know Mrs. Nelson it is time for your siesta. We are supposed to take one every day remember?" Jake said smiling. Jake reached up and cupped her face with his hands and kissed her deeply.

"Aren't we supposed to be sleeping if we are having our siesta Jake?" Catherine asked smiling with mischief.

"Oh we will get around to sleeping eventually honey," Jake said grinning. Catherine's blush returned and Jake had one more thing to laugh about that afternoon.

CHAPTER NINETEEN

On their return to the English Rose, Jake and Catherine sat down with Ramon regarding the information they had learned about his sweetheart Consuela. "Ramon we asked you to sit down with us because we have learned about someone who is very close to you and her brave actions. Ruby McGinnis told us that your sweetheart Consuela was the source of information to the Sheriff and Judge Wilkerson on all of the doings at the Triple B ranch. We know she is out of a job now because of Delaney and Carmichael and well, we would like you to know that she is welcome to a job here Ramon. Miss Catherine will need help around the house and with the babies when they come and we would like to think that we could help you both for all of the support that you have given us," Jake said smiling. He shook Ramon's hand then and thanked him for everything that he had done for both of them.

Ramon was truly speechless at this turn of events. "I did not want to say anything about Consuela to either of you. I knew that you would be very worried for her safety as was I. She refused to back down because she said that she knew there was evil at the Triple B and the only way to stop evil was to face it and to deal with it," Ramon said bravely.

"I told Catherine yesterday that I thought the three bravest women in the valley were Consuela, Ruby and Catherine of course. Ramon if Consuela is interested in coming here to work and if the two of you would like to get married, I can build you a cabin here on the ranch and that way you can have your privacy," Jake continued.

Ramon was again speechless at the opportunity that lay before him. "If agreeable to you both, I will ride to Consuela's family and tell her of your kind offer. I would very much like to marry her as she has been through so very much. You are right senor, Consuela is like Miss Catherine one of the bravest women that I have ever met. It will be my honor to have her for my wife if she will agree to marry me. I know that she will be very happy here as I have been very happy here as well. Thank you both again for this opportunity," Ramon said smiling. He left then on his way to approach Consuela with the job opportunity and with an offer of marriage.

"Well Catherine, it appears we are alone in the house for a spell. I reckon we will be getting used to that in the future. Let's get the boxes unpacked and then we can start planning for the party and for the vow renewal," Jake said smiling.

"I also made a note that I need to make a basket of treats for our native friends when we leave for our honeymoon. Will we take one of the steers with us then also darling?" Catherine asked.

"We will indeed. We will tie a steer to the pack horse and take him with us when we go back to the cabin. Do you have your list started for the trip to the cabin also darling girl? Don't forget to put candles on your list. I don't want to be without candles for this honeymoon," Jake said with a wink. The expected blush began to arise from Catherine's neck and Jake went to the wagon to unload his books and winter clothes laughing and in continued good spirits.

*****

The morning of the cattle drive rose cool and clear. Jake had told Catherine to make sure that the blinds were up the night before as they needed to wake with the sun. There was much to be done on cattle drive day and this year he would be leading two ranches of cattle to the rail head. Because of the number of ranches and the number of cattle to be sold, each ranch had a particular day to load at the railhead. Trinity and the English Rose would load on the same day as they were the closest to town and the rail head. This was the first time that both ranches had sold on the same day because they were now bound by the marriage of Catherine and Jake. Catherine relented from her usual dress for town today as she wanted to ride beside Jake when the herd was driven into town. She would need to wear her riding clothes today, but she thought the town would understand as she was a rancher's wife and co-owner of two of the biggest spreads in the valley. As it was her first drive to the rail head, she was as excited as Jake.

She arose before Jake for a change so that she could be dressed and ready with breakfast waiting for him. He smiled when he realized that she was up before him. He knew she was excited as she had talked of little else for the past two weeks. She asked him endless questions again and now that he was used to her questions, he happily answered them as he knew that was how she learned about new things. She was very like her Father in that respect.

Jake had saddled his horse and a mare for Catherine to ride. They would ride together to see the great gathering that was the drive to the rail head. Catherine came down the porch steps with her Spanish style felt hat, riding clothes and a vest and belt. He saw that she had still not gained the weight back from their month of trial, but he knew she had found her appetite again and she was doing everything that the doctor had asked of her. She had the roses back in her cheeks again and the mischief in her eyes, so he was content for her to gain the weight back gradually. He also had learned his lesson about discussing winter weight. He reminded himself every day that he was talking to his wife now and not another rancher when he made those comments.

"So are you ready to see this big event Catherine?" Jake called out.

"I am so excited Jake. I could barely sleep last night just waiting. I was afraid I would over sleep so I was awake before you for a change," Catherine replied with mischief in her eyes. Jake gave her a leg up on her mare and they headed for the oasis. Both herds would converge at the oasis and then head into town. As they waited for the two herds to converge, Catherine noticed that Jake's horse was prancing and was especially active this morning. She knew that Jake could handle any horse so she watched him entranced as he talked to the horse and continued to pat his sprightly head. "Jake, I think your horse is especially active this morning my love," Catherine commented.

"Oh honey he is just frisky because he feels the cool weather coming on. He is feeling his oats and also has been giving the eye to that pretty mare that you are riding. I think he is looking for the sign Catherine. You know what I mean by the sign?" Jake said grinning. Catherine turned her customary blush and smiled in response. Moments later, Jake was giving the signal to the men to head into town with the two herds. Catherine thought to herself that Jake was as frisky as his horse and definitely feeling his oats today. How he could keep his mind on teasing her and leading two herds into town at the same time was beyond her. He had definitely recovered and was in charge today.

Catherine rode along side Jake smiling at the day ahead of them. She had been told about this week's events ever since she arrived in Buena Vista and she wouldn't have missed it for the world. As Jake had told her in the darkest days, look toward the future Catherine; look for the happiness that is ahead of us and leave the despair of the past behind you. No words were truer as she looked at Jake's smiling face today. He lived for this yearly event and to lead two fine herds into Buena Vista today was a triumph of everything that he worked for during the entire year. Catherine had never been as proud of her husband as she was today when he led their men into town. She knew the townspeople would turn out to see this annual event and she was there with the best man in the valley watching it all from her special vantage point. She felt as if she was in one of her western novels then and couldn't believe the beauty of the day and her own happiness. It was like the day that Jake had taken her to the oasis for their first swim. Above them was the big blue sky and beside her was the love of her life in fine form as frisky as the mount that he rode.

As they came into town and neared the train station, she saw Chet Stoner in the distance. Knowing him as she did, she assumed that he would have some tease to make today. She knew from experience that Jake and he only teased people that they liked or loved in Jake's case. All the rest they ignored. She was repeatedly glad that she was one of those that was liked and loved by these two men. They could make her laugh in moments with their gentle teasing. She found that she liked to rise to their challenge and come up with a tease of her own. She was especially adept at that challenge when it came to Jake, but then, she saw him every day so she had a lot of practice.

"Well now Jake and Miss Catherine; this is a fine day for a cattle drive. What do you think of your first drive Miss Catherine? I told you this was something to see and you definitely didn't want to miss it. Of course, there may have been one or two other reasons for you to stay in the valley eh Jake? Do you think she had one or two other reasons to stay?" Chet asked smiling.

"Well Chet, there is Ramon's excellent special cake that I always remark upon. Catherine has become quite a good horsewoman since she has been here and you know I taught her how to shoot. She hasn't been out for a while to practice, but she was starting to get pretty good at it. I guess there might be one or two other reasons why she is still here. What do you think honey; are there one or two other reasons to stay?" Jake replied grinning.

"Well of course gentleman. Where else would I get this wonderful teasing everywhere I go? I have started to get pretty good at teasing back Mr. Stoner so you need to be careful," Catherine replied with a look of mischief.

"Oh she is right about that Chet. You could almost say she has gotten sassy since she has been here, but I guess that is just the company she keeps," Jake said laughing. "Are our buyers here Chet?" Jake asked.

"They sure are Jake; they are around back at the corrals. They are ready for you. I told them that the prize herds were coming into town today and they are ready for you," Chet replied smiling.

Jake got off his horse then and tied him up at the train station. He handed Catherine down from her horse and tied up the mare as well. Taking her hand, they went around to the corrals and he introduced her to the buyers for the big beef companies who were here to size up the herds. The Trinity and English Rose men brought the cattle into the waiting corrals then and the buyers were counting head of cattle as they were rounded into the corral. Jake may have felt boastful, but he knew that Chet was right; theirs was the best herd of the week. They were the closest to the rail head, but they also had the best stock. Catherine listened as they negotiated on price and the buyers wrote out a check for the sale of the two herds. Jake told them that Catherine was the bookkeeper for the two ranches and he would leave it to her to take care of all of the transactions from that point. She was so proud to be Jake's partner in life and in the two ranches. They talked briefly with the buyers and then she and Jake headed down the street to deposit the check for the sale at the local bank. It was the entire year's revenue for the two ranches excepting sale of horses or other livestock. It had been a good sale year and Jake was pleased with the transaction.

As they walked down the street, Jake took Catherine's hand and smiled. It was a good feeling to freely walk down the street again and not feel like they needed armed guards for the privilege. Catherine had told him that she felt like the Crown Jewels walking down the street when they had come to town for the hearing. To him, she was the Crown Jewels and he would do anything to keep her safe and make sure that she was happy. They made their way to the bank and deposited this year's sale proceeds. It had been a very good sale year indeed. It was time to turn their attention towards the party that they would host on the 16th and to the vow renewal with Judge Wilkerson.

As they walked by the General Store, Jake and Catherine went in to pick up the dresses that Mrs. Downes had prepared for Catherine. Jake also placed his order for some books for the winter months. He made a point of winking at Catherine when that order was placed so that he would have his own winter reading materials and not need to delve into the world of lady's novels that he had read during his recovery. Catherine smiled at the previous day's discussions of *lady's things* and thought it amazing that they could communicate so much with just a wink and a smile at this stage in their relationship. It made her think again of the look that she was supposed to develop only for Jake's benefit which in turn brought back the blush from yesterday. Jake was watching her intently and wondered what new magic had brought Catherine's blush without him saying a word. "Do you need anything else today honey?" Jake asked.

"No thank you Jake. I think I have everything for today. Thank you again Mrs. Downes. We hope that you and your husband will be able to make it to the party on the 16th of October. We will look forward to seeing you there," Catherine added.

"So are you ready to head on home Catherine? What did you think of your first cattle drive?" Jake asked smiling.

"It was wonderful Jake. I wouldn't have missed it for the world. I was so excited to see that our herds were considered the best in the valley. That is all a testament to your knowledge and skill Jake. I am proud to be your partner in life and in the two ranches. We make quite a good team I think," Catherine said smiling shyly.

"We do indeed honey. We make a good team in ranching and in life. Now, we need to commit the rest of the week to planning for our party, our vow renewal and our second honeymoon," Jake said smiling. "We will see how the boys are coming along on Ramon and Consuela's cabin when we get home too. We have a lot to be thankful for Catherine. The worst is behind us and we have a lot of happiness in store for us," Jake said. The townsfolk who saw them together that day thought that they had never looked happier and were thankful that they had weathered the storm and come out stronger on the other side.

*****

As Jake had noted, the rest of the week was committed to planning for the party and for the vow renewal. They would set up chairs in the front yard leading out to the large tree that provided shade to the yard. There the Judge would conduct the ceremony. Catherine had been fretting about weather and what they would do as contingency if there was rain. Jake said that the weather would be perfect and that she wasn't to worry. They had tables set up on the side of the house as they had done for Catherine's Father's wake. Ramon and the boys would barbeque half a steer again. There was beer and other refreshments and this time Ramon had Consuela in the kitchen to help him with the potato salad, cole slaw and baked beans and corn bread. It was all in all a very happy household and one that was filled with a great deal of love. If anyone had seen this same group of people one month earlier, they would not have believed the change. Tested and tried and now enjoying the benefits of their new happiness.

Catherine tried on her Mother's wedding gown again and was distressed that it, like most of her clothes, was now too large. She thought that perhaps she could pull in the bodice more so that it would not be so noticeable. Jake came to the door to see what she was doing and she remained behind the screen. "Where are you honey; lunch is almost ready out on the porch?" Jake called out as he came into their room.

"I am behind the screen Jake and don't come behind. I am trying on my wedding gown again and like everything else, it is now too big," Catherine replied anxiously.

Jake stretched out on the bed to prepare for the latest case of wedding nerves from Catherine. "Honey you are going to be so beautiful that no one is going to notice that the dress is suddenly bigger than it was in August. Besides, don't you have some of those lacing things that can pull it in more?" Jake called out.

"Lacing things; is that like lady's things Jake?" Catherine called out laughing.

"Don't make me come behind that screen Catherine Nelson. You know I have already seen your wedding gown so it can't possibly be bad luck," Jake called out.

"You are not to see it again until the 16th Jake. While I think of it, you are not to see me at all on the morning of the 16th until you see me come down the aisle out front; assuming of course it doesn't rain because if it does, I don't know what we will do," Catherine said worriedly.

"How am I going to keep from seeing you when I live in the same house and we share the same room? Don't tell me that you want me to sleep downstairs the night before because that is not going to happen," Jake said laughing.

"No silly, just the morning of the 16th. I can take your suit downstairs and you can dress down there in Father's first floor bedroom and that way you won't see me until I come down the aisle. You see, I have it all worked out Jake if I can just get this dress to cooperate," Catherine replied groaning.

"You need me to help out with those lacing things?" Jake offered again laughing.

"A kind offer but thank you no. I will see if Consuela can help me or perhaps Judge Wilkerson's wife can help again or Mrs. Downes. I will think of something," Catherine replied.

"Well if I could just get you to eat some big meals between now and the 16th then maybe you could gain the weight back and the dress would fit," Jake offered smiling.

"Jake Nelson, just so you don't start talking about winter weight again because if you do, we will have words for sure. You can't talk about winter weight with your wife like you talk about winter weight with your fellow ranchers and with the cattle. It simply is not done," Catherine said primly.

"Oh I have learned my lesson on that one honey. I will not talk about winter weight with you or any other woman as long as I live. I do not know for the life of me why you women are so particular about your weight, but there it is; just one of the many mysteries that make up my beautiful wife like your habit of blushing at the drop of a hat," Jake said laughing again.

Catherine came around the screen then in her customary blouse, vest, belt and gaucho pants. "You see Jake Nelson, you put ideas in my head and then I start thinking about them in the most unexpected places and the blush just starts. I can't help it you know it just happens," Catherine said smiling.

"I know honey; I am just teasing you aren't I? So what idea have I put in your head now Catherine?" Jake said innocently but with mischief in his eyes.

"I think it relates to that whole conversation about the look Jake; you know the look like the one between your horse and my mare?" Catherine said returning his grin with mischief of her own.

"Oh that idea; have you had any luck in coming up with the look yet because if you have, I need to know which look it is so that I know going forward. Remember I can't read your mind honey and after reading some of your novels, I don't know if I should be able to read your mind," he said winking.

"I will let you know at the appropriate time Jake Nelson once I have mastered the look. Perhaps I can put that on my list for our time at the cabin. Now, did you say something about lunch earlier because if you did, I think we should go down so that we don't keep Ramon and Consuela waiting any longer? They have a great deal to do in preparing for the party you know," Catherine said smiling.

"I know that honey. Maybe we should just get out of their way this afternoon and have another siesta. What do you think of that idea?" Jake said laughing and watching her face intently. The customary blush began on Catherine's neck and had worked its way up to her face by the time they went downstairs and out on the porch for lunch. She as always attempted to pretend that she had not been affected by Jake's comment. He laughed all the way down the steps and as they settled in on the porch.

*****

The morning of the 16th rose gray and hazy with a damp fog settled in. Anyone who knew the weather could feel the autumn upon them. Catherine rose in a fit of worry and Jake as always couldn't understand the commotion. She had gotten up and gone behind her screen until he left the room for the morning. As always he was laughing and in good spirits and Catherine was worried sick about the weather and whether or not it would rain and spoil the vow renewal and their outside plans for the cattle drive party. "Honey, I don't know what you are worried about," he called out from the bed while she remained behind the screen. "This is going to burn off and we will have a day so beautiful that it will hurt your eyes Mrs. Nelson. Are you sure I can't get your mind off of all this planning just so you don't get yourself riled up again? I can think of a few ways to relax you until the vow renewal begins," Jake said laughing.

"A kind offer as always Mr. Nelson, but I think I had better start getting ready and I think you had better start getting ready downstairs as per our agreement. Besides Jake darling, you have to greet our guests until the ceremony begins remember? I will be upstairs until the ceremony begins so it falls to you to entertain everyone as they arrive. Can you do that little thing for me Jake darling?" Catherine called out from behind the screen.

"So I am Jake darling again am I? Well that is good to know Mrs. Nelson since I am marrying you again this morning. Just so you know we are already married Mrs. Nelson so you don't have to get all worked up about it. The party will be beautiful, you will be beautiful as always and the weather will be beautiful. That is my prediction for the day and I will remind you of my prediction tonight. I love you Mrs. Nelson even if you do send me out of my own room to get dressed," Jake called after her.

"I love you too Jake. I will see you downstairs darling for the ceremony. I will be the one in the white gown just so you know," Catherine replied laughing.

"I will look for that, so thank you for letting me know honey," Jake replied.

Now that he is gone, Catherine thought to herself, I can truly start getting ready. She quickly made the bed and then began to lay out all of the items that she would need for her wedding ensemble. It was strange but she again felt that same feeling of nerves as if this truly was her wedding day. The first wedding had been so rushed that she barely had time to prepare let alone become nervous about all of its ramifications. Today, they were standing up in front of the whole community and pledging their love to one another. Having weathered the storms of the past two months, this wedding meant even more to her than the first. She knew that she loved Jake even more for having survived so many mishaps with him in such a short time. Since their recovery, they had become inseparable and she had never been so happy. She hoped that he felt the same and suspected that he did since she had never seen him as happy as he had been over the past few weeks.

She sat down first to prepare her hair thinking that she could wrestle with the lacings on her corset and on the bodice of her dress when she had some assistance. She kept thinking back to that first wedding day and her naivety at the wedding night that would follow. She truly had no idea what took place between a man and a woman. Jake had been her teacher in that aspect of her life just as he had taught her so many things since her arrival in May. Ruby had told her that she thought Catherine had grit to have survived since May in Buena Vista. Catherine thought she might have grit, but more importantly she had Jake at her side. As she had said many times, with Jake at her side, she could face anything. She looked at the portraits of her Mother and Father on her dresser again and thought that Jake was the most important gift that her Father had ever given her.

With her hair completed, she heard a knock at the door shortly thereafter. Judge Wilkerson's wife had again come to assist with her wedding finery. "May I come in Catherine? I know I gave you some assistance on your first wedding day and I thought I might offer again," she said smiling.

"That is so kind of you," Catherine replied. "I tried on my gown yesterday and I am having some problems with the lacing. I lost weight over the past month and I will need the lacings on the bodice pulled even tighter so that the dress will fit properly," Catherine replied smiling.

They both knew the reason that Catherine had lost the weight, but neither dwelled upon it. The events of the past month were too monstrous for anyone to want to discuss. The important thing was that they were behind this young couple and that they were doing everything in their power to put the past behind them. The Judge had told her that Jake and

Catherine looked even happier than they had on their first wedding day. Mrs. Wilkerson thought that no two people deserved it more. Mrs. Wilkerson wondered to herself how it was possible that Catherine could be smaller than she was on her wedding day. Why she thought that day that she had never seen a smaller waist. She pulled the lacings tighter on the bodice and they made up the difference so that no one would see the weight loss from the past month's misery. Catherine was as beautiful a bride as she had been two months before and to Mrs. Wilkerson's mind, even more beautiful. Having come through such an ordeal, she must now understand true happiness as never before.

"Well Catherine, I think you look even more beautiful than you did on your first wedding day. Ramon said to tell you that he has flowers for you in the hallway when you come downstairs," Mrs. Wilkerson stated.

"I forgot to ask; has the weather cleared? I was worried that we might have rain with the clouds and fog from this morning," Catherine stated worriedly.

"Oh my goodness Catherine; the fog has cleared and it is such a beautiful day. Why the sun is so bright it will hurt your eyes," Mrs. Wilkerson said smiling.

Jake's prediction comes true then, Catherine thought to herself. I will be hearing *I told you so* in short order. That was the least of her concerns however. She was so happy that the weather had cooperated and that she was marrying the love of her life again in front of the friends and neighbors who had known him his entire life. He was the best man of the valley for sure and the best teacher, guardian angel and the love of her life as well.

"I think you are ready now Catherine. I will go ahead down and let them know that we are ready to proceed. I will see you afterwards Catherine. Best of luck to you again," Mrs. Wilkerson stated.

Well Catherine, two months ago you looked around this room one last time before going downstairs to the library and the quiet wedding. Now you are doing the same knowing more about life both the good and the bad. The one constant has been Jake and he is waiting for you to come downstairs and walk to him, take his hand and say those words of promise to him once again. He said that he would always come after you and he has; he said that he would always protect you and he has; he said that he would always take care of you and he has. He had done all of the things that he promised and you have fulfilled your vows in ways that you never expected only two short months ago.

As she closed the bedroom door and walked down the steps, she was content in the knowledge that fate had led her to this beautiful spot in New Mexico to begin a new life just as her ancestor had begun her new life in Lewes, Delaware in 1811. There had certainly been adventure, there had been tears, there had been anxiety and grief, but through it all there had been love. With this thought uppermost in her mind, she accepted her flowers from Ramon with a smile and walked through the front door, down the porch steps and towards the man who had made all of her dreams come true. She didn't see anyone in the audience although she knew that they were there lending their love and support to the day. She only saw Jake standing next to Judge Wilkerson. He was smiling from ear to ear as he had done two months ago. He had mischief in his eyes as he always did. They would laugh today and she would probably cry and then tonight she would again be beside the love of her life.

Catherine said a prayer in her head as she walked to her vow renewal. *Thank you Father for placing me in this man's care when I first came to Buena Vista and thank you Father in heaven for assuring that we have survived the past two months and all that life has seen fit to throw our way. Guide us and keep us safe going forward and let us be forever in your hands and in your care.* When she reached Jake, he took her hand as he had done two months prior and kissed it. She looked into his eyes and saw all of the love that he held for her and he saw the same reflected in her eyes. No one else existed in that moment. Judge Wilkerson had to clear his throat so that they knew he was ready to begin. Catherine looked surprised for a moment as if she had forgotten that he was with them. Such was the power of the love of these two people.

Judge Wilkerson told the story then not of the evil that had been in their midst, but of two people who had found one another and held onto one another through the trials of life. He said that it was always his pleasure to join two people in marriage, but never more so than when the two people were meant to be together. He said the words over Jake and Catherine, but they had said those words to one another many times in the past two months. When the worst of times was upon them, they had always clung to one another and they had made it through to the other side, tested, tried and not found wanting. When the Judge told Jake that he could kiss his bride, everyone leaned forward to see how this would be accomplished because Jake was so very tall and Catherine so very tiny. Judge Wilkerson knew the answer because he had seen it before. Jake lifted Catherine very slowly off of her feet and she placed her arms around his neck and they kissed as they had done two months before. When they separated, Jake saw the dark blue of Catherine's eyes and he held her for just a moment before returning her to her feet. They walked up the aisle together smiling and happy to share their great good fortune with the community.

The crew quickly gathered up the chairs and placed them at the waiting tables. Judge Wilkerson made a brief speech that it had been a good year for cattle and a year that was improving every day for the valley. Everyone knew what he meant and there was no need for retelling ugly stories on such a beautiful day. Jake welcomed everyone to the English Rose and asked them to enjoy themselves at the cattle drive party for 1885. Catherine stood on the third step of the porch steps so that she and Jake were at eye level. She smiled at

Jake then and he touched his forehead to hers alone again in the moment; alone in the throng of people before them.

Jake and Catherine were led over to the place of honor and they were served their meal so that they could relax and enjoy the day. Everyone else formed in buffet lines to take advantage of the great barbeque, cole slaw, potato salad, baked beans and another of Ramon's beautiful cakes. There was another wedding cake, but Ramon had also made some of Jake's special cake as a groom cake. When they reached that course, Jake said that they would need to take packets with them again tomorrow so that they could feast for the week to come. At that thought, Catherine reflected on the serenity again of their mountain hideaway. She couldn't wait to get back and to recapture the special bond that she and Jake had forged on that sacred mountain.

The party continued on through the afternoon. Their friends came by and wished them well. Chet Stoner commented on the fact that Miss Catherine had found a reason to stay for good and he knew that she was one of them now. She had experienced her first cattle drive party and she was a member of the community for sure. Dr. Martin came by to say that his two favorite patients were both looking well and that he wished them much happiness in the years ahead. All of their friends came to their table to shake Jake's hand and to kiss the beautiful bride. Jake kept his eye on that part of the day because as he had said before, he wasn't used to sharing Catherine and he thought he probably would never be. There were no snakes in this crowd today however, just well wishes and hard working people who loved the land, took care of it and the land in turn took care of them and of their families.

At last the party began to wind down and the last of the party goers headed for wagons and horses to leave and return to their ranches. Jake took Catherine's hand and they headed back inside. The house was theirs for the night as Ramon and Consuela had decided to get married today also. They timed their honeymoon with that of Jake and Catherine's and Hector would be cooking for both crews next week. When they all returned, Ramon and Consuela would move into their new cabin and Jake and Catherine would have the house at night all to themselves.

As they mounted the stairs together, Jake thought back to that first wedding day and the comment that he had made to Catherine about her needing help to change out of her wedding gown. Tonight he would be her help and he was looking forward to the task. They reached their room and Jake stood by the bed lighting candles. Catherine turned to him and smiled as she knew that Jake liked lit candles by the bed. She took off her veil and carefully placed it across the rocking chair. She opened the window farthest from the bed then and pulled down each of the shades. She then came to her husband and he turned her around and started to undo the lacings that had brought in her gown and obscured her weight loss since the August wedding. He found the lacings and slowly undid them, kissing her spine as he did so. He felt the chills cascading down her back and knew the temperature of the room was not the cause. As the bodice came way, Catherine turned to him and took off his jacket and undid his tie.

Jake undid the lacings on the skirt as well and carefully gathered the bodice and the skirt on the rocking chair. He knew that after today, Catherine would preserve the dress and the veil for their daughter. He thought again of the challenges he would face if his daughter was as beautiful as her Mother. He would have to sit on the porch with a loaded shot gun every time she went courting. Those were worries for another day however and not for this day.

Catherine pulled Jake's shirt from his trousers then and he sat on the side of the bed as she sat on his lap and kissed his neck and into his upper shoulder. She looked into his eyes then and he kissed her deeply for the first time since they had entered the room. All else melted away at that moment.

Clothes were discarded and the two made love without another word spoken. They didn't need a word. All was now said with one look and one touch and much love.

They lay on the bed recovering their breath and looking at one another with love as they had done on the day of the celebration of their court case. Both were thinking of that moment before everything started going terribly wrong, but neither wished to speak of it. The day after that happy day was the day of the accident and the accident led to Delaney's death which in turn led to Catherine's miscarriage. One event had spiraled onto the other until they both thought that they had travelled a road of grief that few could recover from. They had recovered however and they were living proof of the fact that life does go on and happiness will again return if you hold firm to that belief.

"Mrs. Nelson, I think you had better get under the covers before you start getting cold honey. I can't have you getting sick when you are about to start your honeymoon," Jake said quietly.

"I am just lying here gazing at my beautiful husband and his beautiful mouth and thinking what a lucky woman I am to be loved by such a beautiful man," Catherine said smiling.

"Shoot honey; I am just a cowboy and a rancher, but I am married to the most beautiful woman in New Mexico. Everyone wanted to kiss my bride today, but I wanted no part of that," Jake said with a smile. "Now, are you going to get under these covers so I can keep you warm?" he said with a raised eyebrow.

"I will very shortly Jake. I am just drinking in my beautiful husband," Catherine repeated quietly.

"I knew I should have added something to those vows about obeying your husband. The Judge and I talked about it and here I am getting sass on my wedding night from my new wife," Jake said grinning.

Catherine started giggling then and then looked at Jake very seriously. "You know Jake Nelson you are not my

Father and I don't have to obey you. I do agree with you when I think that you make good sense and that good sense should be followed," Catherine said grinning again with mischief.

"Does it make good sense to keep from catching cold when I can keep you warm under the covers?" Jake continued.

Catherine sighed then audibly and smiled at Jake. "I guess it does make good sense. I just didn't want to have to move until the morning," Catherine said peacefully.

Jake picked her up then and placed her under the covers, blew out the candles and pulled her up on his chest after he had gotten comfortable again. "Now honey, you don't have to move until morning. I will keep you warm all night and in the morning, we will go to the mountain and we will rest again in the arms of that sacred mountain. Go to sleep Catherine and know that I love you more than anything in the world. I would marry you again and again and each time, I will love you more than the time before," Jake said into the darkness.

CHAPTER TWENTY

The next morning, Jake and Catherine set off for the mountain cabin and their second honeymoon. Everything was relaxed and happy in comparison to the hasty retreat of the first honeymoon. Catherine had sent the basket of treats along with the men of the Trinity to be picked up this morning. She knew they would have more items to pack for this visit and that basket was one less thing to be transported on the pack horse. They had food packages again from Ramon and Catherine had warm clothes packed as Jake told her they may see snow up on their mountain. She was excited to be there again and the thought of snow on the enchanted cabin only added to the excitement. Jake had saddled the pretty mare again from the cattle drive ride and his horse was again feeling his oats. As they rode along to the Trinity, Catherine noticed that Jake's horse was again frisky.

"Jake, what is your horse's name?" Catherine asked.

"He is called Blaze honey and he is my main mount," Jake replied.

"Does my horse have a name?" Catherine continued.

"No honey, I don't think anyone has ever named her. If you would like to ride her from now on, I think you should name her," Jake responded.

"I would like to call her Star for the beautiful star on her face. What do you think Jake; Blaze and Star? I think they make a beautiful couple. I think the whole valley is in love Jake. We started the trend and now the whole valley is in love," Catherine said smiling.

"The whole valley may be in love, but no one has a treasure like me," Jake said grinning at Catherine.

When they reached the Trinity, the steer that would be given to the tribe was ready to be transported and the basket that Catherine had insisted on bringing to them was attached. Jake thought that Catherine was nothing if not mindful of her manners. He was surprised that she hadn't written a thank you note as well, but decided to let that comment drop. He smiled when he thought about her becoming sassy. Like he told Chet Stoner this week, it must be the company that she was keeping.

As before, they rode nearly an hour into the mountain before Jake let out the same call as before. It was answered and the many friends of the tribe came from the surrounding trees. They greeted Jake as before and Jake presented the steer and the basket of treats. He explained to them that Catherine had wanted them to have a special thank you for their kindness in August. They smiled and one man touched his face. Jake turned to look at Catherine then and shook his head. He noted something further to them which Catherine did not understand. They shook their heads in understanding and shook Jake's hand and touched Catherine's hand. She waved shyly and they rode on further up into the mountain to their retreat.

When they arrived, Catherine was struck by the temperature in the middle of the day. She knew that it would be colder by morning, but she knew also that Jake would build a big fire and would keep her warm as he had done so many times before. He helped her down from her horse and she began to unpack the pack horse to take items into the cabin. "Wait just one moment honey; we have a tradition to maintain," Jake called out. He came up on the porch then, opened the door and carried her over the threshold. He kissed her as he placed her back on her feet and smiling she followed him out again to finish unpacking the food items and clothing items for the week.

Jake took off the saddles from the horses and led them over to a lean to that would keep them warm during the cold autumn nights. He laughed then at Catherine's comment that the entire valley was in love. If that was the case, he thought, there would be a lot of babies coming along by next spring. "I will start gathering some wood for the fire and some water for the kettle. Did you bring those candles Mrs. Nelson?" Jake called out to Catherine.

"I certainly did my love. I didn't think that we needed a picnic basket for this visit because I thought it might be too cold to go fishing or swimming for that matter," Catherine replied.

"We will think of something to keep us occupied Mrs. Nelson, have no fear," Jake called back.

I will not blush, Catherine thought. I will not blush. If I keep telling myself this over and over maybe I can stop blushing. She smiled and thought that knowing Jake, that was probably never going to occur. She took her clothing back to the changing area and looked around the cabin that had changed her life. Here she had started her married life and here she had fallen in love with her husband even more than the day that they had married. Now two months on, she could not imagine the trials that had awaited them both when they returned to the valley after their first honeymoon. They had survived them and come to the other side to the happiness that Jake had known waited for them. Hold onto all that is beyond this madness he had told her repeatedly and he had been right as he was about almost everything.

Jake started to gather wood for the fire and water for the kettle. They would need to heat water to bathe and for the warm drinks for the evening. Tonight Catherine would see her first taste of true autumn weather and Jake would hold to his promise to keep her warm. It was a task that he had thoroughly enjoyed for two months and hoped to enjoy for the rest of his life. When he came back to the cabin, Catherine had unloaded the pack horse and was organizing everything for the week ahead.

"Did you and Ramon think that we would be stranded up here for a month honey? I think we have more food than last time and that was a lot of food," Jake said smiling.

"I have to make sure that my husband doesn't blow away and besides, aren't you the one who said that honeymooning works up an appetite?" Catherine said with mischief in her eyes.

"Just like I said last night honey, she has only been here for five months and she is already sassy. What am I going to do with you Mrs. Nelson?" Jake said grinning.

"Just love me a lot Jake; just love me a lot," Catherine replied smiling.

"That I can do honey; that I can do," Jake replied kissing the top of her head.

That evening when the fire was going well, the water heated and dinner complete, Jake put on his jacket to go out and check on the horses. Catherine knew if he had put on his jacket, it was definitely cold as she had remarked before that he washed on the porch without a shirt on a cool August morning without thought to the temperature. She put a blanket down in front of the fire where animal skins lay and pulled out her book to read. She had changed into one of Jake's shirts and a pair of his socks after bathing for the night. She made sure that she had packed extra of both as she loved the comfort of his shirt when they had gone swimming in August and his socks were wonderfully warm. When Jake came back through the door, he found her sitting in front of the fire with her book as though curled up for the evening. He started to take off his boots and jacket which were covered with the first snow of the autumn. "You are going to see your first New Mexico snow tomorrow morning Mrs. Nelson. It is just starting to come down. The horses are in their lean to and love is in the air," Jake said grinning.

"I told you the entire valley is in love Jake. We just started the trend," Catherine said smiling. She had put down her book as soon as he entered the cabin.

"Did you truly bring a book on your honeymoon Catherine? Has the magic gone so soon?" Jake said laughing.

"Oh no sweetheart, the magic is very much with us every day. I brought a book because I thought that you might want to go hunting. You told me that you went hunting and fishing when you came to the cabin in the winter," Catherine replied smiling.

"I used to go hunting and fishing at the cabin in the winter. Any man who goes hunting on his honeymoon with a wife like you in the cabin needs his head examined. I think we can still go fishing, but maybe in the heat of the day and maybe we will have to sit on some skins to keep us warm. Speaking of keeping us warm, what are you wearing?" Jake asked.

"I am wearing one of your shirts and a pair of your socks," she had pulled the shirt over her knees and was doing her best to cover his socks with the shirt as well.

"Does this mean that you did not bring any of your own clothing this time around?" Jake said laughing.

"Of course I did Jake. I just like wearing your shirt because it smells like you and your socks keep my feet warm without me wearing my winter slippers which you teased me about in August," Catherine replied.

"I teased you honey because you were wearing them in August," Jake continued still laughing. "So if you are wearing my shirt because it smells like me, what exactly does it smell like?" Jake asked curious.

"It smells like fresh air and it smells clean and masculine just like you smell," Catherine replied smiling.

"Well that is a real nice thing to say. I don't suppose you would have it on if it didn't smell nice," Jake replied. He started rubbing his back against the door frame then and Catherine sat frowning trying to understand what he was doing.

"Jake, why on earth are you rubbing your back like that; is something wrong my love?" Catherine asked anxiously.

"Oh I am just starting in with my winter skin; nothing to worry about. I have it every year," Jake replied. He had come to the table then as he had removed his boots and jacket.

"I can fix that Jake if you like. You don't need to suffer with that anymore," Catherine replied eagerly.

"That would be just fine honey. What do I need to do?" Jake asked.

"If you want to spread out here and take off your shirt, I will be right back," Catherine replied. She got up then and went to the bedroom and her endless supply of potions and lotions. She came back with a pillow for his head, a blanket and a handful of potions and lotions. "Here Jake, I brought you a pillow. Did you want a blanket?" Catherine asked anxiously.

"No honey; I am lying in front of the fire. Only you would need a blanket in front of the fire." He was lying watching as she was preparing a mixture and wondered what process she was going to do next. Since his accident, he had no doubt of her healing knowledge he just wasn't sure how she was going to make winter skin go away.

"I have a lotion that I make myself which heals winter skin. You see you need to take away the dead skin that is making you itch and then treat the healthy skin underneath. It always works Jake. It does smell like lavender though because you know I always wear lavender. Do you mind it smelling like lavender Jake?" Catherine asked worriedly.

"Of course not honey. You wear my shirt because it smells like me and I will have lavender that smells like you. I don't think I could wear any of your clothes honey because I couldn't start to fit in them could I?" he asked smiling.

Catherine had poured water into a shallow bowl and was letting it cool. She had a sponge and the mixture that she had made lined up in front of the fireplace. Jake was lying on the blanket with his arm behind his head watching her and wondering what would occur next.

"I was just letting this cool Jake so it wouldn't be too hot on your back. Now, if you would turn over, I will get started. You might want to take off your belt so that you aren't lying on it and then you can make yourself comfortable on the pillow, all right?" Catherine stated smiling.

"Whatever you say honey; just sit on my rump if you need a seat while you are doing whatever you are going to do," Jake replied grinning. He stretched out then on the blanket and put his arms under his head and settled into the pillow. He became very quiet and Catherine thought he was falling asleep. She wet his back and then placed the mixture on his back and began to use the sponge to rub the mixture into his back and rub away the dead skin. She then took another cloth and wiped away the mixture and let his back dry. Using her lotion she began to massage it deeply into his back taking special care of the areas that were especially dry that she had just treated. She then took one of his arms and stretched it behind him and began to massage in the lotion there as well. She had done this each day during his recovery, but he hadn't been able to tell her if it was something that he enjoyed or not. She had done it to make sure that his skin did not dry out while he was concussed. She heard his low moan as she massaged and thought that it must be a good thing and that he must be enjoying it. She did the same with the other arm and then put additional lotion on his back where the dry skin had plagued him. When she was finished, she sat for a moment and thinking him fallen asleep, got ready to move from her perch. Jake quietly asked her where she was going.

"I thought you were asleep Jake. You were just playing possum again weren't you? You are awfully good at playing possum you know," Catherine said smiling. "Does that feel better sweetheart? It won't take it away completely as we will need to do it again, but it will make it feel much better and you won't look like a bear rubbing your back on door frames all winter," she said with mischief.

"You have angel hands to go with your angel face. That is what I thought the whole time you were taking care of me after the accident," Jake said quietly. Up until this moment, Catherine and Jake had shared a silent agreement that they had not talked of the accident or her miscarriage ever since their recovery. It was the first time that Jake had mentioned it and it surprised Catherine. She didn't at first know how to respond. Finally she asked if he would like her to put lotion on his chest as well. He turned over then and smiled at her as she started her work. He closed his eyes again and relaxed on the blanket.

Catherine sat gazing at her husband and thought then that she usually didn't have this extended opportunity. During his recovery, she had kept him covered with a blanket and worked on one body part at a time while she had massaged the lotion on him. She thought that in her novels, this would be the point in which the heroine would swoon at the beauty of her mate. Jake lay with his head towards the fire and she noticed as always his beautiful mouth which she had noticed the first time that they had ridden together to the English Rose. The September sun had added blond streaks to his hair and his chest was solid tan from exposure over the past month. His arms were muscled from his lifelong work on the ranch and his shoulders broad. His chest came to a deep v right before the belt area. He was definitely a mate that was worthy of a swoon but she didn't think that Jake would be happy with a mate who made a practice of swooning.

The greatest surprise of her married life so far was the fact that Jake wanted her to respond to him in the same passionate way that he did to her. She had always thought that only the man would find passion in love and she found that she was surprised and pleased to know that she could not only feel that passion for Jake, but that he encouraged her to feel that passion for him. She smiled her cat who swallowed the canary smile as she placed lotion on Jake and hoped that she was not blushing too much and if so, would attribute it to her proximity to the fire should Jake awake. She thought again that he must be asleep as he was so quiet and relaxed. As she finished placing lotion on his chest and on both arms again, she moved closer to the fireplace to let him peacefully nap.

"Where are you going honey?" Jake asked quietly, his eyes still closed.

"I'm not going anywhere Jake; I thought you were asleep again. You were so very quiet that I thought you had drifted off to sleep," Catherine said quietly.

"You used to do that when I was recovering from the concussion. I could feel you do that even before I came out of the concussion. I thought you had angel hands to go with your angel face like I said before. You haven't done that since I came out of the concussion honey. It sure felt wonderful Catherine," Jake said quietly.

"I told you that we would need to treat your back so that the winter skin doesn't come back. I can use my special lotion again if you like . . . I mean when I treat your back of course," Catherine said shyly. "I thought I would like to start an herb garden next spring Jake. I will need herbs for the different lotions that I make or otherwise I will need to send back home for them. If I grow them myself, I can make some of my own lotions and medicines for us to use."

"Jake," Catherine asked tentatively . . . "I was wondering . . . do you think that I will have any problem getting pregnant again . . . I mean after losing our baby?" Catherine asked quietly. The silence of the night meant that they were finally talking about those things that they had hidden away since their recovery. The only sound in the cabin was the crackle of the fire, the night quiet as the falling snow outside.

Jake opened his eyes then and looked across at Catherine who was leaning against the fireplace. He had talked about his accident and recovery for the first time and she was now talking about her miscarriage. The silence of the night and the lack of day to day pressure had once again lifted that veil and they could finally bring their pain out into the open again. He knew as well as she that they had developed a silent language of their own when a look or a touch asked the question. The still rough territory was there to be probed and perhaps it was time to bring it out into the open to let it heal. He placed his arm behind his neck again and watched her intently before speaking. "Honey, you are as fertile as the valley. You were pregnant the first time after we were married for a month. You have to give yourself time to heal; your body, your mind, your heart and your soul. Since you stepped off of that train you have had one grief after another and you have coped with each and every one. You tried so hard and finally your body said enough. Today when the medicine man saw you, he asked if you had been ill. He could see the signs. I told him you were on the mend and you are honey and so am I. We are the best medicine for each other that we could possibly have," Jake said tenderly.

"Jake, when I had the miscarriage, you sang a song to me. I remember you singing it, but I didn't know the words. Was it a lullaby Jake because that was what it sounded like?" Catherine asked.

"It was a song that the medicine man sings when someone is ill. It is a song that asks for healing of the person afflicted. I knew your body would heal Catherine because you are strong and healthy just like the Doc said. I wanted your heart to heal and your soul. When I heard you laugh for the first time, I knew that my prayers were answered. That laugh was better than all of the tea in China honey. At least it was to me. You will get pregnant Catherine when your body is ready and you will be the best Mother in the world. Your ancestor Catherine had five children and your Mother had six children honey. You are from very fertile stock. I should know Catherine because I know all there is to know about stock. That ranch will be like a nursery come spring with calves and foals everywhere you look. Nature always knows what it is doing honey and you will get pregnant when you are ready and there won't be a monster coming at you this time around to spoil what nature has provided. Do you believe me Catherine?" Jake asked earnestly.

"Of course Jake; I always believe you because you are almost always right," Catherine said smiling.

"Only almost always right?" Jake said grinning. "I was right about the weather for our cattle drive party and vow renewal wasn't I?" he said smiling with mischief.

"Yes darling Jake; you were right about the weather," Catherine said rolling her eyes.

"And I was right about you looking so beautiful that no one would notice the difference in your gown?" Jake said laughing with one eyebrow raised.

"Yes darling Jake; you were right about that also," Catherine continued.

"And I was right about Blaze and Star who are working on their new family as we speak?" Jake said sitting up.

"Are they really Jake? Oh I can't wait to see their foal. It will be so beautiful with two such beautiful parents," Catherine said smiling.

"Just like our baby will be beautiful. I thought about our daughter yesterday when I helped you with your wedding gown. I knew that you will save it for our daughter. I thought then if she is as beautiful as her Mama, I will have to sit on the porch with a shot gun every time some young buck takes her courting," Jake said grinning.

"Oh you wouldn't do that Jake. The poor boy would be terrified of you," Catherine said worriedly.

"The poor boy that doesn't yet exist will be terrified of me when I protect the daughter that doesn't yet exist? Is that about right Catherine?" Jake said grinning.

"You are just trying to make me laugh Jake," Catherine said smiling.

"Yes I am Mrs. Nelson and I am also getting ready to come over and rescue you from that corner that you have placed yourself in. This is our honeymoon Mrs. Nelson and as we have said, love is in the air. Come here and finish what you started," Jake said huskily.

"What did I start Jake? I treated your winter skin and I massaged your arms and your back and your chest,"

Catherine said confused. Jake was making his way over to her then on his hands and knees.

He stopped just short of her curled feet and pulled her onto his lap then and looked at her deeply in the eyes. "Catherine, you are like a fever in my blood. If I touch you, I want you; if you touch me, I want you. That is just how it is Catherine. That is how it will always be. When we have been married for fifty years, it will be the same. I might not be as spry or as able to show you then as I do now, but that is how it will be honey between you and me." Jake started to unbutton the buttons of his shirt worn by Catherine.

"I should put on my nightgown Jake. This isn't very pretty for a honeymoon," Catherine said shyly.

"It doesn't matter honey because it is not going to be on for long," Jake said kissing her deeply. He finished unbuttoning his shirt then and seeing the always present corset beneath, slowly undid the strings on the corset until it fell away and only the chemise remained. He moved her hair away from her neck and kissed her neck then hungrily and saw the chills start to rise on her arms and chest. He knew she wasn't cold because she was sitting next to the fire. He knew his touch had started those chills just as her touch had started his response to her. He stopped and waited for her reaction to him. She placed her arms around his neck then and kissed him deeply and he growled deeply at the back of his throat in response. She smiled then at the wolf sound and the dance of love between them.

He slowly and lovingly unbuttoned the buttons on her chemise. His hands came again to rest at the small waist and his fingers traced her side and came up to cup her breasts. "Catherine," he whispered, "I don't think you have lost weight everywhere if that is any consolation," Jake said grinning.

"I'm glad Jake," Catherine said quietly.

"So am I honey," Jake whispered again in her ear. "We need to put blankets in front of the fire at home Catherine.

You are even more beautiful by firelight. Your skin is like alabaster," Jake continued.

There would be many new babies at the ranch that spring and one new baby would be on the way as well. Catherine was convinced of that as her final conscious thought before Jake made love to her before the fire place.

*****

The next morning, Catherine could not wait to go to the door and see the snow on the ground. She asked if they could go to the waterfall again and Jake happily agreed. He saddled Blaze as he had in August so that the two could ride together. When Jake helped her up onto Blaze, Catherine asked if Star could come along as well. "I think she will be lonely without Blaze Jake and wonder why she is being left alone," Catherine said smiling.

"Are you going to be a matchmaker for every creature on the ranches from now on? I just need to know because you will probably want to name every baby born and fuss over it until I won't be able to sell one head of cattle or one horse without your approval," Jake said laughing.

"Not every creature certainly but just Blaze and Star because we brought them together didn't we? Blaze is your mount so he is like you; strong and proud and masterful and Star will just want to be with him won't she especially now when they are newlyweds," Catherine said smiling.

"Alright honey, we will bring Star along with us and then she can watch Blaze be strong and proud and masterful as we ride to the waterfall. Come on boy" he called to Blaze; "let's show off for the ladies," Jake said grinning again. Blaze nodded his head as if he was taking in the conversation. Star followed behind and they whinnied to each other along the route. Blaze was true to Jake's instructions and practically strutted to the waterfall. Jake kept his hand around Catherine's waist and shook his head at his darling wife's fancies.

The approach to the waterfall was as powerful on this morning as it had been in August. The snow gave an even greater magic to the location. Catherine remembered the first time hearing the water as they approached it and took in the sight today with even greater wonder. They had brought a canteen again to capture the pristine, cold water. Both had dressed warmly this morning because they knew the snow had brought out the frost in the air. Catherine watched Blaze and Star and their wintry breath as they approached the waterfall. She saw her own and Jake's and thought like him that winter was not far away. The peace and beauty of this site was just what they both needed. Jake had told her that they would sleep in every day of their honeymoon and do as much or as little as they wanted to do. If ever two people needed to bask in the peace of the mountains, it was Jake and Catherine after their two months travail.

Each day of their honeymoon they enjoyed the simple pleasures that they had experienced on their first honeymoon; visiting the waterfall, fishing at the lake, sleeping by the fire each afternoon and holding each other each night. It was as magical to them as it had been in August. Catherine told Jake that they now had two wedding anniversaries and he would need to remember them both. Jake suggested that she place the dates somewhere conspicuous to help his memory. She told him that she would always remind him of the two dates that had changed her life.

*****

All too quickly, the week passed and they were ready to head back to the ranches. They would stop at the Trinity again to see if there was anything further that Jake wanted to pack for the English Rose. They would then head back to the English Rose and begin their preparations for the upcoming winter. Catherine said she would need to update her brothers again and she had ignored her diary for far too long. She had much to record for her future ancestors. Both the good and the bad needed to be captured just as her ancestor had recorded for her family beginning in 1811.

As they entered the clearing area again, the people of the mountain came to bid Catherine and Jake goodbye. The medicine man stepped forward again to talk to Jake. Catherine had ridden with him again this morning due to the steepness of the incline just as she had in August. The medicine man touched his face again and smiled this time to Jake. Jake shook his head and smiled his agreement. They were thanked for the steer and for the treats that Catherine had provided. She felt that it was now her sacred duty along with Jake to keep the people of the mountain safe against all manner of attack by the modernizing world.

Back again on the Trinity land, Catherine asked Jake what the medicine man had asked. "He said that the mountain had healed you Catherine. He said that you looked better already and that I was to give you a baby over the winter. I told him that I knew my duty and I would keep working at it every day," Jake said laughing.

"You did not tell him that Jake Nelson. You are just saying that to see if you can make me blush," Catherine said primly.

"Is it working honey?" Jake said laughing. "Come on Blaze," Jake called out again; "we need to get the ladies home. We have work to do this winter boy. I will keep you in hay and Ramon will keep me in special cake and we will get this work done," Jake said laughing again.

Catherine shook her head then and leaned back against Jake. As Ruby had told her, she was holding onto a good hand and a good man. Their chapter of the McCullum-Nelson saga was just beginning. There would be many chapters to write; some happy and some sad. But she knew as long as she and Jake were together, they could face whatever life threw in their direction. The English Rose and their Trinity would be the backdrop of their lives.

CHAPTER TWENTY-ONE

Come spring, the English Rose and the Trinity gave all the appearance of a nursery just as Jake had predicted. Star was expecting with her first foal, calves were being born all over the ranches and Catherine was expecting their first baby. If all went according to plan, Jake and Catherine's baby would be born in September. She had written her brothers and asked that if visits were to occur, would they consider waiting for October and the annual cattle drive. That way they could see the best herds in the valley being brought to sale and they could see the best man in the valley in his element. Catherine had sent home a photo of the two of them taken in October at their second wedding. Catherine's brothers thought that Jake was as tall as their Father and as tall as the original Cameron, the husband of the first Catherine. They all thought it ironic that the family trait continued into yet another generation; tall man and tiny wife. Somehow it all continued just as if planned.

Jake planted Catherine's herb garden just as she requested. He also planted a rose garden for his English Rose as he thought it only proper that a ranch with such a name should have a rose garden as well. He made sure the herb garden grew lavender because Catherine would need that for her special lotions. Never again was Jake plagued by winter skin. Catherine had seen to that and he had seen to the blankets in front of the fire in their room. They had spent many a winter night there and now, they had the first baby on the way. Catherine had been right; love was in the air and babies on the way. Jake of course stated that his latest prediction had come true and Catherine agreed that he was almost always right.

The sadness and the pain of 1885 was part of their memory now. As long as they were married, they would not forget the trials of their first year of marriage. As Jake predicted, though buffeted by the winds of life, never again did they have such a year of trials as the year of 1885. As each successive year passed and their family continued to grow, they would return to the sacred mountain and carry their children along with them to the peace of the mountains. Jake built the room for the children onto the cabin he had planned and made sure that he and Catherine had their own time together to recharge and renew. Each year they took two second honeymoons; one in August with the children and one in October for the two of them alone. Blaze and Star carried them to their mountain retreat and then the offspring of Blaze and Star; the circle of life coming round year after year.

Catherine's brothers visited and were in awe of the best herds in the valley and of the beautiful children born to Catherine and Jake. The last of the family born to them was a beautiful girl who was also named Catherine. She had black hair and deep blue eyes. When Jake held her for the first time, she curled her fingers around Jake's little finger. He looked at Catherine and shook his head. "She has me wrapped already honey; just like I knew she would." The next generation's story had yet to be written, but with such a glorious history, Jake and Catherine knew it would be an eventful one.

THE END

Made in the USA
Middletown, DE
10 March 2019